CITY OF
STRANGERS

Also by Louise Millar

The Playdate
Accidents Happen
The Hidden Girl

LOUISE MILLAR

CITY OF STRANGERS

MACMILLAN

First published in the UK in 2015 by Macmillan
an imprint of Pan Macmillan
20 New Wharf Road, London N1 9RR
Associated companies throughout the world
www.panmacmillan.com

ISBN 978-1-4472-8111-5

1 3 5 7 9 8 6 4 2

A CIP catalogue record for this book is available from the British Library.

Typeset by Ellipsis Digital Limited, Glasgow
Printed and bound by CPI Group (UK) Ltd, Croydon, CR0 4YY

Visit www.panmacmillan.com to read more about all our books
and to buy them. You will also find features, author interviews and
news of any author events, and you can sign up for e-newsletters
so that you're always first to hear about our new releases.

To Bella, with love

Acknowledgements

As always, a huge thanks to my editor Trisha Jackson, and to Natasha Harding, Sam Eades and all at Pan Macmillan. Also to Lizzy Kremer, Harriet Moore and all at David Higham Associates.

A special thanks to my daughter who, at ten, wrote a thrilling short story called *The Man in the Kitchen*, and lent me the name as the working title for this book.

My gratitude, too, to all the experts, family and friends who helped and guided me with research. Any mistakes are, of course, mine.

Finally, I have taken some creative licence with geographical locations.

CHAPTER ONE

Now, where to start?

Probably the shoes.

They were the style businessmen wore, but scuffed, as if the dead man, who wore them, had been dancing in dust. The white powder had burrowed into the decorative arcs on the toes, creating lacy caps. Gaps at the heels suggested a poor fit.

Someone else's shoes.

Grace Scott knelt, careful not to disturb the crime scene, and photographed his feet. The heels were square and stubbed, and sported identical worn half-moons at the edges.

No socks.

Her lens trailed to the shoelaces. Brown, lying mismatched against parched black leather, plastic aglets split or missing, but each loop equal in size. Tied with care.

A gap of ankle, with dark, coarse body hair, then the suit.

She moved her lens upwards.

It was navy, pinstriped and, like the shoes and the yellowed business shirt underneath, poorly fitting, suggesting a previous owner. Thin threads dry-cleaned into submission. A shine that suggested a thousand journeys in traffic jams and meetings in baking-hot rooms, sweat infused with stress hormones, and last night's pint and takeaway curry. A hint of buttercup paint on one knee. Perhaps a DIY paintbrush picked up late at night by someone too tired to change after work.

Grace moved her camera lens along the dead man's limbs.

Black gloves. Fingers stiff.

No watch.

No belt.

Light broke into the kitchen. The thunder had subsided, and now a freakishly bright beam blasted between the storm clouds through the window of the Edinburgh apartment. It lit up one sliver of patchy, lucent skin, visible between the strands of brown hair that masked the face. The hair was luxuriously thick, dried like bracken. A substance was spattered across it: tarry and foul-smelling, like the stain on the pale granite worktop.

Blood.

A milky eye stared through two strands.

Trying to keep her hands steady, Grace focused her lens. No hint in it about what had happened. No suggestion that he knew life was about to end.

She widened her angle, shooting the whole body now in the context of where it had fallen. The head below the sink, the feet protruding into the dining area, the kitchen cupboards framing him like a coffin.

Then, for an even wider perspective, she shot from the kitchen door, catching the eerie light, igniting the puddle of broken glass by the smashed back door.

Then the man's black shoes poking out from behind a cupboard.

The wedding presents in the corner he had been trying to steal.

To steal.

Grace lowered the camera.

What was she doing?

Tiptoeing across the scene, she unstacked the dining chairs, and sat. The only sound was her breath, and rain dripping onto the oversized white floor tiles, creating mud-coloured rivulets in the new grout.

Outside was the fire escape he must have climbed. The back-yard of the newsagent's below, and the gate beyond.

The kitchen cupboards were open, as if he'd been looking for food.

They were brand-new cupboards. There had never been any food in them.

That was sad.

She replaced her camera in its bag, checking to make sure she'd caught every angle. He looked like he'd been here for days. A family must be worrying somewhere, hoping for a call.

Undoing the T-shirt she'd tied over her face to fight the acrid smell, she walked to the hall, and rang 999.

'Yes . . . Hi. My name's Grace Scott. I live at 6A Gallon Street by the Crossgate Tower. I've just come back from holiday and found a man dead in my kitchen . . . Yes, lying on the floor . . . No, no idea . . . He looks like he's been here a while . . . Maybe a burglar, the back door is smashed . . .'

Instructions were given. Grace ended the call.

Mac would be at the door any minute, with bags full of shopping from Morrisons that no one would eat.

'Don't worry,' she said into the empty room. 'I'll stay with you.'

CHAPTER TWO

Downstairs, in the rear storeroom of Mr Singh's newsagent's, the man listened to the footsteps in the flat above. Through the barred window, dirty curtains of clouds gathered above the backyard.

They'd found the body.

Focus.

He crouched, waiting.

The cold tickled his throat, and he coughed. A long minute passed.

No response above. They hadn't heard.

Good.

CHAPTER THREE

Mac stood in the hallway, Morrisons bags spilt at his feet. Two oranges rolled along the gold-and-blue Victorian tiles. 'You what?' he said to Grace, hands cupping his nose and mouth.

Grace pointed at the kitchen.

He squeezed past the second tower of wedding presents to the kitchen door and saw the dead man's feet. His lips parted, but nothing came out, as if there were simply no words for this. Tiptoeing to the smashed back door, he turned the key. 'This how he got in?'

'Must be,' Grace replied. 'The kitchen door was still bolted from the hall when I got here, so . . .' Mac's shoes left prints in the dirty rainwater. 'You better come out – we're probably not supposed to disturb anything.'

His eyes flitted to the body, and away. 'Shit. Who is it?'

'Don't know.'

'So, he's broken in – what, after the wedding presents?'

She tried to answer and gagged.

'You all right?'

A second to recover. 'Well, it's not good, is it?'

'No,' Mac snorted. 'It's not good.'

He tiptoed back and hugged her, just as the doorbell rang.

They buzzed in two uniformed officers, their neon-yellow jackets and black hats shiny with rain.

After Grace confirmed the details from her 999 call, the officers pressed past, to peer into the kitchen.

The woman turned. 'Right, can I ask you to wait downstairs, please?'

'Any idea what's happened?' Mac asked.

A hand came out. 'Downstairs, please, sir.'

They carried their holiday suitcases, still packed, down to the communal hall of the tenement. Grace leaned between two oversized oil landscapes of the Black Isle, hung by the artist who owned the top-floor flat. Mac sat on the stairs. His blue eyes, pink-rimmed with jet lag, popped comically against his tan.

Neither of them spoke.

The female PC appeared above them, talking into her radio. 'Delta 42 to Control. We're attending 6 Gallon Street. Person dead in Flat A, first floor. Sign of forced entry at the rear. Looks like they've been here for some time. Signs of decomposition. We're not entering. Can you ask CID and the sergeant to attend?'

Grace sat and buried her face in Mac's chest, trying to use the faint smell of coconut oil on his T-shirt to mask the putrid odour. Her eyelids begged to close. With the plane change in London, it must be eighteen hours since they'd left Bangkok. Twenty-four since they'd slept.

Mac kissed the side of her head. 'What are we going to do tonight?'

'Don't know. Get a hotel.'

The female PC came downstairs, with a notebook.

'Right, that's us, waiting for CID. I'll need a bit more information. Can you tell me what happened when you found the body?'

Grace sat up. 'Yes. It was me. We just got back from honeymoon today, about half four? Mac went to Morrisons, and I came in to get the heating on and make some tea – I found him in the kitchen.'

More questions followed and she tried to focus. 'Yes, my name's Grace . . . Elizabeth . . . Scott, with two "T"s . . . I'm a freelance photographer . . . Yes, we were in Thailand for two weeks . . . No, we haven't slept in the flat yet. This was supposed to be our first night . . . No, we only got the keys a week before the wedding . . . Yes, we did the main removal two days before we left . . . The boxes? They're wedding presents . . . No. They were delivered directly here. There's more in the sitting room, too . . .' She noted the PC's eyebrow lift. 'Yup, big families . . .'

The officer glanced at Mac, who was checking the influx of work emails Grace had banned him from downloading in Thailand. 'And, sir, you are . . . ?'

He pushed back his hair. In the brash hall light, Grace saw now that shock and exhaustion had drained the pigment from his tan. He shook himself upright. 'Sorry. Mackenzie Lowe – L-O-W-E . . . I'm Grace's boyfr— Sorry, husband. Just getting used to that!' The officer didn't seem to find it amusing. 'My job? I design music venues and bars. Just setting up a new one in Leith . . . The previous owner of this flat? John Brock. B-R-O-C-K. He's my boss, actually . . . Aye, here's his number . . . No, John's never lived here, either. It's a refurbishment project. We just bought it off him . . . The previous owners? Think it was a student rental before. John'll know . . . No – no idea who the guy in the kitchen is. Do you?'

If the PC had identified the dead man, she wasn't telling. She returned to Grace. 'And can you run over again what you did when you entered the flat?'

Grace stood up, stretching out her back after the cramped

plane journey. 'Well, I noticed the smell first. I thought a pipe had burst. So I checked the bathroom, then the sitting room, then the bedrooms. Then I unbolted the kitchen door and . . .' Her chest dropped as if it had hit turbulence. As she breathed to control the palpitations, the acrid smell buried deeper into her lungs. A hand flew to her mouth. 'Oh God. Sorry.'

Mac took her hand. 'You OK, darlin'?'

'Yes. Whooh. Sorry. It's . . . Go on.'

The PC paused, then continued. 'Right. You said the kitchen door was bolted from inside the hall? Is that normal?'

'Well, it's the first time we've used it,' Grace replied. 'It seemed like a good idea if we were away for two weeks. John said he put it on to make the flat safer at the back, with the fire escape going down to Mr Singh's backyard.'

'There's no alarm?'

'No.'

'Right. So you bolted the inner kitchen door when you left for Thailand two weeks ago?'

'Yes.'

The PC flipped a page. 'And you arrived, smelt something odd, looked around the flat, unbolted the kitchen door and entered?'

'Yes,' Grace repeated. 'And I know I shouldn't have, but I honestly thought it was a burst pipe. Then I saw the man's shoes and I know it sounds daft, but I thought maybe the leak had gone downstairs into Mr Singh's shop, and he'd somehow got a plumber up into the flat to fix it. And the plumber was lying on the floor, under the sink.' She broke off. Mac patted her leg, eyes still on his phone. 'And then when I saw him, I thought for a moment it was John Brock – he's got longish brown hair like that – and that he'd collapsed. So I went to check if he was OK, and that's when I saw . . .'

The milky eye, fixed and lifeless, through strands of stiff hair.

There was a creak upstairs. The male PC exited the flat. He pointed at the door next to theirs on the first-floor landing.

'Is this a flat, too?'

'No. Cupboard, I think,' Mac said.

'Right.' The PC tried the locked handle. 'And upstairs?'

'Two more flats,' Mac replied. 'Haven't been up there yet.'

'And you, sir,' the female PC continued to Mac, 'did you enter the kitchen?'

Mac nodded. 'Yes, same as Grace. Sorry. Just went over to the back door to see how the guy got in.'

'And did either of you touch anything?'

Grace checked with Mac. 'Don't think so. I mean, the bolt and the door handles, but nothing else. Mac, no?'

'No.' He stroked her leg, and she sat back down.

'And how long was that – between you finding the body and calling the police?' the PC asked.

Grace tensed her calves against her camera bag. 'Uh. A few minutes?'

There was a rap at the front door. The PC shut her notebook. 'Right, well, CID'll want to talk to you, so if you can just wait there, please.'

Grace eased her camera bag further out of sight, as two men in suits entered, introduced themselves and went straight upstairs. Conversations began to blur around her. Energy drained like sand. She leaned against Mac, as he continued reading emails. New people arrived. A crime scene manager and a police surgeon. She fought her drooping eyelids. Barrier tape was put across the door. By the time one of the detectives asked Grace and Mac to come to Lother Street Station to give witness statements, she'd lost all track of time. It could have been twenty minutes since she found the body or two hours.

Outside, a ferocious blast of east-coast wind whipped her awake. With his arm around her, Mac led her to the back seat of a waiting police car.

She realized her hands were shaking.

'It's shock, darlin',' Mac said, putting a seatbelt around her. 'Feeling a bit spaced out myself.' He did his own, then put his arm back around her and hugged her.

The scene from the pavement became distorted through a windscreen glazed by rivulets of rain. Flashing blue lights and yellow street lamps diffused into messy holograms. Curious eyes of onlookers grew and shrank.

Four months ago, she'd never seen a dead body. Now she'd seen two.

Grace shivered, feeling the claws of death clasp round her once again.

She shut her eyes, craving the Thai sun. Willing herself out of a winter that simply wouldn't end.

CHAPTER FOUR

'*Grace? Grace?*'

A tapping sound, insistent – then drumming.

Grace opened her eyes. Unfamiliar black curtains came into focus, edged by light.

'*Grace? Grace?*'

For a wonderful moment, the timbre and tone of the voice promised the world would keep turning. Everything would be OK.

Beyond the bed, a jigsaw of images formed that didn't fit together. A Formica desk and laminated menu card. Striped wallpaper. A wall-mounted TV. Suitcases spilt on the floor.

It wasn't Thailand, so where . . . ?

Grace pushed back the duvet. Raw cold shucked her skin. On the floor, she saw the four empty minibar miniatures they'd downed last night for the shock.

Of course.

Pulling on her fleece, she crawled out and lifted the curtain. The insistent tapping was rain battering the window. Industrial land stretched beyond, a rough prairie of grey weeds and winter grass, barely visible in the low light of a Scottish February. Heavy clouds looked as if they'd been hung out without being spun.

They were home.

In a conference hotel, out near the airport. The only one with a room free late last night after the police station.

She leaned on the windowsill, chin on forearms.

Below, a tight-bodied woman jogged hard alongside cars splashing by towards the airport, her pale grey tracksuit sodden in piebald patches. Rental boards advertised new plots. Tesco and Krispy Kreme clung to the land like wet molluscs.

'*Grace? Grace?*'

Her father's voice dissolved like warm ice in the gloom.

Just a dream.

If she squinted, she could almost see him on the horizon, hiking along on the purple watercolour brush of the Pentlands, eyes bright blue, cheeks ruddy under a white beard.

With a cold fingertip, she traced a circle in the condensation to recapture her father.

A sign below pointed to the tram into Edinburgh's centre. Thailand, it was already becoming clear, had changed nothing. She would have to face the city again. Since he'd gone, it had become nothing but a collection of shadows and echoes. A city of unfathomable thoughts and an uncharted future.

The prospect of her wedding without him had been horror enough.

Now this.

I came home, Dad, and I found a dead body in my flat.

He would never know.

Back in the warm bed, Grace checked Mac was asleep, and turned on her camera to ensure yesterday wasn't a dream, too.

There had been a moment of panic at Lother Street Station last night, when she'd thought the police might keep her and Mac's suitcases, and her camera, as part of their investigation and discover her shots of the dead man. The theoretical argument she'd constructed in her exhaustion had seemed robust.

'That's none of your business. I'm trained in reportage photography. I photograph the story in front of me. You wouldn't question me about photographing bodies if I was covering a war or the aftermath of a natural disaster, would you?'

She'd also imagined their scathing reply.

'But, Ms Scott, you've just told us you photograph people for diet and fitness magazines, and charity fun-run stories for newspapers. Who the hell are you kidding?'

They would have been right. Who the hell *was* she kidding?

The last photo was the best. The kitchen was ablaze with ghostly storm-light. Empty open cupboards buried into the shadows on one side, a wall of wedding gifts on the other; in the central floor area, a diamond-sparkle of wet, broken glass. A range of contrast, of textures, shadow and light. In the middle was a pair of upturned shoes. It was a slow-burn detail that added a shock-pulse to the image, as the implication of the still feet hit home. *Who is this man?* the story in the image asked. *Why is he here?*

The alarm clock on the bedside table said 9.01 a.m. It was sixteen hours since she'd rung 999. They must know who the dead man was now.

Grace crept out into the corridor, imagining the conversation that must have taken place with the dead man's family in the early hours. The shock of waking to a knock on the front door. A grim-jawed police officer bringing life-changing news. She imagined them, right now, like her, staring out of the window on a bleak morning, trying to fathom the first day in a world without their loved one.

'Can I speak to someone about the body at Gallon Street?' she asked the detective constable who answered her call.

'That'll be DI Robertson. He's in an interview, if you want to ring back at ten?'

She used the time to shower, scrubbing away the vestiges of yesterday's smell, which seemed buried into her skin. With no warm clothes to hand, she constructed the sturdiest outfit possible from her holiday suitcase: black leggings, layered T-shirts, a blue hoodie, her aeroplane sleep socks, her fleece and trainers.

Mac slept on, the sun-bleached tips of his light brown hair just visible above the duvet.

She sat and scrolled through her photos again.

The minutes ticked by interminably.

At 9.58 a.m., Grace returned to the corridor.

'Is DI Robertson free yet?'

'No, still in a meeting,' the detective constable said. 'Do you want to leave a message?'

'Not really. I just want to know who the dead man in our flat is. Can you tell me?'

'Do you want to try in an hour?'

A door opened and the drenched jogger from earlier emerged from her hotel room, in a business suit the same beige as the walls. Muzak played. A dour-faced maid rattled a trolley along, replacing yesterday's sheets. Rain drummed on the corridor window.

The old restlessness that Grace couldn't name returned.

The urge to race forwards, yet with no sense of direction.

Thailand had just made it worse.

She had to get out of here.

'No. I'm coming in.'

Without a coat, her fleece and leggings were soaked by the time she reached the tram. Her hair hung in sodden dark blonde rat's tails.

14

Through the steamed-up windows, she watched wet, grey Edinburgh tenements come into view. Raindrops dive-bombed off shop signs onto granite-coloured pavements. An army of umbrellas battled across roads. Car headlights shone through gloom.

Grace disembarked at Princes Street, by the Wallace Monument, which today looked like a medieval sword thrusting into mist. She pulled up her hood as a vicious wind scratched at her face. A lone bagpiper stood outside the art gallery, blowing strains of a reel into the bluster. Two Japanese tourists watched. Their matching rain-capes were circular and white, translucent jellyfish against drenched black stone.

Instinct sent her hand to her camera bag. The contrast of black and white would work in—

Too late Grace saw the puddle. Filthy water broke over her trainers, and flooded her socks to the toe.

Fuck.

Steeling herself for the hill ahead, she cut through a skinny alleyway that smelt of urine and rubbish, trying not to think about Thailand.

The Victorian building that was Lother Street Station sat atop Deansgate, its heavy brown double entrance doors as foreboding as a drawbridge.

'He's just finished. Come through,' an officer said. Grace entered a door behind the counter, and passed a tearful young woman in handcuffs being processed by a desk sergeant. It was a different interview room to last night's. Smaller, but still over-heated and smelling of sweaty feet and cigarette smoke clinging to unwashed clothes. Yelling and banging came from a cell down the corridor.

She hung her fleece on the radiator, and sat at a burgundy

table with a perfect bite mark in it. The door flew open and a new detective appeared with a file. His physical presence immediately eclipsed the tiny room.

'Hello, hello,' he said in a friendly voice she guessed was designed to neutralize the impact of his size.

She guessed he was six foot six. His grey hair was shorn over a balding head, and supplemented with a close-cut beard. Rather than create a row of double chins, his excess weight filled out his face like a balloon. His suit struggled to contain his tower-block frame.

'Hi,' she said, moving closer to the table as steam rose off her damp leggings.

The detective eased down opposite. 'OK, so I'm DI Finley Robertson, in charge of the investigation into the discovery of a body at 6A Gallon Street. And you are Mrs . . . Ms . . . ?'

'Ms Scott.'

There was a faint sheen on his forehead, and he wiped it with a hanky. 'You haven't taken your husband's name, then?'

'No.'

'Why? Has he got a stupid name?'

'No.' She smiled weakly, appreciating his attempt at a joke to relax her. 'So, thanks for seeing me. I just came in to find out about the man in our flat.'

DI Robertson ran a meaty hand over his bristles, and opened the file. Without warning, his kindly expression turned as menacing as a storm over the Pentlands. He tapped the page, and the sun returned. 'Right, no ID. Fingerprints and DNA checks being processed. No match yet for missing persons reports.'

It took her a second. 'You still don't *know*?'

'Oh, he'll be in the system somewhere. It's just a matter of time.'

'But he must have been there for days – how can nobody have reported him?' She didn't mean for it to but her tone emerged cross, as if she didn't believe he was trying hard enough. 'Sorry,' she added, even though she wasn't.

'No, that's OK,' he said evenly. 'These things can take longer than you think.'

She traced a nail along the bite mark. Six perfect teeth. 'Well, could you tell us how he died, at least?'

DI Robertson tapped his notes. 'Post-mortem's this afternoon. While you're here, though, do you know anyone from the Netherlands?'

'Was he Dutch?' she asked, hopeful.

'Not a wedding guest? Someone visiting the flat?'

Her thumb found a matching tooth-print under the table. Six more teeth. 'No. We've not even lived in the flat yet . . . Oh! Hang on.' She raised a finger. 'There were students in the flat before John Brock bought it. Could one of them be Dutch?'

DI Robertson folded his arms. His suit sleeves grimaced at the effort. 'This is John Brock who sold the flat to you?'

'Yes. Mac's boss. Have you spoken to him?'

'Aye, this morning. Said he sold it to you privately?'

Jet lag tricked her – turned her mind blank. Didn't they tell the police that last night?

'Yes,' she said hesitantly. 'John's a property developer – he's an old friend of Mac's mum and dad. He knocked off the estate agent's fee for us as a wedding present. He did it for Mac's sister, too.'

'And he's doing up a warehouse in Leith at the moment?'

'Yes. He's turning it into flats and a restaurant, and a gym. Mac works with him on the ground-floor space.'

'Ground-floor *space*. What's that?' The detective's eyebrows teased her.

She cracked another weak smile to humour him. 'A kind of bar-slash-photography-studio-slash-rehearsal . . . *space* . . .'

He chuckled. 'You've lost me.'

Her smile crumbled at the edges. She didn't want to talk about this. 'It's a sort of integrated venue with a photography studio and band rehearsal space and a DJ area – a bar, art gallery, workshop. A kind of big creative *space*. John got the idea from New York.'

DI Robertson nodded. 'Ah. Very good. And your husband runs that?'

'He will do – he's designing it at the moment.'

'And this flat you bought, 6A Gallon Street, Mr Brock sold that to finance this project?'

'Yes. That's what John does. Refurbishes flats and sells them on. He sold all his flats and his own house in Atholl Crescent to buy the warehouse.'

The detective whistled. 'One of the big Georgian ones?'

'Yes.'

'Right, that's fine. Mr Brock explained this all this morning.'

DI Robertson offered her a pack of fruit chews. She took one, again to humour him. It tasted oddly saccharine. A diet brand.

He chewed, watching her. 'And you're a photographer yourself, right?'

'Yes. Freelance.'

He flipped to another page in his file. He tapped it with his fruit chews. 'Early indication from Forensics is that footprints, probably yours, were all around the body. Remind me again why that is.'

She rested a wet trainer on her camera bag. If he asked her directly, she'd have to tell the truth. Just stick to her argument, although in the cold light of day, it didn't seem quite so robust.

'As I said last night, I walked into the kitchen looking for a burst pipe. Saw a man with longish brown hair on the floor, and walked over to see if it was John Brock. I couldn't see his face, so I had to walk around.'

'Right. And how long did this take?'

'I'm not sure. A few minutes? I was waiting for Mac.'

'OK.' The detective shut the folder. 'That's all fine. Well, thanks for coming in. We'll let you know when we've identified the body.'

That was *it*.

'So, have you spoken to other people at Gallon Street?' she asked.

DI Robertson chewed his sweet three times, and opened the folder again. 'We're speaking to Mr Singh today who runs the newsagent's underneath you . . . Top floor's owned by an artist who mainly rents it out as a holiday flat. Empty since New Year. And . . . the geologists above you, on the second floor. They're offshore at the moment, I believe?'

'Yes. John said they work a few weeks on, a few weeks off.'

'Aye. So we'll be speaking to them today.' He shut the file again, and pushed back his seat.

Determined, she kept her elbows on the table. 'And where is he – right now? The man who died?'

'Mortuary in Cowgate.' The detective stood up, the table creaking as he leaned on it, making her elbows bounce a little.

Reluctant, she got up, and retrieved her damp fleece from the radiator. 'I just don't get it,' she said. 'If my dad was missing for a week, I'd have reported it. Isn't that weird?'

DI Robertson extended a long arm to open the door. 'Well, I'm afraid not everyone's lucky enough to have family looking out for them. But don't worry – as I say, we'll get there.'

Then before she could think of another question, he ushered her out.

Grace's plan had been to return to the hotel to dry off, but DI Robertson's news had thrown her.

How could they not know who the man was?

Without purposely planning it, she found herself, twenty minutes later, on the corner of Gallon Street, drenched through.

A police car and a white van sat outside Mr Singh's newsagent's. A woman emerged from number 6, peeling off a forensics oversuit.

Grace's mobile rang. *Mac.* 'Hi.'

'Where are you?' he asked, voice cracked with sleep.

'Went to Lother Street Station. They still don't know who he is.'

'Who?'

'The dead man!'

'Oh.' Mac tutted. 'Ach, don't worry about it. He'll just be some junkie after the wedding presents.'

A lorry thundered by, splashing gutter water onto her leggings, and she wasn't sure if it was that or Mac that irritated her. 'Are you still at the hotel?'

'Yeah. John's picking me up. We're going to get some booze for the party.'

A van turned into the road and she stepped back. 'What party?'

'Our party, knob-head. The house-warming?'

Grace froze. 'Oh God. No. I completely forgot. No way. We can't.'

'What?' he exclaimed.

'We'll have to cancel it.'

'Why?'

The road cleared and she picked her way across puddles. 'What are you talking about, Mac? The flat's full of forensics people. I'm here now.'

'Well, the guy at the police station said they'd be out Thursday, Friday latest,' he replied. 'And he's given me numbers for cleaning firms who'll go straight in. So what's the problem?'

There was a whooshing sound from above and fresh rain came cascading down onto her head, bouncing up from the tarmac like a thousand tiny ballet dancers. 'The problem? Er . . . the dead man in our flat?' she said, reaching the other side. 'Seriously, Mac. We're not having a party. For God's sake. His family doesn't even know yet.'

Mac's voice remained on its default setting, midpoint between laconic and laissez-faire. 'Well, I'm not cancelling it. Asha's booked to DJ. And anyway, it'll be good for us – get the flat back to normal after the police have cleared out.'

Outside the newsagent's, she stopped. 'Mac! Will you stop being ridiculous? A party is not going to take my mind off this. It's going to make it more stressful. Listen, you need to tell people it's off. If you don't, I will.'

She ended the call, and ran into number 6, shaking rain from her fleece for all the good it did. At the top of the tenement stairs, a PC guarded their door. Police tape stretched across it. She showed him ID, and asked to pick up clothes. As she hoped, he rang the station to check, filled in a crime-scene entry log, and pulled up the barrier tape.

The flat was freezing. Her drenched clothes iced onto her skin. Through the kitchen door, she saw crime markers between the muddy footprints and broken glass. Another forensics officer was brushing dark powder off the back door. It tumbled onto the brand-new white floor tiles.

'So this is the outer cordon,' a PC was saying, pointing to the kitchen door. 'There's no traces of the deceased outside the kitchen. So you're fine in this part of the flat, but not in the kitchen.'

The black shoes were gone. *Of course they would be.*

'And still you've no idea who he was?' Grace said, in case something new had happened in the past half-hour.

'Sorry.'

Frustrated, she took a rucksack, warm clothes and coats from the bedroom, then crossed to the front sitting room.

Death seeped through the flat like sea-mist. Mac was insane. She wasn't sure she'd be able to *sleep* here, to say nothing of hosting a party. She stuffed her laptop in the rucksack, and leaned against the front bay window. The frame, freshly stripped by John's guys, was waxy and smooth on her cheek.

Raindrops battered on. She peered down, and saw Dad's navy Ford was parked at the end of the street.

Her stomach lurched. For a second, there was hope; then she remembered.

Of course. It was her car now, along with a box of his and Mum's old love letters, his work diaries and photos, her gran's display cabinet, two pairs of reading glasses and the £4,213.23 left from his savings account.

A silver car pulled up beside Dad's. Two police officers climbed out and entered the newsagent's below. Pushing against the window, she tried to see. Perhaps Mr Singh knew something. The dead man had come in through his backyard after all.

She zipped up the rucksack, and headed back out.

Somebody somewhere had to know something.

CHAPTER FIVE

Downstairs, in the rear storeroom, the man stood behind a tall stack of crisp boxes, trying not to cough.

It had gone quiet upstairs at about 2 a.m. Nobody had come to search. But they were definitely coming now.

He stood still behind the box-stack, trying to make out the distant voices.

The door from the shop into the corridor outside opened. Voices grew. Footsteps approached.

Mr Singh jangled the lock of the storeroom.

'And what's in here?' a male police officer said, walking in.

The man formed his lips into a long 'O' to control his air intake.

Mr Singh now. 'Just the storeroom – and toilet.' Nerves twanged in his voice like a worn guitar string.

A drop of sweat from the man's forehead fell to the floor.

A vice closed on his foot. Cramp.

Face contorting, the man pointed his toe, and pulled it back sharp. His other leg struggled to balance. Tensing every muscle in his body, he tried to stay still. One inch to the left and he'd crash through the boxes.

Then a female officer's voice. 'The TV and fridge – do you stay here sometimes, Mr Singh?'

'No, no. It's just a wee break room. Somewhere to get out the way when the wife's doing the accounts!'

The police officers laughed. No doubt Mr Singh's white teeth were flashing too hard in his dark beard.

The man's eyes darted left and right.

There was a sharp tap by his head. The female officer's voice again. 'See, if I worked here, I'd be on that *Obese: A Year to Save My Life*.'

All three laughed again.

Footsteps moved to the back door. It creaked open.

'Right, so the backyard belongs to you, Mr Singh?' The male officer again.

'Aye. You think the guy came over my gate?'

'Forensics'll tell us,' the woman said. 'Have you had any problems in the past with people breaking in, or anything unusual happening at the back?'

'Not really. A bit of graffiti last year when the . . .'

The voices faded and vanished.

The man allowed himself three long, slow breaths, and one muted cough. The sweat from his chest landed on the plastic bag by his cramping foot.

He knew what they were looking for.

They wouldn't find it.

CHAPTER SIX

Doph, doph, doph . . .

On Saturday night, six days after they had found the body, Grace stood in the kitchen of Gallon Street, in a throng of people. Mac's DJ friend Asha bobbed at the decks in the corner, a hand on the headphones atop her pink crew cut. There must have been fifty or sixty people in the kitchen, spilling out into the hall and onto the fire escape. They were dancing, straining to hear each other over the music, laughing, heads thrown back.

Someone had strung fairy lights round the handsome neo-Gothic back door and the heap of wedding presents, which would wait there unopened until they had some more storage. John's fancy dimmer switches gave the place a sophisticated glow; cold wine and beer were stacked in the built-in silver fridge. Wedding-present candlesticks glowed above the plates of food Mac had miraculously arranged.

She knew what it looked like: the fantasy kitchen of property programmes, designed to 'entertain family and friends'. The clean-up company had done an expert job yesterday, too. Every surface, hinge and crease had been deep-cleaned and disinfected. The smudges of fingerprint dust had vanished, and the white walls and tiles shone.

Yet right now, she wanted to be any place but here.

Grace took a stray coat from a chair, and squeezed through to add it to the pile in the sitting room.

If only they could steam-clean her mind.

Gently, she shut the door and sat on the sofa. There were more fairy lights round these wedding presents. Their new curtains covered the front bay window. It looked quite homely. A new framed wedding snap of her and Mac sat on the mantelpiece, brought by a friend tonight. A rainbow blast of confetti billowed in their faces outside the registry office, hiding Grace's strained smile. Mac's arm was round her waist. He was waving to guests out of shot, ready for the evening reception party.

She scanned their eyes, hers dull with grief, his bright with the occasion.

Her eyes strayed to a photo of Dad and, in a rush, the panic of that last day returned. The growing sense of unease as she rang him all day, knowing he'd never miss a hospital appointment. Finding herself at his front door, gripping Mac's hand, taking a last breath before they opened it together, instinct telling her to savour the last few seconds of life as she knew it. That there was something bad on the other side. An *unfathomable* sight.

Tonight, why wasn't Mac thinking of the dead man's family? Rubbing her face, Grace pulled the evening paper from under a cushion, and turned to page six.

BURGLAR DIES AT GALLON STREET

A man has died while breaking into a flat in Gallon Street.
The owners of the flat returned from holiday to find a body
in the kitchen. Police say the intruder, who was in his forties
and had been drinking heavily, died from a suspected fall.

They are not looking for a third party. Anyone with any information about the man's identity should contact the following helpline . . .

Six days now, and no news.

Somewhere, his family were waiting for him, wondering why he wasn't calling.

She thought about the weeping Australian woman she'd seen on the TV news yesterday morning, appealing for information about her husband, who'd gone missing outside Edinburgh in January, hiking in snow. It had made her think of Dad, and how often he'd caught tourists like that wandering haplessly onto Carn Mor Dearg or Aonach Beag mid-afternoon, without hiking survival equipment or even a compass, and turned them back.

If anyone remembers anything, however insignificant, please call this helpline . . . the Australian woman had said to camera, fighting back tears.

Her husband. The dead man in Grace's kitchen.

Dad.

All these families, grieving.

Trapped together in this horrible winter.

Back in the kitchen, the party hit a furious pace. The floor shuddered as Asha rammed up the volume further. More people arrived. Grace waved at Ewan from last year's journalism MA course. He was doing some terrible hand-waving dance by the kitchen door, a head and shoulders above everyone else.

'Heard anything yet about the dead guy?' he shouted down, brushing away sweat.

'Not yet,' she yelled back, wishing everyone would stop

asking. She changed the subject. 'Heard who your new boss is yet at *Scots Today*?'

He rolled his eyes. 'Sula McGregor.'

'Who?'

'Used to be on the *Mail*. Been away freelancing somewhere and just got back. Shit-hot crime reporter, but a right fucking nightmare, so— Hi, girls!' Two of Mac's bar staff, in their early twenties like Ewan, danced close by. Ewan's eyes strayed. His terrible hand-dance restarted, hopefully.

Grace walked off, knowing she'd lost him.

This party was the worst idea Mac had ever had.

It'll be good for us, he had nagged all week. *Honestly. Trust me, darlin'. We'll forget the guy was even here.*

It wasn't good. Not in any way.

She should never have given in.

They were dancing on that poor man's grave.

A cheer went up. John Brock entered the kitchen door, in a sharp suit, longish dark hair pushed back from his face, holding up a bag of beers. With him was a younger woman, with a snub nose and red hair woven in a plait. Mac pushed through the crowds, and he and John clapped each other's shoulders.

Grace turned back to the sink, but it was no good.

A shout. 'Grace!'

John approached, champagne held above his head. 'Find a place for this,' he yelled over the music. 'It's for you two, not this lot.'

'Thanks,' she mouthed.

'How you doing?' he shouted, planting a dry kiss on her cheek. A waft of citrus aftershave.

She shrugged and mouthed, 'OK.'

'Still no news about your guy?'

Not *another* one. 'No,' she yelled over the music.

'Bloody weird, eh?' John looked serious. 'I'm sorry for you. But the flat – it's all right, eh?'

She reminded herself to be grateful. 'No. It's great. Don't worry, we'll forget it happened.'

He grasped her hand in alliance, then walked away, setting off a row of smiles like Christmas lights in the women he passed.

Grace reached up to put the champagne in a top cupboard.

A drunk couple jogged her, making her slip off her tiptoes. Reflex made her grasp the granite worktop – exactly where the dried blood had been. She jerked back.

Air. She needed air.

Squeezing between the dancers, Grace escaped to the fire escape and rinsed her hand in rainwater.

Back through the window, Mac danced with Anne-Marie, the pair of them regressing, as they always did, to the lunatics they'd been at high school, as if college and careers, babies and mortgages had never happened.

As if the dead man had never happened.

His family still didn't even know.

They should have been able to come here first. See where he died. Pay their respects in peace.

Lights twinkled in the high-rise flats that towered at the back of Gallon Street. She scanned the windows, wondering if they were keeping people awake. A faint bluish light drew her eyes down. It was dancing on Mr Singh's back gate. It pirouetted, shifted, faded; returned, and danced on.

Where was that coming from?

Grace bent over the railing and saw the back window of Mr Singh's shop.

A pale green glow, now, illuminated the glass, then melted back into blue.

Somebody was in there.

If she'd been looking for an excuse, finally she'd found one. Grace pushed inside and motioned Asha to turn down the volume. The thumping beat juddered to a halt. Faces turned.

A glance exchanged between Mac and Asha. 'What's up?' he said, pushing towards them.

'Mr Singh's downstairs,' Grace said. 'He must be doing a stock-take or something. We need to call it a day, anyway, Mac. It's after two.'

Mac held out his hand. Unable to refuse in front of all these people, she took it and let him lead her into the hall.

'Did I tell you you look gorgeous, by the way?' he whispered. 'Listen.' He cupped her cheeks with his hands. 'I know you're having a hard time, darlin'. But it's a house-warming. Mr Singh'll understand. Want me to get him up for a drink?'

'No,' Grace said, placing her hands over his. 'I don't. I just want this to stop right n—'

A bass beat crashed across the kitchen like a sonic boom, drowning out her last word.

'No, Mac!' she yelled, the dancing restarting en masse. 'I want everyone to *go home. Now!*'

In his eyes, she saw a struggle about who to please. 'Darlin', John's just got here. Come on. Have a drink and relax and—'

'No!' She pushed him away, ran into the bedroom, slammed the door, and crawled under the duvet.

She knew he wouldn't follow. He couldn't. His boss was here; their friends were here.

Asha bloody what's-her-face had given up a paid gig to be here.

The music thumped through the bedroom wall, and she clutched a pillow round her head, saying sorry to the dead man's family for letting this happen.

It was wrong.

Everything right now was wrong.

CHAPTER SEVEN

Downstairs, the man sat on a stool watching a documentary about a shark. The shark could detect prey miles away from faint signals.

Music pumped through his ceiling. Heels clattered on the floor and laughter shrieked from the fire escape above.

With a growl, he clenched his fists, and climbed on his stool to look at the back gate.

He shut his eyes, imagining climbing over it and heading for home.

The music increased in volume, making the beams above his head judder, and he punched the wall.

What did it matter now, anyway?

His lips parted, and all those days and weeks of holding everything in erupted into a mighty yell.

The force of it propelled him backwards off the stool.

Three months later

CHAPTER EIGHT

'OK, Shona, look at the camera for me, please – head up, chin down. Maybe do something with your hands. Like this . . .' Grace motioned the subject by the window to turn, and took a few shots.

The woman's facial expression had settled somewhere between discomfort and the required appreciation for this free makeover. She rubbed her modest mouth, unused to the sting of the greasy lip-plumper. Her newly reduced curves were temporarily hosting a beige-and-purple geometric wrap dress the stylist had talked her into; six-inch nude heels stretched out what she nervously joked her father called her 'rugby player' calves. Her dark hair was glued into a painful-looking chignon that lifted up her neck hairs.

'Right. Just hold that for me . . .' Grace fired off four more shots. Then, knowing the diet and fitness magazine down in London would want an alternative, said, 'OK, super. Let's do one in the garden.'

The woman hobbled outside like an injured horse. Grace watched her go with sympathy. She'd rather have photographed her an hour ago when they'd arrived: smiley, and natural, her round face creased with laughter lines, dark hair soft and glossy,

35

comfy in her jeans, playing with her dog. By the time the magazine had PhotoShopped Grace's image from today, there would be nothing left of the original woman at all.

The May sky above Edinburgh was blue today, and filled with soft nets of clouds. After the shoot in Stockbridge wrapped, Grace headed on foot to *Scots Today* to her next job, to edit the shots she'd taken last week of the newspaper's new gardening correspondent. She forced herself to avoid the mortuary on Cowgate, as she had for the past month, and turned up past the volcanic hulk of the castle on Castle Terrace, calculating. If the *Scots Today* picture editor was happy, this would be her last freelance job till John's restaurant opening on Sunday night.

There would be time to finish a few jobs in the flat.

As usual, the *Scots Today* office was buzzing with tapping keyboards and the high-energy chatter of a daily newsroom. She waved at Ewan on the news desk, and headed to the Picture Department. She and the picture editor had just made a final decision on the new gardening correspondent headshot when a ball of paper hit the back of her head.

'Oi,' she said, turning round. A second hit her on the chest.

'Scot-*taayy*. What you doing here?' Ewan said.

'Working,' she said, chucking it back at him. 'You should try it.'

'Oh, I'm hiding,' he said, crouching down beside her, his long legs folding like a grasshopper's under the chair.

'Who from?'

'Her.'

A door flew back and a tall woman emerged from the stationery cupboard. She had wild bird's-nest grey hair, black glasses, skinny jeans and a leather jacket. She walked like a gunslinger entering a saloon.

'Oh God. Is that her?' Grace asked.

'Aye. Fuckin' terrifying,' Ewan said.

'Serves you right.'

'You know she smokes in there?' he said, indignant, 'and nobody *says* anything.'

Grace made a horrified face.

He dug a finger in her leg. 'So what are you up to?'

She pointed at her gardening correspondent headshots. 'This. Then I'm finished till Sunday. Mac's away on a golf trip with his dad, so I've got the flat to myself.'

He sighed. 'Lazy fucking freelancers. When are you gonna pitch us some reportage ideas, then, eh?'

'Too busy.'

He tutted. 'Those crappy mags pay you too much. Well, hurry up. We're waiting.' He stood up. 'Hey. I saw your DI Robertson at a police conference yesterday. Still nothing on your dead guy at Gallon Street?'

Her smile vanished. 'No. Heard anything here?'

'Nothing on the news desk. I'm listening out, but . . .'

A shadow fell behind them.

'Ewan, what you doing?'

It was his new boss. Her accent was Glaswegian. Her demeanour suggested a general lack of tolerance for mucking about.

'Grace,' he said, starting back, 'this is my new boss, Sula McGregor, senior crime reporter. Sula, Grace Scott, freelance photojournalist. Grace was a *mature* student on my journalism MA last year – though some might say that was debatable, eh? Ha!' He laughed nervously.

Sula hooked pale yellow-green eyes into Grace, like an eagle spotting a rabbit. Grace ignored Ewan, and held out her hand. Behind Sula's back, Ewan shook his head, mouthing, '*Nooo!*' She dropped it.

37

'Poor you,' the woman said, holding out a digital recorder. 'Right, Ewan, hurry up. I need this transcribed.'

'Yes, master,' he said, trotting away, deflated, mouthing, 'Help me,' at Grace.

Back at Gallon Street, the flat was quiet with Mac away. Grace stored her camera equipment, turned on the kettle, and opened the rear door to let in the afternoon sunshine.

Next door's magnolia tree was in full blossom, its delicate pinky-white petals blowing into Mr Singh's yard. Her gaze rose to the eighth floor of the Crossgate high-rise flats as a curtain drew back. The naked man she saw most days stretched and yawned. She had been tempted to snap him and post the photo through his letterbox anonymously, but suspected he might relish it.

She made tea, then wrote a list of jobs for this afternoon. The first was to open and put away the last few wedding presents; the second was to order bedside lamps; the third to frame and hang her photos from their Thai honeymoon in the hall.

From the original three towers of gift-list wedding presents, only ten or fifteen boxes remained now, stacked against the kitchen wall. The rest had been unwrapped one by one, and squeezed into the airing cupboard, the tiny second bedroom-cum-box room where they kept their bikes, and the new cupboards and shelves they'd had built last month in the sitting room and dining area of the kitchen.

These last gifts would have to cram into whatever space was left. She started with the small boxes on the top, unwrapping Sabatier knives from Auntie Marjorie, photo frames from Mac's cousin in Ullapool and a plastic carriage clock from Dad's old neighbour at the flats. A thin, rectangular package made her laugh. It was a photo Anne-Marie had had blown up on canvas of Grace and Mac on the beach at Lower Largo. They were about sixteen years old, jumping off a rock holding hands, peroxide hair obscuring his face, hers screwed up like a troll, both in their skinny Britpop jeans and lumberjack shirts, her with a badly cut Justine Frischmann bob.

How the hell could that be nearly twenty years ago?

Next, she started on the bottom row. The first large box was a microwave from Mac's gran. The second was heavy and flat.

An envelope was tucked inside its white ribbon. *GRACE SCOTT*, it said on the front.

Grace removed it, wondering why it was addressed to her and not Mac. The envelope was already torn across the top, and empty inside. Whatever had been in there had gone.

That was odd.

Tossing it aside, she undid the wrapping. A frying pan poked out.

'Ooh dear,' she muttered. Instead of the black from their wedding-gift list, it was a violent canary yellow. It also contained a second envelope, addressed to *Mr and Mrs Mackenzie Lowe*, containing a card from Mac's elderly great-aunt Peggy in Canada. Well, the colour might be hideous, but it was sweet of her to go to the trouble.

Grace opened the last few boxes, discovering a kitchen recipe-holder, two more picture frames, two pillows, a juicer, a ruby tartan throw and a white cotton duvet cover.

Considering they'd only invited a small number to the registry office, the evening guests had been unbelievably generous, as if, feeling helpless in the face of her grief, giving her a beautiful gift was all they could think of to reduce the pain of a wedding without Dad.

She gathered the wrapping. Heading for the recycling bin, she bent to pick up the discarded envelope addressed to *GRACE SCOTT*.

And stopped.

On the back, was writing.

It was fussy and looped, and reminded her of her French school pen pal's letters.

The words listed sideways, and were difficult to read.

I am not . . . that man . . . Luc-ian . . . Gra-bol-e.

Lucian Grabole – who was that?

Mentally, Grace summoned the guest list. She'd been so immersed in grief in the months before the wedding Mac had arranged it all.

The name was not familiar.

She texted Mac: 'Do you remember Lucian Grabole at the wedding?'

She waited. No reply.

If he was out on the golf course, it could be hours till he saw it.

She crumpled the envelope with the wrapping paper. Maybe it was a cousin or a friend's boyfriend. A plus-one who'd only known her name, not Mac's.

Losing interest, she threw it away, picked up the unwrapped gifts, and headed for the hall.

Into the airing cupboard she squeezed the new pillows and duvet cover. Then she tried the ruby tartan throw on the Victorian red velvet chaise longue she'd bought for the sitting-room bay window with a little of Dad's money.

She bent down to put the frames in a cupboard and—

Lucian Grabole.

It sounded foreign. Italian or French, maybe.

From nowhere, a thought crashed into her head like a coin in a slot.

Dropping the new frames, she returned to the kitchen and yanked out handfuls of recycling, sending tins clattering onto the tiles.

Flattening out the torn envelope, she checked the handwriting. Blue ink, back and front. Grace waved it under her nose. Why was it empty?

The forensics people had fingerprinted and checked *around* the wedding presents in the kitchen, but as none was missing, and all were sealed, no presents or cards had been opened.

As she sat, thinking, a text arrived from Mac. 'Nope. Why?'

That was disappointing.

'Found his name on a present. Just wondered.'

His reply pinged back. 'No idea. See you Sat ☺ <3 <3 xxx.'

Grace sat at the kitchen table with her phone.

At some point, after the dead man was found, DI Robertson's voice had become less patient when she'd rung to ask about progress.

No, still nothing, I'm afraid. Still making enquiries.

No, nothing since last week, no.

No, nothing for you, sorry.

It had been two months now since her last call, to ask why he hadn't issued an e-fit to the local newspapers. His tone had grown terse as he schooled her on shrinking police budgets, wasting resources on weak lines of enquiry, and murder investigations taking priority over non-suspicious deaths.

When she'd found herself passing the mortuary at Cowgate every time she was in town, in a warped vigil for a dead stranger, she'd known she'd have to let it go, before it drove her insane.

The envelope sat on the table in front of her.

But if there was any chance, any chance at all . . .

She picked up her phone.

41

It wouldn't hurt to remind him they'd been waiting three months for news.

His voicemail promised to ring her back.

She'd just put the plastic carriage clock in a charity-shop box when he did.

'Hello, Ms Scott. What can I do for you?' His kindly tone had returned.

'Oh, hi. I just wondered if there was anything new on our guy.'

'Hang on.' A rustle of paper, but no sigh, like last time. 'Let's see where we are. Right. No match for DNA, fingerprints or physical markings. No match with missing persons reports. Checks done with homeless hostels, bail hostels, social services, hospitals, prisons, immigration and . . . The list goes on here. Hang on . . . and let's see . . . No, all negative.' A pause. 'No, I'm sorry not to have anything new for you. It's very unusual, I have to say. We've flagged up alerts with European police forces, but I wouldn't hold your breath. It can take months, especially if the death's non-suspicious. But we'll get there in the end. You were told about the post-mortem, right?'

'Just a few things, in case we knew him: his height and age; a tattoo of a wolf on his shoulder; the signet ring with a green stone. And you said there was a chance he was working here without being legally registered, and that he possibly had Eastern European or Dutch connections. And you said he was starving and that he'd been drinking heavily.'

'That's right. Pathologist said he fell and hit his head. "Blunt-force trauma" on the granite worktop. Subdural haemorrhage. Fiscal called it "non-suspicious". So I'm afraid that's where we still are.'

'Right.'

'But he's not going anywhere. He'll stay in the mortuary till we get a hit, or someone notices he's missing. Don't worry, we'll get there.'

'OK,' Grace said, wondering how many times he'd said that.

'Anything else?' DI Robertson asked.

'Well, it's probably nothing, but I found something in the flat this morning.'

'Oh?'

She described the note.

There was a rustle of a sweet wrapper and she wondered how his diet was going. 'Have you had many people in the kitchen since the body was found?' he asked.

The back gate opened and Mr Singh walked in carrying a box. She saw him give a slight nod in the direction of his shop, and wondered who it was to. 'Quite a few. We had a house-warming party in February. And our friends and family are round a lot.'

'Anyone else?'

Where was this going?

'Uh, plumber for the washing machine . . . Oh, and the two flats upstairs – they all came in for a drink. Mr Singh downstairs brought up some post. So, yeah, quite a few. Why?'

'So, in theory, any one of those people could have stuck the envelope on the present?' he asked.

'Well, yes, but I'm pretty sure they didn't. Why would they?'

'Well, it's just that we'd need to eliminate each of them. And who touched the presents before they were delivered?'

'The people at the wedding-list firm?'

DI Robertson's tone sharpened. 'And would they have, say, grouped your presents together, maybe on a pallet?'

'I suppose so.'

'And what name did you put the wedding list under?'

'I can't remember. Possibly mine – Grace Scott.'

He continued, 'So a warehouse worker could have scribbled, GRACE SCOTT, on an old envelope, and stuck it on there, to keep your pile separate?'

She fingered the envelope, trying to work out if GRACE SCOTT, in capitals, was written in the same hand as the lower-case message on the back. 'Yes. But why would they write that? *That man is not me Lucian Grabole.*'

'You know what it sounds like to me?' he asked.

'What?'

'A crossword clue. No punctuation.'

'Like an anagram?'

'Are any of the letters crossed out?'

'No. But—'

'So, just in theory, a guy in the warehouse, doing his cross-word – or the delivery-van driver – writes down his clue. Then he needs to separate your gifts, turns it over, writes, GRACE SCOTT, on it and sticks it onto the nearest box.'

'Right,' she said.

'No?'

'No. It's just . . .' She sighed.

'What?' he asked.

'Well, is it not worth considering? I mean, it's been three months now and . . .' *It's more than you've come up with*, she wanted to add.

DI Robertson's tone softened. 'Listen, it's frustrating for us, too. Thing is, if your guy's from Europe – and we don't even know he is – that's a lot of different systems to check. And we still don't even know if he entered the UK legally. But why don't you spell this new name out for me and I'll run it through our systems – see if we can get a hit, even just to rule him out? And I'll get someone to chase up those European police checks. See where we are. OK?'

44

'Thanks.' She spelled it, not feeling optimistic.

'And drop that envelope in to me.'

'Will do. Thanks.'

'And don't worry, we'll get there.'

After the call, Grace made herself lock Lucian Grabole out of her thoughts. There was nothing else to be done now. She decided to go out and buy the bedside lamps at a shop to distract herself.

She walked around the kitchen fetching her keys and coat.

Her eyes strayed back to the envelope on the table.

It could be days or weeks till DI Robertson checked the name Lucian Grabole. For all she knew, budgets would force him to wait for the European checks first.

She *would* drop the envelope in to him – in her own time.

She threw down her keys, sat, opened her laptop, and typed two words into Google.

Lucian Grabole.

CHAPTER NINE

That afternoon, Sula McGregor burst into the office of *Scots Today* from a meeting with the minister in charge of cyber-crime and stopped.

A gang of people were huddled around the printer, eyes on the floor. Shouting came from the editor's office.

'What's going on there?' she said to Ewan, throwing down her bag.

'Oh, you'll find out,' her assistant said, pushing his greasy hair out of his spots.

She sat down. 'I know I will, because you're going to tell me.'

'I know I am.'

'But first you're going to get me a coffee.'

'That's not in my job description.'

'Neither's being an arse. Off you go.'

He stood up. 'Would you like that coffee with one or two bodily functions?'

She ignored him, piling her interview notes and voice recorder onto the desk. A muffled shout came through the partition wall from the editor's office. She recognized the agitated tone of the sub who'd misspelled a headline on her story last week. Sula opened up her screen.

Ah well. He'd had it coming for a while.

She could have told him the trick to longevity in this job was knowing where the bodies were buried.

Sula was just finishing up her report on proposed amendments to Scottish cyber-crime law when Ewan held up a hand.

'Sula, seen this?'

'What?'

He pointed at the Police Scotland Twitter feed. '"Body found at Auchtermouth."'

'No. Is that right?' She typed the last sentence quickly and looked over.

'Think it could be that Australian hiker David Pearce?' Ewan said.

'I think it could, son.'

The old instinct came to ring Donnie or Joe. Not for the first time, Sula cursed bloody Leveson and the fear of God he'd put into her coppers.

All above board now, Officer.

These days, a woman had to be creative.

Sula filed her story, stood up, and grabbed her bag. 'Right. I'm going up there. Stay on Twitter, Ewan. Check the Pearce family Tweets in Australia, and Twitter from around Auchtermouth – shops, library, the usual.'

This was the missing hiker David Pearce up on that cliff – she knew it.

The sun disappeared as Sula drove out of the city up the coast to Auchtermouth, and she wondered why David Pearce would have been here, when he'd told his father he was miles away, hiking in the Pentlands.

'Oh, hello. Now, where've you come from?' Sula muttered, as

she pulled into a lay-by, by a police car. A serious-incident vehicle had parked just in front of her. A PC climbed in the side door, presumably to set up an interview space for any passers-by with information about the discovered body. Sula checked around to see who else was here. This would have made sense for a murder – 'I've just remembered, Officer, I saw this red car outside my house last month, acting strangely' – but for a pensioner who'd gone missing hiking in bad weather? What use was that?

With her binoculars, Sula searched the body recovery scene up on the cliff, behind blue-and-white barrier tape. Every time she attended one of these, some smart-arse had found a new way to hide it from any passing nosy parker with a camera phone and a Twitter account.

This time, a black crime scene barrier flapped in the east-coast wind, in front of the roof of a white evidence tent. Just to make sure, a police van and a four-by-four were parked either side of the barrier screen.

Sula put down her binoculars.

Something wasn't right here. She checked the police Twitter accounts again. Nothing new. Still saying 'a body' had been found.

Maybe this wasn't Pearce.

She checked her GPS. To the left of the crime scene, the coastal cliff dropped steeply down to the fishing village of Auchtermouth. She'd already seen two dog walkers. Must be a path. If this was Pearce, and he'd collapsed in the snow on a hike, how the hell had the old fella lain here for four months without being seen?

Three more cars drew up and parked on the verge. The usual suspects from the local media got out of two, and walked to the police tape with cameras and recording equipment. From the third came two detectives she didn't recognize. They pulled wellies on over their grey Slaters suits and spoke to the PC in the lay-by.

Right. Time to go.

Sula grabbed her hiking stick from the back seat and followed them. At the barrier tape, she turned left towards the locals milling around, bored dogs at their heels. Their expressions said they were terribly sad, and terribly curious.

Making like she was off for a refreshing walk on the cliffs, Sula arrived among them.

'Oh dear, what's happened here?' she said to a wifey with a poodle.

The woman told her that a body had been found by a woman 'from the village' walking her dog. She was 'very shaken up'. No, she didn't know her name.

Sula sized up the scene.

Down in a dip stood another PC on guard duty.

Derrick Gillespie.

Bingo.

He was guarding a vulnerable spot at the bottom corner, where the tape ran out by a gnarled tree. He stood, hands wrapped in front of his neon-yellow jacket, with the pinched features of a man who'd guarded a crime scene for hours without going for a piss.

Sula turned on her heel. No harm making him wait.

Back in the car, she wrote a draft of a short news story that a body had been found on the cliff above Auchtermouth by a female dog walker.

Then she logged on to the Twitter accounts of David Pearce's brother, other Pearce family members, and the 'Find David Pearce' campaign. All was silent. It was night-time in Australia, though. Next she checked Twitter news alerts from Edinburgh, and Australia, to ensure nobody was getting ahead of her.

Nothing new.

It would be ten o'clock in Perth, right now. She emailed David Pearce's brother, hoping he'd still be up.

'Body found on cliff outside Edinburgh. Do you have a comment?'

Two of the journalists drove off, clearly deciding there was nothing else to do now till a news conference was called.

Fine by her.

Sula grabbed an insulated bag from the back seat, removed two still-warm bacon rolls from the cafe in Auchtermouth, unwrapped and took a bite of one, and headed back up to Derrick Gillespie with the other.

'God's sake, Derrick,' she called. 'This weather. Can't make its mind up.'

His eyes were defeated, his nose pink. 'You're right there, Sula.'

The smell of warm bacon wafted between them. His eyes flickered with longing, then away.

'Been here hours?' Sula said, taking another bite.

'Coming up five.'

'I don't know how you guys do it, Derrick.'

'Bladder like steel, Sula.'

She laughed. 'Just like your dad. How is he?'

'Oh, good, thanks, fine.'

'Enjoying his retirement?'

'Aye.'

'Good for him.' She looked around. 'Have you seen that daft new assistant of mine?'

'No, sorry.'

She tutted. 'He should come with an instruction manual, that

one. Brought him this up an' all. Gonna have to eat it myself.'
She held the packet out in front of him. 'You don't . . . ?'

Derrick's nostrils quivered.

'Can't eat on duty, no?'

'No.'

'Shame. Never mind.' She took another bite of her roll.

Derrick sniffed to stop his nose running. He sighed. 'Oh, go
on, then, Sula.'

'Sure? I'll stand in front of you. Nobody's looking.' She took
a ketchup sachet out of her pocket. 'Want one of these?'

'Cheers.'

He unwrapped the roll, squirted on the sauce, turned to the
bushes, and demolished a third of it in one bite. Sula sneaked a
look to the back of the crime scene. That was odd. Two guys
who looked like Mountain Rescue, with hard hats and coiled
ropes, were heading into the tent.

She wrapped her coat around her. 'Nearly didn't make it up
here – traffic's mad on the bridge.'

'Aye?' Derrick chewed fast, cheeks bulging.

'Better tell your Fiona if she's bringing you up some nice
warm soup later.'

He snorted. 'Ha! I'll be lucky.'

'Oh, it's like that, is it?' she laughed. 'Right. Well, looks like
he's not here, so that's me, Derrick. I'm heading off. You here a
while longer?'

'Aye. Few more hours.'

Sula pointed to the dog walkers passing by. 'Poor woman with
the dog, eh?'

Derrick nodded, eyes ecstatic as he chewed.

'I tell you, who needs Search and Rescue?' Sula said. 'Wifey
with a cocker spaniel, that's what you need.'

51

'Could have found him from space this time, Sula,' he said through the last mouthful.

'Oh. That bad?'

He rolled his eyes.

'Is it our walker guy?'

'Need to ID him first.'

Him.

Sula didn't blink. 'Know when there'll be an update?'

'Morning, maybe.'

'OK, well, you have a good night, then.'

'Thanks for the roll.'

'No bother. Hope the rain holds off for you.'

She returned to the car. An email was waiting from David Pearce's brother, Philip. 'Can you tell us more?' it said.

She tapped her reply. 'Unconfirmed reports man's body found on cliff above Auchtermouth. Comment?'

Ten seconds. 'We're hopeful for news.'

Two minutes later, Sula filed her story.

A man's body has been found on the cliff above Auchtermouth
by a female dog walker. The family of Australian tourist
David Pearce, 60, who disappeared on 29 January while
hiking in snow, are 'hopeful for news'.

She wound down her window, chucked out her half-eaten roll, and drove off.

CHAPTER TEN

That night, in Gallon Street, Grace tossed in bed, unable to sleep.

During the afternoon, she had just meant to Google the name 'Lucian Grabole'. But when 'zero results' had appeared, she'd decided to add each European country alongside the name, and search for that. Also with no luck.

She'd then found herself going through a list of Edinburgh's homeless shelters, her phone at her ear.

'Hello. My name's Grace Scott. I'm trying to find a homeless man who might have stayed with you a few months ago – called Lucian Grabole?'

The answers had fallen into four categories.

'*My manager's not here right now. Can you call back later?*'

'*Please leave a message and someone will get back to you.*'

'*Sorry, we can't give out that information on the phone.*'

'No, sorry, nobody knows that name.'

Grace had clicked her pen on and off, meaning to stop.

She was supposed to be going out to buy bedside lamps.

Each time, she rang just one more number.

By the time she'd gone to bed that night, she'd rung thirty-six numbers in total. After the homeless shelters, she'd tried food banks and homeless charities. Then repeated the process in Glasgow, Stirling and all other towns of any size within an hour of Edinburgh. Nobody she spoke to had heard of Lucian Grabole.

Maybe DI Robertson was right. She got up, turned on the main light, and wrote, *I am not that man Lucian Grabole*, on a piece of paper. Then she wrote each letter in a random order, and moved them around, trying to spot the answer to an anagram. It would be difficult without a clue.

A memory came of Dad using a computerized anagram solver when he was struggling with his daily crossword.

She walked into the hall fumbling for the light switch.

A noise made her stop.

Eech, eech, eech.

It sounded like bed springs bouncing in the neighbouring flat.

Disorientated, she turned on the hall light. But the geologists' bedrooms were above theirs, not the hall.

Grace leaned forward.

It was coming from the kitchen.

Eech, eech, eech.

Almost beneath her . . . *feet?* She knelt and placed her ear over the doorway onto the tiled floor.

Eech, eech, eech.

Downstairs.

That couldn't be right. The shop was shut. She'd seen Mr Singh leave through the back gate and get into his van at 7 p.m., as he did every night.

Water pipes? Old plumbing?

Too tired to work it out, she stood up to switch on the kettle, found an anagram-solving program on her laptop, and entered, '*I am not that man Lucian Grabole.*'

An animated wheel spun.

'Zero results.'

The kettle hissed noisily in the still night. She made tea and walked to the window. Three lights on in the tower block tonight. She wondered who they were, and why they were up at this hour.

It had taken months to lose her raw fear of night-time. That she'd be woken again at 2 a.m. by the image of Dad dead in his chair, thinking it was a nightmare. Realizing it wasn't.

Sipping her tea, she realized she hadn't thought about Dad all evening.

It should have been a relief, she knew, to feel the lid of grief finally lifting, even for a moment.

Yet as the lid peeled back, she realized she was starting to remember what had been lurking there before.

CHAPTER ELEVEN

Downstairs, in Mr Singh's storeroom, the man stood in the darkness, on cold tiles, breathing shallow, each wrist wrapped round the ends of a towel straddling the ceiling beams above, sweat dripping off his shaved head.

A light patter of footsteps crossing the ceiling was followed by the sound of a door shutting.

They'd gone. He waited ten minutes for whoever it was to fall asleep again, and turned his head torch back on.

Twenty still to go.

Gripping the towel ends tightly in each hand, he lifted his body weight between them, his straining neck, biceps and shoulders forming a cross of hard muscle.

The ceiling beams protested on each lift.

Eech, eech, eech.

CHAPTER TWELVE

Sleep hadn't come till after 2 a.m., but Grace was still back at her laptop early the next morning, eating a slice of toast, compiling a new list of phone numbers, watching the clock.

When it clicked round to 9 a.m., she gave Ewan a few minutes to take off his coat in the *Scots Today* office, then rang.

'It's me,' she said. 'If you were trying to track down a homeless man in this area who might have not been registered officially anywhere, and you'd had no luck with homeless shelters and charities or food banks, what would you do next? If you had a name for him?'

'Good morning, Ewan. How are you this fine day?' he said.

'Good morning, Ewan. So what's the answer?'

He tutted. 'Did you not do the same journalism course as I did?'

'Yes, but you've got all the contact numbers in the office. It'll take me hours to find them. I'm thinking bail hostels, hospitals, social services. Can you think of anything else? And could you email me them?'

'Hang on . . .' He broke off. She heard Sula's voice in the background. A minute's pause. 'OK, I'll ask her,' Ewan replied, 'but my mum's not happy with you, Sula.' He returned to the phone.

'What's that about?' Grace asked.

'Don't ask.'

'OK, so can you help?'

'Is this your dead guy, the one you're not obsessing about anymore?'

'Don't judge – you didn't find him in your flat.'

'OK, but you'll need to wait. There's a story breaking, and I've got Frankie Five Fingers here giving me daggers.'

The first list Ewan sent Grace arrived half an hour later, giving her time to shower and dress. It included hospital and clinic numbers in the Edinburgh area, and social services. It was followed by bail hostels and Immigration.

Grace dived straight in. By 11 a.m., she had made seventeen more calls, without a single hit.

Flagging, she rang the wedding gift company.

'Are you sure?' she pressed at the news they didn't employ a Lucian Grabole. 'Or do any of your staff do cryptic crosswords? One of the drivers, maybe?'

That had given them a laugh, at least.

Dispirited, she popped downstairs to Mr Singh's to buy milk.

The door jangled as she entered. Normally he looked up, but the counter was empty. She walked to the fridge and took out two pints.

A door at the back of the shop opened. Mr Singh jumped when he saw her. 'Oh, sorry. Been there long?'

'No, no.' She took the milk to him. 'How are you?'

'Can't complain, thanks,' he said, ringing it up. 'Saw your husband heading off with his clubs yesterday.'

She handed him a five-pound note. 'Yeah, Blairgowrie. He goes every May with his dad and uncles and cousins. They've been doing it since he was wee.'

'Very good.' He handed her the change.

She put it away. 'I don't suppose you've heard anything new about the dead man upstairs, have you?'

'No. You?'

'Still waiting. Taking forever, isn't it?'

'Aye, seems to be.'

'Right, see you later.' She stopped at the shop door. 'Oh, by the way, Mr Singh, there was a weird noise in the flat last night – a sort of creaking under the floorboards. You haven't noticed anything, have you? Old water pipes or something?'

For a moment, she thought he hadn't heard her. He stood still, as if listening to something far away.

''Cos obviously we don't want it to turn into a leak,' she added.

He unfroze. 'No. Right. I've heard nothing.'

'OK, well, let me know if you do and we'll get a plumber on it.'

'No problem.'

She exited and unlocked the front door to the tenement. There was a click behind her. Vaguely she wondered why Mr Singh was locking the shop door at this time of day.

She was standing by the kettle a minute later, humming to herself, when the red blob on the answerphone caught her eye.

Banging down the mug, she ran. The caller had an English accent.

'Hi. This is Ebele at Riverside Shelter. Um. You can ring me back!'

Riverside? She found her list. It was the fifth number she'd rung yesterday.

The same girl answered.

'Hi,' Grace said, a little breathless. 'You rang me. Grace Scott. I called about Lucian Grabole?'

'Oh yes, that's me. Ebele. I'm a student volunteer here.'

'Oh, hi. So . . .'

The girl continued, 'You're looking for a Lucian?'

'Yes. Well, Lucian Grabole?'

'Well, I don't know if it'll help, but we definitely had a Lucian in last year.'

Grace doodled the word 'Riverside'. 'Really? Can you remember what he looked like or where he was from?'

'No, sorry,' the girl said. 'I'm not sure I even met him. I just remember his name in the register.'

'Lucian Grabole?'

'No, as I say, "Lucian". I only noticed it because my cousin called her son Lucius, and I know it's stupid, but I . . .'

Grace drew stars round the word 'Riverside', hope already fading. Yet until she thought of more places to try, what else was there to do?

'Could I come over now?' she asked.

'Sure!'

The girl gave her directions.

Riverside Shelter was located on the eastern outskirts of the city in an area Grace had rarely been. Rain started as she drove up in Dad's car, and parked in a gravel car park beside a red-brick church hall and two tower blocks that had seen better days. The door of the hall was unlocked. Inside, it smelt of antiseptic and cheap washing powder.

A girl was leafing through a ledger. She had a long braided ponytail, and wore a home-knitted red jumper. She gave Grace a bright smile.

'Hi,' Grace said, holding out a hand. 'I'm Grace.'

'Oh, hi! I've been trying to find that name for you. I'm just thinking, it must have been last summer, because I was—'

A side door opened. A tall, pale boy with limp hair pushed in a bike. He had that consumptive poet's look that worked well fronting indie bands but could be insipid elsewhere.

'Stuart,' the girl said. 'This is Grace Scott. I'm trying to find that Lucian we had in. Do you remember?'

Mild irritation crossed his face as if he had much more important things to deal with. 'What's this about?'

'Hi. Grace Scott.' He shook her hand reluctantly. 'I'm trying to find information about a homeless man who's died. He was possibly called Lucian Grabole and might have stayed here.'

Stuart walked behind the counter. 'And you are?'

Too late she realized she didn't have a good answer. 'Um. I'm actually a freelance photojournalist. I was there when he died and I've sort of become involved trying to track down his family. They don't know yet.'

It was vague enough not to be a complete lie.

'Stuart's the co-coordinator here,' Ebele said to Grace, her dark-brown eyes shining, making Grace wonder if Ebele volunteered here because he did.

'Lucian? Uh. Yeah. He was the one who persuaded Joel to have a shower.'

Ebele's eyes widened. 'Oh my God – was that him? I remember you telling me.' She stuck out her bottom lip. 'Aw, we have this lovely old guy called Joel. He doesn't like taking his shoes off in case someone steals them, so he won't go in the shower. I remember that guy Lucian – you said he was lovely to him, Stuart, didn't you? Really patient.'

Stuart flicked through the ledger. 'Yeah. Haven't seen him for a while, though . . . Yup, May last year. There.'

There was a list of men's names.

One stood out, halfway.

Lucian Grabole.

Grace's stomach lurched. 'Oh my God,' she said, double-checking, in case she'd misread it. From her pocket, she pulled out the envelope from the flat and checked the spelling. 'That's him.'

The pair glanced at each other.

'Sorry, I wasn't actually expecting it to be him.' She composed herself. 'Right . . . Can you remember the last time you saw him?'

Stuart frowned. 'As I say, a while ago. Last summer. Maybe earlier. May.'

'And can I check – was he about five foot ten, brown hair –' she held her hand under her chin, then pointed at her shoulder '– wolf tattoo here, signet ring with a green stone?'

Stuart took off his jacket. 'Don't remember a tattoo or a ring. The rest of it sounds about right – though, to be honest, it matches a lot of our guys in here. The police were in asking with the same kind of description a few months ago. Told them, too. Could be half our lot.'

'So it *could* be Lucian.'

'Could be.'

'Can you remember where he'd come from, or where he was going?'

He took down an apron and put it on. 'I think he mentioned being in Paris. But no idea if he came from there.'

'So he was French?' Grace said, praying for any kind of clue.

Stuart hesitated. 'I thought you knew him?'

'No, as I say, I was there when he died. That's how I got involved trying to trace his family.'

'Right. Again, I don't know. He spoke English here, so . . .'

'With an accent?'

62

'Yeah. Don't know what it was, though.'

Stuart picked up a large steel pot from behind reception.

Grace pointed at the double doors. 'Is that where the men sleep?'

'Yup.' He was once again starting to look as if he had more important things to do.

'Stuart, I'm sorry to bother you when you're so busy, but would you mind if I looked around?' she asked. 'Maybe Ebele could show me?'

He frowned. 'Um. As long as the guys are not there.'

'No, absolutely.'

'Come this way!' Ebele took the ledger, and led Grace into a large main hall, the doors swinging back behind them.

It smelt of school dinners and jumble sales. Around the edges were twenty beds, stripped bare, with folded blankets and bare pillows. On the wall was a large colourful painting of a robed Jesus, his hands parted. Four tables formed an E-shape for communal eating, and a large, clunky television stood in the corner. An insistent electronic beeping came from a door into a small kitchen.

'So, how does it work, Ebele?' Grace said.

'Well, we have twenty men most nights. We open at eight and do dinner. Then we sit with the guys and chat and play board games and maybe watch a film or TV. The guys have a shower and sleep. In the morning, we give them breakfast and a packed lunch.'

Grace watched the hatch, imagining the man who'd died in her kitchen, in his shabby pinstriped suit and scuffed shoes, queuing for food here. It fitted.

Ebele lowered her voice. 'Honestly, I thought it was going to be depressing, but it's actually quite nice. Like a little community.'

The electronic beeping continued in the kitchen.

Ebele pointed. 'That's the dryer – I've just got to put some more sheets in.'

'Sure.' Grace checked for Stuart. 'This might sound strange, but would you mind if I photographed the room? In case the dead man is Lucian and I can find his family. Then I can show them where he was. I'm not sure they even know which country he was in.'

Ebele looked anxiously at the double doors.

'While the guys aren't here,' Grace repeated.

'I suppose, as long as they're not here, it should be fine,' Ebele said uncertainly.

The minute the girl entered the kitchen, Grace photographed the bed below the painting, the hands of Jesus parted benevolently above a green waterproof mattress. Then she shot another bed in focus, with the six identical ones beyond blurring into the distance. She turned to photograph the dining table, and noticed that Ebele had left the ledger open. Grace fired off three shots of Lucian's handwritten name, focusing in tight so the other names were blurred.

'Aw, it's really sad,' Ebele called through. 'How did he die?'

'Well, as I say, I'm still not sure it *is* Lucian, but the man who died had been drinking and hadn't eaten. They think he collapsed and hit his head.'

'Can the police not find his family?'

'They are looking, but it takes ages for all the foreign police checks to come back.'

'Shame.' Ebele returned with an armful of sheets. 'But if you're not sure it's Lucian, why don't you just contact someone who knows him?'

Grace put away her camera. 'I wish it was that simple.'

Ebele pointed at the ledger. 'Can't you just ring them?'

On the facing page, Grace saw a list of phone numbers – one opposite Lucian Grabole's name. She swallowed. She'd completely missed it. 'Lucian wrote that number?'

'We ask all the guys for a contact, even if it's just their social worker.' Ebele folded the sheets and dipped her head coyly. 'Actually, I'm thinking about journalism when I graduate.'

Grace wrote down the number. 'Well, if you do, give me a ring – I might be able to help.'

'Really? Wicked!'

The fire door opened and Stuart carried in the catering-sized pot, eyeing her with suspicion.

Grace slipped her camera behind. 'Well, listen – thanks. That's so useful. I'll leave you to it.'

'So will you let us know if it is Lucian?' Stuart said. 'Joel might like to know.'

'Absolutely. And if you hear anything else, would you ring me?'

She gave them her freelance card, and headed into the corridor. Through the door-window, she saw rain and reached for her hood. As the fire doors slammed behind her, something fluttered. It was a pinboard, crammed with notices. In between health-advice posters and charity helplines, a gallery of photocopied faces stared out.

Missing persons notices.

'Kevin', a spotty nineteen-year-old from London in an army uniform, had gone missing in December. 'Anna and Valentin', a blonde woman and child, were just 'missing', the message in English and another language. 'Aiden', a ruddy-faced man in a wedding suit, had last been seen in Dublin in 1989.

All these families not knowing if their loved ones were alive or dead. Lost in a city of strangers. Grace whipped out her camera and shot the board.

The fire doors banged open and Stuart came out. He saw her camera.

'God, raining again,' she said, pulling up her hood and leaving.

She arrived back at Gallon Street around midday, and sat at the table, examining Lucian Grabole's contact number, unsure of what to do next. *0208* . . . That was a London code.

Grace lifted the receiver, then replaced it, considering the gravity of what she was about to do.

If this *was* Lucian Grabole's family and he *was* missing, she'd potentially be giving them life-changing news.

She tapped her pen.

She could always just *ask* if they knew him. Then if it was Lucian's family, ring DI Robertson with the information so he could inform them officially.

She made a cup of tea, drank it, and decided to go for it.

On the fourth ring, someone answered.

'Hello?' she said.

A pause, then a woman's voice, a foreign accent, quiet and suspicious. 'Hello.'

'Hi. I'm sorry to bother you. I'm looking for someone called—'

A click. A muttered conversation. A new voice appeared. A man.

'Hello?' His accent was thicker, his tone equally wary.

'Hi. Sorry, do you speak English?'

'Yes.'

'Hi. I wonder if you can help. My name's Grace Scott. I'm trying to find a man called Lucian Grabole.'

Silence, then more whispering.

The phone went dead.

She looked at the receiver. 'What the . . . ?'

Grace rang again with no reply. She tried three more times. Nobody picked up.

Her eyes strayed to the floor. The light from the back window caught a faint rubber shoe mark imprinted on the white tiles. She leaned down and rubbed at it, thoughtfully, wondering who'd been on the other end of the line.

CHAPTER THIRTEEN

The day dragged on into early afternoon. Grace made herself a sandwich and ate it, pondering her next move.

She could just ring DI Robertson right now, pass on this new information, and go and buy her bedside lights.

Yet each time she lifted the phone to ring Lother Street Station, she put it down.

Once she'd given them him this number, it would be his. He could do what he wanted with it. And as his interest in the torn envelope and the name Lucian Grabole appeared to be about zero, she found herself reluctant.

Grace clicked her pen off and on till her thumb ached, then rang another number. 'It's me.'

'Oh God. Piss off, Scotty. I'm *busy*,' Ewan said, tapping away.

'Do you want to hear what happened or not?'

The typing stopped. 'What?'

She told him.

'OK, now I'm interested,' Ewan said. 'What you going to do?'

'I don't know.'

'You know what you *should* do?'

'What?' she asked.

'Do it as a story.'

'What do you mean?'

'Write it. "I Tracked Down the Mystery Man Who Died In My Flat." There's loads of that stuff in the papers right now – all that catfishing stuff: "I Tracked Down My Internet Troll"; "I Tracked Down My Internet Stalker and Discovered It Was My Ex"; "My American Internet Boyfriend Turned Out to Be a Granny In Hull." It's good – human interest with a –' he mimicked a posh arts-programme presenter '– twenty-first century urban-alienation angle. Go for it. Do the story *and* the photos.'

She frowned. 'Hmm. Not sure how that would work.'

'It's easy. Come on, Scotty. You're always talking about wanting to do the big stories. You need to hurry up. You'll be retiring soon.'

'I'm thirty-five, Ewan. But cheers.' She doodled on her pad.

'Look, if you do it as an investigation,' he continued, 'you're in control. You're not under obligation to tell the police anything. Not till you're about to go to press.'

That was true. 'Yeah, but who's going to commission me to write a story based on an old envelope?'

'Do more research. You've got all week. Then pitch it. Pitch it here. It's got the Edinburgh angle. Editor might go for it.'

She screwed up her nose. 'I'll think about it. Will you do me one last favour, though? Can you get an address for this number in London?'

'Hang on.'

She gave it to him and heard tapping.

'Right, it's 137 Easter Way. East London postcode. Name's "Cozma". C-O-Z-M-A.'

'Cozma? Not Grabole?'

'Nope. I'll email it over.'

'Thanks.'

'So, are you going?' he teased her.

'Where?'

'London. Knock on doors, ask questions . . .'

Sula's voice appeared in the background again. 'Ewan, will you get off that bloody phone? I need you to . . .'

'Fuck. Frankie's back. Gotta go.' Ewan cut her off.

She sat back thinking about what he'd said. *London. Do the story* and *the photos.*

She circled the address. That was a stupid idea. Yes, Lucian Grabole might exist after all, in real life – she'd had a lucky break with that – but he was still just a name on an old envelope. It didn't mean there was a link to her dead man.

She made more tea, imagining what Mac would say if he was here.

Don't be nuts. It's a stupid idea. That Ewan talks bollocks.

On a whim, she checked the online balance of the money Dad had left her. Then, on another whim, she looked up flights to London.

The next one was 4.15 p.m.

Grace glanced out of the back window at the locked gate, and the tower block looming above, cutting out the afternoon light.

It was Tuesday lunchtime. Mac wasn't back till Saturday.

She could be down to London and back before anyone even noticed.

The envelope sat on the kitchen table.

I am not that man Lucian Grabole.

What the hell did that even mean?

She clicked her pen on and off.

CHAPTER FOURTEEN

'Come on, big man, where are you?'

That same afternoon, Sula sat in the car park of the police station nearest to Auchtermouth, checking her watch. The 5 p.m. press conference on the discovery of the body on the cliff would start in ten minutes.

She checked each approaching car till she spotted a familiar one.

A green saloon pulled in and parked in the corner. DI Robertson hauled himself out, a hefty arm on the roof for leverage.

When he'd entered the police station, she moved her car next to his, then went inside.

Today's conference was held in a hastily located small room. It was already packed with cameras and lights, and people jostling for space for their mics on the desk. Sula stood at the back.

As she'd expected, it was mostly Scottish press, with a few stringers for the Australian media. If this body was David Pearce, nobody else would be bothered with a missing retired walker.

'All right, Sula?' a voice said beside her. One of her old cronies from the *Mail*.

'How you doing, Kenny?' she said, squeezing by.

'You're back, then?' he said, letting her past. 'Someone said you were away down in . . . Where was it? Man—'

'Mind Your Own Business Land?' she said, watching the side door.

Kenny chortled. 'Oh, come on. What was it? Bit of freela—'

'Here we go,' Sula said, cutting him off with a hand.

A door opened and three people trooped to the front. The senior investigating officer, Detective Superintendent Lady Muck, with her sparrow frame and plastic bob, took centre stage, as usual. To her left was that irritating wee press officer Vani, whose catchphrase was 'I'll get back to you' and never did, then Lady Muck's deputy, DI Robertson, towering above them both. Christ. The big guy looked like he was going to eat them for his tea.

Lady Muck waited for silence.

'Right, thank you for coming. I'm now going to read a state-ment. Yesterday at 7.40 a.m., a dog walker discovered a body on the cliff above Auchtermouth. I am very sorry to say that we can confirm that the deceased is David Pearce. Mr Pearce, an Austra-lian tourist, disappeared while hill-walking in poor conditions on 29 January.' She paused to allow a ripple of reaction. 'Mr Pearce's body has now been removed from the site, and his family has been informed. I would like to thank the many local volunteers who joined the extensive search for Mr Pearce. At this time, I am not able to give you a cause of death.'

There was a rush of raised hands.

Lady Muck glanced at DI Robertson and he nodded.

Sula's hackles raised. *Oh aye – here we go.*

Lady Muck cleared her throat to get their full attention.

'While recovering Mr Pearce's body, a second body was dis-covered at the scene.'

A collective hush filled the room. Recording lights were double-checked, mics pushed closer.

Sula's hand reached for the door. Two bodies in the same spot. The story would go national in minutes.

'As yet we do not have an identity for the second body,' Lady Muck said. 'We are currently removing the deceased from the site. I will update you when we have further news. That is all for now.'

A flurry of hands and calls.

'Is the second body male or female?'

'Is it an adult or a child?'

'How long has the second body been there?'

'Is this an accident site or a murder site?'

Sula crept out and leaned against her car. Ten minutes later, following their useless one-to-ones with the detectives, the other journalists spilt out, along with Vani, who climbed into a silly wee button-sized car. Next came Lady Muck, clicking past, nose in the air, to her waiting driver. Soon enough, the big guy came towards her.

Here we go.

Sula rang the old pager inside her bag. It beeped.

'Ach, where is it?' she exclaimed.

She turned the bag upside down as if taking a closer look inside. The pager and some pound coins kept for this exact purpose crashed onto the tarmac.

'Oh God, what am I like?' She knelt down.

'Here you go, Sula.' DI Robertson stood on a coin as it approached a drain, and helped her grab the rest with a grunt.

Sula stood up, hand on her back. 'Thank you. Getting old here, Fin.'

'No problem,' he said, opening his car.

Sula kept her tone casual. 'Well, that's some news, eh? Two men dead. They'll all be here tomorrow, eh? Sky, BBC . . .'

DI Robertson chortled. 'Sula, you're something else. Try it on someone who's not been round the block a few times.'

She dropped the grin. 'Oh, come on, Fin. Is it another guy?'

'You'll have to wait like everyone else.'

She zipped her bag up crossly. 'You lot are tighter than a cat's arse these days. Can't blame a woman for getting creative.'

He squeezed himself inside. 'Oh, I don't. In fact, it's very entertaining to watch.'

'See you,' she said, waving a dismissive hand. 'On your way.'

He chuckled. 'See you soon.'

She watched him heading out of the car park, his car listing to the right with his weight.

'You'll see how creative I can get, big man.'

CHAPTER FIFTEEN

London

Grace stood on the Tube platform at Heathrow Airport, not quite believing what she'd just done. An hour after her phone call with Ewan, she'd found herself in a taxi to Edinburgh Airport, rucksack beside her, passport in her camera bag for ID, fighting the urge to ask the driver to turn round.

In the end, she'd left Mac a handwritten note, on the off chance he came home from Blairgowrie early and freaked that she wasn't there. If she rang him now, it would only cause an argument. His patience with her obsession with the dead man had run out at about the same time as DI Robertson's. *You've spent your dad's money on* what?

She boarded the next Piccadilly Line train to King's Cross, then took more Tube and overland train connections to East London.

Out of the window, she watched as the city shape-shifted. Multicoloured new-build flats slotted into every conceivable space along the track. Seventies tower blocks stood like wild oats among fields of Victorian terraces. The train turned a bend and the sun glinted off a hundred high-rise windows like a discoball. A curl of dual carriageway veered above her head and vanished.

Residential homes gave way to warehouses, and wasteland. Evening sun gathered in golden puddles on a scrubby marsh. Two roof-running teenagers somersaulted in silhouette off an industrial shed.

She wondered if Lucian Grabole had seen this. Even sat in this carriage, doing the journey in reverse to Scotland. If he had, what had been on his mind?

So ensconced in thought was she, she nearly missed her stop. The platform was quiet, the rush hour finished. She climbed up to a scruffy street, and turned past overflowing bins, a funeral parlour offering foreign repatriation, then a row of cheap international call centres and fried chicken and kebab shops.

The hotel she'd booked was five minutes' walk.

'Lovely,' she muttered as she approached.

It was a double-fronted porridge-coloured house. Its plaster was crumbling, the '0181' London phone number on its sign years out of date. It had cost per night the same as the Edinburgh conference hotel she and Mac had stayed in while Forensics were in their flat. A sullen man on reception showed her to her room. Once a double, it had clearly been divided in half into two thin singles, the middle section carved into a minute shower room and wardrobe for each side. A ridiculously narrow corridor now led past the wardrobe and shower room to a seven-foot-square space by the window, crammed tight with a single bed.

She threw down her rucksack, wishing Mac could see this. There was a cheap telly on the wall, and a lamp on a Formica shelf above her head.

Rubbing her eyes, she sat on the polyester bedcover. A plastic cigarette wrapper lay on the floor. Through the wall, a man held a phone conversation in a Slavic language.

She lifted the grey voile curtains. Men were working on a car in a repair garage at the back. The sun had dipped, but it would be light for at least another hour.

She turned on the television. The digital signal flickered weakly, and cut out to a black screen. A squealing noise came from the repair garage.

The prospect of an evening in here was not appealing.

Her map had said the Cozmas' house wasn't far. She checked her watch. If she went now, she might get an answer tonight. Even be on the morning flight home.

According to her phone's GPS, Easter Way was a half-mile walk. The route took her along the main road, then left at a church whose spire was half missing into a labyrinthine housing estate. Teenagers kicked a ball under a 'No ball games' sign. Clothes hung on balconies. Metal gates were locked over front doors. Three elderly women with floral headscarves sat on the grass. Intrigued, she saw they were cooking over a handmade fire, chattering in a language she didn't recognize. She itched to ask to photograph them, but carried on, knowing it would be dark soon.

The estate opened out the back onto a quieter road, lined on one side by a tall fence with an industrial building behind, and scrubland on the other. Giant river cranes loomed in the distance. According to her GPS, Easter Way led from this road to the river. This looked right.

The road fell quiet, just the odd truck or van speeding past. Grace reached the right turn into Easter Way, and stopped to check. This *didn't* seem right. Smaller industrial buildings stretched along it towards the cranes. The scrubland either side was littered with dumped fridges and sofas, and broken bottles. Street lights were unlit.

Where were the *houses*?

She double-checked the map in case there was another Easter Way.

No, this was definitely it. Cautiously, she turned in, and began counting numbers. The estate seemed shut for the night. Up close, she saw the brick buildings were small clothing and packaging factories, with corrugated iron roofs, and side entrances secured by barbed wire and chained shut. A guard dog barked somewhere in the distance.

Counting numbers, Grace found number 137 by a junction into a side road, opposite a closed cafe. A security light triggered as she approached, illuminating a red-, yellow-and-blue plastic sign that said, 'Cozma's.'

It *was* a factory. Lucian's former place of work, maybe?

Taken aback, she stopped. Apart from a faint light behind the front door, there was no sign of life. A tired mannequin sat in its shop-style front window, with a drawn brown curtain behind. Its false eyelashes were long and defined, hair missing. A split silver sequinned maxidress parted at plastic orange legs.

The evening sun dimmed into a beautiful crystalline glow, scattering the road with gold dust. Grace looked around. If she did do what Ewan suggested and turned the mystery of Lucian Grabole into a freelance story, she'd have to start recording now. And this light was too good to miss.

Behind her, there was a sharp crack at ground level.

She spun round, peering into each shadowy alleyway and doorway.

A fox maybe.

As sure as she could be that nobody was watching, she photographed the factory, with the long row of shuttered buildings beyond it down to the black stork-like cranes. Then she shot the mannequin, and the barbed wire above the side entrance. Using the harsh security light, she photographed the factory sign from below, lending it the look of an American neon motel sign.

It was when she bent down by the window, for an alternative angle, that she heard the rumbling.

A mechanical noise, insistent and rhythmic.

Inside.

Stepping closer, she listened at the window.

Someone was in there.

Grace checked her phone. Nearly nine o'clock.

Probably too late, but no harm trying. She walked to the door and knocked.

The rumbling continued.

She rapped harder.

This time, it stopped.

She stood expectant, listening to the distant horn of a boat on the river, carefully forming her words about the possible bad news about Lucian Grabole.

The sun dropped in the sky, like a plane coming in to land, and the gold haze she'd just captured dissolved into a harsh cold blue. With a pop, street lamps came on beside her. A rat ran across the road. 'Come on . . .' she muttered, shivering.

Nobody came to the door.

'Hello?' She rapped the window this time.

Nothing.

Running out of ideas, she rang Lucian Grabole's contact number from the Riverside register. A phone rang out inside the factory.

This was definitely the right place.

But still nobody answered.

From somewhere a car started up. Backing onto the pavement, she was just in time to see a people carrier with blacked-out windows emerge from behind Cozma's and accelerate up towards the main road.

'No. Stop!' She waved uselessly.

It didn't.

At the junction, it turned left and disappeared along the main road. Inside the factory, she now saw the faint light was off. If the building hadn't been unoccupied before, it certainly was now. Had they really not heard her?

Aware of how fast darkness was falling, she marched back in the car's direction, wanting to escape the deserted little industrial estate and its unlit doorways. She'd have to come back tomorrow.

It was as she reached the junction that Grace saw the people carrier again.

It was parked on the kerb, hazard lights flashing.

Shadows seemed to watch her from the windows.

She started to raise a hand and it roared off again.

CHAPTER SIXTEEN

Edinburgh

'Right, you, stupid head – it's time.'

Shortly after eight the next morning, Sula opened her car door in the lay-by at Auchtermouth, and regarded the miserable greyhound on the back seat, doing a good impression of a kidnap victim. Good. The sun was coming out, which should make what she was about to do easier.

'Come on.' She grabbed its lead, and set off onto the cliff.

The police cordon was still there, but now both bodies had been removed, the four-by-four and the white van were gone. Any chance of a journalist – or bystanders – photographing something that would upset families, and lead to a lawsuit, had passed.

As she'd calculated, Derrick had been replaced down in the dip by a new PC. She didn't know this one, although from the misery on his face, she guessed he'd just done a night shift and was as likely to rip her arm off for a bacon sandwich as Derrick had been.

'Morning,' she said, approaching the officer.

'Morning,' he replied, standing to, finally with something to do.

She pointed further up the cliff. 'Officer, is it OK for me to take my dog up there?'

'Aye, that's fine. Just stay to the side of the cordon.'

'Thank you.' She pointed to the tent. 'It's a terrible business, eh? That poor man.'

'Aye, it is.'

'Do they know who the second man is yet?'

'No. Won't know that for a while.'

'OK, well, thank you.'

Two men? Up yours, Fin.

Further up the cliff, at an elevated point, Sula hung the dog's lead over a rock, and ducked behind a bush. Crouching, she focused her binoculars back down the slope. The evidence tent was side on from this angle, its flap closed. She settled on the ground, and the dog did the same, head on paws. Half an hour later, there was movement. The flap opened as a forensics officer exited. She zoomed in.

The flap closed.

She blinked, pulling back. What the hell was that?

Sula waited for him to return. This time, he opened the flap for longer, calling back to a colleague at his van.

She focused tight and knew she was right.

Instead of the shallow gravesite she'd expected, there was an existing fence surrounding a hole in the ground. An official-looking sign was stuck to it. The fence had been removed from half the hole.

Above it was a cable winch, a rope dangling inside.

Maybe it was the perspective from here, but the hole looked only a few feet across.

Ewan was on his way out the door to work when she rang. 'Stop where you are, get on your laptop, and find something about the geological or geographical structure of this cliff up at

Auchtermouth. I want to know if there's a well or a natural hole in the ground.'

'Yes, boss.'

She sat and smoked two fags, waiting. The dog whined and chased its tail miserably.

Ewan rang back. 'You know how good I am, don't you?'

'Go on.'

'There's a twenty-foot-deep pit cave up there. Council's fenced it off for safety, so might have a sign on it, or a grate over the top.'

'Pit cave? What's that?'

'Well, according to my expert, Professor Wikipedia, it's a natural cave that is found in the ground or in caves, usually made by water erosion in limestone.'

'How can a cave be on the ground up on a cliff?'

'Because it's not a normal cave. It's vertical, not horizontal.'

'What, like a chimney in the ground that goes down the way and not up?'

'God, that's beautiful,' he sighed. 'Has anyone ever told you you should be a writer?'

'Thank you, smart-arse.' Sula turned off her phone. 'Jesus,' she said out loud.

The hole she'd glimpsed had been two or three feet across. One guy she might have bought, falling in there by accident. But two? And if someone *had* put them in there, there was only one explanation.

They'd been buried upright.

One on top of the other.

Sula wasn't in the business of spending much time thinking about the victims of her stories, but in this case, she hoped the poor bastards were dead first.

CHAPTER SEVENTEEN

London

Easter Way looked very different in the morning sunshine.

Grace walked along, trying to find her bearings from last night. A constant stream of vehicles ran through the industrial estate. Trolleys rattled along the pavement. Radios blared from doorways. Rails of clothes were loaded onto vans, and bales of paper and cardboard dropped by gates. On the corner, by the cafe from last night, men in overalls climbed into an unmarked minibus.

The cafe was open now, windows steamed up with a breakfast crowd. The curtain at Cozma's was still drawn, though. So far, there had been no movement.

Grace leaned against the cafe wall, wondering what to do. Either the Cozmas really hadn't heard her last night or they were purposely avoiding her. It occurred to her that her phone call about Lucian Grabole had rattled them yesterday lunchtime and they were now on the lookout for strangers. But why?

Hoping the machine noise had just drowned her out last night, she crossed the road, undoing her camera cover and turning her phone to voice record to save time if someone answered.

At the window, she listened out. No rumbling.

She checked her watch: 8.55 a.m. If that was the evening shift last night, maybe the day shift started at 9 a.m. She knocked, to be sure.

With the sun out, and nobody around, she decided to risk a few more shots. The factory sign looked different under the blue sky. She knelt down to shoot it and— A sharp rap at the window made her jerk back.

The Cozmas' curtain had been yanked back. A woman was watching her, from behind the mannequin. She had olive skin, and short brown hair, the deep groove between her eyes accentuated by an astonished frown. Behind her was a long industrial table. On it were sewing machines. *The rumbling noise.* Beside it, a rail of clothes covered in plastic slips.

A tall man appeared beside the woman.

'Oh, hi,' Grace said. She waved at them, and pointed at the front door.

It flew open seconds later, and, to her alarm, the man charged out, his face furious. He had thick greying hair that started low on his forehead, and wore a navy pinstriped suit. The woman, she guessed his wife, rushed after him. Behind her came another older, white-haired woman who shared the man's low hairline.

'What are you doing? Why are you photographing my business?' the man yelled.

She took an involuntary step back, raising a hand in peace. 'Oh. Hi. I'm so sorry. I didn't know anyone was here. I'm a photojournalist, Grace Scott.' She held out a card and he snatched it from her. 'I've come down from Edinburgh to speak to you. Do you have a minute?'

'About what?' the man asked, thunder in his voice. Behind him, down a corridor, she saw a back exit, and the people carrier parked outside. His hand chopped the air like an axe. 'My business is legal.'

'No, no. Please. I'm not here about that. At all. As I say, I'm a

85

freelance photojournalist. I rang yesterday. I'm trying to track down a man who might have worked here.'

His eyes slanted with suspicion.

'He left your phone number at a night shelter in Edinburgh,' Grace added. 'Was it you I spoke to yesterday?'

'What man?'

'Lucian Grabole.'

The man's hand wilted mid-air.

Grace pushed on, less sure than she'd been a minute ago. 'I'm just worried something might have happened to him. I'm trying to find his family. That's all.'

With his eyes fixed on Grace, the man spoke in another language she didn't recognize. The women crowded behind him, eyes widening with anxiety.

'What about Lucian Grabole?' he snapped.

Grace composed herself. 'Well, I don't want to worry you unnecessarily, but a man died in Edinburgh three months ago, and I found the name "Lucian Grabole" written on a note near his body. It's completely possible he is nothing to do with the dead man, but I'm trying to find out.'

The man's face flickered, as if trying to check he'd heard correctly. 'Lucian is *dead*?'

The women peered up at him.

'No, no, no,' Grace said. 'Sorry, that's the point – I *don't* know. That's why I'm here. I'm trying to find out. So, it would be incredibly helpful if you could eliminate the Lucian Grabole you know, so I can look elsewhere. I mean, have you seen him recently? In the past three months, say?'

She saw a calculation take place in the man's eyes. His face was turning pale in front of her, as if he were giving blood.

'What did he look like, the dead man?'

She shifted, increasingly uneasy. 'About forty. Brown hair, to here.' She touched under her chin. 'About 1.78 metres tall, wearing an old navy pinstriped suit –' her eyes flicked to his, which was not dissimilar '– and black lace-up shoes. Oh, and he had a tattoo of a wolf on his shoulder. And a signet ring with a green stone on his little finger.'

A gasp escaped the man's mouth.

'Oh my God,' Grace said, taken aback. 'Is it him? I'm so sorry. I really didn't think it would be.'

Before she could speak again, the wife fired off questions in an agitated tone. The words weren't familiar, but the sense of panic was. The man answered sounding like he was in shock. A wail came from the wife's mouth. She pulled at his jacket beseechingly. The older woman, Grace suspected his mother, cupped her face, tears filling her eyes.

This was awful. Grace held up a hand again. 'Listen, I'm so sorry. Can I ask, are you Mr and Mrs Cozma? Are you Lucian's family?'

But the wife was becoming increasingly hysterical, her voice rising, hands gesticulating. The man pulled her into him. '*Nu, nu, dragă*,' he murmured.

Grace gave him a second, then tried once more. 'Again, I'm so sorry, but please, if this sounds like the Lucian you know, could I ask where he was from, and what he was doing in Edinburgh?'

The man let go of his wife. His eyes bored into her. A tone of disbelief entered his voice. 'You want to know this for a newspaper story?'

His wife tugged at him again and he translated. Her eyes grew wide, and she marched towards Grace, planted her feet firmly, and started to talk even faster. The words flew like gravel. Startled, Grace took a step back.

The man grappled the woman into his arms again. 'My wife is very upset. You must leave.'

Leave? Grace put out a hand. 'Listen, I'm so, so sorry, really, but, honestly, writing a story about this is not the most important thing. Not at all. I'm not even sure I'm going to write it. I just want to find Lucian's family. I need to be sure that it's him who died in my flat. And if it is, I want to make sure they know, because—'

Without warning, the wife ran at Grace again, shouting, her face contorted with distress. Grace stepped further back into the road. 'Please, I'm trying to help you. I can give you a name. Tell you the authorities to contact in Edinburgh and—'

But nothing she said worked. The man now turned on her. 'You will do *nothing* else here,' he said, gathering his wife back into his arms. 'Thank you for bringing this news, but from now, this is not your business. Now please, I must ask you to go. Please leave my family in peace. We will not speak to you again.'

Fuck, fuck, fuck.

What had she done?

So close to an answer about Lucian's identity and yet so bloody far.

Grace returned to the cafe, and put down her rucksack. Those people knew who Lucian Grabole was. And she'd completely messed it up.

She couldn't go home, not yet.

Hoping he was at work, she rang Ewan.

'Scotty. Wassup?'

'I've just blown it,' she said, describing the past five minutes.

He listened without interruption. 'Wow. But it's the same guy?'

'Well, it sounds like it. They acted like they recognized his description and hadn't seen him for a while. They make suits and the dead guy was wearing a suit like Mr Cozma's. I swear it's the same one but much older.'

'Well, that's good, isn't it?'

'No, because then they got upset and wouldn't talk. I think they thought I was from the tax office or I was writing a tabloid story about illegal workers or something.'

'Sounds like you're on to something, though,' Ewan said. 'Where are they from?'

'I didn't get to ask.' She sat on a low wall. 'They were really upset. I'm thinking I should ring DI Robertson. Then he can send someone to confirm it officially with them.'

'Scotty – no!' Ewan shouted. 'Don't be stupid. There's a good story here. You've got to go for it. You've got the personal angle of finding the body – in Edinburgh – then an international angle. Then this big mystery about who the guy is. I'm telling you – an editor's going to go for this.'

'I don't know, Ewan—'

'Think about it,' he interrupted. 'If their Lucian Grabole is the guy in your flat, and they're so upset that he's dead, why haven't they reported him missing? It doesn't make sense.'

It was a good point. 'I don't know. Because he worked for them cash in hand, maybe? And they don't want to get into trouble?'

'Well, something's weird about it. Don't do anything till you're sure.'

She leaned over. She loved Ewan like an annoying little brother, and she'd forever be grateful for the way he'd not cared she was in her thirties and partnered up with her with such friendly enthusiasm on their MA course while the rest of the twenty-one-year-olds ignored her. But he had no idea of the way grief smashed your life into pieces, then left you scrabbling to put them back together in a way that made sense. Even she couldn't explain it. She just knew that finding the dead man's family would replace one piece for her.

'Ewan, I know what you're saying, but honestly, this is personal for me,' she tried to explain. 'The guy died in my flat, and finding his family's the most important thing. They need to know. When my dad died, I spent ages in his flat, thinking about that day he died there on his own. Wondering what he'd felt, if he'd been in pain. What the last thing he saw was. You need to ask these questions. It's part of the process. I want to find out why Lucian Grabole was in my flat, but I want to help his family, too.'

'Oi, Scotty!' Ewan snapped. 'You're talking to me here, not a girl. Focus! Let's backtrack. Where are they from?'

She rolled her eyes. 'I told you: I don't know. I can't work out the language – definitely not French.'

'Right. Well, what about neighbours?'

Factories stretched in a ragged line from where she sat, down towards the river cranes. 'I suppose I could try a few.'

There was silence. Then tapping.

'Ewan?'

'Sorry. Something's come up on Sula's story. Gotta go. Scotty?'

'What?'

'Don't you *dare* give up this fuckin' story.'

The phone went dead.

She picked up her rucksack.

Maybe he was right.

What was the harm while she was here?

CHAPTER EIGHTEEN

Edinburgh

Now Sula knew what was inside that evidence tent, she wanted more. She continued along the cliff, following her GPS. It was half a mile down to Auchtermouth in the cove. It was after nine now. From what she could gather, a lot of these dog walkers went out after they'd dropped the bairns at school.

The greyhound whimpered as she marched along. 'Come on, you.'

Sula walked in a circle until she saw a woman with black curly hair in wellies and glasses coming up from the village, with two Labradors.

Sula waved. 'Hello there. You going up the hill?'

'Yes,' the woman said, wary.

'They've just stopped me on the path up there. The police have shut it off. I don't know why.'

The woman relaxed. 'Ah. They've found two bodies, actually.'

'No!' Sula exclaimed. 'Have they? Who?'

'It's been on the news – that Australian tourist David Pearce and some other poor soul.'

Sula tried to look appalled. 'Oh, I remember David Pearce. That's terrible – who found him?'

'Penny, down in the village. She's in quite a state about it.'

Sula covered her mouth. 'Poor thing. That's terrible. Well, the policeman said it would be open in an hour, so it looks like we'll be going this way today, eh, Rover?'

'Thanks for letting me know,' the woman said, turning in the opposite direction.

Sula waved her on, then sat on a rock and lit another fag. Ten minutes later, two more dog walkers appeared and she led the greyhound onwards. These two were posh, in insulated waist-coats and Hunter wellies, one in her sixties and one in her thirties. They had identical thick-cut bobs, one grey, one brown. Mother and daughter.

'Hello there,' Sula repeated, adding a touch of Kelvinside to her own voice. 'I've just been turned back up there. The police have blocked it off.'

'Oh, have they?' The mother looked suspicious. 'I thought they'd opened it up again.'

'He said they're just finishing up,' Sula replied. 'Gosh, it's a dreadful thing, isn't it? Poor Penny.'

'Oh, do you know Penny?' the daughter said, eyes hungry for gossip.

'Well, just through school, of course.' Sula took a bet that Penny had at some point had something to do with a school. 'I was going to pop in and see her later. Do you know how she is?'

The older woman leaned towards Sula conspiratorially, her daughter listing at an identical angle. 'I'm not sure she's having visitors, to be honest. She's quite sick with the shock. The dog was barking and barking. The fence was broken round the hole and she thought maybe a sheep had fallen in and . . .'

'She looked in with her key-ring torch and saw the top of a head,' the daughter finished.

The women regarded each other with fresh horror, as if it

hadn't been all they'd been discussing for the past twenty-four hours.

'Oh, I know, I heard,' Sula said, screwing up her face like them. 'It's just a nightmare, isn't it?'

Her phone rang in her hand. 'Oh, excuse me.' Her accent reverted back. 'Ewan, what?'

'They've released the ID of the second body. Colin McFarlay.'

Sula's mouth fell open. 'What? That scuzzy wee dealer, went missing in October?'

The mother and daughter shot each other warning glances, and she walked off without looking back.

'How do you remember so much when you're so old?' Ewan asked.

Sula ignored him. 'Why would an Australian tourist be buried on top of one of Edinburgh's finest drug dealers?'

'Kinky sex gone wrong?'

'Months apart, Ewan – assuming they both died when they went missing?'

She heard him tap his keyboard.

'Nothing obvious. Though this is interesting. David Pearce was on holiday here from Australia, but he was actually born in Edinburgh. He was visiting his father, Thomas Pearce, in Colinton.'

Sula panted as she climbed back up to the body recovery site. 'Pearce grew up here? So they could have known each other?'

More tapping.

'Unlikely,' Ewan replied. 'McFarlay was twenty-eight, so he'd have been born eleven years after Pearce went to Australia. Last address listed was Smack Row. And Colinton is nowhere near Smack Row.'

Sula stopped to catch breath, watching frothy white water

bang into black rocks below. She never understood why people liked the seaside. Cold and windy and boring.

'Well, drug dealers don't go hiking, so something – or somebody – brought Colin McFarlay up here.'

She reached the road, and saw a little pizza cart run by an enterprising guy had been set up in the lay-by.

'Right, keep looking. I'll be back in an hour.'

'How's Betty, by the way?' Ewan asked.

'Who's Betty?'

'The dog, Sula.'

'Oh, is it? Stupid. That's how she is.'

Ewan sighed. 'Sula, my mum doesn't like people being rude about Betty.'

She reached the car. 'Aye, and she also knows I'm the only one stupid enough to give you a job, so . . .'

'Fair enough. By the way, that friend of mine, Grace, who was in? She might have a story.'

'Listen, you, keep your mind on this. Not your girlfriend.'

'Oh, hark at you, all jealous.'

'Jealous, my big fat arse.' Sula ended the call.

The dog climbed onto the back seat, and dropped its head back onto its paws.

Sula sat in the driver's seat, and rang the police press office. Vani answered.

'Vani, Sula McGregor here. What's your comment that David Pearce and Colin McFarlay were buried upright inside a twenty-foot-deep pit cave?'

There was a muffled exclamation. 'Where did you hear that, Sula?'

'I cannot possibly reveal my sources.'

'Sula, I can't—'

She cut across her. 'It's going online in an hour. You know where I am.'

Sula started the car and threw a biscuit to the dog.

'Right, Fatty. Our work here is done.'

CHAPTER NINETEEN

London

After an hour stomping up and down Easter Way, Grace returned to the cafe, and dumped her rucksack on the pavement.

She must have tried twenty factories, to say nothing of five pedestrians, two men on forklift trucks and a woman on a bicycle. Not a single one had heard of Lucian Grabole or could tell her where the Cozmas were from.

Either they didn't know or weren't telling.

She couldn't let this go now.

She had to know.

The steamy window of the cafe had cleared, the workers vanished. She went inside to have a cup of tea and a think. It smelt of bacon and steam. Capital Radio blared.

Grace took a window seat opposite Cozma's.

A man with dark curly hair, and oversized features that looked like they'd been sculpted out of bread dough by a child, emerged from a door behind the counter and called over, 'What can I get you, love?'

She read the menu, not hungry after the hotel's greasy breakfast. 'Actually, can I just have a cup of tea, please?'

'No problem.' The man picked a mug off a shelf. 'Scottish?'

He said 'Scottish' in a guttural London accent, with no 't's.

'That was quick.'

'Get used to it round here. Everyone's from somewhere. Where you from? Glasgow?'

'Edinburgh.' She willed him to stop talking. To give her space to think, to decide what to do next.

'Thought so.' He winked as he poured, then opened the hatch, revealing an apron smeared by tomato sauce.

'Thanks,' she said, taking the mug. The tea was orange and milky, and she gulped it, already wanting a refill. Did the Cozmas know Lucian's family? Would they tell them? What if they didn't, or the family didn't know how to get in touch with the police in Edinburgh?

The responsibility for this stranger's death was becoming all-consuming. As if the closer she got to an answer, the stronger her need to see it through. A bereavement counsellor, she suspected, would probably have a name for it. *Projection* or *transference* or something.

The man cleared dirty plates. 'Down for a job?' he said, nodding at her rucksack.

'Just trying to find someone, actually,' she said, struggling not to sound irritable.

'Round here? Who's that, then?'

She pointed across the road. 'A man who worked there.'

'Cozma's?'

The mug stopped inches from her lips. 'Do you know the Cozmas?'

He snorted. 'I know everyone around here, love.'

Grace lowered her tea. 'You don't know where they're from, do you?'

'Romania, innit?'

Romania?

Eastern Europe.

She banged down her mug.

'Yeah, they'll be there now, if you wanna speak to them,' the man said, placing some dirty mugs on the counter. 'He's there all hours, Mr C.'

'Hmm.' She grimaced. 'Can't do that.'

'What? Not answering?' he asked.

'No, they're there, but they won't speak to me. I've upset them.'

'How've you done that, then?'

'Long story. I think the man I'm trying to find has died, and I've managed to cock up how I told them. They're a bit angry with me.'

'Yeah? Aw. Who's that, then?' he said, flipping a tea towel over his shoulder.

'A man called Lucian Grabole?'

The big doughy eyes stretched wide. 'Lucian? No bloody way!'

Grace stared. 'Do you know him?'

'Course I do. He was here for a few months last year. Always stopped in for a chat and a cup of tea. Lovely bloke. Jesus. What happened to old Lucian?'

He knew him.

Re-energized, Grace sat up and explained what had happened, hope returning.

'Aw no!' the man exclaimed. 'Thought I hadn't seen him for a while. And there was me thinking he was back in Amsterdam.'

'He's from Holland?' Pieces of the puzzle were starting to fit together.

'Nah, nah, nah. Romania, like the Cozmas. They're old friends of his from the village back home. Amsterdam's where he was *living*. Before he came here.' He lifted the hatch, and put the dirty mugs in the machine. 'That's taken me right back, that has.

I'm in shock. Cozmas didn't say nothing. What about his wife, then? What's happened to her?'

Grace scrabbled for her phone's voice recorder. 'Lucian had a wife?'

'Well, that's why he was here, innit, looking for her?'

'Sorry, um . . .'

'Ali.'

'Ali. Would you mind if I recorded this? I'm a freelance journalist investigating what happened to him. This is all new information.'

'Yeah, no problem.' He came out, turned a chair backwards to sit, gave her his name, repeated what he'd told her already, then continued. 'Yeah, so Lucian told me him and her got split up in Amsterdam. An immigration bust or something, during the night when they were sleeping – they all run off, different directions. Police took the phones when they cleared the house, and Lucian couldn't find her. She'd scarpered with the kid. Someone told him they'd come here, to London, looking for him at the Cozmas'. So that's what he was doing – staying with them, doing a bit of work, waiting in case she turned up.'

'So he was working here without being registered, too?'

Ali looked coy. 'Wouldn't like to say, love.'

'So, did he find them?'

'Never seemed to. But I don't know now.' Ali shook his head. 'Shame. Lovely bloke.'

'When did you last see him?'

Ali whistled. 'Ooh . . . now you're asking . . . Maybe a year? And you're certain this is him, this dead bloke in Edinburgh?'

'No, not yet, but I'm more sure than I was yesterday. Mr Cozma definitely seemed to recognize his description.'

Ali nodded at each detail she repeated, and touched his shoulder. 'Yeah, and a wolf here. Ring with a green stone. That's him. One of Mr C's pinstripes. Bloody hell, sad that is . . .' His eyes darted above Grace's head. 'Tell you what, she might still be here, though.'

Ali reached over and lifted up leaflets on a pinboard. At the back was a poster of a blonde woman and child. 'Anna and Valentin: missing.'

Grace felt the floor shift under her. 'Oh my God. I've seen this. In Edinburgh. At the homeless shelter Lucian stayed at.'

'There you go, then.' Ali handed it to her, pleased.

On second viewing, she recognized the phone number now. It was the Cozmas' landline.

Lucian Grabole had been searching for Anna and Valentin in Scotland – staying with friends in London to find her.

An elderly, hunched man entered the cafe wearing a hat with earflaps, despite the sunshine.

'All right, George? Tea?' Ali said. 'George is one of my regulars.'

Grace nodded politely, rereading the poster. 'So Lucian's wife, Anna, might not know he's died?'

Ali went to make tea. 'Aw. Sad, innit? Why don't you scribble your number on there, love? If she comes looking for him, she can ring you. You can tell her what's happened.'

Grace repinned the leaflet to the board, photographed it in situ for the story she might write, then did what he suggested. With Ali's permission, she took a few more shots with him in the background handing tea to George.

She paid for her tea, and picked up her rucksack. 'Listen, thanks for this. It's been really helpful.'

'No problem. But try Mr C again,' Ali said, pouring tea. 'Probably just caught him at a bad time.'

Grace opened the door. 'I don't know. He was pretty upset.'

'I'm not surprised. Lucian was an old friend of theirs. Go on – see what he says now he's had a chance to cool down.'

Grace looked across at the Cozmas'. 'Thanks. I might do that.'

It was a lie. She would, but not right now. Now, she wanted to find Anna.

CHAPTER TWENTY

Edinburgh

'It's Wednesday, midday, and here's what's happening with the weather where you are!'

The man sat on the stool in Mr Singh's storeroom, headphones on, wanting to punch the babbling weather presenter in the teeth, as he taunted him with reports of 'intermittent showers', with 'broken spells of sunshine later today'.

In a moment of weakness, he let himself imagine the taste and feel of fresh water not tainted by chlorine. A place where sunshine toasted his skin, not a ferocious blast of sickeningly hot electric air from a machine. Where the breeze was gentle and scented, and didn't sweep in uninvited under a door, bringing the stink of rubbish and petrol fumes, and dog shit.

A check of the clock.

A minute after midday, now. Fifty-nine minutes to go.

Hunger yawned. He walked to the window to distract himself, and saw the same dirty clouds from yesterday. A blackbird took off from a garage roof, and became smaller and smaller as it flew into a round, soggy cloud past the tower block. The effect was of a dilating pupil.

A naked man with a large belly stretched in the window on the eighth floor, displaying himself to the city.

Pig.

He checked the clock again. Fifty-seven minutes.

Unable to stop himself, he opened the fridge and regarded the two plates of tinfoil-covered food on the shelf. As usual, he'd switched them round and pushed them to the back, so that when it came to choosing, there would be an element of surprise. A moment of sharp anticipation in the sludge that was each day.

He made himself shut it, and returned to the window, stomach rumbling.

What would it be? The egg-and-cucumber sandwiches, or the pasta and bacon?

The naked man had gone now. A new set of curtains opened on the tenth floor. A bodiless arm was pushing them back. It hung in the air for a second, then vanished.

An English voice filled his headphones. Someone who'd designed a new vacuum cleaner.

He let the details about its unique detangler fill his head. It took his mind off things.

At lunchtime, as his saliva glands readied themselves for action, the man heard a noise.

He threw off the headphones and crouched, ready to fight.

There were footsteps in the corridor outside; then the door handle twisted three times.

'It's me,' a quiet voice said.

He unlocked the door, and shuffled backwards.

Mr Singh stood in the doorway with a plastic bag. The grey in his beard was spreading like a rash. 'Sorry I couldn't come yesterday. My wife was doing the accounts.'

The man took the bag hungrily, and checked inside. A new

pack of tinfoil. A loaf of bread. Three more pasta salads. A cucumber, tins of meat and cheese.

He gave his rubbish bag to Mr Singh.

The newsagent's brow, as usual, wrinkled as he tried to find a way to word his concerns. 'Listen, my wife needed to use the toilet yesterday. I said I'd left the storeroom key at home. Last week, I said the corridor was blocked with a delivery. I'm running out of excuses.' Singh pointed to the upstairs flat. 'And now this – the wife hearing you the other night.'

The man put the food away, saying nothing.

Mr Singh sighed. 'The husband's away playing golf till Saturday, and the wife left in a taxi with a rucksack, so I imagine you'll be all right to move around a bit for a day or two, but then . . .'

But then.

The words died away.

The man said nothing. He didn't have to. He and Mr Singh both knew they had no meaning. He was going nowhere.

CHAPTER TWENTY-ONE

It was lunchtime when Grace reached a hipper-looking part of East London. She disembarked the overland train, and looked for a Tube station to return her to King's Cross and Heathrow.

Her thoughts were now consumed by a new piece of the puzzle.

Where were Anna and Valentin?

The London air was muggy and warm. For a second, she sat on a polka-dot bench outside a vintage clothes shop, to check her GPS.

A couple in their twenties cycled towards her on matching old-fashioned bikes, he with a handlebar moustache, her in a summer skirt covered in foxes. Grace took out her camera and photographed them. If they noticed or cared, they didn't react. She guessed this happened a lot round here, with all the fashion spotters and hipsters.

The GPS told her she was one street away from her Tube station.

Now all she had to do was book her flight home.

For a reason she didn't understand, Grace didn't move.

A group of black-clad emos in vertiginous platform shoes towered over a tiny pensioner with a blue-rinse perm and a shopping trolley, asking for directions. She photographed that, too.

Her phone rang in her pocket.

'Hey. What's happening?' Ewan said.

She updated him about Ali, and the news about Lucian's missing wife and child.

'Seriously?' he exclaimed. 'Ace. So what you doing now?'

'Coming home, I suppose. Start looking for Anna and Valentin. Obviously Lucian didn't find her in London, so he went to Edinburgh. He must have had an idea she was there.'

'But if he'd found her in Edinburgh, wouldn't she have reported him missing when he died? Or rung the police when she saw his description in the paper?'

'Would she report it, though,' Grace replied, 'if they were both working without being registered? She didn't report it in Amsterdam when they got separated.'

'True.' Ewan hummed for a second. 'Hang on, are you sure she was even in Edinburgh? Just because there's a poster there . . . There's one in London, too. For all we know, Lucian's put them in shelters all over the country.'

'Good point.'

'You know what you need to do?' Ewan said.

'What?'

'Go to Amsterdam – work backwards. Find out what Lucian Grabole was doing over there. Anna could be back in Amsterdam, looking for him. If that's where they were living originally, somebody over there must know them.'

'Amsterdam?'

'Why not? What else are you doing this week?'

'Er . . .'

She heard him typing furiously.

Ewan returned to the phone. 'Amsterdam. Five thirty, from

Gatwick – sixty-seven pounds single. Oh, come on, Scotty! This could be the big break.'

She sat thinking. It wasn't *impossible*.

'When's Mac back?' Ewan asked.

'Saturday.'

Mac would never do something this spontaneous. Or expect her to, either.

'Oh, go *oooonnnn!*' Ewan goaded her.

'You know what,' she said. 'Fuck it. I'm going to go.'

'Yay! Want me to book it? I'll do it on my credit card and you can pay me back.'

'Sure?'

'Yup. Got your passport there?'

'Hang on.' She gave him the number, and held on as Ewan booked her flight, not believing what she'd just done. If Mac were here, he'd be shaking her shoulders, telling her to stop being a loon and wasting her dad's savings.

A spraying noise started behind her.

In a side street, a wiry, shaven-headed man, dressed in a black leather jacket and trousers, was urinating by a railway arch. He zipped up and walked off. Everything about him was pointed: ears, black leather boots, chin, skull. With the sun ahead of him, he turned into a sharp-angled silhouette. There was something primal about the illusion. A human city-rat, his dark stain marking the wall. Grace fumbled for her camera, and fired off one shot. As if he sensed her, the man began to turn. Grace shot him once more, from the side, catching his jagged profile, and turned back before he saw her.

Ewan returned. 'Right, I'm emailing you the booking – try and print it out somewhere or the bastards'll charge you a fortune at the airport.'

'Thanks. I'll sort out the money at the weekend.'

'No bother. I'll book you a hotel, too. And I'll ask around – I think someone in Pictures has got contacts in Amsterdam.'

She stood up to go. 'You're a star.'

'Aw – all shiny and lovely?'

'No, all pointy and sharp.'

It was the first joke she'd attempted since Dad died. Whether or not he found it funny, Ewan, to his credit, laughed, and she joined in, because for the first time in months, for reasons she didn't really understand, she felt like it.

CHAPTER TWENTY-TWO

Police Race to Solve Mystery of Two Dead Men Buried In Pit Cave.

That afternoon, Sula sat in her car reading her freshly posted online story on the *Scots Today* website.

Vani had already glowered in her direction on her way into this afternoon's press conference.

This would be interesting. Maybe they'd reveal the link between the two victims. Sula followed her in.

As she'd suspected, the number of journalists had doubled overnight.

DI Robertson was on his own today. He glared at her, too, and she winked back.

'Right, I'm here to give you a quick update on the discovery of the bodies of David Pearce and Colin McFarlay.' He scanned the room for impact. 'This is now a murder investigation.'

A shocked murmur rippled through the room. Sula rolled her eyes at her colleagues – what did they think it was, two guys having a cheese sandwich on a rock to enjoy the view and – oops! – both fell down the same hole?

DI Robertson hit his flow. 'Colin McFarlay was last seen on CCTV in Edinburgh city centre at 2.30 a.m. on 19 October last year. David Pearce went missing on 29 January, after telling family he was hiking. Both men were found on the cliff above Auchtermouth on 4 May.' He took his time looking around, making eye contact individually. His gaze came to rest on Sula. 'Now, two men have died. I'm sure you can appreciate this is a very difficult time for both families. So we will *not* be confirming news reports regarding the circumstances of the men's deaths *or* giving out any more information at this time.' She held his stare. 'We will, however, be appealing for anyone with information to come forward. In particular, we would like to speak to anyone who knew Mr Pearce or Mr McFarlay, or knows of a link between these two men. Thank you. Any questions?'

Sula put up her hand, while his eyes were fixed on her. 'Sula McGregor, *Scots Today*. Did they die at the same time?'

'No. Next question.'

'Can you give us *cause* of death?' she called out.

'I've just said, not at this time. Now, is—'

'Were the men dead when they were buried?'

The room fell silent.

When you angered Fin Robertson, his eyes blackened and hardened like a shark's. If he hadn't been a police officer, he had a great look for a serial killer, and she felt sorry for any poor bugger who tried to play him in an interview room. There was a hushed snigger around the room as he fixed those shark eyes on Sula for three long seconds.

'As I said, Sula, we will not be releasing information at this moment about the nature of the murders. Next question.' He pointed at the back.

Jesus, Sula thought, she was right. Poor bastards.

*

Sula charged back to the office to find Ewan eating a late lunch of Quavers, Coke and a Twix, his big googly eyes fixed on an email. When he saw her, he shut it quick.

'Put it away, whatever it is,' she snapped. 'I need addresses for both men's families in Edinburgh.'

Ewan held up a sheet of paper. 'Sometimes I think you underestimate me.'

She took it. 'Brown Oaks Nursing Home – that's Pearce's father?'

'Aye, Thomas Pearce, aged eighty-eight,' Ewan crunched, carrying on typing.

She scanned down. 'And 6 Banister Road – that's McFarlay.' Sula tapped her pen. 'Or, as it's so charmingly called, Smack Row.'

She scratched her head. 'Tell me again how the hell these two met.'

Ewan clicked his mouse. 'Let's see . . . Oh, hello, handsome.'

Sula bent across. It was the police shot they'd printed when Colin McFarlay went missing last October. It was everything you'd expect from a lowlife like him. Vacuum-packed cheeks, greasy hair, eyes drained of life after years of pushing crack to bairns. A face full of plooks.

Beside it, Ewan placed a photo of David Pearce. It was his photo from Perth University Engineering Department. It was everything you'd expect: beard and glasses, suit, club tie, expression of authority.

'Something's not making sense here.' Sula's eyes darted between them.

'You said it, Batman.' Ewan bit his Twix. 'By the way, there's a message there for you.'

'Uh-huh?' she said, not listening.

'From your daughter,' Ewan said.

Sula kept her eyes on the photo of Colin McFarlay.

'She said, can you ring her back?' Ewan continued.

Sula picked the pink Post-it note from her keyboard, without reading it, and placed it in her pocket.

'I think that's a Manchester code,' he continued, crunching his Twix. 'How did I not even know you had a daughter? Is she single?'

Sula glared over her glasses. 'Ewan,' she said, 'if I'm Batman, who are you?'

He stopped chewing. 'Your girly sidekick.'

She reached over, grabbed the Twix, and threw it in the bin. 'Right. Concentrate. Somebody put those poor bastards down that hole, and I'm guessing from Fin Robertson's face that they were alive when they did it. And we're going to find out who before he does.'

CHAPTER TWENTY-THREE

That evening, Grace changed pounds to euros in the arrivals hall of Schiphol Airport, realizing she hadn't eaten since breakfast. She switched on her phone and found a cryptic email from Ewan about her hotel.

'Lindenkade 401. Go there and . . .' It ended abruptly, as if he'd sent it before it was finished.

She texted him.

No reply.

'Hmm,' she muttered, not convinced by the unfinished instructions. There wasn't even a hotel name. She turned off her phone, in case Mac rang and heard the unfamiliar European ringtone. She was too tired and hungry right now to have an argument with him about her 'weird obsession' with the dead man at Gallon Street, and, most likely, her 'irrational' decision to fly here. Outside the terminal, people sat in outdoor cafes and on ornamental-flowerbed walls, drinking beer and coffee and chatting. It was even warmer than London. She tied her jacket round her waist, found a taxi, and curled up on the back seat.

The freeway sped past sprawling business centres, and apartment blocks tucked neatly behind trees. The sun was setting. Armies of cyclists on sit-up-and-beg bikes ran alongside them as it became more residential, legs moving to the same hypnotic rhythm. A dark glint of water appeared as they crossed a bridge. The taxi turned sharply down a narrow, square-cobbled street.

'Lindenkade,' the taxi driver said, pointing at the street sign.

'Thanks.' She paid and exited onto the canalside.

OK. This didn't look right.

On one side, under elegant old lamplights, there were four-storey red-brick canal houses with tall white windows. On the other were houseboats tethered on the canal, their roofs peeking over the bank. Untidy rows of bikes and cars were scattered above them, among mature lime and elm trees.

No hotel signs.

'OK. Not good,' Grace muttered.

The first house number she checked was 110. The canalside vanished towards a distant bridge lit by dim street lights. Three hundred more numbers till she reached 401?

A car raced past playing drum and bass. A long, slow whistle came from the open window, and she hid her camera bag under her jacket and quickened her pace. Still the house numbers only progressed in twos. Number 401 must be a mile away.

She checked the email again. 'Lindenkade 401. Go there and . . .'

Maybe Ewan had sent that email by mistake. Or it was a typo.

Then a small wooden sign by the canal caught her eye: '423'.

A houseboat?

She worked her way back to a pretty blue one that said, '403'. It *was* a houseboat.

Number 401 was next to it. But still there was no hotel or B&B sign.

No. This really didn't look right.

She rang Ewan again. It went to voicemail.

Number 401 was tar-black, and anonymous, with a long curved roof and featureless windows draped with voile curtains. A low light shone inside.

What was the alternative? Walk through the night with her camera bag till she found a taxi or a hotel? She didn't even know which part of Amsterdam she was in.

Not sure what else to do, she crossed a ramp to the front door.

Faint music came from inside.

This definitely didn't look like a hotel.

To be sure, she knocked.

Steps approached; then the door flew open. A tall, bare-chested man in jeans stood in the doorway. He was deeply tanned like the beach backpackers in Thailand, with dark curly hair, a close-cut beard and dark brown eyes so intense they made her take a step back.

'Hey,' he said.

'Oh – sorry. I must have got the wrong—'

'Come in. Leave your bag there,' he said, walking off. Feeling hesitant, she followed him into a living room, furnished with a grey sofa, a woodstove, a scarlet Afghan rug and walls crammed with framed photographs, paintings and artwork. It smelt of cooking and spice.

'Take a seat. I'll be with you in a minute,' he said, heading into a room off the left of the sitting room. His accent was unplaceable, a mix of American, Antipodean and London.

'Who are you?' she mouthed at his back, as he disappeared. Through the gap in the door, she saw the corner of a bed.

'Nicu,' an unseen woman said, followed by something in Dutch.

The man replied fluently.

Grace stood up to take a closer look at the prints. These were amazing. Seriously good reportage. The work she'd dreamed about at college before real life and paying rent took over. A creak and the man reappeared, pulling on a black T-shirt, still speaking in Dutch.

Behind him came a woman wearing a bandana over two dark plaits, and a summer dress. She was pulling on a cardigan.

She nodded coolly at Grace, who returned it, uncertain. Then a second woman appeared. Blonde hair was looped in coils on her head. On her shoulder was a bag. She also nodded.

What the hell was this?

The girls were nearly as tall as the man. The blonde one took his hand and made a sulky face, pulling him towards the door. He held up five fingers. The darker one said something harsh-sounding. He waved them off and returned.

Had he just slept with both those women?

The man towered over Grace, and she pushed back against the sofa even though there was plenty of space between them.

'OK, I've got ten minutes,' he said. 'So what do you need?'

She stared. 'Um, I'm not quite sure what . . .'

'*Scots Today* said you need help with Romanian contacts in Amsterdam.'

'*Scots Today*?' she said, starting to breathe again.

His brown-black eyes were so intense she couldn't read any expression in them. 'Yeah. Ewan Callow at *Scots Today*?' he said, mild irritation appearing on his face.

'Right. Sorry,' she said, wishing she could get hold of Ewan. 'How do you know *Scots Today*?'

'They syndicate my work and . . .' He put down the pen. 'You don't know who I am, do you?'

She bit her lip. 'No. Sorry. Or why I'm here, actually.'

A ripple crossed his face that might have been amusement. 'Nicu,' he said, holding out a hand. She took it. He had huge

116

hands, with long tanned fingers and leather bands round his wrist. 'Nicu Dragan.'

With a jolt, she recognized his name. He was a reportage photographer. Internationally renowned. His stuff appeared in the nationals and Sunday supplements. She'd seen his work in an exhibition.

She tried to remain nonchalant – 'Grace Scott. Freelance' – positive he wouldn't have heard of her. 'Sorry,' she said. 'It's been a really long day. OK. That's great, thanks. Yes, that's right. I'm trying to find the family of a Romanian man who lived in Amsterdam, possibly working under the radar, without registering legally. You think you might be able to help?'

'Don't know – see what I can find. Hang on.' The man headed to a tiny office off the compact wooden kitchen.

Grace scanned the room quickly. There was a sheepskin over the sofa. The paintings were a colourful mixture of abstract and brash outsider art. A bowl piled with aubergines and peppers sat on the kitchen counter. It was singly the most intriguing room she'd ever seen.

'So what's the name?' he said, returning with a pen.

'Oh. Lucian Grabole. His wife and child are Anna and Valentin.'

His pen froze mid-air. 'Grabole's not a Romanian name – you know that?' His tone was questioning her.

'It's not?' she said, taken aback. 'Sorry, how do you know that?'

'Because I speak Romanian,' he said. His demeanour was laid-back, yet his eyes seared into her, as if measuring the angle of her bones and the light on her skin – photographer's eyes. She shifted uncertainly.

'Oh. OK. That's odd, but anyway . . .' She gave him the rest of the information.

117

'And that's it?'

'So far,' she said.

'OK, well, I'll see what I can do. '

'Thanks.'

Nicu picked up his keys and wallet from a table. 'Right. I've got to be somewhere, but if you're hungry, there's a place on the corner.'

'Actually, I need to find a cheap hotel,' she said. 'Is there one nearby?'

'Oh. Yeah. Here.' He beckoned her outside, took a key out of his jeans and opened the blue boat next door.

He turned on the light and ushered her inside. To her delight, she saw it was his studio. More prints hung on the wall. There was a desk and printer, a light box, tripod and shelves of books. In the corner was a bed, a tiny kitchen and a shower room. It smelt delicious, of Indian oil and pine and woodsmoke.

'Here,' he said, holding out the key. 'Make yourself at home.'

'Seriously? I can stay here?'

'Yup,' he said, shutting the blinds.

'Wow. That's great. So do I pay you for it now?'

Another bemused look. 'Ewan said you're working on spec?' He chucked a bag off the bed. 'Don't worry about it. We've all been there.'

'Oh. That's really kind. Thanks.'

'No problem.' He reached out his hand. Not knowing what else to do, she shook it. 'Oh,' he said, smiling, 'I was just going to . . .'

She turned and saw the outside light switch he'd been reaching for.

'Sorry.' She pushed back into the wall. There was something unsettling about him.

'This is really great,' she repeated.

'See you tomorrow.' Nicu Dragan walked off, hand in the air, heading for a green Jeep.

She scanned the studio. That was a lie. This wasn't great. It was far better than great.

She waited till he roared off, then headed out to find food. The bar he'd mentioned was down an alleyway, and buzzing. People sat in the warm evening drinking globes of beer at outdoor tables. It was after 10 p.m., and nearly full. Starving, she entered. It had a hippyish vibe, with vintage wall lamps, and mismatched tables and chairs. At the bar, she found a stool and menu, ordered a cheese *pannekoek*, salad and beer, and listened to the Dutch, English, American and French voices above the music. A group of Australians sat on a communal table in the middle. It wasn't dissimilar to the backpacking area in Bangkok where she and Mac had eaten in February.

Her order arrived, and she took a sip of beer. Maybe it was the hit of alcohol in her bloodstream, but a sharp rush of excitement went through her.

She was in Amsterdam investigating a story.

Staying with *Nicu Dragan*.

Re-energized after her food, she wrote, *Thursday*, in her notebook, and sketched a plan for tomorrow. Nicu might have contacts, but she couldn't rely on them. Somebody in the city's Romanian community must know Lucian, Anna and Valentin. They couldn't have existed here for any length of time without contact. Her notes went as follows:

1. *Chase up Nicu's Romanian contacts.*
2. *Track down Romanian community groups, especially those for mothers and children, at a central library.*
3. *Ask Dutch police about recent raids on illegal workers.*

She started the internet research on her phone at the bar, adding possible Amsterdam numbers and addresses to her notes, then, when weariness set in, packed up and went to find the toilet. A sign pointed down a dimly lit corridor into a back area, stacked with extra tables and chairs. There was one tiny toilet. The walls were a dull oyster-pink, and covered in graffitied messages. Inside, she squirmed to undo her jeans. When she was finished, she unbolted the door and pulled. Nothing happened.

Tugging, she tried again.

Music from the bar drifted under the cubicle door. She held the metal handle, kicked the bottom, and pulled again.

'Come on!' she muttered, the cramped interior closing in on her.

It was then, in the gloomy light, she saw the smiley-face sticker on the door, written in three languages, one of them English: 'I stick – please don't close me!'

'Oh God.' She bent down in the minuscule space, feeling ridiculous, and tried to look under the door.

'Hello . . . Is anyone there?'

Nobody came.

Table and chair legs came into sight, but no human ones. Far away, she saw people in the bar, down the long corridor.

'Hello?' she shouted, waving a hand under the door.

Nothing. She looked left and saw shadows. Then she looked right.

A pair of man's boots rested against a table.

'Oh. Hello?'

The boots didn't move.

'Sorry. Do you speak English? I'm stuck in here. Could you push the door?'

Nothing happened.

Guessing the man was wearing earphones or was on his

phone, Grace banged the door. 'Hello! Sorry! Could you kick the door, please?'

Footsteps came towards her. Finally.

She stood up.

When nothing happened, she ducked down again. The boots were walking away.

'Wha-*aat*? Excuse me, I'm stuck in here!'

The man kept going.

Something familiar about him tugged at her mind, but she was in such a panic to get out, it slipped away.

It was four more long minutes before help finally came, by which time she was starting to imagine being locked in there all night.

'Stand back,' called a cheerful Australian man. He kicked the door twice.

Grace thanked him, and escaped.

The customers outside had drifted away, and a waiter was chaining up chairs. She turned back onto the shadowy canalside, and walked towards Nicu's boat, shivering, despite the warm evening. It had been a long day. She needed sleep. Her thoughts turned happily back to the tranquil blue boat with its private exhibition of Nicu Dragan's work, which she could devour at leisure.

Up ahead, there was a flicker of movement.

By a tree was the outline of a man. He stood close to Nicu's boat, wearing a hoodie. His posture unnerved her. Perhaps because he was standing still, not leaning. Not moving his hands, or speaking.

Grace crept into a doorway to watch.

Lights had gone out in most of the houses and boats.

Still the man didn't move. She could see even less of him from this angle.

Voices sounded behind her. To her relief, an Australian couple from the bar approached arm in arm. The man didn't react, didn't look round.

Grace crept out, and stayed close behind them till she reached the blue boat, then crossed the ramp and let herself in before the couple were out of earshot.

With the light still off, she opened the blinds a centimetre.

The hooded man was walking away, as if he'd spotted a taxi he'd ordered up on the main road.

'Calm down,' she said out loud. Her nerves were shot today. Too much adrenalin.

She turned on the lamps, showered, then, wrapped in a towel, took a walk around Nicu's prints. There was a stunning one of a teenage acrobat in a wrinkled leotard, with huge false eyelashes, hanging from a rope above a tiger, in a story about Central Asian rural circuses. Another of an Arab woman in white running along a flat-rooftopped building dragging her children, while a hundred men ran in the opposite direction on the ground, guns in the air.

Each was a work of art. She remembered now. Nicu Dragan's work was powerful but incredibly intimate, as if he'd lived for years with the people he photographed. The kind of work she'd aspired to once.

She pulled on a clean T-shirt, and climbed into bed, thinking about her encounter with him. Did he really have two girlfriends? She imagined them all in some cool, seedy bar in Amsterdam tonight. His life, clearly, was not conventional, like hers. Maybe it couldn't be when you worked and travelled like he did.

Before she knew it, the boat was rocking her into a lull.

Then, just as she drifted into a delicious sleep, Grace's mind fired an image at her, sharp as glass.

The back of the man disappearing into the bar.

Her eyes fluttered open.

No. That was impossible.

She tried to focus on it again; then reality and dreams began to merge and it was Anne-Marie she was watching from behind in the bar, and Dad waiting at a table with Auntie Marjorie for her to arrive, worried about where she was. Before she could call out to tell him everything was OK, sleep devoured her.

CHAPTER TWENTY-FOUR

Edinburgh

Dot, dot, dot.

Now night had fallen in Edinburgh, the man prepared himself for his task.

He appraised his drawing, and finished the eyes as he always did at the end. With the fine black pen, he dotted her irises, building them up, with a relentless tapping motion, recalling the fragile blue that always pierced his heart. The defiant expression that appeared when his arrogance pained her. Then he dotted back through the eyelashes to thicken them, recalling the flutter of them against his cheek.

There. It was done. Two hours, a thousand dots.

Standing up, he took down yesterday's drawing of her, the one with the hint of crow's feet around her eyes, her hair short to her chin, and replaced it with today's. In it, her hair was soft around her shoulders, dark as when he had first met her, waved and gentle on the jutting clavicle of her chest and slender shoulders.

The usual ache for her power-punched him in the stomach.

The night stretched ahead.

With the woman upstairs away, he did his exercises earlier than normal, the towels wrapped round the creaky ceiling beams. Then, for tomorrow, he switched the food plates around in the fridge and marked up his TV schedule, both with eyes closed. When that was done, he sat on the stool, turned off the lights, and settled down to watch.

As it did every night around this time, the tower block came alive.

A hive of lights.

Curtains shutting, lights switching on and off. Faces at the windows, watching other people's lives, hiding tears, searching for a night-shift partner or parent, hoping for more, wishing for someone else.

He could almost hear it. A cacophony of blaring televisions and radios, shouts into kitchens and bathrooms, screams and cries, barking dogs and boiling kettles, washing machines and electric guitars and video games, banging walls, the endless whoosh and ping of lifts.

On the fourth floor, a hand ran a toy plane across the window, the owner's mother at the next window, ironing, presumably unaware of the wide-awake child.

Two men hung over the balcony two floors above, hands pointing down.

When you saw this many people gathered in one place, after a while, they stopped being people. They became like his drawings, a thousand tiny dots, faces as indistinguishable as ants.

Nothing defining.

Just like him.

A man without a voice. A man without a name.

CHAPTER TWENTY-FIVE

Amsterdam

Grace woke the next morning in a sweaty tangle of sheets, grabbing air, as she was shunted gently by the wake of a passing boat.

Where was she?

She sat up, eyes puffy, trying to remember.

Someone was knocking.

'Hello,' she croaked. Wrapping a blanket round her, she fumbled to the door. Sunshine exploded in.

Nicu Dragan stood on the doorstep. 'Morning.' His reaction to her disarray was hidden behind sunglasses.

'Sorry. What time is it?' She squinted into the sun behind him.

'Nine.' He jiggled his car keys. 'There's a guy at City Hall owes me a favour – I'm going to see if he can find an address for your Lucian Grabole.'

She rubbed her eyes, trying not to drop the blanket. 'Thank you. Should I come?'

'I need to get going – see you later.' He waved again, and walked off. A man, clearly, of few words.

'Thank you.'

She dressed, wishing she'd set her alarm, and headed out. The cold, shadowy Amsterdam of last night had vanished. The canal was a ribbon of taupe-coloured silk. Haphazard window boxes were filled with cheerful hollyhocks and roses, the road bustling with life. She saw now that the doorway she'd hidden in last night was tiled with pretty antique blue-and-white tiles, the doors made of delicate black ironwork.

At the bridge, she fell in alongside the troops of cyclists, their bikes piled with bunches of flowers, children, laptops, shopping bags and even a guitar. The cafe was at the far end, with outside tables that wobbled on square cobbles. She ate a pastry and coffee, sucking herself in as moped riders with no helmets and bikes zipped round the corner inches from her back. There was a shout below. A woman watered pots on the canalside, waving at her twin sons in a street park as they leaped across a series of flat-ground trampolines like frogs.

She took out her camera.

Ever since she'd arrived in London, she'd wanted to shoot everything. Maybe it was just the change of scene, but she hadn't felt like this in years.

When Nicu arrived back, after ten, Grace gave him a few minutes, then went round to his boat.

He answered, bare-chested again, eating an apple. 'Hey. I have an address for you.'

'Really?'

She followed him, unsettled once more by his casual attitude to T-shirts.

Sunlight flooded through voile curtains. The boat smelt of ground coffee. Nicu lifted a pot from the stove.

'Want one?'

'Thanks. So what did you find?'

He poured two cups and headed across the sitting room. 'Come through.'

To her astonishment, he entered the bedroom.

'Um.' Unsure, she waited, then crept forward.

What was he doing?

There was a bag on his bed, and a pile of folded clothes, travel items and camera equipment. But no Nicu.

A soft breeze caressed her arms.

Tiptoeing forwards, Grace saw lush greenery pressed against the bedroom window – then an open door off the back of the boat.

A garden?

Walking out, she saw a floating deck, a few metres deep, harnessed across the whole length of the black boat. Pots of bamboo and other tall plants screened half the frontage, creating a perfect urban jungle. Nestled in the middle was a wrought-iron table and chairs where Nicu had placed the coffee. A ginger cat sunned itself.

'Wow. This is amazing.' She took a seat.

'Yeah, it's good. I copied theirs.'

Next door, she saw a fit-looking couple in their late seventies, her with a white crop in a potter's top, him bald with a white beard, watering plants on their own deck. Further up the canal, a young couple sat smoking on an old leather sofa, on a much smaller version, floating on tyres, two bikes lying by their feet.

It was beautiful. Blissful.

Nicu picked up a wine bottle and three glasses, and passed them into the open kitchen window. Grace bit back a smile as she sat down.

The two women last night had been on the deck when she arrived – not in his bedroom.

'It's so quiet,' she said.

He lifted a hose. 'You have to be. Noise travels on water. Especially at night. Not that anyone's told Hugo and Magriet.'

His eyes signalled the elderly couple, and the comment was so unexpected she choked on her coffee.

If he noticed, he didn't react, pumping water and spraying the plants. At the water's edge, a black-and-white coot and her chick swam by, creating deep 'V's in the silky water.

She composed herself. 'So, that's great about the address – where is it?'

'Oud-Zuid. South. I don't know if it's your guy, though,' Nicu said, stepping round the cat.

'Why?'

'Because he's registered to work. Or was. He hasn't lived here for over a year.'

There was a flutter above. Shielding her eyes, Grace saw a tall heron on the roof.

Nicu carried on, seemingly oblivious. 'He'd registered his address at City Hall, and had a BSN number – like National Insurance, so . . .'

She reached to stroke the cat. It kicked her away with a cross paw.

'Oi.' Nicu bent down beside her and stroked it. 'Be nice.' This time, it stretched out, happy.

'But worth checking, you reckon?' Grace asked.

Nicu pushed up his sunglasses. His brows were dark and defined, his lashes long. They accentuated the intensity of his gaze. Today, she saw a shimmer of warmth in it, but it made it no easier to meet.

Photographer's eyes.

Did she do that to people, too?

'I don't know. It's your story,' he frowned.

She stared at the bottom of her cup as if there was something interesting in there. 'Thing is, I'm not sure it is yet. It's Ewan's idea to pitch it to the editor at *Scots Today*. Right now, I just want to find out why this guy died in my flat.'

He stood up and turned off the hose. 'Why?'

'Because he died in my flat. And I want to know why he was there. That's the angle of the story, anyway, if I write it. And if I don't find out, there's no story.'

He sipped his coffee. 'So the police have no idea?'

'Well, they're checking the name Lucian Grabole, but there are loads of other avenues to try, too. It's not a murder enquiry, so it'll take time.'

'So, nothing to stop you checking it out, then?'

'Nope. Anyway, thanks for that. Have you got the address?'

He handed her a slip from his pocket.

'Thanks,' she said, reading it. 'Where are we now?'

'Oud-West. West.'

'And is it far?'

'Twenty-minute drive.' Nicu checked his watch. 'I've got to go to my gallery this morning. I'll drop you, if you want?'

'Really? Thank you.'

'And use the computer in the kitchen office if you need to.' His mobile rang and he went inside, ducking his head.

There was something about the way he moved that intrigued her. He was tall, but his movements were lithe and easy, as if he was comfortable in his own skin. *Unhindered.*

She re-read the address he'd given her, her stomach fluttering at the thought of what she might find.

Nicu drove south through Amsterdam, an elbow on the window-sill, seemingly unbothered by the gangs of bikes constantly cross-ing their path. He tapped his fingers to the music on the radio.

'So are you off on a job soon? I saw you were packing?' she asked.

He slowed at a traffic light. 'Yeah. Colombia.' He said it casually, as if he was going to the office for a meeting.

'Wow. What's the story?'

'A female vigilante group in Bogotá.'

'Cool. For a newspaper?'

'No time.'

'No time for what?'

He looked bemused again. 'No, *Time*. Magazine?'

'Oh, *Time*! God. Sorry. How long are you going for?'

'Not sure yet.' He turned up the music. She took it as a cue that he didn't like small talk.

Streets of four-storey apartment blocks gave way to wider, leafier roads. Nicu turned into a broad avenue that overlooked a private park, and pulled up by a large detached house. Number 1 stood behind a wrought-iron gate, a manicured courtyard and a fountain.

Grace checked around. There were five more houses, equally as grand. Next door was the embassy of a small Middle Eastern country.

This was not what she'd been expecting. She saw a quizzical look cross Nicu's face and wondered if he was thinking the same.

He handed her a gallery card. 'Listen, I'll be there for an hour.' He pointed ahead. 'Left at the junction, fifteen minutes' walk straight. Otherwise, see you back at the boat. And I'll see what else I can rustle up, contacts-wise.' He slammed the gearstick back into drive and waited, expectant, as she got out.

'Thanks.' She stood outside the elegant house as he drove away, already guessing this was a waste of time. She'd bet her flat in Gallon Street that the dead man in the scruffy suit and shoes had never lived anywhere like this.

*

131

Ten minutes later, Grace was glad she hadn't made that bet official.

Lucian Grabole's former address was fronted by large cast-iron gates. When she rang the bell, a woman in her sixties in a housecoat and sandals, grey plaits on her head, came to the front door, and called out in Dutch.

Grace replied in English. To her relief, the woman switched languages, and introduced herself as the concierge, Mitti.

'I'm sorry to disturb you, Mitti,' Grace said, 'but I'm trying to trace a man who lived here a year ago, called Lucian Grabole.'

The concierge's expression transformed. She clapped like a child. 'Lucian? Wonderful! How is Lucian?'

At least she knew him. This should make it easy to eliminate Nicu's legal Lucian Grabole from her list.

'Could I come in for a minute, please?'

Mitti invited her in to sit by the stone fountain, beside a flower-bed of tall purple puffballs and ruby stalks, as vibrant as a butterfly.

'I'm pretty sure I'm wasting your time here,' Grace started as she began to describe the details of the dead man in her flat in Edinburgh. At first she thought it was her imagination, but each time she added a new detail – that the man was Romanian, his height, colouring and age, the wolf tattoo and the signet ring with a green stone – Mitti's smile diminished further.

Then, to her astonishment, as she finished up, the Dutch woman's expression dissolved into grief.

'This is the same man?' Grace said, in disbelief.

'Oh!' The concierge nodded, dabbing the fleshy skin around her eyes, as tears formed. 'This is terrible news. Poor Lucian.'

'Oh no. I'm so sorry to upset you,' Grace said. The phrase was becoming familiar. 'Mitti, I'm trying to find Lucian's family.

132

I can see you're really distressed, but could I ask you to tell me something about Lucian so I can tell them?'

Mitti fought back tears, nodding, as Grace asked permission to use the voice recorder and switched it on. 'Uh. He came from Romania.' The woman's skin was a little loose, as if it had been lifted, stretched and dropped back. It gave each expression more depth, as her features gathered like curtains. She sniffed hard.

'Anything else?'

Mitti wiped her nose with a tissue. 'He was young. Only forty years old. He lived here for a year.'

'A year? Till?'

'Last spring.' Mitti blew her nose. An unexpected anger entered her voice. 'This makes no sense, that he would steal from your apartment. Lucian was not a criminal. See here?' She pointed at the rubbish bins, tucked discreetly into a corner. 'Every Tuesday he woke early to help me put these on the street. And in the garden.' She pointed behind the house. 'He worked here, too. Not for money. Because he liked to. He didn't steal.'

'What was his job?' Grace asked.

Her eyes brightened. 'Oh, a painter. A decorator. Come.'

She led Grace into an opulent communal hall, with a marble floor, and century-old oil landscapes adorning an ornate sweeping staircase.

Mitti pointed to the intricate lace coving on the ceiling. 'You see. He filled the cracks. He was so patient – little, little, little.' She mimed Lucian daubing.

They stood beside a polished walnut unit with six shelves with brass nameplates. Each held post for one apartment.

'But he worked outside the house, too?' Grace asked, wondering how on earth Lucian could afford this place.

'Oh yes. He painted the new shopping mall outside the Ring.'

133

The concierge circled her finger. 'The road round the city? He worked at night. He said it paid very well.'

Grace took in the long silk curtains at the hall window. Even a night shift wouldn't pay for this, surely, unless he and Anna rented just a room here, rather than an apartment.

'Would you be able to show me where he lived, Mitti?'

Mitti led her up three floors to a handsome wood-panelled door with a heavy brass knocker. The nameplate said, 'Dr De Jonker.'

'This was it?' Grace asked. 'Really? Could I look inside?'

'No. The doctor is away,' Mitti said. 'I can't.'

Along the rear landing was a window. Grace walked to look out and saw a manicured lawn and pretty rose garden. More bountiful flowerbeds lined the boundaries, and a rope swing hung from an oak tree. This made no sense.

'Mitti, I'm a little confused. Can I double-check a few things?'

'Yes.'

'So, Lucian Grabole was a Romanian man of around forty, and we've agreed what he looked like?'

Mitti's eyes were rheumy now with tears. 'Yes.'

'And he was a painter and decorator, and he lived here for one year?'

'Yes.'

'With his family – a wife and child, also Romanian?'

Mitti frowned. 'Please repeat.'

Grace did.

Curtains of flesh gathered on Mitti's brow. 'No. No. Lucian was not married. He lived here alone. Always.'

Grace thought she'd misheard. 'He wasn't married? He didn't have a wife called Anna?'

'No. Never,' Mitti protested.

134

Stumped, Grace tried again. 'So there wasn't a police raid here – looking for unregistered foreign workers? They didn't just disappear during the night?'

Mitti became indignant. 'Here? Of course not. No, Lucian left because his mother was ill. In Bucharest.'

Two pink dots appeared on her plump cheeks. She dabbed with increased effort at her tears as the news sank in.

It was time to go and leave her in peace.

'Mitti, listen, I'm so sorry to have upset you.' Grace patted her arm. 'I promise I'll get back to you when I have official confirmation. Until then, could I possibly ask you to ring me when Dr De Jonker returns? In case he found anything in Lucian's apartment?'

'Yes.' Mitti led her back out. 'But I hope you *are* wrong. Lucian was a good neighbour to us. A friend to me. We liked him here very much.'

It wasn't professional, but Grace held out her arms, and Mitti fell into her with a sob, then waved her off with a wet tissue.

Grace walked to the junction, stumped. If this was the same Lucian Grabole, why didn't Mitti know Anna and Valentin?

Each mansion on the avenue was as grand as Lucian and Mitti's, set back from the road, with private parking. It seemed impossible that a painter and decorator could afford this.

The road was empty apart from a gold executive saloon parked in front of the Middle Eastern embassy.

Grace approached, pensive.

There was a flicker in the wing mirror.

She looked up, expecting to see a Middle Eastern driver in a uniform, waiting for a visiting dignitary.

Instead, it was a pale face in a green hoodie, stainless-steel eyes locked on her camera bag.

Grace's heart skipped. Diving behind the car, she crossed over and walked quickly to the junction, gripping her camera strap. She needed to be more careful if she was travelling alone.

When she arrived at Nicu's gallery, an assistant told her he was still with the owner but to look around. One room featured a photo exhibition of Syrian refugee camps by an Italian female photographer she'd heard of; the other was Nicu's.

At the door, there was a biography and she sneaked a quick look. He'd been born in Romania, brought up in New Zealand, and studied at prestigious art schools in both New York and London. His work had been shown in a number of major galleries and featured in publications around the world.

There were eight shots in his exhibition, each three metres high, hung in a purposely claustrophobic room. They were portraits of London rioters in 2011.

She swivelled in the centre, taking in each one. He'd shot them close up, so their faces filled the frame. The combined effect was of giant heads surrounding and leering down at you. One rioter had a gashed head, and a glittering gallery of gold teeth. Another blew a kiss from split, bloody lips. One man peered through a gap in a white balaclava fashioned from a looted babygrow. A woman stuck her tongue between a pair of trainers, the sales label hanging off them.

At first, their expressions appeared incendiary and threatening, but in their eyes, Grace saw more. They'd let Nicu steal inside the madness of those nights; revealed their frustration and sense of disenfranchisement.

Her phone rang out in the silent gallery. 'Hello?' she answered.

Nobody spoke.

'Hello?'

An office door opened. Nicu exited, looking taken aback to see her, as if he'd forgotten she existed.

He motioned to the front door, and she followed him out to the Jeep.

'Hello?' she repeated into the mobile. Still nobody answered. She climbed in.

'How did you get on?' he said, starting the engine.

'Weird – it *was* the same Lucian Grabole. Thanks for getting the address,' she said, putting on her seatbelt. 'Apparently, he worked as a painter and decorator. Do you think that's odd that he lived in that house? A doctor lives there now.'

Nicu waited for bikes to pass. 'I reckon even a doctor would be hard pushed to afford that road. Maybe he was house-sitting or subletting.'

'Maybe.'

'Yeah. So what you going to do now?' he said, pulling out.

'I've got numbers for two Romanian community groups. I'll see if they can help me track down Anna and Valentin. Maybe there's a mother-and-baby group or something. And I thought I'd ask the Dutch police about raids on unregistered foreign workers.'

Nicu scratched his close-cut beard, and that shimmer of warmth returned to his eyes. 'Want me to do it? Might be easier with the language.'

'Really?'

'Yup. I've got nothing on till I go to Colombia next week.'

'That would be great, thanks.' She went to retrieve the numbers and saw her phone was still running. The call was on two minutes and fifty-six seconds.

'Hello?' she repeated.

The call ended.

Nicu glanced over.

She shook her head. 'I'm wondering if that was the concierge at the apartment, or someone I gave my card to in London.'

'Recognize the number?'

She shook her head.

Unknown.

CHAPTER TWENTY-SIX

At Nicu's suggestion, Grace used the computer in the tiny office, while he sat on the deck to ring the community groups and his own contacts from a recent immigration feature in Amsterdam.

It was hard to concentrate. On the walls were more of his prints. Above her was a black picket-fence line of hand-silhouettes across the print, raised in dance against a background of roughly hewn rock ablaze with green and pink laser lights. A rave of some sort, she guessed.

She enlarged her photos onscreen and transcribed Mitti and Ali's conversations, then ran back the clip of her calamitous chat with the Cozmas.

'Who's that talking, Grace?' a call came from outside.

She got up and found Nicu leaning in the kitchen window.

'Uh, Lucian Grabole's Romanian friends in London. The Cozmas. They come from the same village. That's Mrs Cozma. She got really upset. I kind of charged in, thinking it wouldn't be him, and it was. They were so upset they wouldn't speak to me anymore.'

'Can you run it again?'

'OK,' she said, taken aback.

His dark curls fell forwards as he listened to Mrs Cozma's hysterical wails.

'She doesn't like you . . .' he said, lifting his chin.

Grace smiled ruefully. 'No, I guessed. I probably should have—'

'And she doesn't like him,' Nicu interrupted.

'Who?'

'Lucian Grabole. She hates him. Did you know that?'

Grace paused the voice clip, privately questioning how good Nicu's Romanian was. 'No. That can't be right. She was *devastated* when I said he might be dead.'

Nicu came round into the boat, and joined her in the tiny office. She squeezed against the desk as he towered over her to take the phone. At least he was wearing a T-shirt. He replayed the clip, then paused it, lips pursed in concentration.

'Yeah. She's emotional – but it's with relief, not grief. She's happy the guy's dead.'

'I don't understand – why?'

'Listen.' He held the phone closer to her so their hair was almost touching. The snatch of fast Romanian repeated. 'This bit, here,' Nicu said. '*Monstrul este mort . . .* ?'

'What does that mean?'

'It means "The monster is dead."'

CHAPTER TWENTY-SEVEN

Edinburgh

Sula sat outside a red-brick building in the Edinburgh suburb of Colinton, guessing it wouldn't be much longer.

The building was the type she'd seen before, thrown up by developers with no conscience about squeezing old folk into kennel-size 'retirement apartments' and taking their savings to pay for it.

She'd put herself over a cliff before living in a place like this, letting some numpty wipe her arse.

The door opened and a familiar face exited and climbed into a car.

'That's it – you get off to have your lunch,' Sula said, watching the woman drive off.

She walked into the reception and flashed a card quickly.

'Sula McGregor to see Mr Pearce. Is DS Foley still here?'

'That the family liaison officer?' the receptionist said.

'Yes.'

'No. You've just missed her, sorry.'

'Have I? That's annoying – is Mr Pearce still here?'

'Yes. Do you need to see him?'

'Just for five minutes.'

'Sure, this way. He's having his tea.'

An old wifey with spools of purple hair sprouting from a bald scalp was slumped in the living area, her bottom lip out, as bairns from the primary school sang songs. She fixed her eyes on Sula, desperate for escape.

Mr Pearce's room was down a long, featureless corridor, but his living quarters were more homely. Tidy. A comfy armchair, family photographs, bird ornaments on the windowsill. A photo of his son David Pearce as a primary-school pupil, fresh face and innocent eyes. Mr Pearce was smartly dressed in a button-up cardigan and slacks, his white hair brushed for his earlier visitor.

'Mr Pearce, I'm Sula McGregor – here to speak to you about your son.'

'Hello. Come in,' Mr Pearce said, struggling to stand. He was hardly any taller when he did, so bent was he.

Sula shook his hand.

'OK, Mr Pearce?' the receptionist said.

'Aye.'

'I'll leave you to it,' she smiled, closing the door.

'Sorry to hear what's happened, Mr Pearce,' Sula said.

'Aye. It's a bad situation.' His voice was indistinct, as if he was struggling for breath. He threw his chin up with each word as if trying to shake it out of his exhausted neck. 'Are you here to find out what happened?'

She touched his arm. 'Now listen. Mr Pearce. I'm not the police. I don't want you thinking that. I'm from the paper. I'm trying to find out what happened to your son, and Colin McFarlay. Do you understand?'

'I do.'

'And you're OK with that?'

'Aye. I want to know myself.'

'Good.' Sula turned on her tape. 'Now, I'm sure the police have asked you this, but your son wasn't a drug user, no?'

142

'Ach no.' Mr Pearce swatted the air. 'He was not. He was a lecturer, at the university.'

Sula nodded. 'And he hadn't been here for a while? He stayed in Australia, is that right?'

'Aye, in Perth. And my other son.' He pursed liver-coloured lips. 'It was my fault.'

'What was your fault?'

Mr Pearce coughed, a rattle in his throat. 'Excuse me. Well, we went there, for my work, in 1959, when my boys were wee. I'm an engineer, too. We came back to Scotland in 1972, when they were nearly finished high school. But they wanted to go back to Perth. Felt Australian by then, you see . . .'

'Right. And when David visited, did he always stay with you here, at your house in Colinton?'

Mr Pearce's wispy grey brows met. 'No, no. David never was back in Scotland. Not for forty years, apart from his mother's funeral. He was always too busy with his work. Him and my other son, Philip, paid for me and her to go over there. Once every year or two. But it's a long way. And when my wife died, well . . .'

'Did you not fancy going over to be with your sons?'

'Ach, well, you don't want to make a nuisance.' He pointed at the bird ornaments on the windowsill. 'They keep getting me these. I don't even like birds. It was my wife.'

'Right. So this was new, was it, David coming to Scotland to see you?'

'Aye.' Mr Pearce coughed again, and his eyes watered.

'And why did he come?'

Mr Pearce waved a bony hand. 'He was angry.'

'Angry with you?' she exclaimed.

'Aye. I sold my house and the boys weren't happy.'

'Why?'

'Well, no point me having the money sitting in a house when the grandkids could use it. But my sons didn't like it. Think they wanted to sell it after I'd gone. Didn't want me spending all the money on this place!'

'So what—' Sula started, but the old man cut across her, anger entering his voice.

'But it was ma house! Treating me like an old man. I was angry. I told David, don't come here and tell me what I'm doing wrong, when you're not even there when your mother dies.' A look of astonishment entered Mr Pearce's eyes, and his voice broke. He searched around again, only moving his upper body.

Sula crossed the room for a box of tissues. 'Here you go, Mr Pearce.'

'Thank you.' He dabbed at his eyes. A low wail came from his mouth. 'Who would kill my son? Who would do that to him?'

Sula counted to ten, waiting for it to stop. It wasn't that she wasn't sympathetic; she just had a story to file.

'I don't know, Mr Pearce, but I can promise you the police will be doing everything they can to find out. But you're sure David – or you – didn't know Colin McFarlay? Or his family?'

'No . . .' His head dipped, and she knew she'd lost him.

He pointed at a pot of tea. 'Want a cup?'

'No, thanks.'

'A wee half-cup?'

'No, but I'm going to leave you to yours.' Sula stood up, guessing time was running out. If the FLO had popped up to the local shops, she could be back any moment. 'Listen, I'm very sorry for your loss, Mr Pearce. And anything I find out, I'm going to let you know, OK?'

'David's wife and my other son are arriving on Sunday, for the . . . to do the . . .' He stopped, and used his tissue.

'Your son Philip?'

'Aye.'

'That's useful to know,' Sula said. 'Thank you.'

She reached the door.

Mr Pearce's voice wavered over to her. 'They talked about the dog finding the top of my son's head in your paper. Down the pit cave.'

Sula held the door handle. She knew the report. She'd written it.

Mr Pearce's eyes drifted away. 'It made me think about him, when he was a wee boy, in the bath. He had this curly hair, and he'd hold his breath under the water, and his head would pop up . . .' His cheeks filled with air, then released into a sorry smile. He patted an imaginary child's head.

Sula nodded. 'It's no' a fair world, Mr Pearce.'

His watery eyes tried to hold her there, no other power left to him. 'Will you find out who did this?'

'I promise I'll do my best. So will the police. You've got one of the best on this case. DI Robertson. I know him. Now you take care. Enjoy your tea.'

She left the retirement home and walked towards the car, phone to her ear. DS Foley passed her with a sandwich bag, her expression turning stern as their eyes met.

'Ewan,' Sula said into his voicemail, opening her car door. 'Find out how much David Pearce's father sold his house for in Colinton. I want to know how that money was split between the family. Dad says the grandkids got it and David Pearce wasn't happy about it.'

It was nothing, but maybe something.

CHAPTER TWENTY-EIGHT

Amsterdam

Grace sat in Nicu's office, her research plans for the story disintegrating in front of her.

Mrs Cozma *hated* Lucian?

Nicu translated the rest, as she typed at his Mac.

'So it sounds like Mrs Cozma comes up while you're talking to her husband and says, "What do you not understand? . . . He was hunting for them. This woman and her child. They were hiding. Running for their lives." Who's she talking about?'

'Anna and Valentin – his wife and child,' Grace said, halting. 'Hang on. She said they were *hiding* from Lucian?'

'Yup. Then she says, "This man. He's a monster. You want to know who Lucian Tronescu was? He was—"'

Grace cut in. 'Who's Lucian Tronescu?'

Nicu paused the clip, leaning over the desk. 'I don't know, but "Tronescu" is a Romanian surname.' He played it again. 'Now her husband's trying to stop her talking to you, but she's angry. She says, "Listen to me. Lucian Tronescu was a killer, just like his father . . . Two months he forced us to keep him here, in London, or his people will hurt my family in Rutaslava. I thank God he's dead. I'll thank God every day . . ."'

Grace typed on, baffled, and then heard Mr Cozma, now in

English. 'Please leave my family in peace. We will not speak to you again.'

Her hands flew to her head. 'I don't understand, Nicu. Why are they calling him Lucian Tronescu? I clearly said I was looking for Lucian Grabole.'

He sat against the desk, folding his arms. 'Sounds like they know he has another name, too.'

Grace shook her head. 'That doesn't make sense. The guy she's describing sounds like a psycho. Everyone who knows Lucian Grabole loved him. They keep saying what a nice guy he was.'

She smelt a faint scent of the Indian oil as Nicu reached across her for the mouse and summoned a Google map of Romania. A boat puttered past, and Grace felt an urge to jump out of the window and escape on it, away from these increasingly disturbing revelations about Lucian, and this cramped room and this physical restlessness she felt around this man.

Rutaslava, the village Mrs Cozma mentioned, appeared. It was isolated in a mountain area, a single name in a mass of green emptiness, with just one hair's-breath road passing through it. Nicu zoomed out.

'Wow, that's remote,' Grace said.

Nicu reduced it. 'These places are cut off.'

Other villages appeared at the corners, linked by the road, but equally rural. Eventually, a major road appeared, then a major town, maybe fifty miles from the village.

'Ah. OK. I know this town,' Nicu pointed. 'One of my cousins works at a hospital there. I'll ring her. See if she knows anyone closer to the mountain.'

'Thanks.'

Needing air and time to think, she went out to the deck, and swirled a rotten yellow leaf through the water, considering the new revelations.

Two names for the dead man. If Lucian Tronescu was a violent criminal who'd entered and worked in the UK using the false surname Grabole, it would certainly explain why the Edinburgh police hadn't identified the body yet.

Inside, she heard Nicu talking in Romanian. He appeared a few minutes later, stretching up to hold the door frame. 'She doesn't know Rutaslava, but one of the nurses at her hospital drives in from that mountain. She's going to ask if she's heard of any Tronescus up there.'

'Thanks,' Grace said weakly.

Last night in the cafe, she'd started to plan her research. Now, with Nicu's help, the story was twisting ahead so rapidly she couldn't keep up.

Partly that's because he was treating this like a story.

Yet, for her, it wasn't just a story. It was personal.

Nicu squinted. 'You look worried.'

'No,' she lied. 'I just realized I forgot to get more euros. Is there a cash machine nearby?'

Her resolve not to tell Mac what she was doing had dissolved the minute she heard the dead man in their flat might be a murderer.

She walked quickly to the bridge, and rang him.

He answered after three rings. 'Hey, darlin', how you doing?'

'OK. How's the golf?'

'Great. Sun's been out. Got burned today. We're just having dinner at the clubhouse. What's up?'

'Can you talk?'

Three minutes later, she wished she hadn't bothered.

She'd expected him to be pissed off. But not to go mental.

'Amsterdam? You're fuckin' joking me? This dead guy again. I can't believe you, Grace. How much is this costing us?'

When she'd mentioned the dead man might be a murderer, it only got worse. 'God's sake. Why are you getting involved with this? Get back and let the police do their job. I mean it. If you don't, I'm ringing DI Robertson and telling him what's going on.'

'Mac, I just rang to tell you what was happening. You don't have to—'

'Grace. Just get home.' For the first time in their lives, he slammed down the phone. She headed back to Nicu's boat, cursing under her breath. What had she expected? That he'd say, 'Hey, darlin', good for you – hold your nerve and go for it. This could be your big break.'

He never had before.

Nicu met her at the door with significant news. The hospital nurse his cousin knew was friends with someone who lived in the next village to Rutaslava and had a brother working on a building site in Amsterdam. This guy had agreed to meet them after his shift tonight.

'I'll take you, if you want.'

She grabbed a pen, her resolve returning. 'That's fantastic. What's his name?'

Nicu took out peppers from the fridge. 'He doesn't want you to know.'

She lowered her pen. 'Why? Is he illegal?'

His knife froze above the red flesh, and he frowned. 'Yeah, he's illegal. Causing trouble. You've read the headlines. That's us Romanians.'

She flushed. 'Sorry. That was stupid. I didn't mean that to sound . . .'

Then a smile appeared, and he laughed.

'Don't,' she said.

He tapped the pepper with the knife. 'Want some food?'

'Oh. No,' she said, realizing what he was doing. 'Please, let me make dinner, or buy it for us, or something. You're already putting me up for nothing.'

He cut off a piece of pepper, threw it up and caught it in his mouth. 'Don't worry about it. I'm intrigued now, anyway. "Who's the Guy?" It's a good story.'

'Thanks,' she said, touched. Why couldn't Mac have said that?

Nicu turned on music, gave her a beer, and began to cook. Grace wandered outside, deciding the least she could do was give him space, and thought about her fight with Mac.

Mac did this too often.

Story or no story, she'd decide when she went back. Not him.

CHAPTER TWENTY-NINE

The plan was to eat, then go and meet the Romanian builder by the flats where he was working, at five o'clock. Halfway there, however, he rang Nicu to change location to a bridge, half a mile away.

Ten minutes later, he changed it again.

'Why's he doing this?' Grace said.

Nicu reversed the Jeep in a dead end. 'Don't know. Sounds nervous.'

'Why?'

'No idea. Why don't I talk to him first?'

The final location was an alleyway in De Wallen, the red light district. Nicu parked by a church near the canal. The street was packed with tourists making the strange trail through back alleys displaying windows featuring women in underwear.

'I'll be back in five,' Nicu said, getting out.

Through the windscreen, she saw him enter the alleyway and shake hands with a figure in the shadows. They moved out of sight. A trail of cigarette smoke was the only proof they were there.

Waiting with her recorder and camera, Grace tried to imagine what more new revelations there might be about Lucian Grabole/

Tronescu. There was a movement to her left. A curtain opened in a window, and a girl sat down on a stool, her legs splayed, her décolletage a little sweaty. Where had she come from and how had this become her life? How many countries did these girls come from? Did their families know where they really were? She watched the trail of stag parties, egging each other on, laughing too loudly, bouncing on the balls of their feet, nervous.

Inside the open door of a church, opposite, an elderly lady prayed at the altar. In the candlelight, her face was pained, framed by the arched door. Grace picked up her camera and—

A rap on the taxi window made her start. Nicu jumped in the driver's seat.

The alleyway was empty.

'What's happening? Where is he?'

Nicu started the engine, his face serious.

'What's happened?' she repeated.

'He's not going to speak to you.'

'Why?' She twisted round, desperate not to lose this lead.

Nicu drove off through throngs of tourists, beeping to move a large party of men, who jeered and lifted their cans at him. 'Because he's freaked out.'

'Why?'

'This guy, Lucian Tronescu. He knows him. Or knows *of* him.'

She twisted behind her. 'Oh God, please, Nicu, go back. He might know something important.'

Instead, he turned onto a main road. 'Listen, he's not going to speak to you. But he says Lucian Tronescu definitely sounds like your dead guy – 1.78 metres tall, forties, wolf tattoo, Romanian.'

Grace turned on her voice recorder. 'And what else?'

Nicu checked in his rear-view mirror. 'Well, it's kind of crazy. He says Lucian Tronescu's family are infamous on that moun-

152

tain. Right across the region, actually. We'd probably have found people in the town who knew them, too. Back in the '70s and '80s, Lucian's father, Drac Tronescu, did freelance jobs for the Romanian Securitate.'

'What – the secret police?'

'Yup. He was a paid assassin for them.'

Her mouth fell open. 'I thought the secret police killed people themselves?'

'Apparently, Drac was freelance – a kind of self-employed psychopath. Did the high-level jobs when they didn't want to rock the boat politically. Party members planning a coup. People they wanted rid of without alienating Western trade partners. Mistresses with too much inside knowledge, that kind of thing . . . The rumour was that Drac had a line in pushing people off bridges and trains, so it looked like suicide or an accident.'

Grace listened, astonished. 'What, a kind of state-licensed serial killer?'

'Yeah, but apparently he killed for kicks, too, around the mountain, and nobody stopped him. Like it was his perk.'

'Do you think it's true – not a myth?'

Nicu glanced over. 'Me personally?'

'Well, did you live in Romania under Ceauşescu? Do you remember the secret police?'

'My parents did. We left when I was three.'

'But these things did happen?'

He shrugged. 'A lot of things happened. There's books about it – you might be able to verify it somewhere, though I'm guessing not all the records survived.'

'So where does Lucian fit in?'

Nicu cut through an alleyway to avoid the tourists. 'Right, so Lucian Tronescu is Drac's son. They worked together – father-and-son assassins. The guy says people are still scared of them up there, even after twenty-five years. I wouldn't be surprised if Drac was a nickname for the father – it means "devil" in Romanian.'

She imagined breaking that particular news to Mac. 'So what happened to them?'

'Drac was hanged during the uprising in 1989, two days after Ceauşescu. But Lucian escaped.'

'When?'

'Same time – he was a teenager . . .'

'So he'd be –' Grace swallowed '– about forty now. Like the dead man in my flat.'

'Yup.'

'And the guy back there, did he know Lucian Tronescu?'

'No. Never met him. But his aunt knew the Tronescus. When Lucian was a kid, he threw her dog down a well. Took five days to die.'

They stopped at traffic lights, and a man vomited in a gutter by Grace's window.

This man had been in her flat?

'Did he know where Lucian is now?'

Nicu drove on. 'Said he escaped to Paris, and went underground. Changed his name. That was the rumour. Lucian's mother stayed on the mountain. That's what she told people – her son was in Paris, though apparently she was mentally ill, so who knows?'

Grace held up a finger. 'At the Edinburgh night shelter, they said Lucian had been in Paris.'

'Right. So it fits.'

'So maybe that's when he changed his name to Lucian *Grabole*, to hide out?'

Nicu slowed to a crawl as they hit a row of shops selling giant clogs and windmill pencils, and tourists crossed between them.

'Maybe. But the interesting thing is – I'm guessing why he spoke to us tonight – he says Romanians in Amsterdam swear they've seen Lucian Tronescu here.'

'Here?'

'Yes.'

'But how would they know,' she protested, 'if he was a teenager when he left Romania? He'd be twenty-five years older now.'

'Apparently, he's the spit of Drac. Remember, they were famous up there. He's been seen here by a few people, using a false name.'

'So the Lucian Grabole who lived in Mitti's apartment block *could* have been Lucian Tronescu using false papers and a false name?'

Nicu tapped the wheel. 'Maybe. The guy's going to ask around, if you keep his name out of it. But he won't meet you – people are scared of these guys.'

'So why don't they just report him to the Romanian authorities?'

'Same reason, maybe. Maybe they're hoping the police or a journalist like you will do the job for them. Then they can stay out of it.'

She wondered how much experience Nicu thought she had. 'OK. Well, thanks.'

'No problem.' Nicu swore as the Jeep got stuck behind a horse-and-carriage tourist ride.

Grace sat back.

Out of the window, she watched a street performer tiptoeing across the square, doing an exaggerated version of the gait of the pedestrian in front to make the cafe customers laugh.

Two names now for the dead man in her flat.

One Lucian described as a kind, family man, the other Lucian a violent killer.

The clown copied the pedestrian's confused glances at all those laughing at his expense.

What was she looking for now, two different men or one man with two names who changed his character to order?

She rewound her voice recorder, put her earphones in, and listened back to what Nicu had just told her.

He threw her dog down a well. Took five days to die . . . It means 'devil' . . . The guy says people are still scared of them up there, even after twenty-five years.

What the hell was happening to this story?

The message she'd found on the wedding present returned to her. *I am not that man.*

But which man?

Amsterdam seemed less friendly this evening. A fire engine raced past them, sirens blaring.

Roadworks appeared ahead, and a cyclist, forced onto the pavement, had an argument with a pedestrian who objected to his presence there and blocked him. A fight broke out, and Nicu swerved to avoid it.

Soon, she spotted the play park from this morning. The trampolines were empty. A second fire engine streaked ahead.

A wisp of smoke blew in her window and she coughed, winding it up.

A second, thicker ribbon of smoke crossed her window. Nicu said something.

She took out her earphones. 'Sorry?'

'Where's that coming from?'

Grace craned to see.

Without warning, thick black smoke flew up from the water below onto the bridge they were crossing, twisted demonically in front of them, then smashed into Nicu's windscreen. He swore and braked. More sirens came, from behind. A police car cut in front, and swerved to the left.

Down on the bank, lights flashed blue. The acrid smoke parted. People were running – a jet stream of water was aiming at the corner of a—

'Oh shit – Nicu,' she said.

He'd already seen it. With a swerve, he accelerated past a bike, and down past the fire engine onto the bank, then jumped out, running towards the fire. The smoke parted and her fears were confirmed.

Two fire engines were aiming water at the far end of Nicu's black boat, where his little office was.

All his beautiful photos.

The smoke demon contorted on the boat, fighting with the thick jet spray. It twisted and dived away, over the water in swoops of black, then was captured. It broke away into mini plumes, and fought on. The jets corralled it. Then it was over, just like that.

The air was thick with the stench of burned tar and wood. She saw Nicu, hands on his head, being held back by a fire officer. Guessing what he would do in her situation, Grace opened the door and took a few shots.

His next-door neighbour Magriet walked towards her, holding the ginger cat in a box. The woman's face was tense with fear, soot in her white hair and a stripe across her face. Grace photographed her, too.

'Is Nicu here? Are you OK?' the woman called.

'Yes. Are you? Do you know what happened?' Grace asked.

The woman pointed a trembling finger to Nicu's boat. 'A man. A man did it. He threw petrol and ran to—'

'Petrol?'

'Yes!'

'Where is he now?'

'I don't know,' the woman said. 'Hugo and I were trying to use our pump to put out the fire till the fire engines got here, but . . .' She coughed, three long, hacking coughs, and Grace patted her back.

'Are you OK?'

'Yes. I need water.'

'Did you see what the man looked like?' Grace asked, reaching into Nicu's Jeep and finding some.

'Thank you.' She drank it. 'It was so fast. A hood, maybe.'

They watched Nicu remonstrate with a fire officer about entering the boat.

The new information drip-dripped into Grace's consciousness.

A man in a hood.

Then, as the woman rejoined her husband, she dropped down into a doorway and leaned against the antique blue-and-white tiles, unease crawling through her.

A crowd gathered on the canalside as news spread along Nicu's neighbours. She saw the two tall girls who'd been on the boat last night arrive and put their arms around him.

At first, she wasn't aware of the boy.

There was just a growing sense of a presence behind her. A creak made her turn.

The black cast-iron door of the canalside house was open. A blond boy of about twelve was peering out, his clear blue eyes alarmed.

'Oh, hello,' she said, hoping he spoke English. 'Are you OK?'

'I'm looking for my mom.'

'Are you expecting her?' Grace said, glancing at the police.

'She's late coming home from work.'

'Well, listen, don't worry. The police have stopped the traffic because of the fire. She's probably stuck in it and will be here very soon. And don't worry, it's all over now.' She held out a hand. 'I'm Grace. What's your name?'

He shook it. 'Luuk. Where is the man?' His eyes darted up the street, terrified.

'Which man?'

'Who made the fire.'

Grace stood up. 'Did you see him, Luuk?'

He nodded.

'Don't worry. He's gone now. Can you tell me what you saw?'

His body remained concealed in the doorway, head poking out. 'I was waiting at the window for my mom. He went to the blue boat. He was wearing a green hood. Then he went to the black boat with a can and put the boat on fire. Then he got in a car.'

'You saw his car?'

'Yes.'

'Can you remember the colour and the shape?'

He shrugged. 'Big and brown?'

Grace searched for help. The police were with Nicu. 'OK, Luuk, I'm going to stay with you till your mom gets here, so don't worry. Then you can tell her what you saw, OK?'

'OK.'

On the bridge, she saw a blonde woman in a suit pushing a bike past the frozen traffic, waving frantically.

'Is that her?'

Luuk squeezed out, and his shoulders melted with relief. His mother pushed the bike down the bank, and threw her arms around him, talking in Dutch. She looked anxiously at Grace.

'Your son said he saw the man who set the boat on fire. He was wearing a green hood and driving a brown car,' Grace said.

159

The woman repeated her words in Dutch and the boy shook his head.

'Gold,' the mother translated to Grace. 'He means gold. Where are the police, please?'

Grace pointed.

'Thank you,' the woman said, leading Johann away.

A man in a hood, in a gold car.

At the door of the blue boat.

Fear settled in her stomach like concrete.

The canalside was chaotic now. Hugo and Magriet were bringing a tarpaulin from their boat. Other neighbours arrived with brushes, buckets and mops.

Head down, Grace slipped through them into the blue boat, hoping she was wrong.

She wasn't.

On the floor lay an envelope.

On the front were two words: *GRACE SCOTT.*

CHAPTER THIRTY

The fire engines left soon after. Traffic started up across the bridge. Nicu's canalside neighbours hammered a tarpaulin onto the burned end of his boat.

Grace sat on the bed in the blue boat.

Ewan answered on the third ring. 'Oh, hello th—'

'I'm sending you something,' she said.

'That's nice, not even a "Hello, and thank you, Ewan, for hooking me up with a world-renowned reportage photog—"'

'Ewan. Open the email.'

Muttering. 'Right – what am I looking at?'

Grace held up the photo, feeling sick. 'It's me interviewing the concierge at Lucian Grabole's old apartment today – taken from a distance. Same guy set fire to Nicu Dragan's boat half an hour ago, and left it for me.'

Ewan whistled. 'Wha-aat? Oh God. Have we burned his boat?'

'It gets worse.' She relayed the revelations about Lucian Grabole's alter ego: Lucian Tronescu, fugitive killer.

'Shit, Scotty. You OK?'

'Not really. Bit shaken up.'

'But you're carrying on, right?'

161

A pause. 'Ewan, I really want to, but—'

He saw where this was going. 'Scotty – no!'

Silence.

'You're not giving up the story?' he lamented.

'Ewan, it's not a story. Not yet. Nobody's commissioned it. And it was supposed to be a human-interest story about me finding this man's family. Now I seem to be tracking down some crazed killer who was dodging the police and murdering for kicks. With another psycho following me, warning me to lay off.'

'Scotty . . .' His tone was ripe with disappointment.

'And it's not just that, Ewan. Mac's found out I'm here doing this and he's really angry. If I tell him about what's just happened now, he'll go nuts. He already thinks it's too serious – that we need to ring the police now.'

'Scotty! No!'

'What?'

'Fuck's sake. It's a good story. Don't give it up.'

'What if Nicu had been on his boat?'

Ewan groaned. 'But he wasn't. It's probably just a warning. Come on, Scotty. When are you going to stop shooting all these fatties on watermelon diets and Z-listers doing fun runs? When I met you two years ago, you were doing a journalism MA because you were bored as you'd never used your photojournalism degree and it was bothering you. Well, this is *it*!'

'Ewan!'

'Well, what?'

'I'm not sure I did actually say that. And if I did, it was at that bloody student party you made me go to with those Jägermeister cocktails. It's not that simple.'

'Yes it is.' He was almost hoarse now. 'You're a bloody good photographer, you've got a great instinct for a story, and you're not using it. You finally get an exclusive story that you could pitch to the nationals – words *and* photos – and you give it up.'

Her fist clenched. 'Ewan, I'm not you. I'm not twenty-three and living with my mum. No offence. It's not that easy to go off and take big risks like these when you've got a mortgage and commitments. I could waste all my dad's money on this and not even get commissioned.'

'Commitments?' he said sarcastically. 'What, Mac?'

'Ewan, don't.'

'This is Mac who stopped you taking that assisting job with the big photographer in Glasgow who travelled in Asia a lot, after your first degree?'

'When did I say that?'

'At that party.'

'God! I was *drunk*, Ewan. I said lots of things. I probably told you I fancied you, which tells you exactly how off my head I was. Mac *didn't* stop me. He just didn't want me to be away all the time. I *decided* not to do it. There's a difference.' Vaguely, she wondered why she was defending Mac about something she'd secretly blamed him for for years.

'Right.'

She tutted. 'I'm not discussing this. I'm coming back tonight. It's just not worked out.'

A huffy breath. 'If I pitched this now to the editor, with the Edinburgh angle, he'd commission you. I know he would.'

'Ewan, I just booked a flight home.'

A second's silence. 'Well, that's it, then.'

'I'll come in tomorrow and we'll talk about it, OK?'

'Whatever.' The phone went dead.

Before she could change her mind, she texted Mac her flight number and a message. 'Coming back tonight. We should talk to the police tomorrow.'

His reply was instant. '☺ ☺ ☺ Gonna leave Blairgowrie now, pick you up at airport. LOVE Mxxx.'

His abrupt change of mood made her bristle.

Mac had got his own way again.

Somehow, he always did.

She always let him.

The door to Nicu's black boat was ajar. Despite the open windows, it was still choked with smoke. Soot smattered his beautiful silver prints and artwork, and a rain of ash covered the Afghan rug and grey sofa. Through the door in the kitchen, the office wall was charred, a blue tarpaulin visible through the hole.

She found him in the bedroom, checking his cameras. This room had escaped the worst. The soot smudged on his cheek was the same colour as his hair.

He looked up. 'You OK?'

'Yeah. How are you?'

He raised his eyebrows wearily.

'What did the police say?' she asked.

'Ah, probably some right-wing fuckwit making a point about the immigration story I did.'

She leant against the wall, dreading what was to come. 'I need to speak to you.'

'OK.'

'The fire's my fault.'

His brown-black eyes seared into hers.

She held out the photo and envelope. 'The guy who threw the petrol? He left this for me.'

Nicu took it.

'I saw him sitting outside Lucian's old house this morning. I think he followed me back here.'

164

'From Grabole's apartment?'

'Maybe. Or even from the airport last night. There was someone hanging around outside your boat last night, too. I think someone's trying to warn me off tracking down Lucian's identity.'

Nicu examined the image.

'I feel so bad, Nicu.' She gestured at the charred plants on the deck. 'You were helping me out, and then this happened. I'm sorry.'

He gave back the photo. 'What are you going to do now?'

'Oh,' she said, disconcerted by his lack of reaction. 'Go back to Edinburgh tonight, to talk to the police. I'll help you clean up before I go, though. And I can give a statement, if it helps for your insurance?'

He frowned. 'You're giving up the story?'

'Nicu. They burned your boat.'

He held up his phone. 'So you don't want to listen to this?'

'What?'

'A message from the guy we met earlier. He rang back.'

'What did he say?'

He held the phone away, teasing her.

She sat down beside him. 'Please.'

He put it on loudspeaker and began to translate what emerged. 'So he's spoken to another guy he knows in Amsterdam from that region in Romania who swears he's seen Lucian Tronescu here. At a strip club called Ritzy. He's a bouncer. Other people have recognized him, too. He says Tronescu uses a false name when he comes, but he's ninety-nine per cent sure it's him.'

'What's the false name? Lucian Grabole?'

'No.' Nicu listened again. 'No, a different name – François Boucher.'

'François Boucher?' A *third* name.

Nicu continued, 'He says Lucian Tronescu – or François Boucher, or whatever he calls himself – comes and goes from Paris a lot. He's into dirty stuff. Bit of a gangster.'

'What else?'

'That's it,' Nicu said. 'But he says be careful. People are terrified of this Boucher-Tronescu guy. The bouncer never lets on that he recognizes him. Says it wouldn't be "good for his health".' Nicu stopped the message. 'Still sure you want to give up the story?'

She blew out her cheeks. 'No. But I'm going to.'

His eyes flicked over her, clearly wondering what she was made of. 'OK, well, I'll drop you at the airport.'

She stood up. 'You don't need to. I can get a taxi.'

'It's fine. We'll leave in twenty minutes.'

'OK. Thanks.'

His easy smile had disappeared.

He got up and headed past her into his burned office, and she took it as her clue to leave.

François Boucher now?

Three names for the dead man in her flat.

Grace returned to the blue boat, updated her notes for DI Robertson, then packed her rucksack, thinking about her decision.

Through the rear window, two men were making dinner in their boat. Tonight she'd be back in her own kitchen, overlooking Mr Singh's backyard and the Crossgate tower block, Mac chuntering on about golf, her gearing up for another week of photographing stories that would end up in the recycling bin, consumed once and forgotten.

She took a last look at Nicu's prints. In the tiny spare room at Gallon Street was a box of reportage features like these that she'd been cutting out since she was fifteen. Nobody kept her photos.

She locked the blue boat, and waited by the Jeep. The early evening canalside lights were diffused by the silver velvet ribbons of smoke that still hung in the air. Sooty flakes of ash tumbled gently in the evening breeze.

She thought of Gallon Street.

Nicu came out, carrying a travel bag and his cameras.

'Ready?' he said.

'Yup.' They climbed into the Jeep. 'Are you off somewhere?' she asked, handing him the keys.

He started the engine. 'Paris.'

'Paris?'

'Yeah. Ewan Callow spoke to the editor at *Scots Today*. He's asked me to pick up the story,' he said, starting the engine. 'With the Romanian angle, it makes sense. I can delay Colombia till Wednesday, so . . .'

A furious protectiveness of her story reared up inside her.

He saw her face as he reversed out. 'Grace, come on. You dumped it.'

'No. I know. It's just that I was going to speak to the police in Edinburgh tomorrow and tell them what I've found.'

Nicu headed for the bridge. 'Well, the editor's asking you not to – till next week. But they might run a photo or two of yours, and give you a credit on the piece – unless you're worried about putting your name on there? In case Mr Psycho Killer tracks you down, and hangs you out of a window.' There was a gentle tease in his voice that right now she didn't appreciate.

'No, I'm not worried about that,' she said, a lump in her throat. 'It's fine.'

*

Nicu diverted down a dead end, then reversed, to check the gold car wasn't following, then took the fast road out of town.

Grace didn't speak. She didn't know what to say.

The evening sun was dropping gently over Amsterdam, turning the high-rise buildings into smudged rectangles against a soft navy sky. In a few hours, she'd be driving towards the tower blocks of Edinburgh, Mac at the wheel, all chirpy again, now he had her back.

'When's your flight?' she said to fill the silence.

'I'm driving. It's five hours this time of night.' A train shot past on a track between car lanes, the electricity wires above twisting into the sky like lines of starlings. 'So, can you get me up to speed?'

It hurt, but she agreed.

'So,' Nicu started, 'a guy dies in your flat in Edinburgh. Police think he's a homeless burglar. Accidental death. Can't ID him. Three months later, you find a note near his body that says, *I am not that man Lucian Grabole?*'

'Yes.'

'Police promise to check it out. Meanwhile, you find a Lucian Grabole at a homeless shelter in Edinburgh, last seen about a year before. Apparently, a nice guy. You follow his trail to London. Guy called Ali tells you, yes, the Lucian Grabole he knew in London fits the description of your dead guy in Edinburgh. Also says he was a nice guy and a Romanian, illegal worker from Amsterdam, searching for his wife and kid. Then the Cozmas throw a spanner in the works. Tell you Lucian Grabole is the false name for a "monster" called Lucian Tronescu. This guy's not harmless at all. He's a killer, and a conman, hunting down a woman and kid?'

'Yes.'

'Right. So you come to Amsterdam, find Lucian Grabole

again. Again, his concierge, Mitti, tells you he's a nice guy – but now he's both unmarried and legal, and living in a million-pound apartment. Nothing makes sense. Because, as we now know, he's a conman. Then we check out his name Lucian Tronescu with Romanians in Amsterdam. They confirm they've seen him here, and he's a gangster. He's also based part-time in Paris, and uses a *third* pseudonym, François Boucher. Someone starts following you, clearly wanting to warn you off going further.'

'Yes,' Grace said, not wanting to give him her story. Wanting to wrestle it back and tell him to get lost.

Nicu shook his head. 'Tricksy little fucker, isn't he?'

A car with Turkish plates overtook. She imagined driving to Turkey from here, through Belgium, France, Italy and Greece. A Dutch camper van pulled ahead, bikes on the back. It could be going anywhere: Morocco, Switzerland, Spain.

Unlike her.

She was going home.

She always went home.

Nicu tapped the wheel. 'So tell me again why you think your dead guy in Edinburgh is Lucian Grabole.'

'Well, the note, obviously. But his physical description the police gave us also matches Lucian Grabole's, according to Ali. Same height, age, colouring, wolf tattoo and green signet ring. The police also hinted he had Eastern European connections, and Dutch. I don't know why.'

'Clothes labels, maybe. Surgery or dentistry. They used different fillings in Romania back then.'

'Really? Also, the pinstriped suit the dead man was wearing was handmade, with no label. I think Mr Cozma was wearing the same suit. I think he made it.'

A blast of violet rocketed across the darkening sky to her right.

169

The street lights came on and she imagined what the journey would be like to Paris.

'But beyond that, nothing else you've heard about Lucian Grabole matches this Tronescu-stroke-Boucher gangster guy?' Nicu asked.

'No. They seem to have very different personalities and life-styles.'

'Right.' Nicu took the sign towards Schiphol Airport. 'OK . . . so what about this . . . ? What if it's not one man but two? What if teenage psycho killer Lucian Tronescu escapes Romania in 1989 or 1990, when Drac is executed, and changes his name to François Boucher in Paris? Hides out in the criminal underworld for twenty-five years. Decades later, on some dodgy business in Amsterdam, he's spotted by Romanians from back home and knows he's blown it. Thinks he's going to be hauled back to face murder charges.'

Grace listened, intrigued. 'Go on . . .'

'So, he finds a Romanian guy in Amsterdam who matches him physically: in this case, hard-working, single Lucian Grabole, a painter and decorator, working here legally. Tronescu steals Grabole's identity and papers, and kills him to hide his tracks. Makes up a fictional wife and kid for Lucian G. as cover to travel. Maybe hides out in London with his new ID, till things cool down. Puts the screws on his old pals the Cozmas to hide him. Then when they kick off, say they're going to report him, he moves to Scotland. Starts again.'

Grace stared. 'And what – burgles my flat because he's run out of money and dies by accident?'

Nicu glanced over. 'You don't look convinced.'

'Well, it's a bit of a stretch. Surely if he's dealing drugs and stuff, he'd have money stashed somewhere. And it doesn't explain the note. *That man is not me Lucian Grabole.*'

'True.'

Grace slapped her knee. 'Oh God, Nicu. What if *Lucian Grabole* was in Edinburgh for a legitimate reason, maybe work, and Lucian Tronescu killed him in our flat? What if Lucian Grabole knew he was going to die? Knew that Lucian Tronescu was planning to steal his identity, and hid that note? *That man is not me.* Signed, *Lucian Grabole.*'

Nicu glanced over. 'And *my* idea's far-fetched? I thought you said it was an accident, anyway?'

'Well, the fiscal called it "non-suspicious", but there were so many DNA samples from the old tenants, then all the builders and workmen, it just meant there was no *clear* evidence of a third party when he died. Lucian was drunk and starving, and I think it was the most credible explanation – that he fell and hit his head.'

'So it's *possible* he was murdered.'

Out of the window was a second sign for Schiphol Airport. A thought hit her. 'Well, if he was, that means Lucian Tronescu is still alive – maybe even hiding out in Edinburgh.'

Nicu whistled quietly. 'Which might explain who's trying to stop you investigating this. The last thing Tronescu wants is the whole thing coming out in a newspaper. You'd blow his cover again. He's probably relying on Lucian Grabole not being ID'd – waiting to see if his cover is still safe.'

'So what will you do in Paris?' she said.

'Track down François Boucher. Ewan's hiring a French fixer tonight to get things going. Can you leave anything else: transcripts, photos, contacts . . . ?'

Reluctantly, Grace retrieved her folder. A familiar image appeared as she opened it. A print of the city-rat-man shot, from East London, which she'd uploaded onto Nicu's Mac.

'Did you do this?' she said, stunned.

He glanced over. 'Yeah. Good shot. Shame it's not part of the story.'

He'd cropped out the archway, and pushed the image so hard that a single slash of sky above the city-rat man was harsh white, his body twisted, and blackened against it, like a tree struck by lightning. The five points of his boots, chin, skull and elbow made a perfect pentagon. It was a powerful, urban nightmare.

It wouldn't have looked out of place among Nicu's own stories.

What the hell was she doing?

The sign said it was a kilometre to the airport. The road had widened to five lanes heading for Rotterdam and Den Haag.

Nicu crossed to the exit.

Planes hovered, coming in to land. Mac would be on his way to Edinburgh Airport now from Blairgowrie.

Stars appeared ahead, lighting the way south to Belgium.

Half a kilometre to the turn-off.

'I want to come,' Grace said.

Nicu acted as if he'd misheard, then shook his head. 'That won't work.'

She twisted in her seat. 'I know they've commissioned you now. And I don't care about the money. I'll do it for nothing. For the experience. But I want to do this story. I want to find out who the dead guy is. Please.'

Nicu's eyes hardened. He was becoming irritated with her, wanting her gone so he could work alone. 'Sorry. Can't do it.'

'But it's *my* story.'

He scratched his head. 'Listen, I need to be in and out of Paris in two days and . . .'

The exit approached.

She should never have rung Mac.

He talked her out of everything.

172

'It won't work nearly as well without the angle of me finding Lucian in my flat,' she protested, fighting the urge to grab the wheel. 'Nicu! Really. There's no point. I'm not getting out. You'll have to drag me out of the car screaming at the airport, and then you'll get arrested.'

Nicu pushed back his hair. The exit was upon them. Without warning, he swerved back onto the motorway. There was a flash of lights, and horns beeped behind.

Crossing over, he accelerated into the fast lane.

He was taking her.

An iPod came flying at her from out of his side pocket. 'OK, but no more talking,' he said. 'And no more bloody lie-ins.'

The airport disappeared behind them.

A wave of excitement crashed through her.

CHAPTER THIRTY-ONE

Edinburgh

The dream was always the same.

It had been for years.

A dark forest, impenetrable with thick-boughed fir and spruce, the light sucked out. A bluish icy mist obscured the sky and slope of the mountain beneath his feet. Then him, running over the snow, the smell of burning behind him, trying to find a way out and being blocked by twists of branches.

The man woke, sweating, and scrabbled off his bedroll, knowing something was wrong.

Muffled voices broke into the room.

The clock said 4.12 a.m. Heart thumping, he crept into the toilet, shivering, without his blanket.

A cough rose in his chest, and he held his hand over his mouth.

Two voices.

His ears strained.

In the backyard?

When he'd wrestled his cough under control, he crawled to the stool under the window, and slid onto it, bent double.

Unfurling his body like a snake, he peered over the windowsill. The backyard and tower block were blacked out. Even the street lights were out.

Then, in the backyard, a shape.

A figure in a white hood, face mask and forensics suit walked into the light. A second stepped out from behind him.

Breath emptied from the man's body, and he struggled to refill it.

He sucked and sucked, but the air wouldn't enter his locked lungs. A grating noise filled his ears as he tried to rip his chest open with the effort.

His snore thundered through the storeroom and the man sat up on his damp bedroll, heart racing. The storeroom lay in darkness.

The clock said 1.02 a.m.

He leaped up and checked outside. The backyard was bare. Four lights on in the tower block.

It was a dream.

All of it.

But he also knew it wasn't really a dream. It was a premonition.

They'd be here soon now.

Coming for him.

CHAPTER THIRTY-TWO

Edinburgh

The following morning, Sula arrived at Banister Road before 9 a.m., even though she knew there wasn't much point. The junkies would all be sleeping.

It was worse than she remembered.

She scanned the street for a police cordon, and found none. She wondered why, if Colin McFarlay's body had just been discovered, and this was a murder investigation.

Locking her car, she set off. Only one house had an intact number, so she worked up the street till she found number 8. The front door lay open, a curtain pulled across. A bed base of rusty orange springs lay in the garden, but no mattress. A suspicious stinking mess puddled by the drain cover. A toddler played on the step, singing to herself as she chewed on a piece of cardboard.

Next door was what was left of number 6.

So that's why there was no cordon.

Colin McFarlay's last known abode was burned out, the white walls and black ash interior like a coconut turned inside out. Purple graffiti of fat letters that made no sense daubed the wall.

A teenager in a zebra onesie appeared at the door of number

8, her hair tied up in a huge topknot. She picked up the toddler, and glared at Sula. Sula sighed. She'd seen it all before.

'Know when this happened, doll?' She pointed.

'Depends.'

'On what?'

'You the polis?'

'No, no. I'm the good guys.' Sula held up a card.

'Aye, right.' The girl grinned, revealing a missing front tooth. She came over, toddler in her arms, and took the card. There was a reek of dirty nappy. Sula tickled the toddler's chin and got a gummy smile.

'Was it burned out before or after Colin McFarlay went missing?'

The girl looked up the street as if she kept a tab on every movement that took place here. 'After – he was away by then.'

'Was he? You know where he went?' Sula said.

The girl turned down her mouth, transforming her pretty face into a grim mask. 'To his mother's, someone said – to get off the smack.'

'She here, his mother?'

The toddler's nose was running onto her lip. 'Nah. Colin wasnae from round here.'

'No? So how did he end up here?'

'Who knows? Living the dream, eh?'

Sula grinned. 'Right, well, thank you.' She held out a tissue to the teenager, and a fiver to the baby. The little girl grasped it with grubby fingers. 'Get your mammy to buy you some sweeties, OK?'

When she arrived back at *Scots Today*, Ewan was slouched over his desk, a tumbler of coffee by his hand.

'What's up with you?' she said.

'Up late, sorting out a fixer in Paris – editor's commissioned Grace's story, chasing down the dead guy in her flat. Nicu Dragan's on it with her now.'

He yawned, watching her curiously. 'So, Sula, what's your daughter called? Is she my age? Is she single?'

'Oi, you. Listen.' She clicked her fingers, cross. 'I need you on this now. That address you got for McFarlay's is way out of date. Get me one for his mother – apparently he was living with her when he disappeared. Probably nicking everything the poor cow didn't nail down.'

'Yes, sir,' Ewan said, sitting up straight.

He battered the keyboard for a few minutes, as she checked her emails. 'Right, here you go . . . So that's . . . OK . . . That's officially weird.'

'What?'

'Number 66 Bowling Road, South Queensferry.'

'So? What am I missing?'

'Well, the one down the road went for £1.1 million last month.'

Sula leaned back. 'Colin McFarlay's family live in a million-pound house?'

Ewan stuck out his bottom lip. 'Looks like it. Hang on.' He typed some more. 'Right. Colin McFarlay – mother, Anne McFarlay, father, Morris McFarlay, died 2013. Owned a printing equipment distribution company, sold it in 2011.'

'Are you joking?' Sula checked his screen. Her eyes sailed through the details, then juddered to a halt. 'Am I seeing things?'

Ewan followed her finger. 'Pupil at . . . No way!'

'That is bloody weird.'

If Ewan's sources were correct, Colin McFarlay had attended one of the most prestigious boarding schools in Scotland.

'How did we miss that, last year?' she asked, returning to her desk.

''Cos he was a junkie gone missing – who cares?'

Sula slapped the desk. 'Hang on. Did David Pearce go to that school?'

Ewan tapped away. 'Urrr . . . nope. He was at school in Australia, then just one year in Edinburgh at the local . . . Oops . . . excuse me –' he yawned again, and she rolled her eyes '– high school.'

Sula tapped her pen. 'How the hell does a posh boy like Colin McFarlay end up in Smack Row?'

'Is this a quiz?' Ewan said, sitting up, bright-eyed. 'Are there prizes?'

'Aye – your job at the end of the day.'

The editor passed by with a nod, his tail in the air. Sula knew that look. It said, *Exclusive.*

Maybe Ewan's wee girlfriend was on to something after all.

CHAPTER THIRTY-THREE

Paris

A couple strolled hand in hand down the Paris boulevard in the pink frosted light of dawn. She was dainty, with a delicate-boned bare back in an elegant, white-beaded dress, heels over her shoulder, silver-blonde hair. He wore a suit with the collar undone, dark hair pushed back from a tanned, chiselled jaw. In her hand was a glittering designer handbag. Across his white tuxedo was painted the word 'REVOLUTION', in foot-high red paint.

Grace contemplated the graffitied billboard through the greasy window of her hotel in a north Paris suburb. This had been her idealized image of Paris till last night.

A lot had changed in twelve hours.

Last night, Nicu had turned up the music, and fixed his gaze on the motorway out of Amsterdam. They'd stopped briefly at a service station to grab fuel and coffee, and do a final check for the gold car. For the first hour, she'd ricocheted between exhilaration and panic, and trying to imagine how Mac would receive the text she'd just sent to say she wasn't flying home. Then, as they passed into Belgium, the darkening sky filled with orange flares and damson clouds. She'd watched it, mesmerized, lulled by the music and the diesel hum of the Jeep. In northern France, she'd watched scatters of house lights that looked like low-lying stars in the blackness of the night, dreaming about who lived there.

At 2 a.m., they had entered the north-west of Paris following directions for the hotel booking Ewan had emailed her at midnight.

For a moment, she thought she'd fallen asleep and was dreaming. Instead of the Paris she knew from the odd weekend trip, this was an area of colossal tower blocks. They stretched into the distance like an abandoned space colony. Graffiti coated walls, and subways and bridges; a relentless pouring-out of nonsensical swirls. It was as far away from this advertising image of the romantic dawn stroll through Paris as you could get.

Nicu had only turned on his satnav in the last mile to bring them to a street, mainly inhabited by their hotel, a few North and West African restaurants, and a line of shops selling bright costume jewellery behind iron bars.

She'd stretched her arms. 'How do you know this so well?'

'Lived in Paris for a while. Did a job here last year,' he said, rubbing his eyes.

He followed a handwritten parking sign into a narrow alleyway, and reversed into a space between two skips and the hotel's fire escape.

Bags in hand, they entered the building from the front. Nicu spoke in brisk French to a receptionist with the bloodhound eyes of a night-shift worker.

The hotel was shabby, and smelt of trapped air. Five exhausted-looking men crammed in the lift with them, and disappeared into a room stacked with bunk beds.

Their own rooms were on the fourth floor, at the rear.

'Right, see you in the morning – early,' Nicu said.

'Don't worry.' Grace smiled, closing her door. At the back was the alleyway, and Nicu's Jeep. A baby cried somewhere. The room had a mould patch on the wall, and smelt of cheap air freshener.

With Nicu out of the way, she steeled herself and turned her phone back on.

There were four new voicemails from Mac.

She was right. He hadn't taken the news well.

'What the hell are you doing?' one message said. 'I've just cut my golf week in half to get back. Fuck's sake. Ring me.'

The later ones – the last at 1.06 a.m. – were even more pissed off.

Maybe it was exhaustion, but Mac's voice was starting to squeeze around her, make her feel like she couldn't breathe.

Before she turned it off, she checked a second email from Ewan at 1.17 a.m.

Hey, Scotty,
Look at you, on a job!!! Your fixer in Paris is HENRI TAYLOR
– freelance crime correspondent for French/UK press. Contact
number attached. FYI: Henri Taylor KNOWS OF FRANÇOIS
BOUCHER – it was his idea to book you into Hôtel Dacoin (so
don't blame me if it's shite). It is opposite François Boucher's
family bar on Rue Dacoin – PEPINE'S.
More later, ma peteet amee.

She climbed into a lumpy bed with unaired sheets, wide awake again in anticipation of tomorrow.

Henri Taylor *knew* of François Boucher, the third name for the dead man in her flat. It was another major step forwards.

The light from the alleyway shone through thin curtains, and she lay watching the shadow of the old fan light on the ceiling.

All those years of finding excuses not to do this and it turned out it wasn't that difficult after all.

Grace sipped bitter coffee in the too-hot breakfast room the next morning, and watched the Bouchers' bar across the street. The shutters were down, its name just legible in unlit neon above it. *Pepine's*. Women passed by with bags of vegetables from a street market that had sprung up overnight, a riot of colourful cheap tracksuits and children's clothes fluttering like flags against a blue sky.

Her phone buzzed. Ewan again.

RISE AND SHINE, SCOTTY!! Meet Henri Taylor at 2 p.m. at Café de Flore on Boulevard Saint-Germain. FYI: Henri says François Boucher is KNOWN TO FRENCH POLICE – but no record of the other two names your guy used, Lucian Tronescu or Lucian Grabole. Editor's authorized Henri to do private background check on Boucher. In the meantime, this is Boucher's last known address (from two yrs ago – no record since then).

Nicu arrived downstairs half an hour after her, his dark hair damp from a shower. He ordered coffee in French, and sat opposite.

'Morning,' she said. 'How was your lie-in?'

A faint smile played on his lips. 'Any word from the office?'

She updated him about Pepine's and Henri Taylor. 'And I've swapped my room to the front to overlook the bar.'

'Good.'

Maybe it was her imagination, but his shoulders seemed to relax, as if he realized she wouldn't be a liability, after all. The waiter returned with coffee. Nicu ordered breakfast in rapid French.

'How many languages do you speak?' she asked.

He gulped the coffee like fuel. 'Romanian, English, Dutch, French, bit of Greek if I'm in trouble.'

'Do you get into trouble a lot?'

'Just in Greece.' It sounded like an attempt at a joke to make up for his grumpiness.

'It's there, by the way – Pepine's.'

He leaned past her. 'OK.' His dark eyes trailed to hers, and stayed for a second.

A photographer's gaze, she told herself again, reaching for her phone to break it.

'I'll find out what time it opens,' she said.

Together, they made a plan for the day, Grace keen to show this was still her story. After breakfast, they'd visit the last known address for François Boucher to ID his most recent description to see if it matched Lucian Grabole's, and possibly source a photo. Then they'd meet Henri Taylor in central Paris, and stake out Pepine's tonight.

Back in her hotel room, Grace regarded her professional camera bag. It was bulky. The type you took to real-life shoots for magazines, where everyone knew you were a photographer. Here, it would stick out a mile.

Before she was due to meet Nicu, she visited the street market, wandering through a melee of shouted Arabic, French and African languages, tinny radios, shoppers browsing vegetables, and clothes and electrics stalls. It was the most utilitarian market she'd ever seen. A mound of bags were simply piled up in a jumble on a table, like the chaotic beaded shoes next to them, no attempt at pairing. She buried through till she found a black leatherette rucksack, and waited to pay. An African man beside her was selling corn-on-the-cobs cooked in a barbecue pot, secured inside a shopping trolley. She asked him in school French and he nodded, letting her fire off ten shots, with him both looking at the camera and away, the roasted yellow of the piled corn filling the centre of the shot. Pleased with herself, she then bought cheap sunglasses, a light black beanie and more T-shirts and underwear, at another stall, and met Nicu back at the Jeep.

It was warm and they opened their windows as he man-oeuvred the Jeep through the thin corridor between stalls. The dusty air carried in diesel fumes and rubbish and spice. They drove past the colony of tower blocks from last night. Her fingers itched to shoot more. A hundred balconies were crammed with satellite dishes, ironing boards, bikes, plants, rugs, flower bas-kets and lines of washing, as if they'd been blown out of the flats. Some tower blocks were clean with new windows; others were old and tatty – the outside shutters broken and hanging, concrete mottled, blankets used for curtains.

The tower blocks were soon replaced by sloped-roof houses. The avenues grew smarter, the buildings shorter, the fronts better painted.

The appearance of François Boucher's former apartment was as unexpected as his suspected alter ego, Lucian Grabole's Amsterdam one. Shiny black pillars stood guard either side of a double-height black door in a white terraced mansion block. Pristine nineteenth-century railings bordered well-tended shrub-bery. The cars parked outside were sleek and low.

'OK. So François Boucher was loaded, too?' Grace said.

They climbed marble steps, and rang an elegant black door-bell. The door opened and a balding concierge in his seventies peered out. Nicu spoke French and she heard the name 'François Boucher'.

In Amsterdam, Mitti's face had lit up at the mention of Lucian Grabole.

François Boucher had the opposite effect.

This concierge whispered as if he didn't want anyone to hear, then retreated, a hand extended in apology, before it vanished.

'What just happened?'

Nicu pressed the buzzer again. 'Doesn't want to talk.'

'Does he know François Boucher?'

'Said he couldn't remember.'

'Why's he lying?'

'Scared, I reckon.'

Grace looked up. A curtain tweaked.

'Well, we can't leave. We need a photo – or at least a description of what he looked like, to confirm he's Lucian Grabole.'

Nicu started to photograph the house.

'Don't you need to ask permission?'

'It's a public place. If they don't like it, they can come and talk to us.' He shot off five more. 'What forensics are there on your dead guy in Edinburgh?'

'DNA and fingerprints – they're searching for them with European police systems at the moment.' She paused. 'We need a photo to confirm they're the same man, don't we?'

'Henri Taylor might have one,' Nicu said, climbing the railings for a different angle. The movement exposed a stretch of tanned back.

'Do you want to try the bell again?' he said, turning.

Grace ducked as if searching in her bag. 'Yup.'

One by one, she tried the apartment buzzers for all eight residents. 'What, now nobody's in at all?'

Nicu jumped down. 'Old guy's told them not to answer, I reckon. Come on – we'll try later.'

Deflated, they returned to the Jeep, and drove on into central Paris to meet Henri Taylor. The white terraces gave way to the Paris she recognized, where people conversed over coffee in street cafes, shopped in boulangeries and walked tiny dogs. Café de Flore was located in the grand Boulevard Saint-Germain, surrounded by expensive designer stores and graceful apartment buildings. The balconies here were empty, she noted: lacy, antique wrought iron and simply ornamental. A million miles, not just a few, from where they'd started this morning.

Henri was waiting at an outside table opposite a Louis Vuitton store. He was in his forties, stocky, with a round, pleasant face, smartly dressed like the men around him, in a suit, with an open shirt. He explained his Welsh accent by way of his father coming from Aberystwyth. He ordered them all citron pressés from a waiter in a white shirt and bow tie, while Grace turned on her phone recorder, hoping to pick up his voice above the chatter from other tables and the traffic.

'Right,' Henri started. 'So . . . François Boucher. You're aware of the Boucher family's reputation in Paris?'

'No,' Grace said. 'We know nothing. Just that the Bouchers own Pepine's, which frankly looks well dodgy, and that there's no record of François Boucher living in Paris for two years.'

Henri poured a carafe of water into glasses of fresh lemon juice. 'OK. When I say "family", I mean *family*. François's father-in-law, René Boucher, was a big gangster here in the '60s, '70s and '80s. A kind of Godfather in the French criminal world. He ran all sorts of rackets: trafficking, drugs, prostitution, gambling. The bar was his. He named it after his daughter, Pepine, and she still runs it today. It was quite the place, back then. Film stars, celebrities . . .'

'But it seems so run down,' Grace said.

'Well, the area's changed. René's sons, Luc and Marc, still operate out of Pepine's, but they very much live off Papa's reputation these days. From what I can see, they do sod all themselves – just survive off René's cash and get the local youth off the housing projects to do their dirty work – and not very well, at that. I'm guessing the only thing between them and jail is a bit of witness intimidation and an expensive lawyer.'

'Does their reach extend outside of Paris?' Nicu asked.

'Good question.' Henri lit a cheroot and exhaled. 'I don't know. René's certainly did. Back in the day, he had fingers in pies all over Europe. But when he died, I know the family lost power. Albanians and Russians moved in on his supply routes. It's hard to tell how far their reach goes now. But don't underestimate his sons. René had a code of ethics. Luc and Marc don't. Really, they're trouble.'

'So where does François Boucher fit in?' Grace asked.

He tapped his cheroot. 'He's more of a mystery. As I say, he's René Boucher's son-in-law. He married Pepine in 1992. Don't ask me why he took her surname and not the other way round. The rumours are that François ran René's dope route from Marseilles. René relied on him like a son. Maybe more. It would be hard to be more useless than his real sons.'

Grace stirred sugar into her drink. 'Henri, we have information that François Boucher is not French, that his real name is Lucian Tronescu, and he's a criminal who escaped the authorities in Romania in late '89 or 1990. And that until recently he was using a third name, too, Lucian Grabole.'

Henri exhaled smoke. 'Oh really? I've never heard that.'

'You haven't?'

'No.'

Nicu interrupted. 'Any idea why François Boucher left Paris?'

Henri tapped ash into an old-fashioned ashtray. 'Well, it's only a rumour, but apparently when René died, François started working in Amsterdam . . .'

Grace stopped stirring.

'I spoke to a retired police contact of mine this morning. He thinks that François left for Amsterdam two years ago, with another of René's thugs, a bruiser called Mathieu Caron. Really, you don't want to meet Caron on a dark night. He killed a man with a broken bottle when he was fourteen – did eight years for it. What those two get up to in Amsterdam I don't know, but I doubt it's charity work. I do know, though, that François and Pepine Boucher are separated. She's with a Bulgarian guy now.'

Nicu nodded. 'OK. Henri, we need a photo of François Boucher to confirm he's the man we think was using the name Lucian Grabole.'

Henri put out his cheroot. 'I'll do my best. Give me twenty-four hours. The background check should be back tomorrow. But listen, can I ask you guys to get direct authorization for the payment, so I'm not covering it upfront? I'm sure you know how these things drag on when you're freelance.'

'Of course. Want me to do that now?' Grace said.

'Please.'

Grace stood up. She motioned to the drone of traffic. 'I'll ring Ewan.' She went inside and wove between waiters and red banquettes up to the quieter first floor. In private, she turned on her phone. As she was dreading, four new messages had appeared from Mac since last night. She texted Ewan Henri's financial request, then sat at an empty table and steeled herself.

Mac answered on half a ring, already angry. 'What's going on *now*?'

'Calm down. I'm in Paris.'

'Wha-aat?' His disbelief was so exaggerated it sounded as if he were joking.

'*Scots Today* commissioned my story.' She waited for him to congratulate her.

Silence.

'I got a new lead, so they're paying for it now. I decided to keep going.'

'Fuck's sake.'

An elderly woman sat at the next table reading a novel with a glass of red wine, looking as if she had nobody to please but herself.

'Mac, what is this?' Grace asked, suddenly irritated. 'I'm trying to work it out. Why are you so upset about me being here? This is my work. I don't complain when you and John go clubbing in London as "research". Or go off on golf weekends with clients.'

'It's nothing like the same,' he exclaimed. 'You're travelling halfway across Europe on your own, pretending you're Kate fuckin' Adie. I don't even know where you're staying.'

'Then I'll tell you. It's Hôtel Dacoin on Rue Dacoin.'

'How do you spell it?'

'D-A-C-O-I-N. And I'm not on my own.'

'Who's with you?'

Too late she realized her mistake. 'Another freelancer.'

'Who?'

'Nicu Dragan.'

'*Nicu?* What, a girl?'

The strap tightened further round her chest. 'No, a guy. He's a photojournalist. And another freelance journalist, Henri. So can you stop panicking? They're both experienced. And I won't be here long. I just need to find more evidence and I'll be back.'

There was a gentle intake of breath, then an exhalation.

'Mac! Are you smoking?'

He did it again.

'That's fourteen months! Why would you start again?'

Then she knew why.

He was punishing her.

'Listen, forget about that. I don't want you doing this. I want you to leave it to the police and get back.'

'But this *is* my job, Mac. This is what journalists do.'

'Not what *you* do.'

'No, but what I *want* to do. Do you understand what this could be? An exclusive criminal investigation, with a Scottish angle, commissioned by a Scottish newspaper, possibly a joint byline with Nicu Dragan – he's huge. It could even go international, with all the Romanian and Dutch and French connections, and Nicu's American contacts. It's a huge deal, Mac. This could be a major break for me.'

'What are you on about? Major break – break to what?' Sarcasm spiked his voice and she saw now he wasn't angry. He was scared. He couldn't deal with her being away.

'Mac,' she said. 'Please. Just support me on this. I'm keeping my wits about me. I'm not on my own. I'll be back on Sunday to do John's restaurant photos. It's all fine.'

'Yeah. Whatever.'

She bristled. 'Why are you talking like this?'

An infantile tone entered his voice. 'Because frankly I think you've gone nuts. Sorry, darlin', but since your dad died, you've been acting like a loon. Going on and *on* about the dead guy, like you know him or something. Like you owe his family. You don't. They're just skanks like him, probably. You need to let this go.'

'Mac. Shut up! This has got nothing to do with my dad. It's

you never wanting me to do what I want to do, and me getting sick of it.'

A long exhalation. 'Whoa! This is because of *me* now?'

'Yes. No. You *and* me.'

'What the fuck does that mean?'

'It means, you don't like me being away. You never do. Like when I got that chance to assist that photographer in Glasgow who went to Asia a lot, after college, you went on at me till I pulled out.'

'You're still fuckin' going on about *that*? It was fifteen years ago! I didn't stop you.'

'No, but you sulked till I didn't go.'

'Well, of course I didn't want you to go.'

'No, but you should have *told* me to go. Made it easier. Like now – you should be telling me to go for this story. Supporting me. Not making it more stressful.'

The elderly woman looked over her pince-nez.

The phone went quiet.

Grace sighed. 'We're not getting anywhere here. We'll talk about it when I get back.'

He laughed.

For a moment, she thought he knew he was overreacting and was going to be reasonable. Instead, his sarcasm hit a new gear. 'You know, I love your timing, Grace. You wait till we can afford to buy our own place and start talking about kids, then – hang on . . .' He mimicked her voice. '"It's been fifteen years since I did my photojournalism degree, but now I want to get serious." Jesus Christ, darlin'. I'm telling you, I don't know whether it's your dad or you're having a midlife crisis, but you *have* gone nuts.'

'Oh, shut up, Mac!' she retorted. 'I didn't say I'd decided I wanted kids. You have.'

There was another long exhalation of cigarette smoke. Loud and clear.

This was hopeless. It wasn't something to discuss on the phone. Nicu and Henri were waiting. She adopted a conciliatory tone. 'Look, let's just leave it. I'll be back at the weekend. We'll talk then. And I will talk to the police. I'm just not doing it now. And I don't want you to, either.'

A metallic clattering echoed onto the line, followed by Mac swearing.

'What was that?' she said.

'Nothing.'

She waited, but he had clammed up. 'Are you OK?'

'Yup.'

'I'll ring you tomorrow.'

'Yup.'

'Bye.'

A foot-high model of an old-fashioned French waiter sat beside her inside a glass cabinet. Downstairs, art deco mirrors lined the walls. She was in Paris, sitting in Café de Flore, once frequented by Ernest Hemingway and Simone de Beauvoir. She was here on a job with Nicu Dragan. Yet Mac had managed to travel seven hundred miles through a phone and drag her back to where he wanted her to be, in just a few minutes.

Your choice, a voice said in her head. *Either you keep letting him do this or you don't.*

CHAPTER THIRTY-FOUR

Edinburgh

It was twenty-four hours early, and the wrong time of day, but the man had become unsettled, so changed his routine for once.

That afternoon, he squirted shaving foam on his head and, with practised movements, ran a razor over a week's worth of grey fuzz, working round his ears, skimming over scars from previous nicks.

A loud clanging noise burst into the room.

He crouched, razor in hand.

He waited.

Nothing more.

Drying his head with a towel, he stood on the stool.

An intruder was bent over in the backyard. The expression on his face was thunderous, a cigarette in his lips, a phone in one hand. He was picking an ashtray from the ground.

This was no dream.

No.

Scrabbling to the side, the man hid, scanning the room, to see the view from the window. A sleeping bag on a bedroll. The TV on. A plate with an empty tinfoil wrapper. The drawing of a woman's face pinned to the wall.

Fool.

After all this time. To be this careless.

Tensing for a kick on the door, he shut his eyes.

Nothing came.

A mobile rang outside the window and he held his breath.

'Hello?' The voice of the intruder drifted through the glass. 'Yeah, I've just spoken to her – she's in Paris.' The voice faded. The fire escape creaked.

Upstairs, a door slammed.

The man sank down.

He was safe.

It was the husband from the couple upstairs.

Music started up through the ceiling.

Sweat ran down the man's face, bringing with it the pine-scented watery residue of dried-on shaving foam.

This time, he'd been lucky.

One day, that would change.

CHAPTER THIRTY-FIVE

Paris

Back at Hôtel Dacoin early evening, Grace spread out the press cuttings Henri had brought about René Boucher, pushing Mac firmly from her thoughts. He'd have to deal with it.

The cuttings were mostly from the 1960s and 1970s. François Boucher's father-in-law had been handsome, with hooded, long-lashed eyes and a heavy jaw, wide shoulders, groomed thick hair. A famous American film actress stood by his side. The news story implied a possible affair.

The report said René had been jailed in 1952 for ten years, for racketeering. There was a more recent cutting of him, dated 2008, bloated, his hair gone, the power of his eyes hidden by loose skin.

There were no cuttings about his children, Pepine, Luc and Marc, or his son-in-law, François Boucher. His family stayed below the radar.

She showered, dressed in her new clothes from the market, wondering again why François had taken Pepine's surname, and not the other way round, and prepared her camera at the window.

Pepine's was still shut, the steel shutter closed.

The street market had vanished as magically as it arrived, the only evidence a pile of empty boxes on the corner, ready for pick-up.

Her phone rang.

'Mac Work,' it said on the caller display. His number at the warehouse in Leith.

She checked the time. Ten minutes till she met Nicu. 'Oh, Mac. Leave me alone,' she groaned. 'What?' she said, answering it.

A second of hesitation. 'Grace, it's John.'

'Oh, John. Sorry, I thought you were Mac.' Why was he ringing her? 'Is everything OK?'

'Fine, darlin'. Just wanted to give you the heads-up – I've had that daft man of yours on the phone. He's on his way to Paris.'

'*What?*'

'Ach, I think he's just worried about you. Got it into his head you're in trouble.'

The constriction round her chest tightened again. He wasn't worried. He just wanted her home. 'John, I'm fine. He can't do that.'

'I know. I've told him it's a bad idea, but he's not listening.'

She checked outside, panicked at the idea of Mac appearing and dragging her off in front of Nicu Dragan. 'John, he can't come here.'

'Darlin', I've told him. I've tried. To be honest, I need him here tomorrow, on site. Got the architect in.'

'Oh God, sorry.'

'Ach, don't worry about it on my account – he's just got himself in a state.'

The lie emerged before she considered the consequences. 'The thing is, John, I'm not in Paris.' She picked at an old sticker on the windowsill. 'We left this afternoon. We're driving back to Amsterdam now.'

'Amsterdam?'

'Yeah, but I'm not even sure we'll make it tonight. It's five hours, so we might stop off in northern France or Belgium. So it's just stupid, him coming. Pointless.'

He tutted. 'Listen, I'm going to get off the phone – see if I can catch him before he gets on that plane. He said it was delayed, so we might be lucky.'

'Thanks,' she said, grateful. 'Sorry to ask. But if I ring, he won't answer in case I try to talk him out of it. And, John, will you tell him I'll be home tomorrow night? And that I'm fine. Safe.'

'OK, leave it with me, darlin',' he said cheerily. If he was cross with Mac for skiving off work to go and find her, he was hiding it from her. 'And listen, good for you. That's you with your big break, huh?'

'Well, I hope so.'

'You're doing well, darlin'. Proud of you. We all are. I know your dad would be, too.'

'Thanks, John,' she said.

After the call, she pondered that thought. What *would* Dad think about this? He'd probably be so worried, too, he'd be in the car with Mac on the way to the airport. They'd always been as bad as each other.

She leaned on the windowsill. To her right, she saw the space-colony high-rises in the distance, and wondered how far you could see from the top floor.

At eight, there had still been no word from John to say if he'd stopped Mac, so she went to meet Nicu. Even if Mac was already on the plane, she hoped that he'd never find his way out here tonight. It was miles from the airport, and a long walk through the space colony from the train station.

198

The restaurant was at the corner of Rue Dacoin, with a limited view of Pepine's.

Nicu was at the door, watching a man load two mannequins into a van from a shop. She liked that about him, she realized. He never had his eyes on his phone screen like everyone else; always on the world.

He raised his eyebrows in greeting and opened the door for her. It was North African, the tables communal, the air heavy with spice. Arabic music pounded towards them and waiters spun between tables with large plates, calling out to each other in Arabic and French. It was packed with families and groups.

They were waved to a spot side by side on a bench, beside a family with teenagers. A plate of pistachios, peppers and bread was put in the middle. Nicu ordered *couscous berbère* and she asked for the same, checking out of the window.

'So what do you want to do about Pepine's?' she said, to distract herself from Mac.

Nicu chucked a nut in his mouth. 'Get in there. Act like tourists stumbling into the wrong place. Then go back tomorrow night, when we know what's going on.'

'OK. I was just thinking that—' Her phone buzzed and she stopped to read the text.

'Hi, Grace. Caught him! Back at the flat now – give him a ring when you can. JohnX.'

'THANKSXXX,' she texted back.

'News about Grabole?' Nicu said.

'No. No, just my husband, sorry,' she said, turning it off. 'He didn't know where I was. But it's sorted now.'

Nicu called for water. 'Is he a photographer?'

They'd been together a couple of days and it was the first personal question he'd asked her. 'No. He designs clubs and bars.' The teenage girls opposite were listening, eyes round and curious. 'He works for his dad's friend. John refurbishes old buildings into flats and venues. Mac oversees the venue side.'

A waiter opened the door into the alleyway and a warm breeze blew in. The pounding drumbeat was replaced by a haunting wail. She realized she didn't want to talk about Mac. More people arrived, forcing her and Nicu to squeeze up, their legs jamming together.

'Can I ask a work thing?' she said, trying to ignore it. 'With this job, how much time do you spend away?'

'Depends – a day, a month. Two. Why?'

She bit a green pepper, bitter and sharp. 'So, how does that work with family? Relationships?'

Nicu watched her side on. Their eyes danced together for a second, and she turned away to find nuts.

'Why do you ask?'

The teenage girls opposite whispered again and their mother called out in Arabic and they looked away, admonished.

'Just wondering.'

He shrugged. 'You need to be with someone who understands. My last girlfriend was a painter. She liked having the place to herself for a while, so it worked out.'

A painter.

'Is she in Amsterdam now?'

The waiter arrived with food. Nicu leaned past her to fetch hot sauce, brushing her arm. She waited for him to answer. But he didn't.

'So you don't normally travel?' he said.

'Um, the odd day up north or to the islands, but no, most of my work's in Edinburgh or Glasgow.'

'Why?' he said, eating.

'I get a lot of freelance work there – for the Scottish newspapers, and a few diet and fitness magazines down in London –

people who've had makeovers, done an interview about their small businesses, opened a new gallery, that kind of thing. I've been lucky.'

He looked thoughtful. 'Right.'

'How long have you lived in Amsterdam?'

'Three years.'

'Straight from New Zealand or—'

Nicu waved his fork. 'Now, see, this always happens.'

'What?'

'Dinner with another journalist. Turns into a two-way interview.'

She grinned, feeling relaxed in his company for the first time since they'd met. 'I'm interested! I've never travelled – unless you count two weeks in Thailand. I mean, where did you learn all those languages?'

He chewed, thoughtful, then spoke. 'Got my first job in London.' He named a well-known photographer he'd assisted after college, which made her bristle with envy. 'Then I travelled. Mostly across Asia. Lived in Greece for a year with a girl I met in India, then Paris for a year, at an agency. New York for five, then Amsterdam.'

He took a forkful of food. 'Right, my turn. So why this guy? Why marry him?' He stuffed it in his mouth.

'Mac?' she said, surprised he was interested. 'Um, we've just always been together.'

'Always?'

'Since we were sixteen. But I've known him since day one of primary school.'

He reached for water. 'And you're still together.' He sounded incredulous.

'Well, we've never had a reason not to be. We both went to college in Edinburgh and moved into student flats together, then

201

rented our own. It just sort of evolved. We bought a place this year.'

'So when did you get married?'

His interest confused her. 'February. Why?'

He put down his fork. 'What, after . . . how many years?'

'Nineteen.' She traced a path through the couscous, realizing she was too nervous about Pepine's to eat. 'We never talked about it before, but my dad was ill last year and wanted me "settled", as he called it, so we did it for him, really. Then he died a few months before the wedding and we just went ahead . . .'

'Shit. Sorry,' Nicu said.

The music changed again. The primal beat of a hand-held drum thumped through their seats. She felt the heat of his leg against hers. The atmosphere heightened in the room. Right now, she could be anywhere. Seven thousand miles from home, not seven hundred. So far from normality her bearings were changing faster than she could keep up.

She fought to stay focused, and asked Nicu more about the photos she'd seen in his boat. He asked about her degree in photojournalism, and they discovered they shared two favourite American photographers. The teenagers opposite were whispering again now, watching with huge, round eyes.

Suddenly, Nicu leaned right across her. 'The bar's opening.'

He was right. The shutters were being pulled up at Pepine's by a blonde woman in a tight black dress. Nerves punched her insides.

'Do you think that's Pepine?' she said.

Nicu motioned the waiter, and pointed at the woman. Grace heard the names 'Pepine' and 'Boucher'. The waiter nodded and looked sour.

'Did you see his face?' Grace asked.

'Yup. I don't think he likes her.'

Pepine Boucher disappeared inside the club, and a heavy-featured bull of a man in a black suit appeared, and planted his feet firmly across the doorway.

Grace stopped eating, the implication hitting home. That woman *knew* François Boucher. She'd been married to him. They were close to a real answer about his identity. This woman could confirm if he was also Lucian Tronescu and Lucian Grabole.

'I don't know how you can eat,' Grace said, pushing back, as Nicu continued to wolf down his food.

'Don't go into battle on an empty stomach.'

The word 'battle' set off alarm bells. 'You don't think they know we're coming, do you? That we're walking into a trap?'

'Because of the guy following you in Amsterdam?'

'What if he's their guy?' she said.

Nicu tapped his fork. 'I'm not convinced.'

'Why?'

'Did you hear Henri? I'm wondering if François Boucher split from the Bouchers when René died. What if there was a power struggle between his three kids and François, the son-in-law? What if François took the Marseilles route for himself and extended it to Amsterdam? Cut out the brothers, Luc and Marc.'

'What, so they're all rivals now?'

Nicu pushed away his plate. 'We know he and Pepine split. Sounds like he got out of the family the minute René copped it.'

She bit her nails, watching the bar. The bouncer was picking his nose.

'What if you're wrong?'

Nicu called for the bill. 'Tell you what, we'll walk past the bouncer. If they know who we are, he looks too stupid to hide it.'

The teenage girls had given up all attempts not to stare. As they stood up, the mother spoke to her and Nicu in throaty

French. Nicu replied with something that made her and the girls laugh.

'What did they say?' Grace asked.

'Nothing,' he smiled.

'Tell me.'

'Sure?'

'Yes.'

He opened the door. 'The mother told them to stop staring at us – she said, "Leave them alone – can't you see they're in love?"'

To her horror, Grace's cheeks went on fire. 'What did you say?'

He waited for her to pass under his arm. 'You'll have to learn to speak French, Grace.'

It was dark on Rue Dacoin now. Mortified, Grace followed Nicu up the road; then they stopped by the bouncer as if checking directions. The bulldog measured Grace's chest with his eyes, then turned away to watch a teenage girl from behind.

'He's got no idea who we are. Right – ten minutes in reception?' Nicu said, as they returned to the hotel.

'Yup,' she said, still embarrassed.

When she returned back downstairs with her camera, calmed down, the black leatherette chairs and grubby glass tables of reception were empty. Stomach still fluttering with nerves, she wandered outside. The red neon light was lit now in the front window of Pepine's. Faint music drifted from inside. The bouncer was on his phone now.

Two shaven-headed men, hands in the pockets of their bomber jackets, appeared out of the shadows and entered Pepine's. The volume of the music increased for a few seconds.

A relentless, sexual, pounding beat. A glimpse of a red-lit bar.
Jowly men.

Then the door shut.

She waited for five minutes, but Nicu didn't come.

Ten minutes after they were due to meet, Grace tried his
mobile. It went to voicemail in English and Dutch, so she went
up to his hotel room. No answer.

'Have you seen *mon ami*?' she asked back down in reception,
touching her chin. '*Avec les cheveux.*'

He pointed out back to the alleyway. '*Alarme de la voiture.* Car
alarm.'

'Our car alarm went off?'

Shit. She hoped they'd left nothing valuable in the Jeep.

Deciding to take the front way in case she met him halfway,
she set off down Rue Dacoin to the entrance to the alleyway. It
looked forbidding. A narrow strip of darkness lined with bins
and parked cars.

Squinting, she saw the Jeep, still parked halfway down. No
alarm rang out. Nicu must have turned it off.

'Nicu?' She entered the alley, cautious, wishing she'd left her
camera in her room. Something glinted beside the Jeep under
the dim light from a window.

As she neared, she saw the Jeep door was open. The glinting
came from a reflective sticker inside it.

'Nicu?' she said more quietly.

There was a scuffling sound to the right, like footsteps on
gravel. Her eyes tried to make out the source.

'Nicu? Please.' She said it with new insistence.

As she reached the Jeep, she saw a smeared dark stain on the
ground.

It looked like oil. A leak maybe? She bent down to see if he was under the engine.

As she did, she touched the stain, and sniffed it.

Blood.

'Nicu!'

A balcony door flew open on the other side of the alleyway. An African woman, wearing a yellow headscarf, appeared, a plump baby on her hip, and glared into the gloom.

'Nicu?' Grace shouted, louder.

The woman's eyes widened. She pointed. '*Là-bas, madame, là-bas!*'

But Grace had already heard a low groan. It was coming from a doorway covered with a fixed porch awning. She raced over. He was on the ground inside it, legs folded in at right angles, his head jammed against the trade-entrance door to the hotel, one arm limp. He was trying to sit up and failing.

'Oh God. Nicu.' She bent down and touched his face. It was warm. Then his arm. Her fingers came away wet.

A faint groan. 'Shit and fuck.'

'What happened? Can you get up?'

He tried to move his foot an inch and his head fell back. 'Shit.'

'That's it. I'm getting an ambulance.' Furious with herself, she realized she didn't know the emergency number in France. She should know it. She shouted up to the balcony, '*Madame. Ambulance? S'il vous plaît?*'

The woman called out in her own language. A man in a silver suit appeared with a mobile and started dialling.

Grace turned on the Jeep lights to see better.

Nicu's face was tight with pain. There were bloody grazes across his forehead and cheek, and his eye was red and puffy.

Blood dripped down his right arm, soaking his T-shirt. Too scared to look further, she took off her scarf and pressed it hard against his arm. The man from the balcony appeared, and in broken English told her the ambulance was coming.

'*Monsieur, s'il vous plaît.*' She motioned him to take over the scarf, and squeezed in beside Nicu, taking his face in her hands. His lip was split. He was shivering.

'What happened? Where's the blood from?'

'Fucker stabbed me,' he whispered.

'No! Where? Nicu, where?'

He moved his shoulder an inch.

Grace squeezed in and put her arms around him to keep him warm. 'The ambulance is coming. Keep talking to me.' The blood was dripping across the ground, and the man in the silver suit pushed harder, shaking his head, talking in French.

'*Merci, monsieur, merci,*' Grace said, wishing she could speak better French. 'Did you see him, Nicu?'

'No.'

She listened for the sirens, scanning the dark alleyway.

This couldn't be a coincidence; it couldn't be.

CHAPTER THIRTY-SIX

Paris

The footsteps seemed to take forever, approaching down a pristine white corridor, lined with tall windows out onto an inner courtyard.

A doctor with a tight bun and long white coat walked with Henri Taylor towards Grace through the Urgences Générales Department of a hospital in north-west Paris.

The doctor stopped, looked at a chart, then began to speak in French. 'He's been stabbed twice, in his shoulder and arm,' Henri translated.

That sounded better than his kidney or liver. 'How bad?' Grace said, hopeful.

Henri translated, 'Superficial. He won't need an operation.'

'That's a relief.'

The translation continued: 'He's also been hit on the side of the head, and attacked with something. A club or piece of wood or something. There's bruising on his torso, back and face . . .' He broke off from the translation. 'Someone's given him a bit of a going-over, frankly.'

'So it's bad but not serious?' Grace said. 'Do you think that's weird?'

'You mean like a warning?' Henri said.

'Maybe.'

The doctor cleared her throat and continued.

Henri translated some more. 'She says they've stitched the stab wounds. Dressings need to be changed in a week, or if they become dirty. Keep them dry, so no showers. If the redness spreads or the wounds become more painful, bring him back in case there's an infection . . .'

He listened again. 'He has a mild concussion but no fracture or signs of extradural bleed, so expect him to be a bit woozy and have a headache. Bring him back if he starts vomiting, seeing double or the headache worsens.'

The doctor spoke again, then lowered the chart.

'She says he's going to be in pain, so she's given him painkillers. He's fine to go home tonight, but, as she says, bring him back if anything changes.'

'He can leave?' Grace said, astonished.

The doctor turned serious brown eyes on Grace, gave her a firm nod, and left.

Henri waited a second for her to disappear, then turned to Grace. 'What the hell happened?'

'I'll tell you in a minute. Where is he?' Grace said.

'The police are with him. They said you disturbed a mugging?'

She motioned Henri outside into the dark courtyard. A man in a dressing gown attached to a drip stand sat in the dark, smoking a cigarette.

Checking behind her, she held up Nicu's camera bag. 'This was beside him, with his camera – if it was a mugging, they need practice. It's worth thousands.'

He frowned. 'So, a warning, then?'

'Not unless I scared them off, but I'm not exactly Rambo, so I doubt it.'

'The Bouchers. How would they know you're here?'

The man with the drip looked over. She lowered her voice. 'Someone attacked Nicu's boat in Amsterdam before we came – we think to stop us digging deeper and doing this story. We think it's an associate of François Boucher stroke Lucian Tronescu in Amsterdam.'

'Why not the Bouchers in Paris?'

'Nicu thinks François has split from them. If he's right, François's associate must have followed us from Amsterdam.'

'So do you want to tell the police now?'

'Nicu needs to decide – it's him they've attacked.'

'Well, a word of caution – the police here'll tie you in red tape for days, so be sure it's not just an inept mugging. The place you're staying has high street crime.'

'So, don't tell them?' Grace asked.

'Up to you, but unless it helps the story, I wouldn't. I doubt Nicu will.'

Through the window, a police officer appeared, looking around. She hid behind Henri.

'Have you seen anyone following you?' he said. 'Cars with Dutch plates?'

'A few, but I've seen lots of Spanish and British ones, too.'

The policeman entered the courtyard, and Grace waved over at him.

'Your call,' Henri said.

Nicu, it turned out, had done what Henri predicted and told the police Grace had disturbed an attempted mugging. Grace verified it. The police officers took details and left. Henri gave her a taxi number, and arranged an appointment the next day.

Yawning, Grace made her way to the emergency-room door.

Through the glass, she saw Nicu perched on the side of a bed, eyes shut, eye and jaw swelling. Two large white adhesive dressings covered the stab wounds. Half his T-shirt had been cut off. Dried blood snaked down his arm and his clothes.

She switched on her camera, opened the door quietly and fired off four shots.

Nicu lifted a swollen eye. She shot again.

'Always take the shot,' she said.

'Bloody journalists.'

She rubbed his good arm. 'How are you?'

'How do I look?'

'Like shit. What did you tell the police?'

He moved his injured arm and winced. 'The truth. That they hit me from behind. Didn't see it coming. No idea who.'

'Was it our guy?'

'Could be. Which means he followed us from Amsterdam – fucker. Must have swapped cars. It was definitely planned. He set off the Jeep alarm and was waiting.' He tried to focus with his swollen eye. 'Thanks for getting me here.'

'What do you want to do now?'

He tried to stand, and stumbled. She took his hand and he tried again. 'Let's decide tomorrow.'

'You want to keep going?' Grace said, offering her shoulder.

He put his arm around her and stood up. 'Someone's trying to stop us and I want to know why, don't you?'

'Yes. But you can hardly move.'

'I just need some sleep. Henri will find most of what we need tomorrow. Then we go back to Boucher's apartment, back to Pepine's, then back to Amsterdam.' They reached the emergency-room door. 'There's a number somewhere on my phone for a taxi.'

'I've got one waiting outside,' she said.

Nicu started to smile, then looked like he was going to throw up.

CHAPTER THIRTY-SEVEN

Paris

They arrived back at Rue Dacoin after 2 a.m. She asked the driver to stop in the alleyway and keep guard till she locked the Jeep and helped Nicu through the back entrance.

In his hotel room, he sat in the bathroom, and she cut off the rest of his T-shirt, and soaked a face towel with hot water and soap.

'Bet you're glad you came now?' he said, as she wiped blood and mud from his arms and face.

'I bet *you're* glad I came now,' she teased.

She left him to change into fresh clothes, grunting, then helped him to the bed. By the time she'd cleaned up the bathroom and thrown away his clothes, he was asleep.

She bent to turn off the light. Dark lashes lay across his cheek. There was a faint two-inch scar across his forehead. An old piercing in his ear. For some reason, she wanted to ask him about all of it. About his life. About everything.

Leaving painkillers on the side, she took his keys to check him in the morning and went to her own room.

It was impossible to sleep.

Too many images flared up as she tossed and turned in the

lumpy bed. She checked her phone and saw three new messages from Mac. Without listening, she deleted them.

Giving up, she turned on the television and lay in the dark, watching a bad American movie dubbed in French. At 3 a.m., she jerked upright, the film just finishing, not sure if she'd been asleep or not. French rap music was playing outside, the bass turned up. A car door slammed and voices drifted up. Grace crawled over to the grubby windowsill, blinking through swollen eyes.

A white four-by-four was parked outside Pepine's.

The rear doors lay open. A man's leg extended from it. Long, skinny and wearing black suit trousers.

As she watched, he emerged.

He was very striking. Well over six foot tall, model-thin, in an expensive slim-cut suit, with a black shirt and tie. His dark hair was cut into a quiff over sharp, angled cheekbones. The only detail that wasn't black was a green and red tattoo on his neck, reaching out of his collar and winding up to his face.

There was a menace about him she couldn't place.

Then, from the passenger door, came someone else.

She blinked. It looked like the same man. Every single thing about him from the tattoo to the suit was the same.

Twins?

Which meant they were . . . brothers?

Luc and Marc Boucher?

Tripping over her shoes in the dark, she grabbed her camera. By the time she returned, a third person was with them.

He was young, and a foot shorter. A teenager, about fourteen years old.

Even from here, she could see the boy was terrified. His shoulders were hunched in defence; sweat soaked his hair and face. One twin put a finger on the boy's chin, and pushed him backwards into a wall. He held him there, like a pinned insect. The other stuck his hand inside the boy's T-shirt. The boy cried out, and tried to pull away. One twin slapped him twice across the face, and replaced his hand. All the while, his brother spoke intently into the boy's ear. His face crumpled.

Grace turned off her flash, and placed her lens between the curtains. The red light from Pepine's, the car headlights and the street light might give her something they could manipulate.

She rested the lens on the ledge to keep it still and zoomed in. The boy was shaking now, openly crying. They were humiliating him. Terrorizing him.

Grace chose the rapid-fire mode and pressed the button.

White light exploded in her room, as five shots fired off.

'No!' She ducked down. She'd fumbled it, not turned off the flash.

Fuck.

Amazingly, scrolling back, she saw one decent image. The twins had looked up at the window at the flash, the boy still pinned to the wall. The quality was poor, but the image was menacing.

The rap music below stopped. Then the car engine.

Did they see which room she was in?

The hotel had five floors overlooking the street. She reassured herself it had happened too quickly.

Giving it a minute, she squinted back through the tiny gap.

The car headlights were off, the pavement empty.

They must have gone into Pepine's.

Maybe it scared them into letting the boy go.

Wishing Nicu was awake, she climbed back into bed, eyes wide open, mind racing.

*

215

She was just starting to fall into an exhausted, restless sleep when voices made her jerk upright again, her heart pounding.

The clock said 3.24 a.m.

A creak came from the corridor outside.

Another whisper now.

Standing up, Grace tiptoed to peer into the eyehole. Night-shift workers coming home, she told herself.

Her eye focused in the hole into the lit corridor outside. And in that moment, her heart tried to bolt out of her ribcage.

The twins were in the hotel corridor, trotting along like skinny wolves, pointing at numbers.

Counting.

Her heart thumped so loudly in her chest she could hear it in the room.

Tiptoeing backwards, Grace tripped on her shoe and fell onto the bed.

Her eyes scanned the dark room. There was no phone to reception. Even if there were, what would she say?

A cold layer of sweat coated her skin.

What if the man at reception had told them?

Anyone staying here with a camera?

She recalled the flimsy lock on the door. A child could kick it in.

Floorboards creaked right outside her door.

Grace covered her face with her hands, willing it to stop.

A soft knock. '*Chérie?*' a call came.

'Go away,' she mouthed. What was the emergency number in France?

Idiot. She still didn't know. She should have found that out this evening.

Expecting the door to burst open at any minute, she picked

up her mobile, tiptoed to the bathroom, and locked herself in, shaking.

She fumbled through her contacts. If she called Nicu, his phone might be heard ringing in the room right beside them.

She found Henri's number instead – he could ring the police for her, if he answered.

Her finger hovered over it, waiting.

One minute. Then four. Nothing happened.

When ten minutes had passed, her breathing began to return to normal.

Tiptoeing back, she checked the spyhole again. The corridor was empty.

They'd gone.

But it was only 3.36 a.m. Still three or four hours till it was light and the staff appeared. Till she felt safe.

Returning to the window, she checked the gap. Below, the twins were crossing the street to the car.

One was on the phone, the other smoking, as if nothing had happened.

At the door of Pepine's, the bouncer flung it wide, standing back with deference.

For a second, she thought she'd got away with it.

But then they stopped.

The twins swung round.

Before she could move, one pointed to his watch at her, and held up a finger.

The other blew her a kiss.

It landed on her skin like snake venom. Gasping, she gathered her camera and valuables, and ran out of her room and let herself into Nicu's.

It was filled with the sound of his laboured breathing.

She put a chair under the door handle, and jammed it tight.

'Nicu?' she whispered.

A rustle. 'What's happening?'

She knelt beside him. 'I've done something stupid.'

She explained and he whistled. 'Shit. You OK?'

'No. They're fucking terrifying. Can I sleep on your floor?'

Nicu moved his body to the left. 'Sleep there.'

'No, I don't mean that—'

'Grace, I'm in too much pain to argue.'

'OK.' She climbed onto his bed, grateful, and pulled the top blanket over.

The street light from the rear alley shone through the flimsy curtains.

At least if they came back, there were two of them now. Nicu could ring the police.

As his breathing deepened again, she watched his outline in the night shadows.

She'd never be able to tell Mac this. How odd. After all this time to have a secret she'd carry from him for the rest of their lives.

Now they'd both have secrets.

CHAPTER THIRTY-EIGHT

Edinburgh

That Saturday morning, the rain-sodden clouds sat heavy over the dull grey waters of the Firth of Forth, the Forth Bridge disappearing into the mist like a red caterpillar.

Sula sat in her car in South Queensferry, outside a large sandstone villa that stood on its own at the far end of an avenue mostly populated by bungalows. Rain dripped on the windscreen, as she waited for the clock to tick to 9 a.m. and a decent hour for calling.

She checked Ewan's notes from when Colin McFarlay went missing last year. He was right. Mrs McFarlay lived in a bloody huge house. There was only one other on the street, at the far end.

There were spiked railings and electric gates in front of the modest driveway, which had room for one car and a garage. Probably to keep out her son.

The car in the driveway was a brand-new Mercedes. Printing equipment had obviously paid dividends. She wondered how much they'd spent on a boarding school for a boy whose career was pushing crack to bairns.

At 9 a.m., she pulled on her raincoat, and rang the gate buzzer.

Through the sitting-room window, she saw one of those stupid fancy mock-chandeliers. Cartoons were playing on a huge wall-mounted TV.

An English man answered the intercom. 'Yes?'

'Sula McGregor to see Mrs McFarlay.'

'Oh, hang on,' he said.

The gate buzzed. She walked in and crossed the wet dark pink gravel. The front door opened. A man in the banker's weekend outfit of chinos and a striped shirt, hair in a side parting, and a smile designed to be charming, came onto the porch eating toast. In his hand was a card. Close up, Sula saw another four-by-four in the garage.

'Hi!' he said in his well-educated voice.

She stood in the rain in front of him, her glasses steaming up. A toddler came running behind him, followed by a slim woman in jeans and a navy cashmere jumper, with a highlighted bob. 'Darling, come here.' She grinned with mock irritation at Sula.

The man handed Sula the card. 'Mrs McFarlay doesn't live here anymore, I'm afraid. We're the new owners. That's the address for forwarding mail.'

'Is that right?' Sula said, taking it. There was a 'Sold' sign stuck down the side of the garage. Bloody Ewan. He'd not updated last year's research – too tied up with that bloody Grace Scott story. From the postcode on the card, it looked like Mrs McFarlay had moved to Stirling.

'Can I ask when you moved in?' she said, wondering if there was any chance their well-to-do manners would include asking her out of the rain.

'Uh, October.'

'Right. Thank you.'

'You're welcome. Come on, monster.' The man turned and

swung the child up in the air, checking back for Sula's admiring look.

'She needs a change, darling.' The woman pushed past him. 'Excuse me, do you know her? Mrs McFarlay.'

'Why d'you ask?' Sula questioned.

'You're not a friend?'

'No.'

'Well . . .' the wife said, adopting a conspiratorial tone.

Rain ran down Sula's face and glasses.

No, don't you get yourself wet there.

'It's just that people on the road keep giving us funny looks and saying things like, "We're so glad you've moved in," as if they're grateful Mrs McFarlay's gone. I was just wondering if there'd been something going on here.'

Sula decided to have some fun. 'Ah, now that sounds familiar. You mean was she a high-end escort?'

The toddler ran back out, chased by the man, now also wearing an expression of fake frustration that really meant, 'Isn't our life marvellous?' The woman turned them both back inside hurriedly. She crept closer to Sula, but still under the cover of the porch. 'Really?' she said, aghast.

'Well, you get them in these residential areas,' Sula said. 'Older madame. Men coming in and out at all hours, upsetting the neighbours.' She pointed. 'Electronic gates to keep out nosy parkers and the police.'

The woman looked up at her spanking-new house with its freshly painted windows and potted olive trees.

Sula lifted her eyes to the first floor. 'God, you can't even imagine what went on.'

'Oh God,' the woman said. 'Do you think?'

Sula shrugged. 'Have you had it checked for hidden cameras, that kind of thing? In the light fittings and bathrooms? You know what these people get up to with their secret filming. If it was me, I'd have the place pulled apart.'

She turned and stomped across the wet gravel. 'Right. Thanks for your help.'

CHAPTER THIRTY-NINE

Edinburgh

Back in Mr Singh's storeroom, the man finished his lunch, starting to believe he'd had a lucky break. The husband from upstairs had not appeared again.

It looked like he'd got away with it for now.

Dropping the paper plate in the bin, he put on his headphones, and sat on the stool to watch his first randomly picked TV programme of the morning: about buying a new house at auction.

The tapping entered his consciousness slowly.

The first house up for auction was a two-bedroom dump in Devon with a rotten roof. At first, he thought the tapping was coming from the television; an off-screen suggestion of the roof being fixed.

Tap, tap, tap.

The adverts broke in and he took off his headphones.

Tap, tap, tap.

The man swung round, to see the husband from upstairs at the storeroom window, polite astonishment on his face.

'Hi,' he shouted through. 'Got a minute?'

A tremor rumbled through the man. His fists balled.

'Listen, man, don't worry. It's just Mac – from upstairs. Wanted to say hello.'

Tap, tap, tap.

The man stood up, and faced his enemy. The husband was in his mid-thirties. He had a stupid cheerful face with pretty girl's eyes; the thunderous expression from yesterday in the yard was gone.

'Hey. There you are!' the husband called out. He stuck up a thumb and pointed to the back door.

The man walked towards the door, each foot dragging as if through thick mud. The silver key in the lock burned his flesh.

He turned it, opened the door and the husband bounded into view like a clown.

'Hey, how you doing?' He stuck out a hand. He was shorter than the man, broad-shouldered but not muscular. The man knew he could knock him over with a finger.

The husband's hand quivered in mid-air like an arrow.

The man didn't take it.

Yet the husband wasn't thrown. He simply turned it to point at the barred window.

'Didn't mean to startle you. Didn't know you lived here. Just moved in?'

The man gave a small nod. Behind the husband, the backyard stretched ahead. People from the tower block could see him. His chest tightened.

'What, last week or something?' the husband said.

The man nodded another lie.

'Funny. We thought this was Mr Singh's storeroom and . . .' The husband's eyes roamed inside to the boxes of crisps and sweets. 'Oh – and it is!' New curiosity filled his eyes. 'So, what, you just crashing here for a while?'

The man fought the urge to knock the husband's stupid smile into the back of his head.

He nodded again.

'Oh, right.' The husband winked. 'Not exactly legal. No bother. None of my business. I just saw you in there yesterday and thought I'd say hello. Did I say – I'm Mac from upstairs, by the way? And you are?'

The man decided to try to speak, knowing it was his only chance to get rid of this fool. Yet it had been so long since he'd spoken that nothing came out. He tried again and a hoarse whisper emerged. 'I . . . can't . . .'

The husband dipped his head. 'Sorry – Kent, did you say?'

The man froze.

'Well, Kent, nice to meet you – listen, don't be on your own down here. Come up and have a cup of tea. Maybe later today? Just give us a knock at the back.'

He blinked again, and the husband took that as a yes, walking off with a wave.

Staggering back inside, the man slammed the door. A breeze pushed its way in with the movement, bringing with it smells that set off a longing so painful it was unbearable.

Through the barred window, he saw the husband clatter back up the fire escape, two stairs at a time.

Then a creak above. Now he was on the fire escape. Seconds later, fresh cigarette smoke drifted in under the door.

The man stood on his stool.

The back gate and the tower block were blurred now, as if a giant had smudged them with a wet finger. He rubbed his eyes to make them focus again, but it was no good.

Somebody else knew he was here.

CHAPTER FORTY

Paris

Heat woke Grace, warming her cheek.

It was sun, shining through the hotel-room window.

She sat up in Nicu's bed, disorientated, her mouth dry, trying to remember why she was here, then remembered.

The twins.

'Nicu?' she said hoarsely.

His side was empty. The curtains were half open. To her shock, her phone said it was lunchtime.

Swearing came from the bathroom. She saw the indent where Nicu had been lying next to her, and felt it. Cold. 'You OK?'

'No, I'm . . . *Fuck.*'

'D'you need help?'

Silence.

She got up. 'That's yes, then, is it?'

He opened the door, a towel round his waist. His hair was wet and she saw he'd managed to have a bath, and wash the rest of the blood off, while keeping his arm dressings dry.

'Here,' she said. She guided him to the window, grabbed her camera, and began to shoot him.

'Jesus,' he said, realizing what she was doing. 'I thought I was bad.'

'All part of the story.' The swelling round his eye was pale blue. A purple-blue bruise the size of a saucer was splattered across his ribs, as if it were food thrown there by a toddler. Smaller blue bruises that looked like toe-prints dotted his back and torso. He held his arm stiff, as if it wasn't part of his body, but made of wood and strapped on.

When she finished, he motioned to it. 'I can't move this. Can you . . . ?'

'You should have woken me,' she said, finding tracksuit bottoms and a T-shirt in his bag.

'You needed sleep.'

She tried to stay practical. 'Can I cut this one?' She held up the T-shirt.

He nodded and she cut away the arm.

'Tell me again about last night,' he said as she turned her back, to let him start dressing. When he'd finished the bottom half, she showed him the shot of the twins, then recounted the story as she stood on the bed, lifting the cut hole of the T-shirt over his injured arm.

'You think they're the Bouchers?'

'Well, they're twins and they were going into Pepine's. And they were nasty bastards, so . . .'

'Well. If they didn't know someone's watching them, they do now,' Nicu said.

'Sorry.'

'No. It's a good shot. I'd have done the same.'

'Thanks.'

He said nothing more. She wondered why. Then their eyes met ahead in the bathroom mirror. She realized her hand was resting on his bare back.

'Right,' she said, pulling down his T-shirt and jumping off the bed. 'So I'll go ring Henri.'

'Good.'

'In my room.'

'Right. Thanks.'

'Welcome. And thanks for having me.' This was getting worse. Rolling her eyes, she opened the door and crossed to her room, telling herself to shut up.

Then stopped.

An envelope lay outside her doorway. *GRACE SCOTT*, it said on the front. Picking it up, feeling sick, she returned to Nicu's room.

'Look.'

It was a photo of them last night in the North African restaurant, taken from the alleyway.

'Right,' he said, 'we need to get out of here.'

They checked out, twenty minutes later, and crept out the back. Grace piled their bags in the Jeep, and went to the passenger side, only to find Nicu already at the door.

'You'll have to drive.'

She froze. 'I can't. I've never driven on the right.'

He opened the door. 'No choice. I can't move my shoulder, and I'm concussed.'

'Shit. OK.'

She walked behind the Jeep. Her foot kicked something metal by the wheel and she stopped.

'Nicu?' she called, confused. 'What's this?'

He came round and stared.

'Fuck's sake.' Leaning down with a grunt, he pulled from under the wheel what looked like a grey rubber tube with long nails sticking out of holes spaced roughly five centimetres along it. 'It's a spike trap – someone's made it. Police use them to blow tyres during car chases.'

'Look,' Grace said, ducking down, not believing what she was seeing. 'There's one under the other wheel.'

Nicu shook his head, throwing them in the Jeep. 'Someone really doesn't want us here. Come on.'

Grace checked the front tyres were clear, then climbed in beside him, and pulled his seatbelt over him, then her own. He grimaced as his bruised back touched the seat. In the driver's seat, she regarded the back-to-front instruments with horror.

'It's as good a place as any to learn,' Nicu said.

'Paris. Is that a joke?'

At least it was automatic. She put it in drive, and drove slowly to the end of the alleyway, nosing out. A motorbike shot past on the 'wrong' side and she slammed on the brakes.

Nicu jerked forwards, and held his rib. 'Ah, you bastard.'

'Sorry. I'm going to kill us.'

'What's your surname?'

'Scott.'

'Right, think, "Scott in the Centre." The Jeep's steering wheel is on the left, and French roads are right-hand drive. So as long as you're nearer the central reservation than me, you're on the correct side.'

Not convinced, she pulled out and made it to the junction of Rue Dacoin, then turned onto the main road, shrieking feebly as cars came at her from unfamiliar directions. Nicu gave her calm instructions, grunting each time she slammed on the brakes in a panic. At the second T-junction, it was easier. At the third, she began to anticipate the turn. Apart from a roundabout, where she tried to go the wrong way, there were no mishaps. When they arrived at Henri's office thirty minutes later, and parked, she felt as if she'd run a marathon.

She helped Nicu out, and into the rattling lift that took them up six floors to Henri's office. He met them with a handshake, and concern for Nicu's condition, then led them to his desk in a shared freelancers' office.

'So, please sit. I have news.'

Outside the turret window was a run of rooftops, the attic windows of the elegant nineteenth-century buildings pinched, as if out of clay.

'Right,' Henri said, pushing across a file. 'This isn't complete yet. The good news is, you were right. François Boucher simply appears in Paris in 1992.'

'From Romania?'

'Doesn't say. But there's no record of him before 1992, so I'm guessing he used false papers. It's not impossible that René arranged the marriage with Pepine to bury François's false ID. Keep his star worker safe from deportation.'

'Lucky Pepine,' Grace said. 'So he definitely *could* be Lucian Tronescu, hiding in Paris, under the name "François Boucher"?'

'Yes. And I have a photo.'

Grace practically tore it from his hand. It was a 1994 police arrest shot. The face was strong-featured and striking. The subject was in his late teens, and had eyes so black they sucked out light. The eyebrows were thick, as if drawn with a marker pen. He had wide cheeks like a bull terrier, a small pointed nose and a defiant stare. His hair was short and brown, the texture thick and tightly curled, like Velcro.

'Is this the dead guy?' Nicu asked.

Grace held up the photo. 'I can't tell. It's too old and I didn't see his face. His hair was this colour, but it was below his chin.' She checked the arrest details. 'But look, the height's the same – 1.78 metres.'

'So what next?' Henri said.

Sun shone into the attic, and Grace realized how pale Nicu was, his skin almost pearly and translucent.

She took control. 'We'll go back to François's old apartment here, and find someone to confirm this is definitely him, and find out what he looks like now, twenty years later.'

Nicu nodded.

'Then back to Mitti in Amsterdam to ID this photo as Lucian Grabole,' she continued. 'If she doesn't recognize it, then maybe Lucian Grabole is an innocent man who got caught up in this.'

Henri peered over gold-rimmed glasses. 'But why was Lucian Grabole in Edinburgh?'

Nicu shifted his arm, frowning.

'Water?' Henri said, offering some.

'Thanks,' he said, and swallowed a painkiller. 'Henri, you said René had drug routes all over Europe. Could you check if that included Scotland?'

'Sure.'

Then, with Henri's permission, Grace photographed the scene for the feature. She shot the photo of François Boucher on Henri's desk among his scattered notes, then the Parisian roof-tops beyond his desk with Henri in silhouette at the window. Then she shot the photo of François Boucher at Nicu's sugges-tion, held by Henri's hands. He had strong hands, with manicured nails and a chunky ring.

'What about Luc, Marc and Pepine?' Nicu said.

'No photos of Pepine, but the Boucher brothers, yes.' He handed them a grainy shot from the file.

Grace focused. 'That's them.'

'What this?' Henri peered over his glasses.

She explained about the previous night.

His eyes opened wide. 'These guys were at your door? OK, listen, you need to be careful. These guys are dicks. Like stupid dogs with a nasty bite.' He pointed at Nicu's arm. 'Are you sure this wasn't them?'

231

'I still don't reckon they know we're here. Or didn't, anyway.'

'So who put the photo of us outside my hotel door?' Grace asked.

Nicu shrugged. 'I'm not convinced it's them.'

Henri took off his glasses and tapped them, thinking. 'Are you sure, Nicu? That they don't have contacts in Amsterdam who could have followed you here?'

'Because . . . ?' Grace asked.

'Because they've heard a newspaper – i.e. you – is investigating their brother-in-law. Remember, François knows the Boucher family business going back nearly twenty-five years – which means he knows, literally, where the bodies are buried.'

'You mentioned François's sidekick, Mathieu Caron – what does he look like, Henri?' Grace asked.

'I can find out.'

'You're thinking he might be the guy following us? Who did this?' Nicu asked, nodding at his arm.

'Could be. Maybe he still works for Luc and Marc, too.'

'It's interesting that he hasn't really hurt you. Not yet,' Henri said. 'Caron's not shy when it comes to breaking legs. Or heads, for that matter.'

Nicu shifted in pain. 'He kills me or Grace, everything changes – there's police all over. He doesn't want that heat.'

'Well, there's a positive,' Grace added.

'I still think whoever's doing this just wants us off the story.'

Henri stretched back. 'Well, be careful. As I said, whatever those Boucher twins do, they always seem to get away with it.'

They ate lunch in a cafe, then Grace drove them back to François's former apartment.

They agreed that Nicu's thuggish appearance wouldn't help, so Grace tried the door buzzers alone.

Again, no answer.

A tiny security camera swivelled above the front door, and too late she guessed the concierge had spotted the Jeep outside.

'I'm not moving,' she said through gritted teeth. From here she could see Nicu had fallen asleep in the front seat.

She waited on the steps, checking her phone. Nothing new from Mac since she'd spoken to John last night. Suddenly she remembered. John had told him she'd be back tonight. There was no chance. She texted him quickly.

'Sorry. One more day. Back tomorrow now. Talk then. Gx.'

A car drew up outside. A woman in an exquisite red coat-dress and black heels was dropped by a driver. She clicked towards Grace, finding her keys in a leather handbag that looked like it cost a month's mortgage at Gallon Street.

Grace waved. 'Hello? Excuse me – do you speak English?'

The woman stopped. A waft of expensive perfume floated over. She surveyed Grace as if a dog had deposited her on the pavement. 'Yes,' she said through perfectly lined red lips. 'Do you speak French?'

From her expression, it wasn't a joke.

'Could I please ask you about this man?' Grace lifted the photo of François Boucher.

The woman's snooty expression changed to abhorrence.

She knew him.

'Is this François Boucher, who used to live here?'

The woman headed past her up the stairs.

'Please,' Grace said. 'I'm trying to gather information for the police.'

The woman stopped.

'*La police?*'

'Yes. Is it him?'

Her eyebrows raised. She gave a short, sharp '*Oui.*'

'And his hair – is it longer now? To his chin?'

She took out keys. '*Oui.*'

'And does he still live here?'

'*Non. Dieu merci.*' She opened the door.

'And—'

The door slammed shut.

'Positive ID for François Boucher, then and now,' she said, waking Nicu back in the Jeep.

Nicu's eyes flickered open. 'Good.' She gave him water, and he drank thirstily.

'You OK?'

'Painkillers just knocking me out.'

'And the concussion probably. Let me just . . .' She lifted his T-shirt and checked the bruises, pressing them and making him wince. The redness hadn't spread. To be sure, she took a pen and drew round the bandages on his arm.

'What are you doing?'

'I like drawing on people.'

He frowned.

Grace used the same stern voice he'd used about her lie-ins. 'Better watch out. Next time you fall asleep in the middle of a story, I'm going to draw glasses round your eyes.'

His baffled look made her laugh.

That evening, they found a coffee shop to hide out in for a while, the owner watching Nicu's bruised face suspiciously.

Grace checked her phone. Predicatably, there were four new messages from Mac. She deleted them without listening to them.

Leave me alone. Let me do this.

Nicu unfolded a map he'd brought from the Jeep. 'What day is it?'

'Saturday.'

'OK . . .' He drew a zigzag line from their current location two miles due south.

'What's that?' she asked.

'Back-up plan.'

'Is it the route out of Paris?'

'Kind of.'

'Can you do one without roundabouts, please?' she asked.

'You'll be fine,' he said.

She tapped the map. 'Do you think we'll need one?'

'You heard Henri,' Nicu said. 'We don't want to hang around in there. If they do know who we are, we need to get out fast. I reckon we go early, when Pepine's on her own. Get her reaction to the photo, then get the fuck out of Dodge.'

She nodded, nerves knotting.

That night, Grace drove back towards Rue Dacoin.

Nicu directed her to the parallel street behind Pepine's, and they parked up, out of sight. When it was time for the club to open, they waited half an hour, then took Nicu's camera and crossed down one street to Pepine's. Nicu pulled down his baseball hat. Her legs began to weaken as she faced the prospect of coming face to face with the twins from last night. The bulldog bouncer was on the door. They waited till a group of men went in, and squeezed in behind them.

Nicu murmured in French. The man glared at Nicu's bruises and then looked away. If he recognized them, he didn't react.

The inner door was made of darkened glass. They opened it into a large red-lit circular room. The relentless thumping beat rushed out. The place smelt of beer and disinfectant and baby oil.

The club was smaller than she'd guessed. The curved walls

were host to red PVC booths. A glittering set of illuminated shelves behind the bar displayed rows of alcohol. Beside it was a platform where a woman danced topless, with tired moves.

The place wasn't even a quarter full. The men who'd just arrived were making themselves comfortable as if they were staying for the evening. Others leaned over beers at the bar, watching the dancer.

'Get a seat,' Nicu said. 'I'll be back.'

'No. Where are you going?'

But he disappeared towards the toilet sign. Grace crept into a booth.

A blonde woman appeared behind the bar from a back room and examined the newcomers. It was the woman the waiter from the North African restaurant had identified last night as Pepine Boucher. Her nose was sharp and curved between vacant, cruel eyes. She shared her brothers' angled cheekbones, and had hard, suspiciously round breasts.

Her eyes braked at Grace, and she shrank back.

Where was Nicu? What time was this to go to the bloody toilet?

Then he was back, easing himself painfully into the booth.

'Right, there's no one else here. Just the bouncer.'

'And her,' Grace said, nodding.

'You ready?' Nicu held out his hand for her to take. She flushed as a volt passed between them. They climbed out and went to the bar.

Nicu ordered them bourbon in French.

The woman's eyes widened, travelled his bruises, then moved to Grace as if auditioning her for a lap-dancing job.

'*Deux bourbons*,' she said in a grating voice.

Nicu pulled out euros. The woman poured the liquid into the glasses, with worked-out, sinewy arms.

The bouncer outside stepped away from the door to speak to someone in the street.

The woman gave Nicu change, with long green-painted talons.

Nicu beckoned Pepine Boucher closer. He slipped the photo of François Boucher on the bar, and spoke in fast French.

The woman stiffened. Her eyes flew to the bouncer.

'*Qui êtes vous?*'

Nicu whispered in Grace's ear. 'Get ready to go,' he said.

'Where?'

Nicu lifted a small camera from under the counter. Pepine Boucher watched it, hypnotized. The flash lit up her amazed expression.

Before she could move, Nicu photographed her twice more. The mask crumpled and she swiped with green talons, with a roar. Nicu kept shooting.

The bouncer returned to the doorway, back to them.

'Go,' Nicu said calmly, heading for the toilet, taking Grace's hand again. They moved as quickly as he could go. Now she saw – there was a fire escape.

'What are you doing?' she gasped.

He pulled her harder. 'Come on. We need to move.'

They stumbled through it, out into the alleyway. Now she understood. The Jeep was parked at the end.

She helped him in, then got in the driver's side and scrabbled to get the keys in the ignition.

'I can't believe you did that.'

There was a bang from the alleyway and the bouncer came flying out of the fire escape.

'Grace, go,' Nicu repeated.

She started the Jeep and screeched out of the parking space. The bouncer ran behind them talking into a phone.

237

'Well, he was faster than I gave him credit for,' Nicu said.

Grace accelerated, trying to control the swerve as they approached a junction.

'Right,' Nicu said, checking the rear-view mirror.

She overtook a cyclist too fast. 'Argh – I'm going to hit someone.'

'No, you're not . . . Fuck.'

'What?'

He was looking in the side mirror.

'Nicu, what?'

'Nothing. Right. Change of plan. Take the next right, straight on, then left at the junction.'

She bumped along the narrow street, then did what he asked.

Nicu was still watching the mirror, not answering.

'Nicu, what is it?'

'Keep going.'

A long beam of light appeared in her rear-view mirror. 'Please tell me that's not them.'

He checked the map he'd drawn on earlier. 'We'll be fine. Just do what I say. Left, then left again.'

Trying to concentrate on not crashing, she followed his instructions for two minutes, turning into a long, dark road lined by warehouses. The beam disappeared in her mirror.

'To the end and left again . . .' Nicu said.

The beam reappeared just as she took the turn.

'They're still there!' she said, starting to panic. 'Nicu! We shouldn't have done that. Ring the police. If they catch us here, they'll kill us.'

'They're not going to catch us.'

'They are!'

Nicu touched the wheel. 'Right, take the next bend up ahead. When I shout, "Now," I want you to turn off your headlights.'

'What!'

'Just do it.'

She raced round the bend, trying to grip the wheel.

The beam disappeared out of her mirror.

Nicu shouted, 'Now!' and she turned off the lights. He pulled the wheel down hard and they shot into the open driveway of a huge derelict building.

The Jeep hit a pitted surface.

'Put your foot down. Keep going.'

'But I can't see!' she said as the Jeep hit a pothole.

'Grace, do not stop,' he said, twisting behind him.

The Jeep hit a brick with a bang and they jerked onwards.

Nicu pointed ahead, squinting in the dark. 'Right. Through that gap.'

In the moonlight, she now saw what looked like the entrance of an abandoned hangar. Just as they entered it, a beam sped past behind them, the other car tricked.

'They've gone!' she said, twisting round.

'Right, turn it round, then reverse up to that.' A sheet of corrugated iron lay against the wall.

She did it and turned off the Jeep. Nicu got out and, with his good arm, started to pull the sheet in front of the truck, hiding its lights and windscreen. She jumped out to help, feet crunching on glass and broken brick, hands shaking. The only sound now was the distant rumbling of a train.

'What if they find us in here?' she whispered, searching the shadows.

'I'm counting on them not knowing this place. Come on.'

He took her hand again, and walked out into the open. In the pale moonlight, acres of dirt and rubble stretched ahead. It smelt of urine. They passed burned-out fires to a wall that was daubed in graffiti. Nicu put his good arm around her and led her on into the building. 'Give them half an hour to check around; then we can head off.'

Inside, it smelt even worse. They picked over more rubble in the dark, keeping each other steady.

Ahead of them, there was a flutter. Two shadows moved. Grace's heart banged in her chest, and the power in her legs simply stalled. She yanked back, hissing, 'There's someone in here.'

'It's fine,' Nicu said, pulling her onwards. Even injured, he was much stronger than her.

'No!'

She tried to pull back, but he pulled her on towards the waiting figures.

CHAPTER FORTY-ONE

The shapes, she saw, as he dragged her on, were teenagers.

The whites of their eyes shone as they watched her. A trembling started in her legs as Nicu pulled her towards them. They were boys, about fifteen. Nicu spoke in rapid French and they replied. One bent down and there was a grating noise. The boy's arm came round her and she pushed him away angrily. 'What the fuck is this?'

'Go with him.'

To her shock, one of the boys simply disappeared.

The second teenager put a hand out to her.

'Go with him,' Nicu repeated.

'No!'

Swearing, Nicu grabbed her hand and gave it to the boy. He pulled her towards him and motioned to her foot.

It was a hole.

He grabbed her ankle and placed it on a metal bar.

Stairs.

'Grace, getting a fucking move on,' Nicu said. 'Climb down.'

Having no option but to trust him, she did what he said. The first boy was shining a torch up, giving him a ghostly appearance. The train rumbling grew inside.

Marginally more scared of the Bouchers right now than these boys, she began to descend, finding more metal bars under her feet. A hand came from below and guided her down into the dark. Her feet landed in stinking water.

Nicu came next, grunting with the effort. Despite her anger at him, she reached up a hand to help. Then the other teenager came last. There was a scraping above and the manhole shut. The light vanished and her heart jolted into a long, slow, painful beat.

She was going to die in here.

Nicu held out his hand and she pushed it away again, panicked. 'What is this? Who are they?'

'Just somewhere to wait till they've gone.' He grasped her hand again. 'Come on.'

The teenagers headed off, taking the only light source with them. Nicu turned on his phone light, and she did the same. A dim glow appeared in the distance.

As they approached, she saw it was a pale orange light dusting the walls. As things became brighter, she realized they were in a tunnel. Except the sides were not the smooth concrete of a sewer, but roughly hewn from rock. They rounded a bend, sloshing through the shallow water, and the lights brightened. Grace pulled back on Nicu's hand.

This made no sense.

Up ahead, a floor-standing candelabra was encased in a rock alcove. A mass of candles burned in its holders. It sat in a volcano of dried wax, as if it had been burning here for years.

The train noise became louder. Yet now she realized it wasn't a train.

'Come on, nearly there,' Nicu said. The water disappeared, and the light brightened further, casting longer shadows on the ground. A stream of graffiti appeared on her left and carried on alongside them. The ground began to shudder with the thumping noise.

Music?

Any will she had to resist was gone now. She didn't understand. She was lost in a tunnel with strangers, being chased by someone who wanted to hurt her and Nicu, for reasons she didn't really understand.

Ahead was a hole in the wall. The teenagers disappeared through.

She stopped at it, not believing what was on the other side.

The tunnel opened like whale jaws into a cavernous hall.

There were people here. A hundred or more of them, their backs to Grace and Nicu.

Dancing.

An astonished laugh burst from her mouth.

It was incredible. Strings of globe lights hung on the ceiling. Laser lights strobed the walls, and a DJ stood at decks at the far end.

By the entrance was an oddly neat row of assorted rubber boots people had clearly used to walk through the tunnel water.

She cupped her face. 'I don't believe this.'

Nicu smiled. 'Come on.'

They continued through the crowd to low rocks by the side, covered in Moroccan cushions, where people lounged. They found a free space and sat beside a woman selling beer at a table. Nicu bought two and came back. They banged bottles, with wry grins.

'How did you know it was here?' she said, relief pumping through her like a tranquillizer.

'This is the job I did here last year.'

She turned, wide-eyed. 'That photo in your office – of the hands at the rave?'

He nodded. 'These subterranean tunnels are all over Paris. There's hundreds of kilometres of them – they used them for illegal raves and artist salons, lots of stuff. Police can't keep them out – there's too many of them.'

The beer hit her system, now, and her limbs relaxed. 'How do they get electricity?'

He pointed up. 'Divert it from the Métro.'

'Amazing.'

He turned on his camera and she leaned in to look at Pepine Boucher. The last image was the best. Cruel eyes, and a sharp nose. Mouth curled in fury.

'You were never going to ID him with her, were you?' She nudged his arm.

'No point. She's not going to tell us anything.'

Around them people danced, hands snaking in the air.

'This is amazing. I can see why you'd want to shoot it,' she said.

Nicu handed her his other camera and took her beer. 'Go for it.'

It was a model she could only dream of owning.

'Really?'

She played with the controls, then stood up and entered the throng. She started to shoot, without a flash, using the laser lights instead. Most dancers ignored her, faces set in ecstasy; others watched her with mild curiosity. She walked and shot, and walked more. She shot a woman with her hands in the air as if praying. Two elegant girls with designer handbags, white-dusted noses, shimmying up to guys in suits, their ties ripped away. The DJ shaking a hand at the ceiling.

Then she sat on the floor and shot up, creating montages of mouths, eyes and chins, against the laser-pink rock ceiling. Above her, a man walked past, his black quiff rising above the crowd like a shark's fin. She lifted her camera to shoot. A second, identical quiff walked into the shot.

Grace dropped like she'd been punched. Trying to breathe away her terror, she crept through the jumping crowd to Nicu. He saw her expression and pulled her in.

'They're here,' she said. Her hands began to tremble. They were trapped.

Nicu put down the beer. 'Where?'

'How do we get out?' she mouthed.

Nicu put his good arm around her, and they moved low against the rock along the side. Through a gap in legs, she saw the bouncer from Pepine's blocking the hole they'd passed through.

She crouched. 'We need to ring the police.'

'No signal down here.'

Nicu motioned a teenager leaning against a wall. The boy came over. They spoke and he nodded. He crept off, waving behind him. They followed, Nicu taking Grace's hand tightly in his. Behind them, suddenly, the music juddered to a halt, the echo swallowed by the rock.

The twins stood on the DJ deck. Boos and shouting started from the crowd, some still swaying even though the beat had died.

One brother took a mic and spoke. A hush fell. A few looked behind them, eyes wide.

Behind her, the crowd parted.

People were looking around, then at each other. The boy motioned her and Nicu into a new tunnel at the back.

This one was smaller. Immediately, the light died. Water seeped into her shoes and there was a rotting smell. She put out a hand to stop her head hitting jutting-out pieces of rock, trying to control the panic. Nicu's laboured breathing came from ahead, as he held his rib.

245

'*Arrêtez*,' came a throaty whisper a minute later in the pitch black. The boy brought out a torch and carried on. It hardly helped. This tunnel was smaller, and she hit her head twice, trying not to shout out. It felt like an eternity, but eventually a hiss came from up ahead. She ran into the back of Nicu, making him grunt.

'Sorry.'

'Come here,' he said.

His hand guided hers onto a metal bar. She gripped it, realizing the boy was already on it.

Praying the rungs would hold on the damp tunnel wall, and the boy wouldn't fall on her head, she climbed after him. Up was good. Up was better than down there. There was a clattering sound above. To her joy, dim blue moonlight appeared. She clambered out behind the boy. Nicu hoisted himself up behind her, with a muffled curse. She and the boy helped him up.

He spoke in French and held out money. The boy grinned and kept his hand out. Nicu gave him another note, then patted the boy's back. '*Merci*.'

'*Merci, monsieur.*' The boy disappeared into the shadows, clearly not risking going back down there.

'Where are we?' Grace whispered.

'At the side, I think. Keep low.'

She could tell by his voice he was struggling, and reached out for his hand. They stumbled across twisted metal, bricks and dirt in the almost dark, to a broken window. Nicu was right. They were at the far right of the industrial plant, on the other side of the hangar that housed the Jeep. From the distant glow of street lights, Grace saw there were now two cars on the forecourt, one of them a white four-by-four. In the other, a faint orange glow flickered. A cigarette.

'There's someone in there,' she said.

'OK. Let's try this way.'

Tripping and stumbling, they arrived round the back of the hollowed-out warehouse and reached the Jeep. They removed the corrugated sheeting.

Panic enveloped her. The cars were parked between them and the exit. They were never going to escape. They were going to die here, in this horrible place.

Nicu reached inside the Jeep with a grunt, came out and spoke in her ear. 'Get in and put the keys in the ignition. Don't do anything else till I get back.'

'Where are you going?' She grabbed his jacket.

'One minute.'

He crept out through the front entrance. She climbed in the Jeep, eased the door gently shut, and forced her trembling fingers to fit the key in the ignition. Dust covered the windscreen and she leaned out to wipe it off. Through a gap, she saw a faint movement at the back of the two cars.

'Hurry,' she whispered.

A minute later, the passenger door opened. Nicu climbed in, face contorted with pain.

'What?'

'Nothing.'

'What now?' she said.

'Start the engine when I tell you, but don't put the lights on. Then reverse like fuck and turn –' he pointed outside '– there. He'll take a minute to work out where we're coming from. Then hit that exit like your life depends on it.'

'Does my life depend on it?'

'Possibly.'

Grace gripped the wheel with sweaty fingers.

'Ready?'

'Yup.'

Nicu dropped his hand and she turned the key. Faltering in the dark, she shoved the gearstick into reverse and accelerated backwards, jolting over broken bricks and wood, the Jeep protesting with a squeal, out into the open.

Lights came on in the white four-by-four.

She reversed the Jeep in a semicircle.

'Right, stop,' Nicu said, flicking on the headlights. 'And go! Fucking go!'

Grace slammed down her foot. The Jeep shot across the forecourt. The four-by-four engine started with a growl.

Foot to the floor, gasping, she sped forwards, the wheels picking up speed.

'He's seen us!'

'Go, go, go!'

There was a loud pop as they raced past the car and she saw the brake lights slam on. Far off to the left, figures ran out of the building.

'Through the gate!' Nicu shouted.

She made it, just, bashing the post.

'Left! Left!'

She swerved into the road.

Nicu checked behind. 'Keep going.'

But Grace's attention was elsewhere. Headlights were coming at them head on.

'Scott in the Centre!' she shrieked. As Nicu turned, she steered out of the path of the oncoming truck into the right lane. A long, angry klaxon ripped through the air.

There was a shocked silence as she righted the Jeep.

'Fucking hell.' Nicu laughed, then touched his arm. 'Ow. Fuck.'

Grace checked the mirror, desperate. 'They're just going to follow us.'

'No, they're not.' He pointed at a road sign ahead. 'Next right. We need to get on the ring road.'

'What did you do?' she said, wiping dust out of her eyes.

'Used the spike traps on their tyres.'

She couldn't help it. A loud laugh burst out. 'Nicu!'

With his good arm, Nicu fiddled with the satnav, smiling. A comforting English voice appeared. 'Turn right at the next traffic lights.'

She followed instructions towards the autoroute, never wanting to leave a place as much as she did now.

Her breathing began to slow. 'What did they say in the tunnel?'

Nicu shifted his back, with a grunt. 'That if they didn't tell them where we were, they'd seal the exits and firebomb the place.'

Grace accelerated. 'OK, now I feel sick. Would they do it?'

'Doubt it.'

He checked in the mirror. 'Right. We've lost them.'

A ridiculous 'Whoop!' emerged from her mouth.

'You did good.'

'I can't believe it. That was . . .' She hesitated.

'Fun?' He turned on his camera. 'Good photo of Pepine, though, huh?'

She smacked his leg, and shook her head at him. His face was streaked with dirt like hers, with bits of crap in his hair. She entered the streak of orange that was the ring road, her damp jeans sticking to the old leather seat, her shoes soaked with tunnel water.

The satnav said four hours and fifty-seven minutes back to Amsterdam. Nicu turned on quiet music, and offered her water from the back. She took it, and saw him throwing back more painkillers.

When they hit the autoroute north towards Belgium, he found a jumper in the back, too.

'Want it?'

'Thanks.'

He put it around her shoulders with his good arm.

'How are you feeling?' She nodded at the other one.

She saw him forcing his eyes open, and knew he was either in pain or struggling against the wooziness of the concussion. His head fell back and he shook himself awake. 'What did you say?'

'Just sleep, Nicu. I'm fine.'

'Sure?'

'Trust me, after today, I won't sleep for about three weeks.'

'I'll stay awake for a . . . In a . . .' She looked over and saw his head had fallen back. His lips were soft, and open.

She followed the satnav, checking in her mirror till she was positive no one was following.

Tomorrow, she could take the photo of François Boucher back to Mitti and find out for sure if Lucian Grabole and Lucian Tronescu were the same man or not.

The story would move forwards again.

The speedometer said a hundred kilometres per hour, but for some reason, it seemed faster. The Jeep flew through the French darkness like a spaceship.

It was unbelievable. An instinct about an old envelope in her flat had led to all of this.

Never in her life had she had such a strong sense of knowing exactly what she was doing.

It was as if her future had always been on this road, just waiting for her to arrive.

CHAPTER FORTY-TWO

Stirling

The following morning, Sula McGregor parked her car in front of a garage that said, 'No parking,' and climbed out.

Stirling was bonny in the sunshine today. Lego figures crossed a distant golf course pulling carts, and a green haze kissed the hills.

She walked up the close, checking numbers.

Number 42, Mrs McFarlay's new place, was a modest bungalow in a group of ten. It was neat and tidy. Red brick, double glazing, a glass 1970s front door. No flowers, just clipped lawn and bushes. A hatchback in the drive.

And no electronic gates.

She wouldn't need them anymore, mind you. Now there was no son turning up at all hours, banging on the door, asking for money, no doubt bringing his scuzzy wee pals with him, with their dirty bomber jackets and pavement-shuffling and permofags. Police asking questions about his whereabouts, and him begging her to lie, and the neighbours craning their necks, blaming you.

Poor cow.

Mrs McFarlay answered, a tall, broad-jawed, handsome

woman in her early seventies, with grey hair. She eyed Sula warily. 'Yes?'

'Sula McGregor.' She stuck out a hand. The woman took it. '*Scots Today.*'

The woman threw it back with a loud tut. 'For goodness' sake, how do you people find me? I've said before, many times, I do not speak to the press.'

'I'm sorry about your son,' Sula said.

'Oh, are you?' she snapped, backing inside.

'Mrs McFarlay,' Sula called out. 'I know what you've been through.'

The door slammed. She saw the woman's reflection inside, leaning sideways against the wall.

'I know he was hard work,' Sula called out. 'Believe me, I've been there myself. But he was your son, and I know you want to know which bastard put him down that hole as much as I do.'

The door smacked open. Mrs McFarlay emerged, her cardigan held tight around her chest. Intelligent blue eyes sparkled with anger. 'Don't give me that. Your paper sells *advertising* off my boy's death.'

'I know it does,' Sula said. 'We can't survive if we don't. But that doesn't mean we can't conduct a thorough investigation for you and the other family. Was his death drug-related?'

'Oh, you . . .' Mrs McFarlay wrung her hands, with a bitter smile.

'There were no drugs found at the scene?'

'No,' the woman retorted. 'I don't know. He'd been clean for ten months.' Sula saw the fight go out of her, as if she'd been battered for so long she couldn't sustain a strong front.

'Ten months? So he was doing well?'

Mrs McFarlay sniffed. 'You know, your readers see boys like mine as scum. You print that photo of him from the police station next to David Pearce in his suit. That's all anyone cares about. People see it and they think Colin caused this. Caused that man's death, too. Colin was trying. Nobody knows how hard it is to stop. I didn't. Not till I saw him try.' She sniffed. 'And he did try.'

Sula nodded. 'Well, *I* know. And I know that ten months was him well on his way. And I'm sorry. It's a shame.'

The woman looked out into the hills, bewildered, as if she still couldn't understand how everything she'd worked for had come to this. A plain wee bungalow on a close full of strangers.

'Mrs McFarlay,' Sula said, 'I'm not going to lie to you. I'm after a story for my newspaper, but I'm not here to do you or your son over. I want the truth, too. Somebody did a bad thing to Colin *and* Mr Pearce, and I want to know why. That person is still out there. We need them caught.'

A man in overalls came out of the house next door and watched, curious.

'Oh, come in,' she said.

The kitchen was cold and soulless. The blue Formica table for one was empty. The sitting room next door was free of ornaments, just a thick novel and glasses on a coffee table by a fake gas fire. It was far from the sandstone villa with landscaped garden and sea views.

Mrs McFarlay made them tea.

'I know you've been asked this a hundred times,' Sula started, 'but do you have any idea if or how Colin and David Pearce knew each other?'

Mrs McFarlay stirred in sugar. 'No. I don't. I've told the police many times – I'd never heard of David Pearce.'

Her cheeks were stiff. Stretched. Sula recognized that look. She'd seen it on parents countless times in criminal trials, as if they'd gritted their jaws so many times at the failure and disappointment of their delinquent bairns the muscles had turned to shell.

'So not from Colin's school, or you and your husband's business? Not someone Colin met on the internet?'

'He sold his computer for drugs.' She said it defiantly, as if nobody in the real world with children and computers understood. 'I'll tell you what I told the police. I didn't know my son very well. After he left school, we hardly saw him. We didn't know his "friends", and most of the time, we didn't even know where he lived. Apart from when he was in prison, of course.'

'But he was at boarding school?' Sula said.

'Yes. That's where it all started. Some of these boys – the money they had.' She shook her head. 'Parents with no sense. One of Colin's friends had access to this big house up in the Highlands that his parents let him use when they were away. Colin begged us to let him go up to these weekend parties. We found out later about the drugs that were going on up there. Colin told me one of the boys had a gun. A handgun. He was impressionable. He wanted to fit in.'

'And the heroin?'

'Maybe when he was about seventeen. That's when he began to change. Drop out.'

'And that's why you had gates put in.'

She regarded Sula drily, picking at the wrapper for the sugar. 'One o'clock in the morning he'd come yelling, crying, doing anything to be let in. He knew we didn't want the neighbours disturbed, so we would. Morris couldn't take it. He'd be working all hours on the business and then come home to this.'

She drank her tea as if nothing tasted of anything anymore.

'You get to the point you can't take any more.' Her eyes

254

closed for a second or two. 'He was coming in when we were at work and stealing. We'd change the locks and he'd break in anyway, steal the radio, TV, chequebooks. He knew we wouldn't call the police. At one point, Morris and I rented out the house and ran the business from the Channel Islands for a year, just to get away. But he kept robbing the house, even when we had tenants in. He knew the way in at the back. Or he'd rob the neighbours' houses. He was stealing from our family, from our friends. My daughter moved her family down to England to get away from it.'

'Did you try rehab?' Sula asked, guessing the answer.

'Did we? Six times. A place down in Cornwall, then one in Galloway. Couple more. Last one was in the Lake District. He was back on it each time within a month. That was when we gave up. Got the gates put in, let the neighbours put up with it for a while, and eventually he stopped.'

'So what changed?'

'Morris dying.' Mrs McFarlay stopped and breathed in and out slowly three times, as if a counsellor had taught her the technique. 'Colin came to me in a state, begged me to help him one more time. I said no, but I was scared of him, to be honest. Without Morris there. People don't know what that's like, to be scared of your own child. To see them intimidated by the people they think are their friends and not be able to stop it.'

'No,' Sula said. They didn't.

'I used every penny of our savings to send him for nine months this final time, to a place in Yorkshire. I did it just to get him away from me, really. I couldn't deal with it alone — it was bad enough with Morris here. But he came back a different boy. I think this time he really wanted off it. Saw what it had done to his dad. A drugs charity put him on a training course fixing bikes and he got a job doing that. Found a room in a hostel.'

'So he wasn't dealing anymore?'

'No, I believe not. He was talking about getting into college and redoing his Highers. He was a bright boy, could have done anything. Morris always wanted him to take over the business. He never quite gave up on that.' She stopped and did the breathing exercise again, pain etched into her features. 'The funny thing was, our finances were in a bit of a mess, because of the business, when Morris died. Colin tried to help me out with it, like a real son. He'd taken every penny I had, and now he was trying to protect me.'

There was a catch in her throat. She rubbed loose skin on her arm. Sula guessed the weight had fallen off her recently.

'Mrs McFarlay, have you got any photos of Colin, before all this happened?'

She shot Sula a scathing look.

'OK,' Sula said, raising a hand. 'I know what you're thinking and I'm going to be frank. The shot of Colin in the newspapers – his arrest shot. Nobody cares about that boy. You know as well as I do they're glad there's less scum on the streets to sell their bairns drugs.'

The woman flinched, but Sula carried on.

'Now, you give me a photo of Colin before this happened, the wee boy that you've told me about, and those same people will see a victim. A wee boy, just like theirs, who became a victim of something bad that could get their kids, too. You tell me about him, before all this happened, and I'll write it up. A story about an ordinary boy from a good family, who fell into bad times, but worked hard to get out. Who tried to make amends and help his mother. I write it. You take control of the way people see your son, and who knows – you might just jog a bit of sympathy somewhere. Somebody might take the time to think of a detail that helps the police with what happened up on that cliff.'

Mrs McFarlay stared at her, and for a moment, Sula didn't know if it had worked or she was about to be thrown out. Then the woman got up without speaking. She returned with a primary-six school photo of a boy with blond curly hair, a shy, cheeky smile and eyes full of fun.

'Aw, look at that,' Sula said, lifting her glasses. 'Those curls.'

'Morris had them, too,' Mrs McFarlay said. A smile started at her lips, then puttered out.

Sula stayed for another hour, interviewing Mrs McFarlay about her son, Colin, until she had enough for a double-page exclusive. Before she left, Mrs McFarlay handed her three more photos, of the family of four on holiday in Spain, Colin on his dad's back in the sea, Colin playing football for the local youth team and then sitting on Mrs McFarlay's knee, aged five, birthday chocolate on both their faces.

'Don't make me regret this,' she said, letting the photos go.

'I can't promise that,' Sula said, 'but I can promise I'll write what you tell me.'

Mrs McFarlay's eyes searched Sula's. 'You said you understood. What I'd been through?'

Sula put the photos in her bag, and opened the front door.

'It would be a sorry thing to lie about,' Mrs McFarlay said.

Sula headed down the driveway. 'It certainly would, Mrs McFarlay.'

Back at the car, she found a furious man pointing at the 'No parking' sign she'd blocked, and got in muttering, 'OK, OK, keep your hair on, pal.'

Leaning over to drop her bag on the passenger floor, she saw the pink Post-it phone message Ewan had taken, crumpled, unread, where she'd thrown it the other day.

How many times had that woman nearly let go of Colin? Thought it was the last time?

Those wee curls.

Ignoring the irate man, Sula picked up the note and wound down the window, to throw it out.

Mrs McFarlay appeared at the upstairs window of the bungalow.

Sula sighed and dropped it back on the seat.

CHAPTER FORTY-THREE

Edinburgh

The man sat on the stool in Mr Singh's storeroom, waiting.

He'd been waiting twenty-four hours now.

The husband from the flat upstairs would be coming back. There was no question about that. It was when, rather than if.

Music had started upstairs at ten last night, and continued till one. Through the window, he'd watched the tower block extinguish like a candle, then start to come alight again around 5 a.m.

The man sat, thinking about what had brought him here, and wondering how this would all end.

By mid-morning, his eyelids felt like anchors were attached. His body was raw and nervy with anticipation.

Unable to continue, he tore a crisp box in half, stood on his stool and placed a ripped sheet of it across the window. The storeroom fell into semi-darkness and he told himself he'd have to bear it.

His vision blurred again; his chest tightened. He must not cough. The husband could knock all he liked, but there would be no answer. No way to see inside now.

It was Sunday, too, so Mr Singh's nephew would be in the

shop today. Even if the husband asked him questions, the nephew would have no idea what he was talking about.

Headphones on, the TV droned on about an Italian pasta recipe. After a while, his limbs felt heavy, so he let them fall to the side.

He didn't mean to fall asleep, but he did.

Which meant he didn't hear the husband return.

'Whoa! Kent, you OK?'

The man shook awake. A tug at his head.

'Kent! Are you all right in there?'

Bewildered, he sat up.

The husband, Mac, his face split in a grin. He was tugging at the headphones.

'You OK? Need some help?'

The back door was open. To his horror, he realized he hadn't locked it last night when the husband came.

He'd slammed it shut and not locked it.

Fool.

'Didn't mean to give you a fright. Just knocked to see if you wanted a cup of tea,' the husband continued. 'Talking to Mr Singh in the shop yesterday. Says you're an old mate, crashing here for a while? Not to tell his missus or she'll go ape? No bother, Kent. Secret's safe with me. If I can help you out, let me know.'

The husband went in and out of focus. The man blinked, trying to breathe.

'Look at this,' the husband said. He pointed at the dot drawing on the wall. 'Who's this? Your girlfriend? Your wife?'

He touched it. Touched her. The curve of her cheek. The volcano started inside the man. He forced his hands down, to stop the eruption.

The husband laughed. 'I drew my wife once. Second year at high school, in art. She went nuts.' He grinned mischievously. 'I drew her like she was an alien. Put antennae on her.' At the window, he stood on the stool, pulled the cardboard away and checked the view, then replaced it. 'She was weird-looking, back then, though. I can say it now. We called her "Casper" at primary – like the ghost. She had these big, spooky eyes and white hair and a wee tiny white face.' He pinched his chin. 'Smooth, you know, like a sculpture? But then she changed overnight. You wouldn't believe it. Walked into school one day in fifth year and – pow! My heart's going . . .' His hand pumped his chest.

He jumped down, checked out the tiny toilet, then sat down on the stool and stretched out his legs. 'Between you and me, Kent, I'm a bit pissed off with her. She's back tonight from Amsterdam, so if you hear a row upstairs, apologies in advance. She's been over there, trying to find out who the dead guy was in our kitchen. Completely bloody obsessed with it. Can't let it go. Police says the guy fell and hit his head, but she thinks someone killed him.'

The volcano pushed up, a thunderous explosion, inside the man. He fought to control it.

'Oh, I forgot. You don't know about that, do you, Kent? You weren't here then, no? It was a weird business. Came back from honeymoon and found a dead guy lying in our kitchen. I was thinking last night, it would have been useful if you had been here. The police would've asked you, though, if you had been. Might have heard something.'

To control the volcano, the man knelt down, and began to draw a new page in his notebook. *Dot, dot, dot.*

'Is that how you do it?' the husband asked. 'Clever.' He sat back. 'Yeah, that would've been useful. Could get this thing cleared up quick so Grace can drop it.'

261

Dot, dot, dot.

'She's a photojournalist. Got it in her head to do a big story about it,' he continued. 'Between you and me – again – I feel sorry for her. At school, she had these dreams about being the big global reportage photographer and it's not worked out for her. Now she's got it in her head again – a sort of midlife crisis. They say it happens when your parents die.'

He stood up and stretched. 'Her mum died when she was sixteen. I stepped in. It's what you've got to do, isn't it? Step in. Now her dad's gone, too. It's just me.'

Dot, dot, dot.

He walked to the door. 'Right. That's me, Kent. Got a big day – restaurant opening tonight. But listen, you think of anything, you let me know.'

The man dotted his page, wanting to stick the pen in his eye.

CHAPTER FORTY-FOUR

Amsterdam

Two swans glided down the canal in Amsterdam, moving to the side as a two-seated boat puttered past. Grace stood at Nicu's kitchen window, trying to wake up, after two sleep-deprived nights and the long drive back from Paris. The cleaner Hugo and Magriet had arranged for Nicu had done a good job. The walls and floor had been scrubbed, the voile curtains washed. The sofa cover and red rug were missing, presumably at the cleaner's. A sorry pile of artwork and prints had not fared so well. They were waiting for assessment and repair.

From here, she could see Nicu through the bedroom door, asleep. She'd checked him every half-hour since she'd woken in the blue boat this morning. Dark shadows were smudged under his eyes; his injured arm was placed awkwardly to find relief, her marker-pen lines still in place, with no sign of spreading infection.

All night she'd woken intermittently at the sound of passing cars, and checked outside, but the canalside had been quiet. She prayed they'd lost whoever had been following them back in Paris. There had definitely been nobody behind them on the road last night.

Fear, exhaustion, Mac – everything inside her felt as if it had been tossed out of drawers and not put back yet.

There was one thing she did know, however.

Out on the deck, desolate and half bare now the burned plants had been removed, she rang a freelance photographer friend Jenny in Edinburgh, then texted Mac and John in the same message, to tell them Jenny would do John's restaurant opening tonight, and she was sorry. She turned off her phone, but not before deleting three new messages from Mac that had arrived last night and this morning.

She wasn't finished here.

He would have to deal with it.

Life carried on, on the canal. People read books and cycled, watered plants and chatted and smoked on their decks.

Flower baskets of vibrant colours hung from the bridge.

Right now, it was hard to imagine ever going home.

She wandered back into the boat, to make coffee. The cleaner had left a pile of singed papers from Nicu's damaged office on the floor. She leaned down to move them.

A smoke-damaged black-and-white photo sat on the top.

Checking for Nicu, she held it to the window. It was a woman, in her early thirties. There was a wildness about her. Thick, messy hair fell about her face. She was scowling, her lip curled like Elvis, a challenge in her eye.

The artist. Was this her? She slipped the photo back inside the papers.

CHAPTER FORTY-FIVE

Early afternoon, she left Nicu's painkillers by his bed with water, and asked Hugo and Magriet to check on him.

Climbing in his Jeep, she followed the satnav. Despite all the bike lanes to navigate, she managed to do a couple of diversions without knocking anything or anyone over and, satisfied she wasn't being followed, arrived at Lucian Grabole's former residence.

In the Jeep, she examined the 1994 arrest shot of François Boucher. Her pulse raced. In a few minutes, one piece of the puzzle would fit.

Lucian's apartment block was busier today. One resident sat in the front garden with a dog, drinking wine and reading a newspaper. A couple were heading out through the gate as she arrived, dressed smartly, she guessed for lunch.

Mitti waved her inside. 'Have you found something out about Lucian?' she asked, her hands clasped. 'Is it good news?'

Grace touched her arm. 'Mitti, this is going to be difficult. Would you sit down?'

Mitti fought back fresh tears. 'OK.' She found a chair.

'I have a photo I need to ask you to identify,' Grace said, 'but it's over twenty years old.'

She held out the 1994 arrest photo of François Boucher, and Mitti popped on her glasses.

'Could you tell me if this man is Lucian Grabole?'

The hall was filled with the heavy heartbeat of the grandfather clock.

Mitti thrust the photo away. 'Yes. It's Lucian.'

Grace tried not to react. 'You're sure – this is definitely Lucian Grabole, who lived here for a year?'

'Yes.' Mitti pointed at his cheeks. 'But it's not a kind photo. His face looks hard here. In real life, it is softer. He has a nice smile. More gentle in the eyes. His hair is longer now, too. But yes, this is definitely Lucian.'

The front door opened and the man with the newspaper nodded at Mitti, and headed upstairs with his dog.

Grace waited, dreading what she was about to do.

A door closed above them.

'Mitti?' She turned. 'I am so sorry, but this man's name is not Lucian Grabole. He's a Romanian criminal called Lucian Tronescu, and as far as we can work out, he was hiding from the Romanian authorities in France for about twenty years under another name – François Boucher. This is a police photo of him, taken when he was nineteen. He is a very unpleasant and dangerous man. A gangster. We know that he moved to Amsterdam two years ago, possibly to run a drugs route here from Marseilles. I think he lived in this house under a false name.'

Mitti's face boiled with anger. She stood up. 'Absolutely not! Incredible. This is not possible.' She flung up her hands. 'You keep saying these things about Lucian. He was my friend. He had a job. Every evening, I saw him leave for work – he had a van, with his ladders, everything. Selling drugs? No!' She held a tissue to her eyes.

Grace pointed around. 'But how could he afford to live here?'

Mitti sat back down with a whump on the stairs, like a sulking child. 'I don't know.' She waved the tissue. 'He paid his rent six months in advance. It wasn't my business to ask.'

Confusion and hurt entered her eyes, as she realized her answers simply made no sense.

'I'm so sorry,' Grace said. 'This must be a terrible shock. Is Dr De Jonker here? Could we maybe speak to him?'

Mitti sniffed and, without speaking, stood and led Grace upstairs. She knocked and a small, tidy man in horn-rimmed glasses and a smart jacket answered.

Mitti spoke in Dutch, her distress clear. 'Come in, please,' he said to her and Grace. 'Let me see if I can help.'

Her instincts had been right. Lucian Grabole's apartment would be beyond most people's pockets. It was expansive, with high ceilings, antique wood panelling and polished floors. The sitting room was vast, with a stately fireplace, and three tall picture windows overlooking the rear rose garden. Antique bookshelves lined the sitting room. Indian rugs lay on polished floors. Elegant objets d'art lined antique tables.

'You have a beautiful home,' Grace said.

'My mother's things, mostly,' Dr De Jonker said modestly. 'Now, how can I help?'

Mitti stood quiet and sad.

Grace explained. 'Mitti is very upset. I wanted to ask if you also met Lucian Grabole?'

'No. The apartment was empty when I arrived.'

'And Lucian didn't leave anything behind?'

He pointed to the bottom shelf. 'Just a few books, but nothing else.'

'What kind of books?' she asked.

'They were all in English.'

What was Lucian doing with English books?

'Really? What kind?'

'Well. A few novels. A dictionary and language tapes. A couple of children's books, and a cooking book.'

'Do you have them still?'

But the doctor's eyes were on Mitti. Her eyes were rheumy again with tears. 'Sorry, no.' He spoke in Dutch, and Mitti sat down.

'OK. Well, thank you. I'm sorry to disturb you,' Grace said. 'I just wanted to make sure that someone was keeping an eye on Mitti today. She's had a bad fright.'

'Of course,' he said kindly.

There didn't seem much more she could ask. She pointed to the rose garden. 'What a beautiful view to have in a city.'

Dr De Jonker smiled. 'Oh yes.' He spoke in Dutch again, and Mitti replied.

One word stood out to Grace's untrained ear. She held up a hand. 'I'm sorry – could you repeat that in English?'

The doctor nodded. 'I was reminding Mitti that I was lucky to find this apartment.'

The concierge nodded. 'That's right. You came to see Anna's apartment on the ground floor . . .'

'. . . and this one came free the same week. We weren't sure if the piano would come up the—'

'Anna?' Grace interrupted.

'Yes.' Mitti nodded. 'Anna lived on the ground floor. For three years.'

Grace froze. 'Did she have a son?'

'Yes. Valentin.'

Trying to stay calm, Grace pulled out the missing poster of Anna and Valentin. 'Mitti, is this them?'

Mitti took it. Fear crossed her face, and she dropped it. 'How do you have this? What is happening here?' she wailed.

Dr De Jonker fetched some water. They waited till she'd drunk it.

Grace knelt down. 'Mitti, I'm sorry, but when I was here last time, I asked you if Lucian's wife, Anna, lived here and you said no.'

Mitti pointed at the missing poster, with a befuddled frown. '*This* Anna, you mean? *This* Anna was not Lucian's wife.'

'But she's Romanian?'

'Who has told you these things?' Mitt exclaimed, hand flying. 'Anna is Danish. A paediatrician at the central hospital. She was never Lucian's wife! Why would you say that?'

'A doctor?' Grace persevered. 'Mitti, what was her surname?'

'Johanssen.'

'Johanssen? And she and Lucian definitely weren't together?'

'No!' Mitti cried, crinkled fingers visibly shaking now. 'They were just neighbours. They spoke in the hall, or in the garden. Yes, maybe Lucian made the tree swing in the garden for Valentin, but . . .' The tone of her voice drifted into doubt, then returned, cracked and defensive. 'But Lucian was friendly with *everyone*. We *all* liked him.'

Grace persisted. 'But Anna and Valentin moved out the same week?'

A shadow of doubt entered Mitti's eyes. 'Well, yes. Anna was offered a job in Copenhagen. Lucian left to look after his mother in Bucharest.'

She spoke anxiously in Dutch again, and the doctor patted her arm.

Grace tried again. 'Mitti, no one's come here recently, have they, asking to speak to Lucian or Anna, or to ask about me?'

Mitti shook her head. That was something at least.

Grace stood up. 'OK. Listen, please don't worry. We are getting closer to the truth, and the police will speak to you, I'm sure, when we know more. Please bear with me till then. Do you have a forwarding address for Anna?'

Mitt stood up, flustered. 'Yes.'

The doctor helped her to the door, and promised to keep an eye on Mitti. Grace followed the concierge to the ground-floor apartment. It was a modest flat, in comparison, but with a comfortable rear sitting room. Mitti rifled through a drawer to retrieve a Copenhagen address. With it came a brown envelope.

'This arrived for Anna only recently,' she said. 'I forwarded it to Copenhagen, but it was returned. Will you visit Anna now? Will you take it?'

It was a brown business envelope, with a typed address label and a London postmark.

'Of course,' Grace said, knowing she now needed to do one of the most difficult things she'd ever done.

She explained her request to Mitti.

For a moment, she thought the concierge might fly at her.

Instead, she acquiesced quietly.

Grace led her to the window. Then she photographed Mitti from behind, looking into the rose garden, the pain of her confusion and betrayal visible in the fingers clamped behind her back, and the sagging shoulders.

'Mitti, I'm leaving Amsterdam soon,' Grace said, packing up, 'but here is the number of a friend of mine, Nicu. If anyone asks about me or Lucian, in the next few days, please ring him.'

Feeling bad for the pain she'd caused, Grace said goodbye with another hug and returned to the Jeep, checking around for the gold car. The road was clear. She placed Anna's forwarding address on the seat and rang Ewan.

'Hey – whassup?'

She explained about Mitti and the positive ID.

'Good God, missus – this is spectacular. Help! I've created a story monster.'

'So, Ewan?'

'Yes.'

'Can I go to Copenhagen?'

CHAPTER FORTY-SIX

Edinburgh

Back in the *Scots Today* office, quiet today with just the skeleton Sunday news crew working on Monday's paper, Sula returned from the stationery cupboard with her cigarettes, eyeballing the old fanny at the PA's desk frowning at her, and waited for Ewan to get off the phone.

'Ewan, enough!' she shouted. 'Let that lassie do her own work. That's the second out-of-date address you've got me for Colin McFarlay and his mother. Banister Road, and now that place she sold last October in South Queensferry. Sort it out.'

He put down the phone, not listening.

'What?'

'Grace's story. It's going mad.'

She rapped the desk. 'I'm not bothered about that. I've just told you that . . .'

'No, but she says—'

'Ewan. Do I look interested?'

'No, but—'

'Well then, will you *shut up*!'

Her assistant went pale and sat back. 'I'm telling my mum on you,' he muttered.

She took a breath. Reminded herself Joanne wasn't this daft bugger's fault.

'Right,' she said, dropping her tone. 'What I'm thinking is, when this person or people put David Pearce and Colin McFarlay down this hole, why did they do it? There's a bloody sign on the fence, telling you how deep it is. It's not that deep. They know this is a route that dog walkers and hikers use. Why put the bodies somewhere concealed, knowing it's just a matter of time before someone finds them? They hadn't even tried to cover them with something. At some point, they must have known somebody was going to notice the smell.'

Ewan stretched back, his pigeon chest broadening momentarily. 'What if he wanted someone to find the bodies?'

'Why?'

'Say it was gangland. Send out a message. Nobody wants to die that way, do they? Gives them a few months' breathing space to set up alibis, clean crime scenes. No forensics left after three months outdoors – footsteps, car tracks, witnesses'll have forgotten everything.'

Sula's brow wrinkled. 'So if that's right, and they wanted them to be found to send out a message, what do these guys have in common to get them into trouble?'

'Drugs. Debts. Gambling? The usual.'

A thought hit her. 'Hang on. Mr Pearce Senior told me his sons were furious he'd sold his house. How much did he sell it for?'

'What was the address again?' Ewan checked his notes. 'Two hundred and thirteen thousand. Last June.'

'How long did he own it?'

'Bought it 1958. Rented it out when they were in Australia, then moved back in when they got back to Scotland in 1972.'

'So we're guessing his mortgage was paid off. Two hundred

grand in the bank. That's a lot of money.' She typed into her own computer. 'What about 66 Bowling Road, South Queensferry?'

Ewan bashed away. 'One point two million.'

'And that's her sitting in a wee bungalow in Stirling?' Sula frowned.

'So where's all the money?'

'She said they had business debts,' Sula replied. 'And all that private rehab doesn't come cheap.' She pointed at her notes. 'Find out how much Brown Oaks Nursing Home in Colinton costs a month.'

'Will they tell me that if I ring up?' Ewan said, unconvinced.

'Say you're asking for your elderly mother.'

'What if we just go up there and say you're my elderly mother? Get them to show us round?'

'Oh, you're funny, son.'

'Actually, my mum says I'm *very* funny,' Ewan said, tapping away. 'And *very* special.'

'You said it. Keep looking.' Sula picked up her cigarettes and headed back to the cupboard. Somewhere out there was a link and she could almost see it. It was that close.

CHAPTER FORTY-SEVEN

Amsterdam

Grace parked the Jeep back on the canal, checking again for the gold car, then stopped to pat Nicu's ginger cat, thinking about what she'd discovered. It fell on its back this time, and she stroked it. The air smelt of summer, of possibility.

Nicu's bed was empty, the back door open. Through the boat window, she saw him, beer in hand, on his laptop. He was showered. A denim shirt covered his bandages and bruising. Despite the angry grazes and swelling on his face, he seemed brighter, more alert.

'Oi. Is that a good idea with concussion?' she called through.

'There's more in the fridge,' he said, eyes on the screen.

Just for a second, she allowed herself to imagine this was her life, and recalled the envy she'd felt seeing the photo of the girl in his things, and knew it was a good thing she was leaving tomorrow.

'So Lucian Grabole is definitely Lucian Tronescu stroke François Boucher? It's all the same guy?' Nicu said, when he came in to cook.

'Yes, according to Mitti,' she said, sipping her beer. 'So now we just need DNA from a police match, or an e-fit to match his

275

photo, to prove he's definitely the dead man in my flat. Then I need to find Anna to establish why he was in Edinburgh. Then I need to verify the official stuff here, and in Romania and Paris. Maybe after all that, we'll know why he was in my flat, and what the note meant.'

The alcohol took the edge off the adrenalin rush of the past two days. She helped Nicu lift down a heavy casserole dish. 'I feel awful for Mitti,' she said. 'Lucian tricked her for a whole year. It sounds like Anna ran because she suddenly became terrified of him.'

'Maybe she witnessed him commit a crime,' Nicu said, finding an onion. 'Or even just picked up his mail, saw "François Boucher" on it? Then he tried to shut her up and she did a runner – maybe to Edinburgh.'

Grace took the onion off him to cut. 'I'm going to Copenhagen tomorrow to find out where she is, or where she went.'

Nicu drank his beer. 'You know I can't come.' He motioned at his shoulder. 'I need to get this rested for Colombia.'

'No, I know.'

'You'll be fine.'

'I know. I'm just going for one day. I'll fly home from there. So no more chance of night-time car chases on my own.'

He threw her onion into the pot with one hand, then spices, and the delicious smell of something she'd never tasted filled the kitchen. She looked out onto this canal that she was starting to love, realizing that after tomorrow she might never see this place or him again.

They ate late on the deck, then opened a bottle of wine and sat by the water. A piece of wood floated past, a bird's nest on it.

'God, I envy your life,' she said, no longer caring what he thought, now she was leaving tomorrow.

'What about it?'

'The freedom to live like this. Travel like this. Live anywhere you want.'

He motioned with his wine glass. 'What's stopping you?'

She stretched out. 'Me, probably. I just never did it.'

He leaned back on a giant plant pot, his legs stretched out near hers. 'Well, you're doing it now.'

She pursed her lips. 'Trust me, just once has caused enough trouble.'

'At home?'

She sat back beside him. 'Mac doesn't like me being away. He never has. And he hates travelling. The only way I got him to Thailand was by lying. I told him my dad had bought us a surprise honeymoon before he died.'

'So again. You did it – that's travelling.'

She made a face. 'Sitting on the beach and doing organized excursions to a temple and a night market?' She shook her head. 'I managed to get him to one of those backpacker areas in Bangkok, where everyone sits around talking about where they're going next and perfect beaches and meeting other travellers. We were on our own, eating our tea in our holiday outfits. Honestly, we were like pensioners playing bingo.'

'I couldn't deal with that.'

She bristled with historic protectiveness towards Mac. 'I'm not saying he stops me. Not physically. I just let myself get talked out of things.'

'Then don't,' he shrugged.

It was easy for him to say.

As night fell, they lowered their voices. She told him about her dad bringing her up after her mum died, and her first photography job after college 'piling people up' for a family photographer in

277

Edinburgh, who liked to take quirky portraits of them leaning into each other on the floor, arms around each other, like a boy band. Nicu was, predictably, scathing. She started to laugh till her sides ached, as he came up with a system of weighing each family member and putting the heaviest on the bottom, layering them up in flat piles.

As the temperature dropped, he fetched blankets and they talked on after midnight, her quizzing him about his travels and New Zealand.

'Don't you miss your family over there?' she whispered as Hugo and Magriet's lights went off.

'I go home for a month at a time, so I probably see as much of them as if I lived there. They come and stay. My sister's coming when I get back from Bogotá.'

'But don't you miss belonging somewhere? That's what scares me. Not having friends or family around if you need them.'

He poured them both more wine. 'There's a community here. You saw it after the fire. Some of the guys sorted the tarpaulin. Hugo and Magriet took the cat. Kiki and Madra helped with the deck. I do the same for them.'

She smiled, the wine loosening her tongue.

'What?'

'The night I arrived, I didn't know this was a garden. I thought Kiki and Madra were in your bedroom.'

It took him a minute. 'Hang on. You thought I was getting it on with both of them – you'd stumbled on a den of iniquity.'

She giggled, and he punched her arm gently.

'God, they'll love that. No, trust me, anyone goes near Madra and Kiki would have them.'

*

The moon shot a white streak down the inky water. They moved closer to hear each other in the still canal, as they discussed more photographers they liked.

At one point, Nicu went in and brought out a stack of photobooks, and a lantern. They lay back against the pot and flicked through, discussing them. At the end was a portfolio of his own photos from America.

'My first project after college in New Zealand – I did it on the way to London,' he said. 'Flew to LA and drove across America staying in a tent. I photographed people on campsites, asked them why they were there.'

'Weren't they just on holiday?' she teased.

He rolled his eyes. 'This guy was good.' He pointed at a photo of a man with a beard leaning on a camping table, smiling, an unnatural brightness in his eyes. A Great Dane leaned beside him. 'He was in his early sixties and his wife had just died. His parents were in their eighties. They'd bought a camper van and were taking him – and his dog – on a six-month trip to help him get through the worst.'

'That's really moving,' Grace said. She flicked on to a photo of two middle-aged women in bikini tops and shorts. They had similar scars on their bodies.

'These two met every year – they were strangers.' Nicu pointed. 'She donated a kidney to her. They went camping one weekend a year together to celebrate it.'

'Wow.'

'You should do this.'

'What?' she said, topping up their glasses.

'Take a month out. Three months. Go somewhere on your own. Do one project. Give a story the chance to breathe.'

She picked at a leaf. 'Nicu. You just shut up the boat, give the cat to Hugo and Magriet. Go. Get paid. I can't.'

'People who are successful in this business have to make it happen. They find the stories. Shoot them. Sell them. Hope to get commissioned again.'

A low moan and creaking drifted out of Hugo and Magriet's boat. Grace and Nicu's eyes met, aghast. She put a hand over her mouth, as a giggle burst out. Nicu threw a blanket over her head, and kept her there, in a headlock, till she stopped.

As the night drifted on, she lay on her front, and told him about Mac, the boy at high school everyone fancied, and how lucky her friends like Anne-Marie considered she was to snare him.

'So you've only been with each other?' Nicu asked.

'*Been* with. Yes.' She checked his reaction. 'Oh God. You look horrified.'

'No, no.' He caught her hand. 'I didn't mean that. I just. No, it's cool. Loyal,' he said, grimacing.

She sat up. 'It's OK. I can tell you think it's a horrendous idea.' She sipped her wine, thinking she should stop soon.

'No. I just . . . Are you not curious?'

She punched his arm. 'I'm not answering that. And, actually, to be precise, *I* haven't been with anyone else; he has.'

'When?'

'Last July.'

'Shit.'

She screwed up her face. 'I haven't told anyone this.'

He rolled onto his side, shifting his injured shoulder. 'What happened?'

'He told me he freaked out that I'd be the only person he'd slept with. He met this girl in a club.'

'Then what?'

'We had a huge fight for weeks. We were in the middle of trying to sort it out when I found out my dad's illness was terminal. He was so worried about me being on my own, as he called it. So Mac proposed in front of him, in this grand gesture of apology, and I said yes.'

'But you didn't want to?'

'I wanted to make my dad happy before he died. I thought it would work out.'

'Did it?'

She emptied her glass. 'I've been with him since I was sixteen.'

They fell into silence.

The deck drifted gently, till the clouds broke pink above the bridge and the dawn arrived. By now they were wrapped in the blankets, huddled for warmth.

'Now you've got to tell me,' Grace said. 'About the artist girl?'

Nicu stiffened.

She nudged him. 'What's her name?'

'Lou.'

'How did you meet?'

'Same gallery in New York.'

'And why did you split up?'

He poured the last of the wine, emptying the bottle. 'Because I came back from a work trip to South Africa and she'd taken an overdose.'

She sat up. 'Oh God. Nicu, I'm sorry. Because you left?'

'No. Because it's what she wanted to do. She was an amazing painter, really fucking talented, but there was always a price for it. It was always on the cards. She'd tried it before.'

'When was this?'

'Three years ago. That's when I moved on – came here for a job and decided to stay.' He shut his eyes.

'Were you angry with her?' Grace asked carefully.

'As I said, it was always on the cards.'

'But were you angry with her?'

A long pause. His words came out clipped. 'Yes, Grace, I was angry with her.'

She prodded his leg. 'Sorry. Are there any of her paintings in the boat?'

'No. They're in storage.'

'Why?'

His eyes stayed shut. 'Because that's where I want them.'

The pink light turned white. Traffic started on the bridge, and a sadness gripped her. It was tomorrow. The day she was leaving.

Grace fetched water for them, and returned to find Nicu's camera lens trained on her.

'Don't you dare.'

'Come here.' He pulled her down, then with a blanket still round her head, began to shoot her. At first she was self-conscious, waving him away. Then he asked her about her story, and Mitti, and what she was going to do next, and she relaxed. She looked in the lens, telling him with her eyes what she couldn't to his face.

'Here.' Nicu pulled her back inside his blanket, to show her the images.

Their hair touched. The blanket fell off his bad shoulder, so she leaned across to pull it over. She wasn't sure whose lips found whose on the way back, but she knew it was her who pulled him up and led him into the boat.

CHAPTER FORTY-EIGHT

Edinburgh

'Kent! Kent!'

The man jerked awake, and tried to push down his sleeping bag.

Somebody was banging on the back door.

What was happening now?

His heart hammering, he rolled over onto all fours and stood up.

'Kent,' the husband shouted through the door. 'Got a minute?'

The clock said 6.01 a.m.

Wrapping his blanket around him, the man unlocked the door. The music upstairs had gone on till 2 a.m., and it looked like the husband hadn't slept since. There was a greasy sheen on his pale skin; his hair was pushed sideways. There was a belligerent look in his bloodshot eyes. He smelt of alcohol.

'Sorry to wake you, Kent. Have you got a smoke? Run out.'

The man shook his head.

The husband pushed in past him and made his way to a box of cigarette cartons. 'Ah, that's what I need. Tell Mr Singh I'll pay him back later.'

The man stood against the wall, imagining hitting him from behind.

The husband swayed a little. 'Wife didn't come back last night, Kent. Supposed to be doing the press photos for my boss's new restaurant, and she didn't bloody turn up. Still out there trying to find this dead guy's family. I'm getting to that point, man . . . I'm . . .' He lifted his finger, then gave up.

He opened the cigarettes and threw down the wrapper. 'You know, I've been thinking. When we had a party a few months ago, Grace said she saw lights down here. That wasn't you, no?'

A tremor broke through him.

The man shook his head.

'Sure?'

The husband repeated the question. ''Cos it seems weird, you know, you just turning up like this.' He swivelled round as if trying to remember which way the backyard was.

Then as quickly as he'd come, he walked out. 'Right, that's me. Off to get myself ready for the day, but I'll pop down later.'

He slammed the door.

The man stared after him. Another tremor followed, almost tearing him in two.

CHAPTER FORTY-NINE

Amsterdam

Her phone alarm woke Grace three hours after she fell asleep in Nicu's bed.

Light footsteps walked across the boat's ceiling.

Nicu lay beside her, his body warm and tangled up with hers under the cover, the sensation of it still unfamiliar and intriguing. She ran a hand down her side, remembering his touch on her. Her body felt raw and tender and new.

There was a small thud and the heron flew off past the window.

Unfathomable.

Another day of a new world, when nothing would ever be the same.

She watched Nicu sleep. Although she wanted to wake him, fall into him again, to talk for ten more hours, she knew this wasn't the time. Her plane left in three hours.

Groggy, she crept next door, showered, dressed and packed up. Then she returned and shot him sleeping with his Polaroid, and found a pen.

As she decided what message to write, a thought entered her head.

She imagined writing, *That woman is not me Grace Scott.*

In the light of last night, of these last few days, in the heightened focus of sleep deprivation, the phrase shifted around in her mind.

New perspectives attached to it.

I am no *longer* Grace Scott.

I was *never* Grace Scott.

I am *not who people think I am*. Signed, *Grace Scott*.

Lost in thought, she pulled on her rucksack, left the Polaroid on his pillow, kissed him gently on the shoulder, then let herself out and, checking around her one last time for the gold car, walked to the end of Lindenkade to hail a taxi.

As it headed to the airport, her chest constricted with the pain of leaving him.

This was not the right time, in so many ways, she told herself.

At Schiphol Airport, she checked in, a shiver running through her body each time she thought about Nicu's touch last night, or sensed the faint smell of him on her clothes.

She was heading for security when her phone buzzed.

A photo came by text. It was one he'd taken at dawn. Her expression, framed by a blanket, was strong and striking. There was a new definition and sureness in her eyes she didn't recognize. The text simply said, 'Scott in the Centre . . . Nx.'

Pain and sweetness welled up together.

She forced herself through the security barrier, so there was no way back.

CHAPTER FIFTY

Edinburgh

Sula had done her sums, which is why she was sitting in the car park of the Brown Oaks Nursing Home from 11 a.m., waiting.

According to Mr Pearce Senior, David Pearce's wife and brother, Philip, were due to arrive in Edinburgh from Australia that weekend.

Sula gave them twenty-four hours to recover and speak to the police this Monday morning, but not enough time for any other bugger to sneak in there and grab her exclusive.

Sure enough, early lunchtime, DS Foley drove up and let out a man and woman, with the granite faces of the bereaved.

'Mr Pearce? Mrs Pearce?' she called across as they walked to reception.

She held out a card. 'Sula McGregor from *Scots Today*. Have you got a minute?'

'Go on, Diane,' the man said, waiting. Mrs Pearce passed through the double doors.

The man looked like his brother, with a beard, but better-looking; the more popular, younger one, Sula guessed.

He motioned her close. His voice was thick with menace. 'If I catch you near my father again, I'm going to take you and your paper to court for harassment. He's an eighty-seven-year-old man with a heart condition whose son's been murdered, and you slip in here pretending you're the police. What the hell is wrong with you?'

'I'm trying to find out about your father's house sale,' she said. 'Was he in debt, to a loan shark or . . . ?'

The brother's face turned livid. His cheeks shook as he spoke, spit flying. 'Let me make myself clear. You are scum, and if I find you here again . . . Actually, don't worry about the police – I will pay someone to remove you. Do you understand me? I will pay for someone to remove you from this place in a way that will make you think long and hard about harassing another family like mine ever again.'

Sula didn't move, wondering if he'd ever met the kind of people – as she had – who would actually carry out a threat like that. 'I am trying to help you find your brother's killer.'

He laughed bitterly. 'The police will find my brother's killer, not you, you fucking moron.'

'Mr Pearce.' Sula held up her phone, the recorder timer ticking. 'I'm sorry for you. I really am. It was a terrible way for your brother to go. And your dad seems like a nice man. It's a shame. But a word of advice. If you're going to threaten someone, don't choose someone who records conversations for a living.'

She held out her card again. 'If you want to talk to me.'

For a moment, she thought he was going to go for her. It wouldn't be the first time. Instead, he ripped it and dropped it on the ground.

'Your dad's got one if you change your mind,' she called, walking away. 'And by the way, your dad? He's eighty-eight.'

CHAPTER FIFTY-ONE

Copenhagen

Grace's plane descended across the green-and-yellow fields of Denmark, then banked round to land. Ranks of giant wind turbines spread across the sea like a defending army, alongside a modern bridge that stretched miles across the water, she guessed to Sweden. Tiny white sailboats whipped along.

Six hours – the time she had to find Anna Johanssen, before her flight home tonight.

Grabbing her rucksack from the luggage belt, she asked directions to Kystbanen, the coastal train line.

The journey north took almost an hour. Another message arrived from Mac, and she again deleted it without listening, consumed by guilt. Not wanting to think about him right now.

She couldn't.

Her mind drifted between the red-tiled houses and trees of the flat landscape, to her night with Nicu, to the mystery of Anna and Valentin. If Mitti knew Anna was living in Copenhagen, why didn't Lucian? Why had he searched for them in London and Edinburgh?

She alighted the train at Humlebæk, and walked a kilometre down a quiet residential road, following signs for an art museum. The white building appeared on a promontory, with views over the blue-grey sea. She found the path down below it, following her phone GPS. The little beach was busy, children playing in the water and hanging off the landing stage with sticks. The path continued for five minutes, the houses spreading out, until she found the address. It was a spectacular house. The home of an industrialist. A white four-storey nineteenth-century wedding cake of a house, with a grey Gothic fairy-tale turreted roof, gold-painted windows and a teetering bell tower atop. At the gate, she readied herself. There was no room for mistakes. If Anna Johanssen was here, she could be the key, finally, to the mystery of the man in her kitchen.

She photographed the house and the view, the path and the gate. With Mitti's letter retrieved from her bag, and her voice recorder switched on, she then rang the intercom. Faint classical music sounded, and a voice answered in Danish. A woman. She sounded older than Grace expected.

'Hello? I've come to see Anna Johanssen.'

An aria drifted through the intercom.

'Who are you?' The voice was suspicious.

'My name's Grace Scott. I've been asked to bring Anna a letter by a friend in Amsterdam.'

'There is a letterbox by the gate.'

Click. The music shut off.

She pushed the bell again. The aria returned.

'No, I'm here to deliver it personally to Anna. Is she here, please?'

Click.

She checked up at the windows, and rang the bell a third time. To her relief, a side door opened at the basement level of the house. A woman in her sixties, slender, in a smart shirt and skirt, hurried down the path, glancing back up at the house. From here, Grace could see her face was strained, grey-blonde hair pulled back in a fierce bun. She made no eye contact as she approached, pressed a release button and walked through the gate.

'Hi,' Grace started. 'Thanks for com—'

But the woman didn't stop. She grasped Grace's arm and led her along the path behind a bush. Close up, the woman's blue eyes were dulled by a yellow film; sagging skin clung tight to a clenched jaw. The harsh lines on her upper lip looked as if they'd been combed through her skin. 'Who are you?'

'I'm a photojournalist, from a Scottish newspaper,' Grace said, removing her elbow from the woman's grasp. She gave her a business card. 'Sorry – can I ask who you are?'

'Why are you looking for Anna?'

'To bring her this letter, from her apartment in Amsterdam. It was returned. And also because I'm writing a story about her neighbour in Amsterdam.'

The woman's lips stiffened into a pout.

'He was called Lucian Grabole?' Grace said.

Now, the woman's eyelid twitched uncontrollably and she put a finger on it. 'No.' She catapulted the word at Grace.

'No?'

A couple appeared from behind the bush with two Labradors. Momentarily, her stance softened, till they passed.

'No,' she repeated.

'Why no?'

The woman held up a hand. 'I have nothing more to say.' She walked back to the gate.

'Well, could you ask Anna to speak to me?' Grace said, following.

The woman strode inside. 'I am the family spokesperson, Anna's aunt. We do not speak to the press.'

To the press? Others had been here before?

Grace stood her ground. 'I'm sorry. I've come a long way and I do need to speak to Anna.'

The woman slammed the gate shut and returned to the house.

Grace called out, 'If you don't help me, I'll wait here till someone does. Till Anna comes home or leaves the house. I can wait all night, if necessary.' She pointed after the couple with the dogs, who'd entered the next property. 'And I'll speak to your neighbours to see if they know where she is. And please don't threaten me with the police. Lucian Grabole is part of a police investigation in Scotland, therefore it is in the public interest for me to come and speak to you.' She had no idea if that held sway in Denmark, but guessed the woman didn't either.

The woman disappeared back into the house.

'Shit,' Grace muttered.

Up on the promontory, in the distance, three women who looked like sisters sat in the garden of the art museum, by a bronze abstract Henry Moore figure, looking out. She followed their eyes out into the pale blue smudge where water and sky met.

Four and a half hours till her flight back.

In front of the house was a tree stump. She sat on it.

Someone inside that house knew something.

It was half an hour later when the old man appeared at the upstairs window. He had white hair and the unnerving stare of a person who had no idea of its effect on the watcher. At first, she thought he was short, then from the way he moved between windows to get a better view guessed he was in a wheelchair. His mouth was opening and shutting.

The basement door opened and the woman strode back.

'Will you please leave?'

Grace lifted her arms. 'I'm sorry, I can't. I want to speak to Anna.'

The woman approached. 'Anna is dead.'

At first, Grace nearly laughed at this ridiculous attempt to make her leave. Then she saw it in the woman's terse expression. It wasn't anger – it was *pain*.

'Anna Johanssen is dead?'

A sharp nod.

'Oh God, I'm so sorry. What happened?'

Disgust ignited in the woman's eyes at the insinuation that Grace knew or cared about Anna. 'I will give you one minute and then you *will* leave, and if you don't, I *will* call the police. My brother is ill and you are harassing him.'

Grace decided not to waste her minute arguing, and switched on her recorder.

'No recorder,' the woman snapped.

Grace took out a pen and notebook instead. 'Could you tell me what happened?'

Anna's aunt's statement was flat, as if she'd given it before. 'Anna and Valentin Johanssen were in a car accident before Christmas in America.'

Valentin too?

'Where in America?'

'Florida. They were visiting Anna's mother. In Miami.'

'Right. So when you say killed . . . ?'

The woman looked out to the sea. 'A car accident. They were hit by a truck at a crossroads.'

Another accident.

'This might sound like a strange question,' Grace asked carefully, 'but it was definitely an accident?'

The woman's gunpowder gaze returned to her. 'What are you talking about?'

'The police didn't question it?'

'No.' Her eyelid twitched uncontrollably again. 'No. Anna missed a red light and was hit by a truck. They were going to the supermarket. An American food truck leaving the same supermarket. It was Anna's fault. The driver had . . . What do you call it? A video camera in his windscreen for insurance, that filmed it?'

'A dash cam?'

'Yes. There was no doubt. It was Anna's fault.'

A rap of glass. The old man at the window.

'Is that Anna's father?' Grace said. 'Is it possible I could—'

'No!' The aunt's anger flared again. 'My brother has lost his daughter and grandson. Show respect.'

Grace judged that her time was running out. 'Anna knew a man called Lucian Grabole.'

The aunt's face hardened.

'I can tell that you know who I am talking about. I need to find out what Anna knew about him. I believe he was hunting for Anna and Valentin before Christmas. Can you tell me why?'

The window rapped again.

'You need to go.'

'No. Please,' Grace said. 'I can't.'

An insistent beat on the glass now.

Muttering, Anna's aunt took out a mobile, rang it, spoke to someone in Danish, then asked for Grace's pen and paper. She wrote a number and gave it to her. 'Go to ree-eed. Ask for Dr Karen Molson.'

'Sorry – "ree-eed"?'

Flustered, the woman wrote, *Riget*, on a piece of paper, and pronounced it again like 'ree-eed'. 'A hospital in Copenhagen.' She spelled out its formal name, Rigshospitalet, then a street address.

'Go now, please.' She returned through the gate.

'But who's Karen Molson?' Grace called.

The old man began to bash the glass. *Bang, bang, bang.*

'See what you are doing!' Anna's aunt rushed towards the basement door.

The man wheeled himself to the middle window, as if trying to get a better view.

In his eyes, Grace now saw a terrible fury.

It was only when Grace was back on the train south to Copenhagen that she realized she still had the forwarded letter from Mitti.

She alighted at Østerport Station in northern Copenhagen, and followed her GPS on foot for ten minutes down streets of willow trees and alongside a pretty city lake, lined with residential flats, and bustling with cyclists and joggers, towards a large park and a modern hospital. This time, she switched on her phone voice recorder and stuck it in her pocket, then rang Karen Molson.

A tall woman with pale red hair and freckles was waiting for her five minutes later at the entrance door, a pack of cigarettes in her hand.

'Here,' she said, pointing at a low wall round the corner. The roses behind were the same colour as her hair. 'I have five minutes.'

'OK,' Grace said, putting down her phone. 'I'm sorry. I'm not sure why I'm here.'

'Herr Johanssen's sister is the family spokesperson. He is ill, so she's asked me to speak to you instead.'

'OK, thanks. So you knew Anna?' Grace asked.

'Yes. She was an old friend from medical school.'

Grace got straight to the point. 'I'm researching Lucian Grabole. Did she ever talk to you about him?'

The doctor lit a cigarette and blew out smoke. It looked odd on someone in a white coat. 'Why are you asking?'

'Because I'm trying to track down his movements. Lucian Grabole was a pseudonym for a Romanian criminal who operated out of Paris. I know he and Anna were neighbours in Amsterdam. I'm trying to find out why he was hunting for her in London and Scotland. Why he told people she was his wife.'

'His wife?'

'Yes. Was Anna in danger from him? Her Dutch concierge said that she left suddenly, the same week that Lucian did. Do you know why? Did she witness a crime?'

Karen tapped ash.

'Was that it?' Grace pushed. 'She was in hiding from him.'

Karen sighed. 'No. No. Anna wasn't his wife, but they did have a relationship.'

Grace stared. 'A romantic one?'

'Yes. For about a year.'

An ambulance drew up, and the doctor glanced over as if assessing if she'd be needed. 'You know who Anna's father is?'

'An industrialist?'

'Yes. A very rich one. Very powerful. Very controlling. She took a job in Amsterdam to remove herself from his influence.'

'And met Lucian?'

'Yes. He was very –' Karen Molson broke off to do a muscleman pose '– tough. But he loved to grow flowers. His mother had taught him. He was gentle and kind to Valentin, shy with Anna. I think she was intrigued.'

'And they began a relationship?'

'Not at first. He really wasn't her type. It happened very slowly. She told me it took her by surprise. They had both had domineering fathers, and I think they found an understanding in each other.'

'Was she happy?'

'Yes, but I worried,' Karen said, taking another quick puff. 'He said they had to keep their relationship secret – he was divorcing his wife in Paris and didn't want her to find out or she'd use it against him in the courts.'

'And you didn't believe that?' Grace asked.

'No. I thought he was married and cheating with Anna.'

'Did you tell her?'

'Once.' Karen smiled. 'We didn't speak for a while. I think she really loved him. I'm not sure why, but she did.'

'So what happened?'

'I don't know,' the doctor said. 'Something bad. She turned up here one day, with Valentin. Very shaken. She said she'd left her job in Amsterdam. She lost weight. Wasn't eating properly. She stayed with her father at first, but then Lucian turned up. He went every day. Banged on the door, rang the bell. It was terrible. The neighbours complained. Anna told him to leave, but he wouldn't, and she wouldn't let her father call the police, either. Then she and Valentin moved in with me for a while, but he began to turn up at the hospital and find me, demanding to speak to her.'

Grace found the arrest shot of François Boucher. 'Is this him?'

Karen squinted through smoke. 'Yes. But he's older now. His hair is longer.'

Grace made a note. 'Was he violent towards her?'

'No. Not that she told me. I think he was just obsessed. In love with her. Eventually, she took Valentin to stay with her mother in Florida, till it blew over. She told me Lucian couldn't get a visa to the States, so it would pass.'

'Did it?'

'No. He wouldn't believe us that she'd gone. He kept going to her father's house, and coming here. Her father was sick with it. He couldn't believe Anna had brought this man into their lives. That's when Lucian disappeared. One day, he was just gone.'

'You don't know where to?'

'No. I assumed he'd believed she was in America and given up.'

Grace tried to take it all in. 'And she never told you why she left him?'

'No,' Karen replied. 'I wondered if he'd cheated on her. Or she'd found he was still with his wife and was too embarrassed to tell me I was right. She seemed angry at Lucian, but heartbroken, too.'

'Scared?'

'I don't know. But she couldn't sleep, and she wasn't eating properly.'

'Do you think that's what caused the crash in America – that she was distracted?'

Karen shifted, uncomfortable. 'I couldn't say.'

'And did Lucian know she died?'

Karen shrugged. 'I don't know. He never came back.' A beeper went off. She checked it. 'I have to go.'

They stood up.

'One last question,' Grace said. 'Do you know why Lucian Grabole would be in Edinburgh?'

'Edinburgh?' Karen said as they headed to the hospital entrance. 'No. Why do you ask?'

'Because he didn't give up. I don't think he believed you that she was in America. He went looking for her in Britain. First London, then Edinburgh,' Grace said. 'That's where he died.'

Karen halted. 'Lucian's dead?'

Grace nodded. 'We're still waiting for DNA confirmation, but yes, I think I found him in my flat, three months ago.'

Karen went pale. 'Your flat? Was it suicide?'

'No. He'd broken in. He was starving and drunk. He collapsed and hit his head on the worktop.'

Karen stubbed out her cigarette. 'That's very sad.'

It hit Grace that it was sad. Anna and Lucian had both died, and neither had known. She gave Karen a business card. 'If you can think of anything else, would you ring me? Where is she buried, by the way – Anna?'

Karen's eyes fixed on a trolley leaving an ambulance. 'In Florida. Her mother wanted Anna and Valentin buried close to her.'

'Was it reported in the Danish press?'

Karen wrapped her arms around her, her expression pained. 'The family made no public announcement. Her father is proud. He doesn't like sympathy.'

Karen's beeper went again. 'Listen, I'm sorry.' The word 'sorry' was laden with guilt, as if she'd caused Anna's death herself. 'And I'm sorry about what happened in your flat. It must have been terrible for you. I know Anna loved him, but I wish she'd never met him.'

Grace bought a sandwich from a cafe in Østerbrogade, then asked directions to Nørreport Metro Station. Her train was unmanned, and she sat at the front, speeding through the tunnel. Karen's words ran through her head as it burst out overland towards the airport.

Lucian and Anna had been in love. They'd lived together in Amsterdam and kept it a secret. Anna had left to escape him, and he'd followed her to Copenhagen. She'd been heartbroken, but angry, too.

At the airport, Grace bought a coffee from a stand, and walked to a contemporary statue of two women peering down at passengers below. She sat beside them, equally still in thought. Why had Anna left Lucian in Amsterdam? Had her father threatened to disinherit her if she didn't leave him?

The departure board clicked over: *Dubai, Beijing, San Francisco, Bangkok, the Faroe Islands, Moscow . . .*

A hunger came to go somewhere else. Anywhere but home.

Nicu would be on a plane to Colombia in a few days. The bittersweet ache for him grew.

A jet raced down the runway, took off and began to rise.

She was going home now.

And in that moment, she knew, she was going to tell Mac.

As she stood up to board her flight to Edinburgh, her phone buzzed again.

It was an email titled 'FAO Grace Scott.'

The email address was new to her, existing of nonsensical letters.

She clicked it, expecting spam. Yet there was no name or introduction – just one line.

An address in Lower Largo, the seaside town an hour from Edinburgh.

As she watched the luggage loading into her plane below, wondering who had sent it, a reflection moved in the glass.

A pair of shoes, sticking out from behind a pillar.

They were sharp and pointed, and belonged to a wiry set of legs.

Pointed boots.

The figure moved.

Sharp, jagged angles appeared in the legs and arms, and then a slice of jaw. A pointed shaved head.

Breath caught in her throat.

Casually, Grace opened her folder to find the print of the city-rat man in East London.

She turned from the window, as if checking the time.

He had his back to her now. A green hood had been pulled up.

She checked out his black-clad bowed legs. The pointed boots.

That night in the cafe in Amsterdam.

She *knew* she'd recognized those legs. It had seemed impossible.

Her heart thudded in a long, painful beat.

This was no coincidence. It couldn't be. Which meant he'd been following her, what – since *London*?

'Flight SK301 to Edinburgh is now boarding,' a tannoy said in Danish and then English.

The man walked to the gate.

Who was he?

Twenty or so passengers stood between them. His hood was pulled up, his gaze resolutely ahead. It was him, she was sure.

She hung back, and rang Ewan.

'Wotcha.'

'There's a man getting on my plane,' she whispered. 'Dark green hoodie, shaved head, pale skin, dark eyes, black jeans and pointed boots. Can you get to the airport and photograph him without making contact with me? I'll walk behind him and point.'

'Why?'

'I think he's been following me.'

'Ooh, how very James Bond.'

'Ewan?'

'Yes.'

'I think he's been following me since London. I think he attacked Nicu.'

'Shit. Really?'

'So be careful. And can you check this out, too? Henri Taylor in Paris told us about a French thug called Mathieu Caron who worked with Lucian in Amsterdam. I'm wondering if this is him. It would make sense if he was hanging around the Cozmas in London, searching for Lucian, and heard that I was digging about for information. Could we get that police arrest photo from Henri?'

'Mathieu Caron.' *Tap, tap, tap.* 'I'm on it.'

'Thank you. See you in two hours.'

The hooded man passed towards the plane. Even though he didn't look back, instinct told Grace he knew exactly where she was.

CHAPTER FIFTY-TWO

Edinburgh

The man stood in Mr Singh's storeroom planning his escape.

The husband would be back.

There was no other choice.

He piled all his possessions behind the stack of crisp boxes, plus the plastic bag, checking not a single trace of him was left.

Then he unlocked the back door, and sat behind the boxes, closing off the gap with some from the top stack. To keep himself occupied, he started a new drawing of her, when she was angry at him, her mouth in a pout, her eyes shooting him down for his arrogance or temper.

What he would do now to take it all back.

To have her here.

At 6.30 p.m., the footsteps started in the flat above. Music pounded down. He readied himself, stomach churning.

He was there for an hour, knowing the husband wouldn't come till Mr Singh had left the shop.

Then the clattering started. A door was flung open at the back of the flat upstairs.

Shoes clanged on metal stairs. A thump on the back door. The storeroom door banged; then the handle turned.

'Kent! You there?'

A cold blast of air seeped through the boxes. Maybe his imagination, but it carried in the sweet, yeasty smell of alcohol. The light was switched on to supplement the small barred window.

The man held his breath, waiting for his absence to become clear. For the husband to give up. Leave.

The back door closed again, much more quietly, and he thought he was safe.

Then there was a scrape of footsteps.

'Where are you?' the husband said quietly.

Noises began around the room. First, door handles being turned. The drawer on the television table opening. The toilet cabinet opened and shut. The fridge.

A squeal as it was moved away from the wall.

The man touched the plastic bag with his toe.

Then a shudder of legs as the stool was pushed over.

He'd do anything to make him stop coming here and threatening everything.

A stronger, more violent tremor went through him.

Outside was the sound of a carton being torn open. A click, then cigarette smoke floating in. A crisp bag opening.

A long, deep sigh.

All of a sudden, the back door opened and slammed shut.

He'd gone.

His eyes fell on her face, on the drawing on the floor. Her eyes watched him, crossly.

The man trembled, realizing what a pitiful creature he'd become.

CHAPTER FIFTY-THREE

Grace arrived back at Edinburgh Airport from Copenhagen, willing Ewan to be on time.

Luckily, the man in the green hood had luggage too, so she kept tabs on him from the collection area, through passport control and customs. Ewan stood among a gaggle of taxi drivers, holding a passenger name board that said, *Mrs J. Bond.*

She nodded at the hooded man. Ewan acted like he was reading a text, presumably snapping him. He and Grace hung back till the hooded man had exited to the taxi rank, climbed in a car and gone.

Grace high-fived Ewan. 'Did you get him?'

'Yup. Certain he's following you? Didn't even look back.'

They checked his phone. Ewan had only managed to get him from the side, but from the sharp angle of his jaw, she was even more convinced it was the city-rat man from East London.

'We need to get a photo of Mathieu Caron to compare it,' she said.

'Henri's on it. So what now?'

She yawned. 'I have to go home and see Mac.'

Ewan gestured towards the exit. 'My carriage awaits.'

Grateful, she followed him to his ancient Mini. Just to be sure the hooded man had gone, she asked him to make diversionary manoeuvres on their return to the city.

'Look at you with all the fancy moves, eh?' he winked.

'Nothing like being followed by a psycho to make you focus.'

'Try working with one.'

'How is Sula?'

He rolled his eyes dramatically. 'Working on this story about these two guys buried in a pit cave up on Auchtermouth – probably some kind of gangland thing,' he said.

She watched Edinburgh come back into view, not really listening.

They pulled up in Gallon Street and she got out. 'Thanks for coming. And for the lift. And for making me do the story – even if you are a pain in the arse.'

'Go, Scotty!' he said, high-fiving her again.

She got out and stood outside number 6. Three nights without proper sleep, the adrenalin rushes, what she was about to do to Mac – it all came together and sucked the energy from her. A force field might as well have existed between her and the other side of the door.

The communal hall of the tenement was chilly despite the warmer weather. Three months ago, she'd sat on these stairs with Mac, the first day in their new home together, embarking on the 'settled' life her dad had wanted for her, yet would never see, a dead body upstairs in their kitchen, dread in her belly.

If she was honest, the dread had already been there when she walked in that day. It had crept up on her on the cramped plane home from Bangkok, as she regretted what she'd done. The differences between her and Mac had never been quite as pronounced as they were over there, away from everything familiar. That same dread had dogged her as they'd tossed a coin on the

306

street to decide who should go to the shop and she'd climbed the steps to their new flat to put on the heating and make tea, knowing Mac would never travel again after that trip. That this was the beginning of the rest of her life.

And now she felt it again.

But this time, she wasn't staying.

She thought of the words and wondered if she'd even need them. If he'd see it on her face. That's what happened if you knew someone your whole adult life. Every nuance of movement and expression was a language.

The stuffy smell hit her as she entered the flat. Mac had smoked, even though she hated it. A full ashtray sat on the sitting-room coffee table, empty bottles of beer beside it and a dirty food plate.

Punishing her.

'Mac?' She checked the bedroom and box room. From the doorway, the kitchen was empty, too.

Then a breeze blew the back door open.

A door slammed down in the backyard, followed by a *clang, clang, clang*.

The top of a familiar head appeared on the fire escape.

He *was* here.

Grace imagined the conversation that was to come and her exhausted body begged for no more.

Not tonight.

Quietly, she closed the kitchen door, grabbed her laptop from the bedroom and Dad's car keys off a hook, and left the flat with her rucksack.

She exited the tenement, climbed into Dad's car and sat watching the dark sitting-room window of their flat, smelling the old mud from Dad's walking boots, and the mints he always chewed. From the glove compartment, she removed his whisky flask and took a swig. A light came on in their sitting room, and she ducked as a figure appeared at the window.

Mac.

If she did what she planned to do, it would mean life now without both Dad *and* Mac.

Unfathomable.

She flicked through Dad's maps, his marked-up hiking routes, tracing his handwriting with her finger.

The lights went out again in the sitting room.

Grace started the engine.

Anne-Marie's cheeks were flushed when she answered the door, a basket of washing under an arm. Laundry smells wafted out.

'Oh, hello, stranger, where've you been?' she said, hugging Grace with her free arm. The ironing board was up in the kitchen, the radio on.

'Where are the kids?' Grace said, kissing her.

'In bed.'

'Is Craig here?'

'Nope. His night in Glasgow.'

Grace dropped her rucksack in the narrow hall and shut the door. 'Can I ask a favour? Or two favours?'

'Go for it.'

'Can I stay the night?'

'Course. What's the second one?'

'If Mac rings, will you not answer?'

Anne-Marie swept dark hair from a pink face. 'OK. Now I'm worried.'

Blown up behind her, Grace saw the photo-booth strip of the pair of them when they were twelve, on a Saturday-afternoon jaunt into town.

'I've slept with someone.'

Anne-Marie's mouth opened. 'Oh my good God. Who?'

'Someone in Amsterdam.'

Anne-Marie dropped the basket and held out her arms. 'Come here.' Grace fell into the girl who'd come to fetch her, alone, from a wall to play on her first day at primary school.

'I don't know how to tell him,' Grace said.

Anne-Marie held her away. 'Is it serious, with this guy?'

Grace shrugged. 'Honestly, it's not about him; it's me. We shouldn't have got married or bought the flat. I'm just so stupid. I knew it was wrong.'

At that moment, her mobile rang out. Mac's name appeared on the caller display.

Sighing, she showed it to Anne-Marie, then turned it off.

'Oh Jesus. Now you're scaring me. Right, come on.' Her friend led her into the kitchen. 'You, me and a bottle of wine. Let's start at the beginning.'

CHAPTER FIFTY-FOUR

'I Keep Asking Myself, Why *My* Boy?'

The following morning, Sula sat in her car in South Queensferry reading her double-page exclusive with Mrs McFarlay in the first edition of *Scots Today*. It was a classy job, if she said so herself. The photographer had taken a good shot of Mrs McFarlay at her window, Colin's school photo in her hands.

She guessed Mrs McFarlay would see it today, and feel the weight of exposure. Hate it. Pick over individual words in her quotes that she hadn't *meant*. Convince herself she'd been tricked into talking and misquoted. It often happened. But it was done now. Maybe some scumbag with information would feel sorry enough for her to make an anonymous phone call.

The sun rose in a blustery blue sky over the Firth of Forth.

As the clock ticked round, she looked at the photo she'd borrowed of Colin McFarlay in the newspaper, with his angelic curls.

Her fingers reached for the pink Post-it note in the well by the gearstick. She uncrumpled it and read it for the first time. It was a different number to Joanne's last one. Probably some mobile that skank Jimmy had nicked for her.

8.09 a.m.

Sula fingered the note, and rang the number. It answered after three rings.

'It's me,' she said quietly, trying to imagine the state of the tiny bedsit she'd rented for her daughter down in Manchester before Christmas.

Her last stand.

A groggy Manchester accent. Male. Not Jimmy. Younger. 'Who you after, love?'

'Joanne. Is this her phone?'

'Yeah. Think so.'

'And are you in her flat?'

'Yeah . . . just for a few days, like. But she's not 'ere.'

'Where is she, then?'

'Haven't seen her. Not since Saturday, I don't think.' Curiosity entered the stranger's tone, wondering, Sula guessed, if there was a buck to be made here. 'What's it about, love? I can tell her you rang.'

Before she could answer, Sula made herself hang up.

Slowly she wound down the window, crumpled the Post-it note and dropped it out.

She glanced at the newspaper photo of Colin on his mother's lap. 'Nobody's to judge us, Mrs McFarlay,' she said quietly.

Her guess was that the new owners of Mrs McFarlay's former home would drop the wee one off at the nursery on their way to the city. Right enough, the electronic gates opened at 8.15 a.m. and a large SUV appeared, with all three in it.

As they sped off, Sula dived out and craned her neck to see the estate agent's sign by the side of the garage.

McDoughty & Steele.

The gates came at her.

Good.

The nearest branch was a five-minute drive. It was a high-end one, catering for the bankers and media types.

A free agent with an eager-to-please face waved her to her desk. 'How can I help you?' she said, casing Sula's jeans.

'Well, I'm just wondering. Bowling Road. Can you tell me what I'd be expecting to pay for a house there?'

'Well, it's all changing at the moment,' the agent said, 'but the bungalows go for about six hundred and fifty thousand.' She grimaced, waiting for Sula to fall over in shock.

'Right,' Sula said thoughtfully. 'Well. That seems very reasonable.'

The woman's gaze refocused. 'What were you thinking?'

'Around a million?'

'A million?'

'But I'd want a view for that.'

The estate agent hid it well, but not well enough. 'Actually, there was a big sandstone villa up at the far end by itself. That went for £1.2 million recently. Great views.'

'Twice as much money. Was it twice as big?' Sula said.

'No. But it was owned by a business who pushed the price quite high and just sat and waited. I think they were lucky to get it. You can do that when you're not worrying about chains and so on.'

'A business?' Sula said, surprised. 'Not a person.'

'Yes. They bought it off the original owner privately.'

Sula remained composed. 'Why would that be?'

'Oh, it was a distressed buyout.'

'What's that?'

'Distressed buyout? It's when firms offer maybe eighty or ninety per cent of the asking price for people needing a quick sale, and pay cash.'

'Right,' Sula said, acting thoughtful. 'OK.'

'So, would you like particulars of other houses?' the woman asked, looking as if she wanted to move on now. 'There's nothing in Bowling Road, but there's some other smashing properties around there.'

'Yes, please.'

She gathered her glossy brochures of dream houses.

'Distressed buyouts. That's interesting,' Sula said, flicking through photos of indoor swimming pools and kitchens drowning in islands and wine coolers. 'My mother's got a seven-bedroom Georgian property in . . .' She named one of the most prestigious streets in Edinburgh. 'But it's got subsidence. She's got herself in a state about it. I said she should just sell it and move in with me. Maybe this would be a way forward. Just sell it for a discount and cash – this distressed-buyout firm could worry about the building work.'

The woman's eyes grew hungry. 'Gosh, well, if she does decide to sell, you'd be surprised how many private buyers are happy to take on building work in the right property, if the location is right. I'm sure we'd get your mother more than eighty per cent. I'd be very happy to arrange a valuation for her.'

I bet you would. Shame she's been dead ten years.

'I'll let her know. Maybe you could do a valuation for her, and I could call these other guys, too – let her have all the options. Who was it?' Sula asked.

'Let's see.' The woman checked on her computer, obviously gambling she'd be able to win the deal if she got her foot in the door. 'Andrew's Equity in London.'

'Andrew's. Right. Thanks very much,' Sula said, standing up. 'I'll be in touch.'

As she walked back to the car, she shoved the brochures of the dream family homes in a dog-mess bin.

CHAPTER FIFTY-FIVE

After eight hours' solid sleep on Anne-Marie's sofa bed, Grace felt her energy return.

Once the kids had piled in on her for hugs and headed off to school, she left mid-morning, checking her phone. Mac had called twice more last night, asking where she was. The frantic anger in his voice had been replaced by a quiet sadness, which just made her more determined to put them both out of their misery.

She crossed out of Edinburgh over the Forth Road Bridge, and stopped a few miles on at a filling station, where she texted Ewan the address in Lower Largo.

Her phone rang back as she stood at the pump. Thinking it was him, she answered with her free hand. 'I was just telling you in case I'm never heard of again.'

Silence. 'Ms Scott. DI Robertson here.'

'Oh, hi.' She stopped and let go of the pump trigger.

'You OK there?' he said.

'Sorry. Thought you were someone else.' If he had any idea what she'd been up to the past week . . .

'Just to let you know, we checked that name Lucian Grabole

on our systems. Nothing came back. But we have had a finger-print hit on one of the European checks.'

'Really?'

A car pulled up behind her. The driver watched her inaction at the pump impatiently.

'Yes, we've got a match in France.'

'Right,' she said, scared to speak in case she gave anything away.

'Our guy's called François Boucher. Paris police say he's known to them, but he's been out of France for a couple of years. What he was doing in Edinburgh we have no idea. We're releasing his name to the press this afternoon, so I wanted to let you know first.'

She stood there, lost for words. 'Thanks. That's great.'

'Told you we'd get there, eh?'

'You did. Thanks.'

'Now, was there anything else?'

She hesitated. 'Not at the moment, but thanks.'

There was another pause. Clearly he was expecting a bigger response after her months of chasing him. 'OK, well, I'm here today if you want to get hold of me.'

'Thanks again,' she repeated, wondering how their next conversation would go when *Scots Today* informed him about the story they were about to run, with her byline on it.

The sea was metal green today in Lower Largo. She drove down a winding road onto the front, and parked up on the narrow pavement in front of a skip, outside a row of nineteenth-century cottages hunkered against the east-coast wind. The seagulls welcomed her with an urgent call.

She checked the address again, recalling who she'd given her business card to this week in London, Amsterdam and Paris. Who was it?

The sun was out, but the wind was strong. It pushed her hair back as she opened the car door, and stole inside her coat. It had been years since she'd been here. Memories returned of Mum and Dad, and weekend trips. Rock-pooling, and digging for lug-worms with sticks, drawing words in the damp sand. Then of trips with Mac, Anne-Marie and their other school friends on a Saturday: eating fish and chips, sitting on the swings, running into the sea in their jeans, screeching, tangled up on rugs together on the sand, her watching the sea, dreaming of the future.

What if she'd known that it turned out like this?

A plane left a trail across the sky and she thought of Nicu.

The address she'd been emailed was a little way out of town, up on a headland lush with vegetation. It was a two-storey cottage overlooking a wide expanse of beach, next to an alleyway down to the rocks and sand below.

Grace stopped before she reached it. There was nothing to give away the identity of the resident. No car outside, or orna-ments on the windowsill. She knocked, and stood back, her recorder and camera ready.

The front door opened.

Her mind whirred, trying to understand what she was seeing.

'Come in, Grace.'

CHAPTER FIFTY-SIX

Sula returned to the *Scots Today* office from her trip to South Queensferry, and yelled at Ewan.

'Mr Pearce Senior's house – sold for what again?'

'Um . . .' He checked his notes. 'Two hundred and thirteen thousand.'

'Did you check – did he sell it, or is that just the last sale figure for the property?

'Don't know.'

She threw herself into her chair. 'Right. I'm betting this firm down in London, Andrew's, sold that house, not him. I'm betting they bought it off Mr Pearce a few months earlier, at an eighty or ninety per cent discount. Same as Mrs McFarlay. Get me Philip Pearce's number.'

Ewan made a face. 'The one that hates your guts.'

'Aye, him.'

'OK.'

Philip Pearce's phone went straight to voicemail. 'Mr Pearce,' Sula said. 'Sula McGregor here. It's about your father. Can you give me a call? It's urgent. I have some important information.'

She and Ewan sat staring at her phone for ten minutes.

'Oh, come on, you bastard,' Sula muttered.

Ewan drummed his fingers. 'Probably out arranging a hit on you.'

She stood up. 'I haven't got time for this. Find the estate agent.'

Ewan tapped away. 'Got it. McGaskill.'

Sula explained what she wanted him to do.

'Got it,' he said. He rang the estate agent, switched to loudspeaker and adopted an accent worthy of *Downton Abbey*.

'Good afternoon. This is Rupert Banker of Andrew's Equity in London. Could I speak to the agent who sold 77 Fry Road in Colinton for us last year, please?'

'Hold the line, please.'

He gave Sula a dramatic wink.

A new voice came on the line. 'Can I help you?'

'Euh, he-llow,' Ewan started. 'Andrew's here. Your company acted as an agent for our property 77 Fry Road last ye-aar?'

A confused voice. 'Oh yes, hello. Sorry, Mr Banker – was it you we dealt with?'

'No, no. That was my colleague.'

A tapping on a keyboard. 'Just looking up your file. That's right. I remember now. Mr Stansfield. Yes. What can I do for you?'

'We-ell,' Ewan said, as if something of huge significance was about to be imparted. 'Mr Stansfield and I are visiting your fine city this week –' Sula banged his shoulder before he went too far '– with the intention of expanding our Edinburgh portfolio. Could we schedule you in for a meeting? Maybe Thursday?'

More tapping, this time faster. 'Yes, absolutely. What about 2 p.m.?'

'That's soo-oper for us,' Ewan drawled. 'Now, I'm out and about at the moment. Could I trouble you to email confirmation of that to our main office?'

'Ah yes, let me just . . .'

'You still have the details?'

'Er . . . yes, got it right here, Mr Banker. It's . . . office@ andrews—'

'Ah,' Ewan butted in. 'I must apologize. My PA's just informed me she's booked us in for another appointment on Thursday. Let me get back to you on that. Toodle-oo.' Ewan put down the phone.

'Toodle-oo?' Sula yelped.

Ewan stood up and bowed. 'I thank you. Oh yes, I thank you.'

But Sula was already typing, 'Andrew's Equity,' into Google.

This was confirmation. Both the dead men's parents had sold their houses to the same firm in London in a distressed buyout. No wonder Mr Pearce Senior's kids were angry – 20 per cent of £213,000 was over £40,000.

This was sounding less of a gangland incident by the minute. And if she wasn't mistaken, she'd just positioned herself one step ahead of Fin Robertson.

CHAPTER FIFTY-SEVEN

Grace stepped into the cottage in Lower Largo, all points on her inner compass smashing into each other.

'Come in.'

She'd recognized her immediately. In her late thirties. Blonde hair pulled back, small nose, wide cheeks and clear blue eyes. Close up, she had fine stress lines on her forehead and around her eyes that the photo hadn't shown.

Anna Johanssen.

Her voice was fragile, eyes and nose pink from crying. The dark interior of the cottage was in disarray. Wet towels lay on the floor, dirty dishes on the table. It was the scene of someone barely coping.

Grace put down her bag. 'I'm so sorry. I must look shocked. Your aunt said that you were in a fatal car accident in Florida. And your friend Karen.'

Anna turned on the kettle. She wore baggy clothes over a too-thin frame. 'I asked them to. They're doing it to protect me. When you told Karen about Lucian, that he'd di—' She broke off and took a breath. 'She rang me last night. I told her to send you. To tell me what happened.' She made coffee and led Grace out onto a terrace that overlooked the beach. Children's play equipment littered it. 'My son,' Anna said. 'He's at school.'

'Valentin?'

Anna dabbed at her eyes. 'I haven't told him about Lucian.' It was then that Grace saw the baby asleep in a buggy. A little girl, around a year old.

'Lucian's?' she said, astonished.

Anna nodded, and fresh tears fell. Grace touched her arm. 'Anna, I'm so sorry you heard the news like this. I need to explain to you that I'm writing a story for *Scots Today*. But it's a personal story, about finding Lucian in my flat and trying to track down his identity and find his loved ones. If I ask you what has been happening, would you be happy to talk?'

Anna shook her head. 'Not on the record. It's too dangerous.'

'Then speak to me off the record,' Grace said. 'But, Anna, please speak to me. The police are releasing François Boucher's name to the press today. François is the name Lucian used. Do you know that?'

Anna nodded, wiping away tears.

'The Scottish press won't be interested,' Grace continued, 'but French crime reporters will be. François – or Lucian's – boss, René Boucher, was famous in Paris. Once they get hold of this, the story will break here, too. And if journalists speak to the people I've met who knew Lucian, it's not going to be good. This is a chance for you to tell Lucian's side.'

'Without my name involved?'

Grace took out her voice recorder. 'I'll make it a condition with *Scots Today* before I file my story. I promise.'

Anna scanned the sea, pale blue eyes glazed with shock. 'Nobody ever spoke up for Lucian.'

'Then you'll do it. Please.'

Anna motioned to a table.

*

The sun was out, but Anna wrapped a shawl around her as Grace set up the recording.

A single tree sat in a pot by the table. 'I kill plants,' Anna said, a rueful smile. 'Not like Lucian – he made things live.'

'He was good at gardening?' Grace settled back.

'Yes, he helped Mitti in Amsterdam. I met him when they were planting lupins. He was too shy to speak, but he played football with Valentin.'

'That's where you met?'

Anna fought back tears. 'I started to sit with him in the evenings, at the garden door, while Valentin slept. I was a little lonely in Amsterdam, and Lucian was trying to learn English, so we spoke it together.'

'And you became friends?'

Anna pushed tears back with her palms. 'Not at first. At first, it was like he was locked behind a wall. His face was hard, but when he smiled . . . Well, when Valentin ran to him, it almost burst off his face.'

'Did he tell you about Romania?' Grace asked.

'Not at first. Later, he told me stories about his father. Horrible things.'

'Like?'

Anna tapped her back. 'He had scars, here. He said it was an accident, when he was a child. Then later, he said his father beat him, and forced him to do terrible things to people. Lucian was petrified of him. The father beat the mother, too. If they didn't do what he said, he'd put Lucian down a freezing-cold well all night. His mother couldn't protect him. Everybody in their village was terrified. The man was deranged. He killed people by tying them up and putting them down wells alive, so that it would contaminate the water supply. He killed animals for fun. Lucian had no friends. He was quiet and sensitive, like his mother. In two years, he never raised his voice to me or Valentin.'

She chose her words carefully. 'Do you know why Lucian left Romania?'

Grace hugged herself tight. 'He lied about that for a long time. He said work. But I found out later he'd had to escape. When the revolution happened, his father paid to be smuggled out by this French gang who traded cigarettes with him on the black market. When Drac was caught and executed, they took Lucian instead. But instead of helping him like they'd been paid to do, they used him. Forced him to work for them. If he refused, they threatened to send him back to Romania to be tried for murder. He was very scared, and alone. He kept trying to run. The third time, they broke his leg with a hammer. He was sixteen.'

'This was the Bouchers?' Grace said, shocked.

'Not at first,' Anna said. 'It was a gang who worked for René Boucher in Marseilles. René took a liking to Lucian at some point when he was there, and brought him to live with him back in Paris. I think he saw his . . . *potential*.'

She sank her face into her hands. 'Lucian's life was so brutal. He said that meeting me was the first time he'd felt love since his mother.' She wiped wet cheeks. 'She loved him so much when he was a child, but being Drac's wife made her sick. She lost her mind. Lucian took her ring when he ran. A little green one. It's all he had of her. He always wore it.'

Grace nodded.

'Did you love him, Anna?'

'Yes.'

'So why did you leave?'

A dog barked below the terrace. A teenager threw a stick and it raced across the sand.

'Because he put Valentin in danger.'

'How?'

A brittle tone entered Anna's voice. 'Because his lies never stopped. About his name. His divorce in Paris. His job.'

'His job?' Grace asked.

'He told me he worked as a painter at night, but it wasn't true. He sold drugs in Amsterdam. Sold misery. I saw those people at the hospital where I worked. Lucian was doing it to them.'

'How did you find out?'

'He came in one night in a terrible state. Frightened. He told me everything. That he had been run by these gangsters in Paris since he was sixteen. And that when René died, his right-hand man, this gangster Mathieu Caron, stole the Marseilles route off René's sons and forced Lucian to be his deputy. Lucian knew it was his chance finally to escape. He persuaded Mathieu to run a second route from Marseilles into Amsterdam, where nobody knew him. While they set it up, Lucian managed to buy false papers from a man he met in a club, and rent a second, secret apartment that Mathieu knew nothing about under a different name.'

'That's when he became Lucian Grabole?'

'Yes. And it worked. For a year, he lived a normal life as Lucian Grabole. Only part of each day, but it was something. He saved money, and his plan was to get an American or Australian visa and escape Mathieu Caron altogether. Just disappear in the night. Then he met me and it became complicated. He kept waiting for the right time to tell me the truth. To persuade me to go with him. But Mathieu Caron found out from one of his contacts that he was trying to buy a new passport under the name "Lucian Grabole". He followed him back to our apartments and found out what was going on. He went crazy and threatened to kill me and Valentin.'

Her face froze, as the waves of shock at his death hit her again. 'I pretended to be calm about it, and told Lucian to go and pack, and we'd run together. Then I slipped away with Valentin and drove to Copenhagen. We left everything in Amsterdam. My job at the hospital. Valentin's nursery.'

'Where did you go?'

'At first, to my father's house, but Lucian broke into the concierge's office and found my address in Copenhagen. He followed me there.'

The softness appeared in her face again. 'He was desperate. He kept saying he was sorry, but I was so scared these guys would follow him and hurt Valentin. I moved to Karen's apartment, but he didn't stop. He made visits, sent me letter after letter. My aunt hated me for what I'd done to our family. Embarrassing them publicly. At that point, I was offered a two-month contract in London covering for a colleague doing a charity sabbatical abroad. I told Karen to tell Lucian we were visiting my mother in Florida. I thought he'd give up. My aunt and Karen and I agreed that if any strangers came looking for me and Valentin, they'd say I'd died in a car accident in Florida.'

'In case it was Mathieu Caron looking for you?'

'Yes.' She wiped the tears with her shawl, and checked her watch. 'I have to fetch Valentin from school.'

'Of course,' Grace said. 'Anna, do you still have Lucian's letters?'

'Yes. Here.' She fetched a bundle from a drawer, took the buggy. She held them back.

'I'll do nothing without your permission.'

Anna handed them over, and promised to return in half an hour.

Grace stared at the handwriting, hardly believing the journey she'd taken. It was the same looped font she'd found in her kitchen a week ago. The language was English, the grammar and spelling unpredictable. Some words and sentences had been scored through and she imagined Lucian poring over this paper with great earnestness, as if this was now all that mattered in his life. Still, the sentiment was clear. Lucian was desperate.

She photographed them carefully, as a pile, and singly, removing Anna's name, in case she gave her permission to use them later.

Random passages quickly confirmed what Anna had told her: *You and my mother are the softness in my life. The light, the love. I won't give you up . . . Do you remember that night Valentin fell asleep by us, and we said we loved each other?*

As she opened each letter, the tone changed. In one, the address was from the Cozmas' in London. *Anna, I can't find you in London. Please answer me. I will make everything all right, I promise. Write to me at this address . . .*

She read on and knew she was reading the private letters of a desperate man, trying to cling on to the one piece of good in his life.

The door of the cottage opened twenty minutes later and a little boy ran in, wearing a blue jumper, wellies and jeans.

'This is Grace, Valentin. She's come to visit us,' Anna said.

He stopped and held his mother's hand.

'Hi, Valentin. It's so nice to meet you.' Grace smiled.

His blond hair was longer, and his cheeks were slimmer than in the poster. When he spoke to his mother, eyeing Grace warily, he had a Scottish accent.

Maybe it was the sea wind or his presence, but Anna's cheeks were flushed now, her eyes brighter.

She motioned to the beach. 'We can let him play down there. He loves it.'

Grace followed her and Valentin down steps off the terrace.

The sun glistened off the sea. The little boy ran onto the sand with a new surety, and she thought of how strange it must have been for Lucian to disappear from his life.

They settled on the rocks, watching him.

'Anna,' Grace started, 'it says in the letters that Lucian was looking for you in London – why?'

Anna placed Clara, the baby, down on a blanket and the little girl crawled across it, gurgling to herself. 'He wasn't stupid. When I didn't come back from Florida, he searched for my name on the internet and found me at the hospital in London. But by that time, I'd already found a permanent job here. I was pregnant . . .' She trailed off.

'In Scotland?'

'Yes. The colleague I'd been covering for rang to say Lucian had been asking for me, so I changed to my mother's maiden name. It took him a while, but he worked that out, too. He turned up here one day, at work. I was seven months pregnant and he realized Clara was his. That just made it worse. I was still terrified of these gangsters looking for us. I told him if he didn't leave us, I'd ring the police – tell them everything. That day he stopped. He just stopped harassing me, but he didn't leave. He wrote to say he'd found a job in Edinburgh. It was as if he was just happy to be near us.'

'What was his job?' Grace asked.

A fragile smile appeared. 'Real work. For the first time in his life. Master decorating. He'd done a course secretly in Amsterdam, and was proud of his skills. He kept writing to me here, and I kept throwing the letters away. Then one night, I was lonely. I opened one. Lucian said he wanted nothing more from me, just forgiveness. I ignored it.' She dabbed her face. 'He told me his love for me had helped him become an honest man. That he'd always be there for us. One day, I couldn't help it. I had a

327

conference in Edinburgh. I went in early to the place he was working and watched him through the window. I returned that night on my way home, and he was still working. He must have been exhausted, but there was a new expression on his face. A satisfaction. I knew he was trying to find a way to rebuild his life. Be there for us if we needed him.'

Valentin ran over to show her a stone, and she talked to him in Danish. Shyly, he showed Grace, too, before running off.

'Not long after that, I went back,' Anna continued. 'I waited for him outside with Clara.' A laugh broke into her expression and briefly Grace glimpsed the woman she must have been before all this. 'He was so happy. He was crying, meeting his daughter. We started to talk. Then I went again. We talked for longer. I couldn't help it. I loved him. I couldn't believe someone who did bad things like that could change, but Lucian started to convince me. One Sunday, I let him come secretly to watch Valentin on the beach. His heart was bursting. When they reunited, Valentin remembered him. The smiles on their faces.' She drew it with a finger like a pen across her face. 'Lucian began to come every Sunday, always early in the morning in case the Bouchers had found him. He left the next morning at five. We started to plan a new life together again, in America, near my mother. But we had to find a way for Lucian to get a passport with false papers. That's what our last conversation was about.'

Fresh tears flooded her eyes and washed away her resolve. Valentin looked over, tapping his bucket with a spade, and she hid her face. 'Then, the next Sunday –' her voice broke '– he didn't come. I waited all night. He didn't answer his phone.'

Grace broke in gently, 'Anna, when Lucian was found in my flat, there was no phone.'

'No phone?'

'No. Did you report him missing?'

328

She dried her eyes. 'How could I? I thought they'd caught him trying to buy a false passport. I knew they'd interview me. I could lose my job. I couldn't involve the children in that. Then I thought Mathieu Caron had found him, and forced him back to Paris, or hurt him. I was too scared to look in case he hurt the children. I knew Lucian would want me to keep them safe.'

Valentin looked over, and she knelt to help him, till he began to fill his bucket again. 'But also, it was so wet that night. The rain was heavy. I thought maybe he'd had an accident on the road coming here. I checked the newspapers for traffic accidents, but there was nothing. Your mind tortures you. I've been waiting . . . hoping, and now . . .'

The baby began to whimper and she went to pick her up.

Grace changed the subject. 'Anna, why do you think Lucian was in my flat that night?'

She kissed the baby's head. 'I don't know. It makes no sense. We were going to leave for America soon. He was earning money. He had a room in Edinburgh. He had us back again. We were just waiting for his papers. The last thing he'd risk was being arrested.'

Grace found her camera. 'I'm going to show you something that might upset you. The reason I knew Lucian was in my flat was that I found a note. I thought it was addressed to me, at first, but now I think he just found an old envelope in the kitchen and scribbled on the back.'

Anna's eyes rounded as she focused on the viewfinder. '*That man is not me Lucian Grabole,*' she read out loud. 'Oh!' she exclaimed. She covered her mouth. She looked like she'd gone into shock.

'What?'

'He must have known.'

'Known what?'

'That he was about to die.'

'What do you mean?'

Anna pointed. 'Look. It's a statement. To the world. About who Lucian was. *That man is not me.* Signed, *Lucian Grabole.* It is a note for his children, Valentin and Clara. He wants them to know who he really was. *I am not that monster Lucian Tronescu or François Boucher. The real me is the man who loves the three of you – Lucian Grabole.*'

'You think someone killed him?'

Anna clasped her hands. 'I don't understand. I thought you said it was an accident.'

Grace shook her head. 'I'm starting to think it might not have been. Anna, I need to go back to Edinburgh and do more digging. I know this is torture for you, but would you give me twenty-four hours to see what I can find out?'

'Yes,' she said, defeated.

'The place where you saw Lucian working – where was it?'

'I'll write down the address.'

They gathered the children and returned to the terrace. As Grace waited, a silhouette caught her eye down the beach. At first, she thought he was a dog walker who'd lost his animal. His eyes were scanning the cottages along the beach, not the sea or the sand ahead.

The sun fell behind a cloud.

Wiry legs, pointed boots. Today in a black leather jacket and a grey beanie.

Air caught in her lungs.

She grasped Valentin's hand and led him inside quickly. Anna turned, confused. Grace beckoned her in and shut the door and curtains.

'Anna, can you put the kids in there?' She motioned to the sitting room.

Alarm spread across Anna's features.

'Please – trust me.'

Anna did what she said, turning on the television, and returned.

Grace pointed outside. 'The man on the beach – I think he's following me. I think he might be Mathieu Caron.'

Anna started to tremble. 'No.'

'I'm so sorry. I thought I'd lost him yesterday, but it's definitely him.' Grace picked up her camera bag. 'Listen. He has no idea why I'm here. Nobody does. So I'm going to leave, quickly, before he sees me. Please stay in here till at least an hour after I go. If you see him near the house, ring the police. And remember, if he did kill Lucian, he has nothing to gain by hurting you now. It's me he wants to stop. He doesn't know how much information I have.'

To her surprise, Anna calmed down, perhaps galvanized by the threat to her children. They agreed that she would watch behind the lace curtains in the upstairs dormer and call for Grace to leave when the man was safely down the beach. When the shout came, Grace returned to her car.

She stopped mid-jog.

A new car, a silver four-by-four, had parked behind her, bumper to bumper. There was an inch of space. With only six inches between her and the skip ahead, she was blocked in.

She glanced in the window of the four-by-four. A green hoodie lay on the floor.

Fucker.

He was clever. He must have double-crossed them at the airport, followed her back to Gallon Street, then Anne-Marie's house.

Shit. He'd been there all night, with her friends' kids in the house.

331

This had to stop.

She jumped in and inched forward and backwards, trying to get out of the tiny gap. By the tenth movement, she gave up and slammed backwards into the silver four-by-four, hoping it was his, and that no one was watching. With a screech of locked tyres on tarmac, it jerked back. She jammed down her wheel and edged out, pranging Dad's wing on the skip. Her phone flew off the passenger seat onto the floor.

From nowhere, the man appeared out of an alleyway between terraced rows of cottages.

He looked as startled as she was.

Close up, their eyes met.

He had a rattish face, as well as body – small eyes, long, pointed nose.

She sped past him down Main Street, taking the road out of Lower Largo. Where was her phone? At a junction, she swerved onto the main road back to Edinburgh, watching in her rear-view mirror.

A camper van pulled out of a junction ahead of her.

'No!'

It lumbered onto the road, forcing her to drop to its snail's pace. A long stream of traffic approached from the opposite direction. There was no way to overtake. The silver four-by-four appeared in her rear-view mirror.

'Come on!' she yelled at the camper van.

It accelerated to forty miles per hour as they passed a links golf course and the sea.

The four-by-four was coming up fast. They'd locked eyes. There was no doubt now. He knew that she knew who he was, and he wouldn't let her get away. Her phone, and the help she needed, lay on the floor.

Ahead, there was a break in the stream of approaching traffic.

A green lorry loomed in the distance. The gap was shorter than she'd usually dare, but right now, the alternative could be worse. Indicating, Grace pulled out and sped past the camper van, making it back in by a hair's breadth.

The silver four-by-four pulled out, then dived back in. He couldn't make it.

Behind the green lorry was a long stream of cars. It would give her a minute. Accelerating, Grace raced along the sea front, praying for a bend to lose him again. In the mirror, the camper van dropped away. She imagined Caron up its back, blaring his horn, swearing.

A sign for the seaside town of Leven appeared. Then a bend, followed by a mini-roundabout.

This was it. Her chance. Grace flew over the roundabout and, instead of carrying on towards Edinburgh, turned sharp right, her wheels squealing, into a small housing estate. One sharp turn into a cul-de-sac and she swung the car round and stopped.

Leaning down, she grabbed her camera and put it on zoom.

The camper van was just approaching the mini-roundabout. As she guessed, the silver four-by-four was an inch from its bumper. The man was perched forward, trying to spot her up ahead.

She fired off three shots and dropped down, hoping he'd missed her. Through the gap in the cul-de-sac houses, she saw him up the back of the camper van, indicator on, trying to force it to let him past.

Good. Giving him a few seconds, she drove back towards Lower Largo at speed, pulling in at a supermarket, and parked among rows of vehicles in the car park. She turned off the engine, hands trembling, and rang Ewan.

'Same guy?' he said, alarmed.

'Yup. But now he knows I've seen him. Should we tell the police?'

'Do you want to?'

'Yes. But if I do, I'll have to tell them everything. Which means the whole story goes to waste. Have you got a photo of Mathieu Caron yet?'

'Henri Taylor's chasing it right now. What you going to do?'

Grace checked around her. 'If he works out I'm not ahead of him, which he will, I reckon he might wait for me at the bridge.'

'So come back the long way. Use the bridge at Kincardine.'

'Might have to. Listen, the police have identified Lucian Grabole as the man in my flat – you'll see a press statement later. I have to be quick. I've got an address for the place Lucian used to work as a decorator in Edinburgh. Could you go?'

'Only if Sula doesn't catch me.'

'Is she there?'

'Popped home for an hour. Is it far?'

'I'm not sure. She doesn't know the exact address. She says she parked on a cul-de-sac with free parking called Ross Turn, then she walked to the corner, and it was the building ahead, about fifty metres on the right – offices or something.'

'OK. So what – just go there, ask if he worked there?'

'Yes, get anything you can. But be careful.'

'Will do.'

Checking every minute for the silver four-by-four, Grace sat back to read Lucian's letters on her phone screen.

If it wasn't for you, I'd stop. Walk into a police station. End this. But I have you now . . . In America, I want to go to college . . . Find a good job. Find a way to pay for my sins . . .

Her phone buzzed. An email from Ewan: 'Heading off now. Henri sent photo of Caron – attached. Ring me when you're back.'

Grace put down her camera, and opened it.

The image unfolded agonizingly slowly.

'Wha-at?' she murmured.

First dark hair, then large brown bovine eyes and a squashed boxer's nose. Full lips, which on this face looked meaty and cruel.

The hooded man following her was *not* Mathieu Caron.

CHAPTER FIFTY-EIGHT

Sula was returning to the *Scots Today* office when she caught Ewaste-of-Space leaping down the escalator. He spotted her and started backing up, long legs reversing, face as guilty as sin.

'Where you off to?'

'To get some . . . nothing,' he said, legs whirring to keep up.

'Then get back up there. I need you on research. How many properties has Andrew's bought up in Edinburgh? Who did they buy them from? There's a pattern here. We need to find it.'

He made a face. 'I was just going to—'

'If this is about Grace Scott, don't even start.'

'Yes, sir.' He ran backwards all the way back up the escalator, like the bampot he was.

It took two hours, but between Ewan and Sula, they'd made enough phone calls and pulled in enough favours to find out this: Andrew's had bought and sold fifteen properties in Edinburgh in the past four years. As they'd been bought privately by Andrew's, only the resale price was available publicly. But after more phone work to Edinburgh estate agents as Rupert Banker,

Ewan managed to find the name of one of the sellers – Mrs Fogarty, aged ninety-one – and the clue she was in a nursing home 'somewhere near Dalgety Bay'.

'Right, Andrew's now,' Sula said. 'Ring them, tell them your mum's looking to do a distressed buyout. Needs the money fast. How does it work, et cetera.'

Ewan rang the landline in London on speakerphone. There was a click, then a long beep. 'Sounds dead to me.'

'Gone under? Bankruptcy?' Sula frowned.

'See if I can find out,' Ewan said, tapping away.

Sula stood up. 'I've had enough of this. Let's go find this Mrs Fogarty.'

They tried three nursing homes in the areas closest to Dalgety Bay before they found Mrs Fogarty, who was not quite as compos mentis as they'd hoped. Her eyes drifted between Sula and Ewan's faces, giving them gentle smiles. She smelt of talc, her white hair neatly brushed, her hand soft as velvet when Sula shook it.

A nurse brought them a cup of tea, beaming.

'How long she been here?' Sula whispered.

'Three years now. It's lovely for her to get visitors.' Her voice dropped to a whisper. 'No family.'

'Is that right? No family to come and see you, Mrs Fogarty?' Sula said.

'No, my daughter died. Meningitis.' She waved her fragile arm as if conducting an orchestra. 'No grandchildren.' Her gaze drifted towards unseen ghosts.

'Mrs Fogarty,' Sula said. 'You had a house in Cramond?'

'Oh, I did.' Her gaze refocused. 'Bought it after the war, me and Archie.' She nearly dropped her cup and Ewan took it from her.

'And you sold that house to Andrew's. Do you remember?' Sula said.

'Yes, I do.'

'Can I ask why you did it?'

'Well, it was the penguins.'

They'd lost her. 'The penguins?'

'Yes. I liked the idea of them, you see. To go and see them. I was going to go on a cruise, you see, to see the penguins.'

'Oh, you mean real penguins?' Sula said, relieved. 'In Antarctica or somewhere?'

'Yes. On one of these big cruise ships, but it was very expensive. I was going to take my friend Rose.'

'Was this Mr Stansfield that bought the house off you?'

'It was! That's right. I was pleased to get rid of it. It was a big old house. Too much for me. Had damp. He said that he'd give me ninety per cent of the price in cash and do all the paperwork for me. He said most firms like his give you eighty per cent, so I was pleased. There was no fees, too.' She smiled. 'I wanted to see the penguins, you see.'

'Did you get a lawyer to look at the contract, Mrs Fogarty?'

'No. That's what made it so easy. Mr Stansfield said I didn't need one because it was a package I was buying. His firm dealt with the legal side of it.'

'OK, and who valued your house, Mrs Fogarty?'

Her eyes widened. 'Well, Andrew's did, of course. The surveyor at the firm.'

Sula glanced at Ewan. 'Did he, now? And can I ask how much it was worth?'

Her lips formed an 'o' as if she had a secret. 'Don't tell anyone, but it was £186,000. Me and Archie bought it for fifty pounds!'

338

Ewan tapped on his phone and lifted it for Sula to see. Andrew's had sold the house the same year for £345,000.

'Mrs Fogarty, did you know how much the other houses in your street were selling for when you sold it?'

She frowned. 'Now how would I know that?'

'On the internet, maybe – these sites that tell you what your neighbours have sold theirs for.'

She looked baffled. 'I don't know. Is that something I should know . . . ?' She trailed off.

'Don't worry,' Sula said. 'Can I ask where you met Mr Stansfield?'

'Oh, he came to the house. Sent me a nice letter saying he was going to knock in a few days; then he made an appointment. You have to be careful, of course, so I had Rose with me, but she thought he was very nice, too.' Her eyes drifted again.

'Did you go and see the penguins?' Sula asked.

Mrs Fogarty made a face as if she'd been naughty. She whispered, 'No. I need all my money to be in here. A thousand pounds a week, you know.'

Sula shook her head at Ewan. The woman had sold her house for half of what it was worth, and it was draining away from her week by week. 'Mrs Fogarty, have you got a copy of that contract? Could I see it?'

With the nurse's help, they spent ten minutes working through Mrs Fogarty's drawers and boxes. In the end, they found it with her will.

Sula flicked through. 'Can I photograph this, please, Mrs Fogarty?' she said, keeping a lid on her tone. 'Not your name or anything. Just the small print.'

'Am I in trouble?' The elderly lady laughed mischievously.

'No, but the company who did this to you might be. Don't go

worrying about it now, but if I find anything out, I'll let you know.'

'Do what you want. I'm too old to worry about these things now.' She beamed. 'It was nice to have some visitors.'

Sula leaned forward. 'You know what, Mrs Fogarty, our Ewan here lives not too far. He loves a chat and a cup of tea. What if he comes to see you at the weekend sometimes? Would you like that?'

'Oh, I would.'

Ewan nodded eagerly, with a fixed grin. 'Oh, me too.'

'Good for the soul, Ewan,' Sula said as they walked out. 'Good for the soul.'

On the way back to the office, she wrangled with the information.

'Right, so we're getting there. These bastards talk old folk into a package where it all looks easy – they get ninety per cent cash straight up, no complications. Except, it's ninety per cent of their own valuation – going by Mrs Fogarty, it was almost half what the house was worth.'

'They must be counting on the old folk not knowing that.'

'So we've got three in the Edinburgh area,' Sula said, taking a sharp bend at speed, ignoring Ewan's dramatic dashboard-gripping.

'And maybe another twelve.'

'So fifteen altogether. Sold their properties to Andrew's cheap at a fake valuation – it sells them on at a huge profit. That's fraud. Need to get a lawyer on that.'

'So what do these three people we know about have in common?'

Ewan lifted a finger. 'One, they're old. Two, they live by themselves. Three, they've got equity in the house, been there long enough there's probably no mortgage. Four . . .' He stopped. 'Don't know.'

Sula braked sharply. He flew forwards.

'No bloody *relatives*, Ewan. No bloody relatives to spot what's going on.'

'David Pearce and Mrs McFarlay had relatives.'

She spun round. 'No, but that's it. They weren't *supposed* to exist. David and Philip Pearce had hardly been in Scotland for forty years. Colin McFarlay – I doubt his mother told anyone about him. She was embarrassed. Told me they'd lost contact since he was eighteen, anyway. She's only just put his photo back out.'

'But why did they sell?'

'Conned into it. You see it in the papers all the time – old folks so lonely they pay five grand to some smooth-talking bastard who turns up at the door telling them their gutter's hanging off. Mrs McFarlay's probably different, though. Probably just desperate to get out of that road after her husband died. Up to her eyes in debt. Can't imagine there'd be many neighbours popping in to check if she was OK, after what her Colin had been up to there.'

'So they're betting these old folk don't tell anyone.'

'That's the point – they've got nobody to tell.' She accelerated through the lights. 'This is motive, Ewan. This Mr Stansfield from London comes up, does his dirty work. Then it goes wrong. Colin McFarlay turns up. Tells him he knows what's going on. Maybe they agree to meet . . . Next thing, Colin disappears. Mr Pearce Senior tells his son what *he's* done and he flies over from Australia. Suspicious about this deal. Demands a meeting with Mr Stansfield to discuss it and – bam! – disappears . . .'

'Wowzers,' Ewan said.

'Mr Pearce Senior's a proud man – who's betting David knew that and lied about where he was going that day? Told him he was off hiking, so he could deal with Andrew's in private, not embarrass his father.'

As they talked, Sula noticed Ewan fidgeting and going quiet. 'What is it?'

He sighed heavily. 'Don't shout, but Grace Scott—'

'Ewan!'

'She's in a bit of trouble.'

'What?'

'There's a guy been following her about this story. She thinks he's followed her round Europe and back here – she saw him in Lower Largo this morning, and she's trapped on the other side of the bridge hiding from him.'

'She told the police?'

'Not yet. She asked me to wait till she'd checked something out . . .'

'And . . . ?'

'I was going to do it when you saw me.'

'What is it?'

'That dead guy in her flat, Lucian Grabole – she's found out where he was working. The police are releasing his name to the press this afternoon, and she's running out of time – and I said I'd ask if anyone remembered him there.'

Sula growled. 'Where is it?'

Ewan checked his phone GPS. 'Ross Turn. Half a mile that way.'

She stuck on her indicator and cut across the lane, causing beeping behind.

'You've got ten minutes.'

*

342

When they parked in Ross Turn, it was clear they weren't the only ones. A number of cars had squeezed into the tiny cul-de-sac to take advantage of the free parking. Ewan led Sula to the corner and pointed over at the building fifty metres to the right. A man at the doorway in a suave suit handed a couple in front of them a brochure and waved them inside.

'Looks like an open day,' Sula said.

Ewan put his arm in hers. 'Let's pretend you and me are just married – you got me off a mail-order website for sexy young husbands, and we're looking for our first love pad.'

'I'll love-pad you.' She retrieved her arm and smacked him round the head.

At the main door, they saw a long hall, painted cream, expensive granite tiles on the floor.

'I like theez house very much, darlink,' Ewan said in a bad accent.

'Shush.'

The man in the suit returned. 'Hello. Welcome. Looking at properties today?'

Sula saw a frown cross Ewan's face. She thrust a card into the man's hand. 'Sula McGregor, *Scots Today*.'

'Oh, hello. How you doing? Is this for the property section? Great stuff.'

'No,' Sula said. 'I'm looking for a man who was working here – Lucian Grabole.'

The man's cheery grin didn't budge. 'Sorry, who?'

'Lucian Grabole?'

'Never heard of him.'

'Well, he was working here as a decorator a few months back, so you should.'

Ewan held up his phone with the French police arrest shot on the screen. Again, Sula saw his eyes searching the man's face.

343

The man put on stupid wee glasses with a designer label to look. 'Oh, him? Aye, I know him. That wasn't his name, though. He was called Youssi something. He was here last year.'

'Youssi?' Sula motioned to Ewan, and he wrote it down.

'Aye – Youssi Jabir or Jaboor or something. He was from Lebanon.'

'Cash in hand, was it?' she asked.

The man appraised her with sparkling blue eyes that looked unnaturally animated within the wrinkles around them. 'The guy was down on his luck. Told us he was saving to get a flight home. His mother was sick. What you gonna do?'

'Right,' Sula said. 'And you are?'

The man turned sideways and pointed his hand diagonally for her to shake in an affected manner.

'John Brock. I'm the developer.'

CHAPTER FIFTY-NINE

'Kent, Kent! You in there?'

The man hid in the toilet.

The coughing had started twenty minutes ago.

The husband had heard it. Run down the stairs.

The man sat on the toilet, spluttering helplessly, wanting to kill him.

'Come on, Kent,' the husband shouted. 'Just want a quick word.'

Stumbling back into the storeroom, the man knew it was time.

Cigarette smoke drifted under the door, making his cough worse.

And that grating voice. It sounded as if he were lying on the ground.

'Come *ooooonn*. Kent! I just want to talk to you. We both know that you were here when the guy died. That was you, wasn't it, Kent?'

The man sat there, shaking. He screwed up his eyes to keep the memory out, but it was no good.

He was back there, that night in February, and it was happening again.

*

It was the noise that woke him. At first, he wasn't sure what it was. It mimicked rain. A drip, drip, drip.

Then all became clear.

Footsteps. On the fire escape outside. Clumsy and staggered. Then, upstairs, the flat door opening and shutting. The faint click of a key turning.

He knew then they were coming for him. That they knew he was hiding and were going to surprise him, and force him out, just like they did before.

His chest tightened as if on a rack, ready to snap and release his thumping heart from his body. He stood up, tiptoed to the stool and peered to see how many there were.

The backyard was shadowy and lit by faint pools of lamplight from the street light in the alley. The tower block was mainly in darkness.

Footsteps moved across the floor above.

He listened, eyes wide on the ceiling.

Upstairs?

It was when he turned back that he saw the masked man.

He was in the yard, approaching the tenement from the back gate. Next door's security light exploded, illuminating him for a second before he dived away. A white suit covered him from his head to his feet, a white surgical mask on his face.

The security light went off.

Now, there were new footsteps on the wet fire escape. Softer, faster. Then a smash of glass. Above, an alarmed shout. The rain thundered outside. Now heavy footsteps across the ceiling. Another smashing sound on the fire escape. A door opening and an alarmed conversation. Two sets of footsteps now across the ceiling. An agonized yelp, then a sound that left nothing to the imagination. A vicious, dull, horrible crack, followed by a thud that shook the ceiling.

Now the footsteps shrank to one person again. Almost balletic, like a child's. They moved around lightly. Then the door on the fire escape shut again.

Now. Was this it? Were they coming for him? Had someone in the tower block seen him through the storeroom window and called the police?

He peered cautiously out.

The masked man was under the fire escape, pulling a plastic bag from his pocket. He placed it on the ground, removed his plastic shoes and stood on it. Then he removed his white gloves, mask and body suit, replaced the white plastic shoes, stuffed the suit, gloves and mask into the plastic bag, and crept off, disappearing over the back gate, into the night.

The man stumbled off the stool. His chest tightened further across his lungs, not allowing them to inflate. He punched at them, inhaling with a grating sound. Dropping to the floor, he gasped, trying to hold on to the stool, but he missed. His head and shoulders fell forward.

Everything went black.

The door in the storeroom banged again, shaking him from his thoughts of that night.

'Kent! Come on, man. Open the door.'

He crept out on all fours.

'Kent!' *Bang, bang.* 'Kent! Come on, man. I need to know if you saw something. My wife's out there, God knows where, trying to find out what happened. And I'm thinking you must know something. I *know* you were here!'

The man crawled behind the boxes. His hands crept over the plastic bag. The one he'd found that night.

*

It was a few hours before he spotted it. First, he woke on cold tiles, head in a vicious clamp, nauseous. Freezing, he'd thrown on a blanket, and stood up, stiff and sore, and staggered to turn on the wall heater.

The night's events returned in a toxic rush.

Climbing onto the stool, teeth chattering, he saw now it had been no dream. Tiny fragments of glass lay at eye level on the fire-escape stairs. He listened, dreading a groan or scraping noise above.

Nothing.

Maybe the other man had gone. Injured, he'd dragged himself out.

Two men, the new occupants of the flat above, fighting over something that was nothing to do with him.

That was it. That was the easiest version to believe.

That way, he was still safe.

Even though he knew it wasn't really true.

And then, as he was stepping down, he saw it. Lying under the fire escape. A solitary white glove, wrinkled up like a used condom, smeared in brown, lying on wet weeds.

The rack began to wind again in his chest. If he left it, Mr Singh would see it. Pick it up, look up. The police would come. The rack tightened.

But if he brought it inside. Kept it. *Just in case.*

He fashioned a pole out of Mr Singh's mop and broom, tied together with twine. It took two attempts to hook it; then he dragged it towards him. The blood was fresh, smeared on the fingers. Before he could think what that meant, he stuffed it in a plastic bag, and hid it behind the fridge.

There. It was gone. As if it had never happened.

He was still safe.

*

'Kent, come on.' The banging worsened on the storeroom door.

Footsteps sounded on the other side of the room, from the shop.

The door handle turned three times as usual.

'OK?' a whisper came. Mr Singh walked in. 'What is going on?'

The man's eyes moved to the door.

Mr Singh looked pained. 'Him again? Go back inside.' He nodded to the hiding place behind the boxes. He waited, then strode to the door and opened it. 'Mac, what can I help you with?'

There was a grunt of surprise. 'Hey, Mr Singh. Just looking for your pal there.' His voice was slurred with drink.

'He's not here. He's left. As I say, he was just here for a few days.'

There was a snort. 'See, I'm not sure that's true. Because I came down here last night and heard him snoring. So, I'm not saying you're a liar or anything, but . . .' He laughed. 'You're a liar! No, sorry . . . Didn't mean it. Are you sure he's just not in here somewhere? Can I just . . . ?'

A new firmness entered Mr Singh's voice. 'No, you can't. And while you're here, I wanted to say, if I find you stealing cigarettes from my storeroom again, I'll call the police, neighbour or no neighbour.'

The husband laughed bitterly. 'Oh, that's fine. You do that. How's council feel about you renting out a storeroom? Pretty sure that's against the law having people sleeping in shops. Taking rent off them.'

Mr Singh kept his calm. 'I helped out a friend for a few days. No rent changed hands. Story over. Now you need to get yourself upstairs.'

Mac continued, 'But I'm not going. Because a guy died in my

flat, and your pal Kent was here when it happened. I know that. And he knows something. I know he does.'

'Kent?' Mr Singh said, aggravated. 'Who's Kent? Listen, pal, you need to get on your way. Last time I'm asking.'

There was a sound of tussling, and the back door slammed.

The hammering started again. The husband began to shout, 'My wife's not here because of you. You know something, and you're gonna fucking tell me what it is.' The door buckled as if he'd kicked hard. 'You've fucked everything right up, you cunt.'

Another kick, then silence. A creak of stairs, then the door slammed up above. Loud music drummed through the ceiling.

Mr Singh whispered, 'Robbie. You OK?'

The man watched him wild-eyed, trying to breathe.

Mr Singh reached out a hand. 'Listen, I'm sorry. I've tried my best for you, but we need some help here. I need to call someone.'

'No!'

'It's getting out of control. I'm not worried about the council. But the guy's right. I lied to the police about you being in here when that guy died, because you begged me to, Robbie, and I shouldn't have done it.' He bent down. 'Are you listening?'

At the sound of his name, the man began to cry. Sobs wracked through him at what his life had become. 'I can't. I can't!'

Mr Singh removed the boxes one by one, and held out a hand. 'Come on, let's fix this, eh? Before it gets worse? I won't let anything bad happen to you, I promise.'

'No!'

The music thudded louder now through the ceiling.

Mr Singh stood up. 'Right, I'm going to shut the shop and make us a cup of tea.'

Robbie rocked forward, anguished. 'They're going to find out. They're going to take me away.'

Mr Singh switched on the kettle. 'Robbie, you can't live here. We need to get that sorted. And it's not your fault. The guy was dead, Robbie. It was nothing to do with you. The police said it was instant. He fell in the kitchen, hit his head. You didn't cause that.'

'No. But . . .'

'But what?'

No longer knowing what to do, the man reached into the cavity and pulled out the plastic bag.

Mr Singh's kindly expression changed as he saw the dried blood. 'Robbie, what have you done?'

CHAPTER SIXTY

Grace spent an hour in the supermarket car park, compiling her transcriptions and notes on her laptop, then drove the long way back to the city via Kincardine, and pulled up at the hotel near the airport that she and Mac had booked after Thailand.

Checking for the silver four-by-four, she booked a room, took her laptop and camera bag upstairs, and sat down at the desk. She rang Ewan and left a message to ring her back if he had news. There were three new messages from Mac. No longer thinking about it, she deleted them automatically.

She opened her laptop. It was time to start writing. This afternoon, a French journalist somewhere would recognize François Boucher's name in a newswire or Twitter feed. Time was running out.

She laid out her photos and wrote a headline, to start herself off – 'Do You Know This Man?'

Then a subhead: '*Scots Today* photojournalist Grace Scott returned from honeymoon to find a dead stranger in her Edinburgh kitchen. Here, she documents what happened when her obsession to discover his identity led her into a world of stolen identities, organized crime and families ripped tragically apart.'

She sat back and played with her photos, wondering which one *Scots Today* would choose as an opener.

Nothing fitted. Not the arrest shot of François Boucher, not the letters, or portraits of Lucian's contacts.

There was only one that *would* work.

She flicked through her memory card, just as she had done here, three months ago, till she found it.

It was perfect.

The eerie light in the kitchen, the dark shoes lying on the floor.

'Do You Know This Man?'

Would *Scots Today* dare use it?

Would she dare show them?

An ache came for Nicu, and his allegiance.

She took a deep breath, hoping *Scots Today* had a good lawyer to work out if she was in trouble for photographing a dead body at a crime scene.

Her fingers hit the buttons: 'I'm not sure when I knew the dead man was in my flat. Just that there was an odd stillness when I opened the door, the sense of a presence, but at the same time, not.'

She typed on, recalling how Mac had tossed a coin in Gallon Street to decide who went to Morrisons to buy food and who entered the flat to make tea and turn on the heating. How her emotions at finding the body were so affected by the recent death of her own father. The depth of the connection she felt to the anonymous man. The need to find his family.

Her decision to photograph him.

Grace typed for two more hours, then sat back, looking out at the industrial landscape, recalling her mood that next day.

Wondering how this story would end.

She checked her phone. Two more messages from Mac.
She wrote on.

Ewan returned her call when she was halfway through.

'Hey, you still hiding?' he asked.

'Yup, in a hotel, writing – and bad news. He's not Mathieu Caron. Must be another of Caron's thugs.'

Ewan tutted. 'OK, well, you need to be careful.'

'Did you go to Lucian's workplace?'

He perked up. 'Aye – it was interesting.' He explained about Youssi.

'Wow,' Grace said. 'So Lucian was using a *fourth* name in Edinburgh, to hide from Mathieu Caron maybe. So what did they say about him?'

Ewan told her. 'Quiet, hard-working. Nobody took much notice of him. It's a big development, though. There's a lot of guys working there. The owner, this John Brock guy, didn't even know who we were talking about for a while.'

Ice crept through Grace's veins. 'What did you say?'

'John Brock. The developer. It's driving me nuts. I know that guy's face from somewhere.'

Her house-warming party at Gallon Street.

'So where was this place?' Grace said quietly.

'Some warehouse development in Leith. Youssi painted the flats, then disappeared. Cash in hand. Nobody spoke to him much.'

'Right.'

'You OK there? Sula nearly took my balls off for doing that for you.'

'Yes. Thanks. How's your story?'

He started to tell her, but she wasn't listening.

Lucian Grabole had worked at John's warehouse with Mac.

'Ewan, I've got to go,' she cut across him. 'If I send over what I've done so far, would you look at it? See what you think of the angle?'

'No problem.'

CHAPTER SIXTY-ONE

Mac knew Lucian Grabole?

Grace sat at her laptop in shock, knowing she couldn't write any more. She sent her part-written story to Ewan, and went to the window.

When she'd asked Mac about Lucian Grabole, he'd said no – was that because he knew him as 'Youssi' from Lebanon?

She folded her arms across her chest.

It was time. She had to face him.

By the time she headed towards Leith, Edinburgh's rush-hour traffic had dried the roads to a slow sludge.

She parked and watched the warehouse, realizing she could see Ross Turn across the street. The warehouse had transformed since her last visit in March. The restaurant was open on the ground floor now, the menu clearly displayed on the wall. The two floors of double-height flats were finished, all sign of work gone, a 'For sale' sign in the window of one.

She craned to see Mac inside the studio space at the far end. No lights.

Tentatively, she lifted her phone.

There was a tap on her window. She jumped, putting it down. John Brock waved.

'Hello, stranger!' he said, as she opened the door. 'You're back. How d'you get on with your story?'

'Um. Not quite sure yet. Is Mac around?'

'Aye. He's in the office on a call with the builder. Come on in.'

John gave her a cheerful kiss on the cheek, and they headed across the road. 'He'll be pleased to see you. Face like a wet rag all week. So how d'you get on? Find your guy?'

She told him scant details as they headed through the giant double doors of the restaurant entrance, which gave access to the upstairs flats. They passed the closed door of John's office, where Mac was on the phone.

'Come on, he'll be a while. I'll show you round while you're waiting – changed a bit since you were last here, eh?'

'Yeah, looks amazing. Sorry I missed the opening,' she said as they entered the restaurant. 'Was the other photographer OK?'

'Absolutely fine – no bother.'

The main seating area was stunning, with John's usual eye for design: hardwood floors and exposed brick, white tablecloths. A specially commissioned blue stained-glass window by a Scottish contemporary artist was the main feature of the room. Tall picture windows overlooked the water. A mezzanine floor with extra seating sat at the top of a spiral staircase, with even better views across the docks.

John walked with the gait of a country landowner surveying his estate. Then he led her to Mac's studio. It, too, was transformed. A vast white space with an ingenious suspended bar hanging in the centre. John explained how it could be moved around the room, depending on use. He also showed her how the walls and floor opened up to create a large photography studio and a DJ corner, and how blocks of the floor raised to create a catwalk for fashion events, or a stage for gigs. A balcony circled the room, allowing space for more spectators, again with views across the water. Three giant gold-and-violet abstract art installations on the wall heralded Mac's entry into gallery exhibitions.

Sadness gripped her. Mac had achieved something amazing here, and she hadn't been listening to him. It had all come together for him, too, finally. His eye for design, his gift for bringing people together for events. His business sense. She'd not believed in this project.

They'd let each other down.

There would be grief when they parted, but this room gave her hope. Mac had his own future to race towards, too. It wasn't too late for either of them.

Grace imagined Lucian up a ladder painting these walls, secretly planning his own future with Anna and the children.

'Right, darlin'. What can I get you? Got a nice Sancerre there.' John pointed at the chiller cabinet. 'Or a cocktail? Or got a Danish vodka, if you're in the mood for that after your trip?'

'Wine's good, thanks.'

He poured her one with a flourish.

'So, is the decorating finished?' she asked casually.

'Aye – bit of tiling to do in the studio kitchen and toilets. Getting the lift in next week and we're done. Come and have a look. Did he tell you we've sold half the apartments?'

'No. That's great.'

'Yup. Reckon after Saturday's open day, we'll get rid of the lot.'

She followed him up to the first floor. Front doors lay open into empty double-height apartments. Everything was white here, too, ready for each owner to make it their own. Kitchen cupboards lay empty; the tall windows over the water were curtain-less. Inside each apartment, more spiral staircases led up to loft-style mezzanine bedrooms.

'What d'you think?' John asked, proud.

'It's beautiful,' she said, touching the fresh-painted walls. 'The finish is amazing. Are these the guys that decorated our flat?'

No answer. She turned.

John looked up from his phone. 'Don't know, darlin'. You'd have to ask the guy that manages the team. Right.' He headed to the door. 'That's a delivery downstairs. Wanna have a wee seat at the bar while you're waiting for Mac?'

'Thanks.'

Back downstairs, she sat in Mac's studio as John exited the front door for his delivery.

Lucian was just part of a team of decorators, she reassured herself.

John had little to do with them.

Even if Mac had met Lucian, he'd only known him as Youssi.

This had nothing to do with him, either.

Lucian must have gone to Gallon Street, knowing it was empty. That Mac was on honeymoon. That must be the link.

She checked her watch, willing Mac to finish his call, dreading it at the same time.

Down the corridor, a key turned in the warehouse's entrance door, and she thought nothing much about it.

CHAPTER SIXTY-TWO

'Robbie, Robbie, look at me.'

The man sat on his stool unable to breathe, the thought of being taken from the storeroom making him want to lash out. Fight.

'No. No. No.' He waved Mr Singh away.

'Listen to me. Robbie.' The newsagent's voice was tired from the last hour trying to persuade him to do what he wanted. 'There's no choice now. What you've just told me is that the guy upstairs was killed. That's serious, Robbie. You've got evidence here that someone needs to see.'

'No!' His head ached.

Mr Singh persisted. 'You're ill, Robbie. They'll understand. You're a good man. You've saved hundreds of lives in your job. I'm going to tell them what's happened here. We'll explain about your crash, and how bad it was for you. And about your Ida dying like that. How you're ill.'

'No!' It was all he could do not to punch him away.

Mr Singh sank to his haunches. 'Listen, Robbie. I had no idea myself how bad this was till you've been staying here. We'll tell them how the bailiffs put you out your house when you were ill, and nobody was helping you. Just tell them how it happened.

That I found you in the street in a bad way, put you up for a few nights here; then you told me you couldn't leave. How you've got yourself locked in here, in your own head. The thing is, Robbie, I'm trying to help, but it's getting worse. You need proper help. A doctor.'

'No!' Robbie held his ears. 'No!'

Mr Singh patted his back and he flinched.

'You and Ida were good neighbours to my mum. And I'm looking out for you now. But we're both getting ourselves into trouble here. I lied about you being in here. I didn't see much harm in it at the time, but if I'd known what you just told me, I couldn't have done it, Robbie. So I'm going up to Lother Street now to see DI Robertson. I'm going to explain everything, and get him to arrange help for you tonight, OK? Maybe get you into a hospital.'

'No!' He gripped the bars on the window.

'Robbie, if this guy Mac upstairs tells them first, it's going to be worse. They'll be charging in here arresting you on the spot. Sticking you in a cell. And me. We'll lose our chance to explain what's happened. Let me go talk to this guy about how ill you are, how I didn't know what to do to help you. He'll understand. OK? The important thing is you tell them now what's gone on upstairs. That's serious.'

Robbie jerked back in a panic, knocking the fridge.

'I'll be back in an hour. We're going to get you through this, OK?' He patted Robbie's shoulder again and left.

Robbie held the bars, watching Ida's face on the floor, beseeching her pencil-drawn eyes to calm him. To forgive him for the coward he'd become.

CHAPTER SIXTY-THREE

'Grace!'

She heard Mac before she saw him. Heavy footsteps ran down the corridor from John's office. The door to the studio flew open and he staggered in.

She couldn't believe the sight of him.

His light brown hair was dirty and dishevelled, shadows underlined his eyes. He hadn't shaved for days, and stank of stale cigarette smoke.

'What's happened?' she said.

He walked past her, behind the bar, and glared.

'Mac? Are you OK?'

'Oh yeah, fuckin' fan-dabi-dozi, cheers.' He opened a beer and the top careered off onto the floor. He leaned on the bar watching her.

In twenty years, she'd never seen him like this. Drunk, yes, but not obnoxious. It was almost like he . . . *knew what she'd done.*

He took out a cigarette and lit it.

'Can you do that in here?' she said.

'Ha!' he snorted. 'Can I do that? Watch me.'

He inhaled deeply, with a contented face.

'Mac, I need to ask you something. The guy who died in our flat . . .'

He flung up his arm. 'Oh, don't fucking start!'

'Mac, what's wrong with you?'

'Fuck off, Grace,' he sneered.

'Mac?' She tried to touch his arm.

'I said, fuck off!'

Astonished, she shut the studio door before John heard and sacked him on the spot.

'Mac, calm down, for God's sake. You've got to listen to me. The guy in our flat *worked here*. He was a decorator. John told a journalist that he was called Youssi. Do you know that?'

Mac stumbled sideways, knocking the chiller cabinet, opening his eyes wide to focus.

She caught his arm. 'Did you know Youssi who worked here?'

'*Youssi, Youssi, Youssi, Youssi!*' he sang to the tune of the Kaiser Chiefs' 'Ruby', lifting his hand from her and above his head.

Something was terribly wrong with him. 'Mac, what's going on?'

He shook his head, almost bewildered.

She felt his arm again, and this time he let it stay there. 'Mac, I'm sorry. We both know we have to talk about us, but right now, this is crucial. A guy died in our flat and he worked here. We told the police we'd never seen him, and that was a lie. I can't write my story unless I know the truth.'

He dragged himself onto a stool. 'Oh, your *story*. I'm sorry. Your fuckin' *story*. Of course!'

She took his hands, and forced him to meet her eyes. 'Mac, you need to sober up before John sees you, and tell me what happened. Did Lucian break in because he heard you talk about going on honeymoon and he knew the flat was empty? Was he on the team that renovated our flat? Because if that's it, then that's fine. In fact, it explains why he was there. Maybe he just wanted somewhere to sleep to save money. It's got nothing to do with you. But I need to know.'

Mac banged down his beer, sending the pale liquid across the counter. His blue eyes were bloodshot and contained an expression she struggled to identify. He pointed at her. 'You're leaving me.'

Suddenly, she saw him, aged sixteen, his tie undone, sleeves rolled up against the rules, charming the maths teacher with a joke and making everyone laugh. Her sitting three desks behind, thinking if Mackenzie Lowe was all she ever got in life, it would be enough.

That was her mistake.

That wasn't his fault.

'Mac, I love you,' she said gently. 'That's not going to stop. You're my best friend. We've been friends our whole lives.'

With one movement, he smashed the bottle sideways onto the floor.

'Mac!'

He jerked away.

'Stop it before John sees you like this.'

'*Sees* me like this?' He laughed bitterly, and his voice broke. 'He's fuckin'—' He broke off. His head dipped to the counter. A low groan came from his mouth. 'Grace, I've fucked up. I've *fucked up.*'

For a moment, she thought she understood. 'Mac. No. This isn't about that girl. In the club. It's really not. It's about us. It's probably why you slept with her in the first place, because things were going wrong. I can see it now. We're just wanting different things from life. Something new.'

'It's not that.' Mac banged the bar, like a teenager whose mother didn't understand him.

'What, then?'

To her surprise, Mac fell into her. She caught him, frightened. 'What's wrong?'

'I wanted to talk to you.' His voice broke. 'I wanted to tell you, but you didn't come back. You didn't ring me. I didn't even know which country you were in.'

She stroked his back. 'OK, but I'm here now, and it's going to be fine. We'll clear things up with the police. And we'll sort things out with us. We're always going to look out for each other. That's not going to stop. I'm so proud of you. This place is amazing. You've done . . .'

Over his shoulder, she saw the Danish vodka. A chill went through her.

'Mac?'

He didn't move.

She prodded him.

'Mac? Where was I when I last rang you?'

CHAPTER SIXTY-FOUR

The *Scots Today* office was in chaos today. The surprise resigna-
tion of a Scottish minister had sent a whirlwind through the
newsroom and the editor marched around, shouting for headlines. In the reviews section, the staff were preparing for tonight's
premiere in town of a new Scottish film with two Hollywood
A-listers in attendance.

Sula slammed down her phone, trying to hear herself think.

'Ewan,' she called across the desk, 'the lawyer says the
Andrew's contract is bollocks. Complete scam. The postal address
is fake, too. Think. If they don't answer the phone, we need something else to get hold of them.'

But he wasn't listening. His eyes were fixed on his screen.

'Ewan!'

He looked up. 'You need to see this.'

'No, I don't. Not right now.'

She lifted the phone and left a message, not optimistic about
a reply.

'Mrs McFarlay, Sula McGregor. Regarding our investigation
into your son's death, we know you sold your house to a firm
called Andrew's. I'm trying to get hold of Mr Stansfield there

and can't. It's urgent. Do you have a mobile for him, or a different address? Or another name maybe?'

She was about to hang up when to her surprise, Mrs McFarlay answered.

There was no greeting. Just a question. 'Why are you asking me that?' Her voice was cold.

Sula stuck her finger in her ear to drown out the newsroom. 'I don't know yet. It's possible there's a link.'

'Are the police following it?'

If Mrs McFarlay rang DI Robertson right now, her lead was blown. 'If there is, we'll give everything to the police.'

Silence. Sula gritted her jaw, willing a reply.

Mrs McFarlay spoke again. 'That headline on your piece – I never said that.' A bitterness entered her voice. '"Why *my* boy?" So self-pitying.'

'Mrs McFarlay, I write the piece; the subs and the editor, they sell it. If you want people to read your story, it has to be sold. What can I say? I fight my corner, but I don't always win.'

A pause. The silence of the lonely bungalow in the background. 'I got a call on my mobile once,' Mrs McFarlay said, 'when I was at the till in Marks & Spencer. It cut off after two rings. I thought it was an emergency about Colin – maybe one of his friends telling me he'd relapsed. So I rang back when I was in the car. Mr Stansfield answered. We were both confused. He was surprised I had the number. I kept it, in case I needed to get hold of him during the house sale, but next time I rang, he never answered. I mentioned it and he said the mobile had been stolen, and always to use the landline.'

'So you think he'd rung you by accident from his mobile, the first time, then cut off?'

'Yes.'

'Do you think his mobile *was* stolen?'

'No. I think he didn't want me to have it in case I harassed him after I realized what he'd done with my house.'

Sula paused. 'So he ripped you off, too?'

Her voice cracked. 'I was widowed. Grieving. In debt. I just wanted rid of it. He was so charming. He sent flowers on the day of Morris's memorial service. Stayed for a cup of tea and a chat. I just didn't know how much he'd taken till Colin came out of rehab and checked on the internet. Saw what the one down the road went for.' A long sigh. 'You feel so stupid.'

'How much did he give you?'

A long silence. 'Eight hundred thousand. It left me enough to buy this place and pay off the business debts, and Colin's rehab. Then Andrew's sold it on for £1.2 million.'

'Did you think of prosecuting him?'

'How could I? It was all legal – he had a solicitor, and a contract. It was my fault for being stupid. Then Colin disappeared and I just wanted out, tell the truth.' A catch came into her voice. 'Did this man hurt my son? Because of me?'

Sula hesitated. 'I don't know, Mrs McFarlay, I don't. But give me today. If I find out what I think I can find out, you can call the police tomorrow, OK?'

'I'll give you one day.'

'Thank you. Now, could I have that mobile phone number?'

'Hang on.' Mrs McFarlay read out Mr Stansfield's contact.

Sula thanked her, and rang it.

The mobile rang out three times; then a cheerful voice answered. Sula pressed 'end call' and stood up.

'Jesus Christ.'

'Sula! *You need to see this*,' Ewan repeated, his cheeks pink.

'Not now.' She waved at the editor, motioned to his office and

marched towards it, the voice from the phone ringing in her ear.
Hello. John Brock.

Ten minutes later, she returned, to find Ewan sitting on her desk,
holding her keypad above his head in one hand and her mobile
in the other.

'What?' she yelled.

'You need to look at Grace's story.'

'Ewan, I'm warning you about that girl. For Christ's sake. We
need to get back to Leith.'

She went to pick up her jacket. Ewan grabbed that, and held
it above his head, too.

'Son . . .' she growled.

'The guy Grace is chasing, Lucian Grabole. The one that
worked for John Brock,' Ewan said. 'He and his father put
people down wells. Alive. Tied them up.'

Her hand dropped to her side. 'What?'

'I've just read her first draft. Lucian Grabole's partner told
Grace that's how they killed people, him and his dad – putting
them down wells alive.'

She pushed her glasses up her nose. 'When did Grabole die?'

'February.'

'After McFarlay and Pearce were killed?'

'Yes.'

'So Grabole could have killed them?'

'Yes.'

Sula blew out her cheeks. 'Know what I've just found out?
John Brock is Andrew's.'

Ewan's eyes grew huge. 'No way.'

'Aye.'

Sula tapped the desk. 'What the hell is going on here?'

Ewan sat on the edge. 'What if John Brock paid Lucian

Grabole to kill McFarlay and Pearce to shut them up after they threatened him with the police?' He hit the desk. 'I know where I've seen John Brock now – a party at Grace's flat.' His hands cupped his face. 'He's her husband's boss. Mac.'

Sula took her jacket off him. 'Ring her. Tell her what's happening.'

'I just did. Her phone's switched off.'

'Where is she now?'

'Holed up at a hotel near the airport, writing up her story. She sent me the first thousand words to look through.'

'But hang on – she thinks the guy chasing her is French?'

'That's what she said,' Ewan nodded. 'One of Lucian Grabole's henchmen from Paris.'

Sula watched the chaos in the office, knowing she was about to bring a new storm to the place.

'What if he's not? What if he's from here?'

They took Sula's car out to the airport, turning off into the industrial estate. Ewan sat forward, no longer appearing to care how fast she drove.

'Hurry up, Sula.'

She overtook a lorry, and screeched to a halt outside the hotel. Ewan ran in, and returned two minutes later. 'She left an hour ago.'

'Right. Get in.'

Sula reversed.

'Where is she, Ewan? Think.'

CHAPTER SIXTY-FIVE

It was half an hour since Mr Singh had left for the police station in Lother Street.

Yet Robbie still couldn't let go of the window bars.

Metal cut into his hot, damp flesh. His vision was so blurred he could hardly see to the toilet door. Each time he imagined DI Robertson turning up here, his grip tightened, turning his fingers white.

Through the window there was a movement.

Was that them – coming for him?

He tried to focus.

A green blur spread across the fence.

He blinked, trying to clear his vision.

The green splodge grew bigger, moving towards him.

The police wore *black and yellow*.

The green turned to white. Confused, he tried to make sense. Like . . .

A groan came from his mouth like a grille being moved from a hole.

A bang landed on the back door.

Not a knock. A kick.

Four more kicks landed on the locked door.

The man in the white mask was breaking in.

Trembling, Robbie fumbled into the centre of the room. There were only two ways out, and the door into Mr Singh's shop would be locked. With nowhere else to turn, he staggered to the door between that and the toilet.

A furious kick rattled the back door. Something metallic fell on the ground.

The man's full weight was on it now.

The fourth door. His last option.

Robbie touched the Yale key in the lock. It burned into his skin, but he turned it and pulled.

A beige blur of carpet and white walls lay in front of him as the door opened.

Behind him, there was a final smash as the back door broke off its hinges. Falling forward into the space beyond, Robbie shut the door behind him, panting.

A new kick landed on this door now. Then another.

He reached out and felt stairs. Inside, his heart was exploding.

'Help me!' he shouted, trying to climb them, but no words came out.

CHAPTER SIXTY-SIX

Sula sped to Gallon Street shouting at Ewan to point out Grace's flat. They double-parked outside a closed newsagent's, and ran to the door of number 6.

'Which one?' she shouted.

'Flat A, I think.' Ewan rang the intercom. No answer. They tried the other flats next.

'Come on, come on,' Sula said. If they couldn't find this lassie, she'd have to ring the police – story blown.

An answer came from Flat C. 'He-llo?' a woman said in a posh Edinburgh drawl.

'Can you let us in? It's an emergency,' Ewan said.

A pause. 'Sorry. Who are you?'

'Friends of Grace Scott in Flat A.'

A longer pause now. 'Is Grace not there? Because I really can't—'

'I've got no time for this,' Sula said, pushing past Ewan. 'We need to get in there now, doll – can you let us in? Life and death.'

A faintly irritated sigh. 'Sorry. When you say life and death, do you mea—'

'God's sake, will you let us in?'

A tut. Then a click.

It seemed to take ten minutes. A middle-aged bohemian woman, her hair piled on her head, in a long skirt and blouson shirt, answered the door.

'Thank you – out the way, please,' Sula said, pushing past.

'Sorry, who are you again?'

'The bloody cavalry. Which one?' Sula yelled to Ewan.

'A – top of the stairs.'

Sula ran up and went to bang on the door.

But she didn't have the chance.

Right that minute, the door next to Flat A flew open, banging into her.

The bohemian woman gasped.

In the doorway was a thickset bald man with old burn marks across part of his head, and on his hands. Behind him were stairs down to a shut door.

'Jesus. Where d'you come from?' Sula said, rubbing her arm.

'That's a *cupboard*!' the bohemian woman said, astonished.

Behind the old man came a banging.

The old fella was mouthing through dry lips. Sula leaned forward.

'*Help me*,' he was saying.

'Help you with what?'

The old man's eyes were unseeing and lost.

'Someone's kicking that door in,' Ewan said, leaning past.

Sula grabbed the old man's limp hand. 'Who's that after you? Down the stairs?'

He groaned again, his eyes fixed beyond her in terror.

'Come on out of there,' Sula said. But he wouldn't move.

The bohemian woman knelt down. 'Can you just come over the step, dear?'

The man shook his head, and began to cry.

'Poor bastard.' Sula turned. 'Ewan, call the police. Someone's after this guy.'

She yelled down the cupboard stairs. 'The police are on their way, pal, so if I was you, I'd give it a rest. And there's four of us here.'

The kicking stopped. She left the old man with the bohemian woman, and sat on the steps, pulling out her laptop and phone.

'What are you doing?' Ewan said, ringing 999.

'Getting a story online before the police get here.'

'What are you like?'

'Show must go on, son,' she muttered. Sula rang the mobile number for Andrew's Equity. This time, she got voicemail.

'Message for John Brock,' Sula said. 'Sula McGregor here, *Scots Today*. Doing a piece about your company Andrew's Equity and its connection to the families of Colin McFarlay and David Pearce. I'm after a quote. Ring me back, please. Thank you . . .'

CHAPTER SIXTY-SEVEN

Shaken, Grace checked John wasn't in the corridor and returned to the bar, where Mac lay, head on his hands.

'Mac.' She tapped his cheek, to make him look up. 'John asked me if I wanted Danish vodka – how did he know I'd been to Copenhagen? I didn't speak to you or John after Paris.'

Mac doubled up like he was ill.

'Mac.' She shook his arm. 'You're scaring me.'

'They're going to kill me.'

'Who?' she said, alarmed.

Up close, she realized how dirty his clothes were. There was a brown stain on his collar. 'What do you mean?'

'It's just kept happening.'

'What has?'

'John,' he said, bloodshot eyes searching the corridor behind her.

'John what? What's he done? Mac? You've got to tell me. I won't be angry.'

He took her hands. 'He's got himself into stuff. Bad stuff. He got himself into a mess with a property thing, scamming old folk. Now he's got this guy sorting it out for him and it's all gone tits up . . .' His voice faded.

She fought the fear rising in her. 'Does this guy wear a green hoodie – drive a silver four-by-four?'

Mac nodded. 'Karl.'

'For God's sake. Mac.' She scanned the corridor herself. 'That guy's been following me. He attacked the journalist I was with in Paris, put him in hospital. He burned his boat in Amsterdam, and threatened me.'

'I know.'

She stared at him, disbelieving. 'You *know*?'

'That's why I was trying to get you home. John told me to get you back. To stop looking into that guy.'

'How did John know I was doing the story?'

'You texted me asking if I knew Lucian Grabole when I was in Blairgowrie – John was up for the day, playing golf with me and my dad. I told him. He went nuts. He sent Karl round to the flat when you were out to see what was going on.'

Grace remembered the faint footprint on the kitchen floor and a chill went through her.

'Then you went to London. He told me to get you home. Find out what you knew.'

'So you knew I was away the whole time?' she said, astonished.

'Aye, but I couldn't let on or you'd guess. John sent Karl after you, and he found out from this guy in London that you were doing a story.'

'Ali? In a cafe?'

Mac shrugged. 'John told Karl to scare you off it. I had to keep ringing and telling you to come back. When none of that worked, John rang and told you I was flying to Paris.' He rubbed his face, anguished. 'But you didn't *listen*.'

Her mind whirred backwards, incredulous. 'John Brock told

Karl to burn Nicu's boat? And what – attack him in Paris? Jesus, Mac!'

Mac's eyes squeezed shut.

'How did Karl even know we were there? Nobody followed us from Amsterdam – we checked.'

'You lost him at the airport. He didn't know where you'd gone. He went nuts.' Grace remembered the flash of lights as Nicu swerved off the exit road at the last second, when she refused to get out of the Jeep.

She held her face, suddenly seeing it. 'Oh God. You asked me for the address of our hotel in Paris – is that how he found us? Mac? How could you?'

A hand came out and touched her arm. 'John wouldn't let it go. He told me he was trying to help you. Get you safe. Get you away from that guy.' Mac's eyes brimmed with a new pain.

'Did Karl follow me and Nicu back to Amsterdam?' she whispered, remembering them wrapped in the blankets on the deck that night.

He nodded, and then she knew John had told him everything.

Bastard.

Mac began to rock. 'Oh, man, I'm fucked.'

She touched his head. 'Mac. Wake up! Talk to me! Why didn't John want me looking into Lucian?'

He staggered up and poured some water, then drank it thirstily. 'He told us one night, in here, what had gone on in Romania.'

'Lucian did? So you knew that was his name?'

Mac nodded. 'He told us he was called Youssi, but then we found him in here one night, crying. He'd got into the booze. He was off his head, sitting on the floor. Told us he had a kid he was never going to see. John gave him more whisky. It all came out about Romania, about his psycho dad, what he'd made him do.

He started puking everywhere, and fell over. John found this ID card on the floor with his real name, Lucian Grabole.'

Grace stared. 'John knew about Lucian's father and what he used to do in Romania, with the wells?'

Mac nodded. 'It was Karl's idea. When John needed Karl to shut up those two guys who were threatening to call the police over the old folk and the houses . . .'

'McFarlay and David Pearce?'

'Aye. John was freaking out. He'd been careful, but he thought he was going to get done for it. Go to prison for fraud. Lose all this. It was Karl's idea to copy it. Said if they killed them the same way Lucian and his dad did it, the Scottish police would link it back to him when they identified his body with the Romanian police. They knew it would take time, and Karl said that was good – there'd be no evidence left up by the cave after the winter.'

Grace let out a horrified laugh. 'The Romanian police would never have identified Lucian, Mac! He was fifteen when he left. They never arrested him or got fingerprints. Lucian Grabole isn't even his real name.'

His eyes grew wider, bloodshot, fearful.

She began to feel nauseous. 'I can't believe this. John and Karl killed Lucian on purpose, in our flat – to cover up what they did to those men?'

'Karl did it. John didn't touch them.'

'But why were they trying to stop me?'

'They didn't want you digging things up, finding people who maybe knew Lucian had been working here at the flats. It would link him back to John, and me, and Karl, and blow everything.'

Blinking as if the light were too bright, she took Mac's hand. 'Please tell me you didn't have anything to do with it.'

379

He dropped his head. 'I just had to leave the back door open. Karl smashed it later to look like a robbery.'

She let go of his hand and he grabbed it back, sorrowful.

'I didn't know what they'd done to those guys till later. I didn't want to know. They set Lucian up. John let him live in one of the new apartments upstairs for a while. I think they locked him in for two days without food during our wedding. Then Karl comes in, all apologetic, acting like it was an accident. Got him bladdered again on vodka to say sorry. Told him the apartment was getting sold now, but as a favour, he could use our flat for two weeks, while I was away. That the back door was open. To help himself to food in there. I think Karl dropped him off, then followed him into the flat and killed him. It was a set-up.'

She stepped back. 'Lucian *knew*, Mac. He wasn't stupid. He knew something was wrong. He left a note.'

He shrugged helplessly. 'I didn't *know*. Any of it. I swear. Not at the time. John asks stuff, you just do it.' He pointed around the studio. 'He's given me this.'

She pushed his shoulders, wanting to shake sense into him. 'Mac! How could you be so stupid? You're an accessory to murder now. We have to tell the police. Now.' She checked on the bar. 'Where's my phone?'

'Why?'

She looked on the ground, and checked her pockets, but it had disappeared. 'It was on the bar, Mac. Where the hell is it? I have to tell someone right now. Otherwise we're both going to get sucked into this.'

Through the bar window, a car drew up. A silver four-by-four.

'Oh God,' she said, alarmed.

'What?'

'We need to get out of here. That guy Karl's here.'

She grabbed Mac's hand and led him out the studio to the warehouse entrance door, and pulled the handle.

It was locked.

'Where's the key?' she said, panicked.

Mac covered his face. 'That's it. We're dead.'

Her heart began to bang in her chest. 'Why?'

'John's not gonna let us out. There was an old guy downstairs from the flat at Gallon Street. I was supposed to find out what he knew, but I didn't. I fucked up. Karl's gone to get him now. They know you know something now, too.'

She realized he was not only unbelievably drunk but in shock, unable to function. 'Restaurant. Quick.' She dragged Mac to the fire escape and pushed the metal bar. It was locked, too. A key turned in the front door. Voices.

'Upstairs, come on,' Grace whispered. They ran to the stairs and tiptoed up two flights. On the second floor, she pulled Mac to the furthest flat at the end, heart racing. 'Up here.' They climbed up to a mezzanine bedroom.

'Where's your phone?'

'John took it off me,' he said, rocking again. She guessed he'd taken hers, too, when he was making the drink for her in the bar. She crouched watching through the balustrade. 'Mac, when did this start happening? With John.'

'Three, four years ago. Started with the coke. He was taking it; then he was dealing it. Then this property business he got into. Now he's got in with Karl. Thinks he's big time. Like some kind of boss. My dad's noticed. Told me in Blairgowrie to give up the job and steer clear of John.' He held his face. 'He's going to kill us.' He groaned. 'Sorry.' Tears came into his eyes. 'Sorry, darlin'.' He touched her face. 'I love you so much.'

'Mac . . .' she whispered.

381

'Listen,' he said, kissing her hand. 'I'm gonna tell him you got out.'

'No, Mac.' She grabbed his hand.

'Stay there.'

His yanked away from her, and she reached after him, but he staggered down the stairs and to the front window of the apartment over the street. He turned and blew her a kiss.

'Grace!' he shouted, banging on the window.

There were heavy footsteps, and voices from below. Through the railing she saw Karl and John appear inside the flat.

'Where is she?' Karl grabbed Mac's shoulder.

Mac pointed outside at the street.

'I just saw her down there – she must have found the key in the office.'

'What?' John yelled.

Karl grabbed Mac and pulled him from the room, and their furious footsteps pounded the corridor.

Grace lay on the mezzanine, trembling. She needed a phone. John's office or the restaurant seemed like the best bet. Creeping down the spiral staircase, she reached the front door of the apartment, and checked the communal corridor.

Silence.

She tiptoed out. A door banged below, and she ran to the next flat along and hid behind its open front door.

All of it had been John. He'd wanted it this way – the anonymous dead body with criminal links to Romania killed in private in their flat, to the victims on the cliff. He'd never have known Lucian Grabole was a pseudonym. All this time, he'd been waiting for the police to get an ID hit on Lucian Grabole in Romania, thinking there'd be a clean link back to the well murders and he'd be in the clear. The last thing they'd wanted was her stumbling upon a link back to them.

There was a yell downstairs, followed by a crash. 'Mac,' she whispered. She leaned out into the corridor.

Scuffling noise and low voices. A cry of pain.

Another, louder, crash.

Then running feet.

'Mac,' she mouthed again.

'Keys are in the drawer. Did you see her go out?' John's yell from below.

'No.'

'Try upstairs. Grace?' John shouted.

Shaking, she hid behind the door. Heavy footsteps came up the stairs. Through the crack, she saw Karl enter the first flat. Holding her breath, she crept past it to the stairs, and leaned down. John was heading into the first-floor corridor.

Hatred rose inside her. She'd always disliked him, the way he'd pulled Mac into his business so early, doing the fake-uncle thing while going out with girls younger than Mac. Keeping his cool young mate around for nights out in clubs.

Holding her breath, she eased down the stairs to the first floor, checked John was searching a flat, then continued to the ground floor and headed to his office.

She tried the front doors again. Still locked. His office door, too.

Trapped now, she ran to the restaurant, praying she could force the fire escape open.

Footsteps thundered along the corridor above her head. Yelling came from the stairwell.

'She there?'

'No!'

She reached the restaurant door, and turned.

A figure caught her eye.

At the far end, through the open door of the studio.

A body on the floor.

A scream came from her mouth. 'Mac! Mac!'

He lay under the balcony, his head twisted sideways.

Footsteps approached down the stairs.

John appeared at the bottom, the hooded man, Karl, behind him.

He saw her face, and followed her eyes.

'Grace, darlin', it was an accident,' he said, hand raised. 'We were trying to find you to tell you. I'm so sorry. He was pissed. Got up on the bloody balcony and fell off backwards. We've just rung the ambulance.'

She backed away. 'Liar! You killed him!'

'Grace, don't be stupid. The boy's like my son.'

'What have you done, John?' she roared at him. 'What have you *done*?'

His hand came out. Grace stumbled back.

Like a cougar, Karl darted from behind him and ran.

'No!' she screamed. She found the restaurant door, and even though every muscle in her body was numb, she slammed it shut and fumbled the lock across it.

Karl's body slammed into the door.

She kept walking, frozen, as the kicking started behind her, not knowing even where she was going.

Kicks and thumps landed on the door, and she knew it was nearly over.

The fire escape was locked.

They were coming for her. There was nowhere to go.

She'd die in this room, without ever seeing anything else again.

It would be made to look like an accident, too. Her and Mac.

She sank to the floor, thinking of Mac, and the dreams she'd never followed, and all that had been wasted.

Then, from nowhere, Nicu's voice appeared in her head.

Scott in the Centre.

The restaurant door began to buckle with the body blows outside.

By the window, she saw a fire extinguisher.

'No,' she said. 'No.'

She stood up, picked it up with shaking arms, and walked to the blue stained-glass window.

'No.'

Behind her the door burst open. She lifted the extinguisher and threw it. It lifted in an arc and hit the window. The main pane smashed into a hundred pieces, raining down on her. A sharp wind swept in from the water, and outside, she saw the lights of the world again.

Footsteps came behind her.

Without looking back, Grace climbed onto the ledge and, not knowing where she was going, jumped.

CHAPTER SIXTY-EIGHT

Seven weeks later

The beach was busy today. Packed for the summer.

The school holidays had started, and children in swimsuits and hats played with spades and nets among the worm casts and bladderwrack.

Someone had made a giant heart of stones on the sand, and the tide was lapping at its edges, as yet leaving it untouched.

The woman walked along the sand, a baby on her back, a child running ahead.

Grace sat on a rock and took a few shots, then headed over, letting the sun warm her face.

Anna turned and saw her.

Grace photographed her again, her blonde hair snaking in the wind, then greeted her with a hug, and a wave for Valentin and Clara. Anna took her arm and they began to walk.

'So, what did you think of the *Scots Today* piece?' Grace said, checking Anna's reaction.

'I thought you did Lucian justice. Thank you. And I thought your photographs were beautiful. Even the one of him in your kitchen – so respectful, so still.'

'Thank you for letting me use it.'

'But the story's not finished?' Anna said, curious.

'I can't finish it. It's going to take so long to get John and Karl to trial – it's complicated by all the property fraud – it probably won't be till next year. So I can't run it until after, in case it's prejudicial. That's why I only wrote the first half – the mystery of who Lucian was. When they're sentenced, I'll write the second half, and put it together. Maybe syndicate it. I couldn't mention the man under our flat in this first part either for the same reason. He's a witness.'

'This is the older man, Robbie, who worked for Mountain Rescue? Is he OK?'

Grace squinted, watching a plane in the distance. 'Apparently. He's still in hospital, but Mr Singh says he's doing better. The good news is, they're not going to prosecute him – they've accepted he was mentally ill.'

'What happened to him – do you know?'

Clara gurgled. Grace saw her eyes had darkened again. They were becoming more like Lucian's, and she wondered if that comforted Anna.

'Robbie? He was in a helicopter crash during a rescue mission in the Highlands about ten years ago. He was the only survivor. He seemed to deal with it OK at the time. Then his wife died last year and it triggered this paralyzing anxiety disorder, but nobody knew because he stopped leaving the house. Then his house got repossessed and he was too ill to explain to anyone he needed help. Mr Singh was trying to help out, but he had no idea how bad it was.'

She tickled Clara's chin to make her laugh. 'But if Robbie hadn't been there, John and Karl might have got away with all of it. The evidence Robbie found in the backyard is crucial, apparently. It puts Karl at the scene. He knew he'd dropped the glove

387

and he'd been back searching for it a few times before he figured out that it was Robbie that had taken it. A guy up in the tower block saw him in the yard.'

Anna squeezed Grace's arm. 'And how are you? How are Mac's parents?'

They stopped to sit on a rock, and let Valentin collect mussel shells in his bucket. Grace took a stick and traced zigzags in the sand.

'His parents are a mess. His dad's threatened to kill John, and the police have had to speak to him about it.' The tears came and she pushed them back. 'I don't know.' She sniffed and Anna patted her arm. 'I still can't believe Mac's gone. That I won't see him again. And I suppose I'm struggling a lot with how much he didn't tell me about what was happening with John. I worry that he must have been scared, and hiding it from me and his dad. I just think he got pulled in by John. Sort of hero-worshipped him. Then it was too late to get out when he realized what John was doing, because he'd become involved in it all.'

Anna watched her carefully. 'You were with your husband at the end, Grace. He wasn't alone when he died.'

They fell into silence. Grace knew Anna was thinking of Lucian, and that dark, wet night in Gallon Street. Valentin turned to watch them, his face puzzled. He lifted two shells and placed them solemnly on his eyes. They both burst out laughing.

'What will you do now?' Anna asked as they crossed the sand back to her cottage.

'That's what I came to tell you,' Grace replied. 'I'm leaving today.'

'Oh?'

'I'm going to the airport now.'

'Where to?' Anna said, taking Clara out of her sling.

Grace shrugged. 'I'm going to decide when I get there. I'm going to take any flight to Europe tonight that still has a ticket. Then, after that, I'll see. I've got no plans. Maybe I'll travel by road or train for a while.'

'Just Europe?'

Beyond the terrace wall, out on the ocean, a sail boat dipped in the wind.

'I don't know. A photographer friend from Amsterdam's been commissioned by an American arts trust to shoot a project on urban regeneration in Detroit. He's invited me to assist next year. So . . .'

'Will you go?'

Grace watched the ferry. 'Maybe.' She put her camera away and saw the envelope in her bag. 'Anna, I forgot to give you this. It was returned to Mitti in Amsterdam.'

Anna read the postcode. 'London?'

'Sorry. It looks like a work letter.'

Anna opened it. A handwritten note came out.

'It's Lucian,' she gasped. 'He disguised it to make me read it.'

She handed Clara to Grace to put in her buggy, and read the final letter from her lover in private. Grace lifted Valentin and swung him on the terrace till his face broke into smiles.

Then she said her goodbyes, and walked back up the beach, to where Ewan waited to take her to the airport, his gangly legs on the wall, phone to his ear, trying to fob Sula off about where he was right now.

A brush of hills lay on the horizon. Grace searched for her father in it, and said goodbye, and told him she'd be back one day, because this would always be home. Then she walked into a shard of sunshine blasting down onto the sand, and felt herself vanish.

The Playdate

LOUISE MILLAR

You leave your child with a friend. Everyone does it.
Until the day it goes wrong.

Sound designer Callie Roberts is a single mother. And she's come to rely heavily on her best friend and neighbour, Suzy. Over the past few lonely years, Suzy has been good to Callie and her rather frail daughter, Rae, and she's welcomed them into her large, apparently happy family.

But Callie knows that Suzy's life is not quite as perfect as it seems. It's time she pulled away – and she needs to get back to work. So why does she keep putting off telling Suzy? And who will care for Rae? In the anonymous city street, the houses each hide a very different family, each with their own secrets. Callie's increased sense of alienation leads her to try and befriend a new resident, Debs. But she's odd – you certainly wouldn't trust her with your child – especially if you knew anything about her past . . .

A brilliant and chilling evocation of modern life, in which friendships may be long-standing but remain superficial.

Praise for *The Playdate*

'I started reading and couldn't stop . . . a must-read that will tap into every mother's primal fears'
Sophie Hannah

KILLER WOMEN

Killer Women is a group of established, London-based, female crime writers that was co-founded by Melanie McGrath and Louise Millar, to represent many sub-genres of crime-writing – from psychological thrillers to procedurals, comic crime, political thrillers and more.

What we offer

Bespoke, ticketed events for festivals, libraries, bookshops and other venues, which deliver more than the usual writer-in-a-room. We will add value and experiential richness to your events.

- **Killer Women** masterclasses and workshops. Between us we have years of experience teaching in universities, festivals and libraries, as well as running Arvon and *Guardian* Masterclasses. We can provide a standalone course or a masterclass or workshop to run before an event.

- **Killer Women** salons and cocktail parties where readers can socialize with crime writers and sample our unique **Killer Women package**.

- Resources for media and bloggers providing quotations, features, listicles and book recommendations.

For more information visit our website at **www.killerwomen.org** or email us at info@killerwomen.org. To keep up to date with **Killer Women** events please follow us on Twitter @killerwomenorg and sign up to our newsletter on our website.

The Hidden Girl

LOUISE MILLAR

How do you look for someone who's not even missing?

Hannah and Will Riley love their London life. Will has a music production company in Shepherd's Bush, and Hannah travels globally for a human rights charity. But there's one thing missing from their lives. And it's destroying them.

So when they find the abandoned Tornley Hall in a remote Suffolk village near where Will grew up, Hannah convinces him that a move to the countryside will help. He can commute. She can devote her time to restoring the property and creating a perfect home. And then everything will fall into place – won't it?

Praise for *The Hidden Girl*

'The creepy, remote village provides a perfectly atmospheric backdrop to the chilling story, and the slow-building tension will ensure you'll be hooked right up until the last page'
Essentials magazine

'A creepy psychological thriller with a great twist'
Sunday Mirror

'No one does creepy quite like Louise Millar. I loved this book'
Tamar Cohen, author of *The Broken*